THE GREAT DIVIDE

Books by Frank M. Robinson

THE POWER
A LIFE IN THE DAY OF . . .
THE GLASS INFERNO (*with Thomas N. Scortia*)
THE PROMETHEUS CRISIS (*with Thomas N. Scortia*)
THE NIGHTMARE FACTOR (*with Thomas N. Scortia*)
THE GOLD CREW (*with Thomas N. Scortia*)
THE TRUTH ABOUT VIETNAM (*Editor, with Earl Kemp*)
SEX AMERICAN STYLE (*Editor, with Nat Lehrman*)

THE
GREAT
DIVIDE

Frank M. Robinson and John Levin

Rawson, Wade Publishers, Inc.
NEW YORK

Library of Congress Cataloging in Publication Data

Robinson, Frank M.
  The great divide

  I. Levin, John.   II. Title
PS3568.02888G7   813'.54   80-5991
ISBN 0-89256-165-3   AACR2

Published simultaneously in Canada by McClelland and Stewart, Ltd.
Composition by American–Stratford Graphic Services, Inc.,
Brattleboro, Vermont
Printed and bound by Fairfield Graphics,
Fairfield, Pennsylvania

Designed by Jacques Chazaud
First Edition

For my brother, Ray
—FRANK M. ROBINSON

. . . and my daughters, Jenny and Sara
—JOHN LEVIN

The authors would like to acknowledge the assistance of many people in researching *The Great Divide* and preparing the manuscript for publication. We hereby gratefully thank the Dean of the University of Santa Clara School of Law, George J. Alexander, as well as Arthur Birsh, Alan Boruck, Dennis and Vivian Callanan, Bill Ewing, Larry Friedlander, Jeff Gordon, Esq., Sally Harms, Jill Hinckley, Gene Klinger, Jane Whitbread Levin, Marvin Lichtner, Alberta Mayo, JoAnne McBride, Debbie Notkin, Dr. John O'Brien, Henry and Eleanor Putzel, Peter Range, Lois Romano, Judith and David Sensibar, Tom Whitmore, and the staff of Representative Philip Burton (D., California). For their faith in the outline and guidance through the subsequent drafts of the book itself, a special thanks to our editor, Sharon Morgan, and our publishers, Ken and Eleanor Rawson.

Solely in the interest of verisimilitude, we have occasionally used the names of public personalities as well as those of real institutions. All names of personnel at such institutions and the description of various policies were invented by us and do not necessarily coincide with reality nor do we mean to imply that they may so coincide at any time in the future.

June, 1981

FRANK M. ROBINSON, JOHN LEVIN
San Francisco, California

THE GREAT DIVIDE

December 14

Steven Hart had to strain to hear what Jerry Wagoner was saying and wondered if Jerry was deliberately pitching his voice low just so he would miss part of the agenda. Hart wouldn't put it past him—Wagoner was a sadistic bastard who'd been on Hart's back ever since Governor de Young had authorized him to reorganize California's delegation to the Constitutional Convention. Of course, it was easier to pick on a political intern than a fellow delegate but why was Wagoner picking on *him*? Hadn't he started the first de Young for Governor campus committee when he was still an undergrad at USC? Hadn't his folks been more than generous with their contributions to de Young's campaign funds?

Hart hunched his shoulders against the chill—it was almost lunchtime but the Feds hadn't turned on the heat in the cavernous Pension Building yet—and cupped his ear to try and pick up Wagoner's words.

"You getting all this, Steve?" Wagoner was staring at him, a faint frown on his face.

"What, Jerry?" He pushed closer, smothering his embarrassment. At one time he had been included in all the caucuses held by the delegation, but ever since Wagoner's arrival he had become little more than a go-for.

"Ostland—he heads up the Montana delegation, Steve—will make a motion to reconstitute the floor committee. If we can get five votes out of Vermont, it'll pass. I'm going to meet with them this afternoon."

Hart nodded, then turned toward the stage as a voice boomed out over the microphone: "It's a privilege and an honor for me to welcome Rhode Island's All-State High School Marching Band." A blue-and-gold uniformed band stepped out smartly from behind the speaker's rostrum and went *oom-pahing* down the center aisle past the almost empty rows of folding metal chairs.

A lot had changed, Hart thought, as he watched the band shuffle through the candy wrappers and styrofoam coffee cups that littered the center aisle. The convention had stalemated months ago, the media had lost interest, and Congress had reduced its appropriations so there wasn't even enough money for regular cleaning crews. The bunting that hung from the balconies along the sides of the hall was dusty and torn, and the huge photographs of past Presidents were water-stained from the leaky roof. Definitely tacky, Hart thought.

He turned back to the caucus, cupping his ears so he could hear over the mangled strains of a Sousa march. Mabel Sweet, a plump, middle-aged delegate from Pasadena, was giving Wagoner an argument. "I still think we're offering them too much," she said. "I can't imagine why anyone would object to the West running the floor committee during the rest of December. After all, the East—"

Wagoner cracked a pained smile. "Mabel, trust me. If we win, dinner's on me—at the Hay-Adams." Wagoner might be a bastard but you couldn't help admiring him, Hart thought. Jerry was smooth, bright, handsome, and definitely not the type to let himself go to fat on a desk job—he had once seen Wagoner jogging on the Mall in forty-degree weather. Somewhere along the line, Jerry had acquired a sense of authority and a tongue he used like a rapier, valuable assets for a former Beverly Hills ad exec in his mid-thirties, though he overused both in his role as delegation chairman.

Wagoner was also the most efficient man he had ever met. As soon as Jerry had arrived from Sacramento, he'd started building a tickler file on every delegate there, not just those from California, and he fed the information into the computer. Jerry knew Mabel not only had a passion for loud print dresses, she was also a sucker for expensive dinners.

Then Mabel's comment sank in and Hart became curious. "What's so important about December, Jerry?"

Maybe everyone in Wagoner's "in" group knew what was going on but he didn't. And he hadn't invested six months in the convention to be kept in the dark just when it looked like things might be getting interesting. Ever since Wagoner had taken over, he had been frozen out. Half the memos that came in over the computer terminal were coded and Wagoner had even brought lock cabinets into the caucus room to replace the regular files.

Wagoner stared at him, disapproving, then fished a bill out of his pocket. "Get me a Reuben and a Coke, Steve. I'll fill you in later."

Hart could feel his face flush. Wagoner was going out of his way to humiliate him. "Sure, Jerry, right away," he mumbled. He struggled up the aisle, angrily pushing past little groups of delegates swapping information, debating votes, or just deciding where to go for lunch. He ought to resign, he thought, he wasn't going anywhere as long as Wagoner was in charge.

He stopped at the entrance to the outside corridor for a last look at the convention floor. An Arizona delegate was on the podium, droning on about the manifest destiny of the West and the perfidy of the federal government. The California caucus had broken up and the delegates were filtering out over the floor—Wagoner was making sure that the votes for reconstituting the floor committee stayed in line.

On his way out, Hart stopped by the California office to pick up his parka. D.C. was a bitch this time of year. That morning, a cold rain followed by the first snowfall of the season had left a freezing dampness in the air.

Ray Griffin, the senior intern, had been working the Xerox and was already putting on his coat. "Watch the store while I grab some lunch, okay, Steve?"

"Can't—Wagoner wants me to pick up a Reuben for him at Reeves."

"Bullshit. Besides, you owe me for yesterday." Griffin hesitated at the door. "Uh, Steve, Jerry asked me to tell all the interns that the files and correspondence drawers are off limits now and briefings will be on a need-to-know basis only."

Hart guessed from his self-important tone that Griffin had just been promoted to the inner circle.

"Meaning I should keep my nose out of where it doesn't belong."

"You said it, I didn't." And then Griffin was out the door and gone.

Griffin was even beginning to dress like Jerry, in addition to acting like him, Hart thought. He was turning into a Wagoner clone.

He poured himself a cup of coffee from the machine in the corner, took a minute to watch the floor action on the closed-circuit monitor and then another to read the bulletin board. Somebody had posted a sensational clipping about the effects of the atomic bomb tests on the people who lived within a hundred-mile radius of the Nevada test sites. The article said that the infant mortality rate was twenty-eight per one thousand live births—almost as high as India's—and that leukemia was the leading cause of death for people under thirty-five. Hart felt another surge of anger, this time directed at the federal government. His older sister and her family lived in Ely. It was bad enough that the Feds were ruining the West with their shale oil projects.

He didn't know what made him sit behind Wagoner's desk. Probably as a show of bravado because he was angry at Jerry, perhaps because Wagoner had a fetish about keeping his desk clean and today there was a small stack of papers in his "in" box.

He hesitated a moment, then glanced quickly through the box: two letters of introduction, an expense account voucher, a Xeroxed profile from Who's Who of the chairman of the Michigan delegation, and an invitation to a reception for Governor Mednick of Utah. Nothing much. He carefully put the papers back in the same order in which he found them.

He looked at his watch. A good twenty minutes before Griffin would be back. He clasped his hands behind his head and leaned back in Wagoner's swivel chair, pressing his knees against the underside of the middle drawer to brace himself. Why the hell was Wagoner such a prick? He had never—

The desk drawer suddenly sprang open and Hart tumbled backward, the drawer and its contents spilling out on the floor. Panicked, he hastily stuffed the supplies and papers back in the drawer, arranging them as best he could. At first he thought that Wagoner had forgotten to lock it, then noticed the bent tongue of the old lock and realized his weight must have forced it open.

He grabbed a cast-iron letter spike from another desk and hammered the tongue back far enough so the drawer would close. By the time Wagoner discovered it a lot of people would have been in and out of the room—he wouldn't be the only suspect.

He had tidied everything up and was feeling relieved when he noticed two letters that had slipped almost completely under the desk. He got down on his hands and knees and pulled them out with the help of a letter opener. He put one back in the drawer but the other had a red "CONFIDENTIAL" stamp on it and he lingered over it, curious. From Sacramento. From Governor de Young's office. CONFIDENTIAL.

He slapped it in his hand several times. It wouldn't take long to steam it open over the coffee machine—Griffin had probably done it a number of times. For once, he'd know what was going on, whether Wagoner wanted him to or not.

"I thought you were going to get me a sandwich, Hart."

Wagoner, followed by Mabel Sweet and several other delegates, had just walked into the room.

Hart slipped the letter into his parka pocket—it was too late to put it back in the drawer—and stood up all in one easy motion, quietly pushing the drawer in at the same time. "On my way, Jerry."

Wagoner's voice was acid. "Don't bother. I'll send Griffin when he gets back. I'd like to have it sometime today."

"Sorry, Jerry, really sorry." He felt sweaty and almost sick. If Wagoner found out the letter was missing, he'd be sent back to California on the first plane. He sidled out of the room, red-faced, aware that the others were staring at him.

Once outside, he headed for the pay phone at the end of the corridor. Who the hell wanted an intern who went through the boss's mail? Nobody would believe it was an accident. Hell, he almost didn't believe it himself. He was almost certain Wagoner hadn't seen him pocket the letter or close the drawer, but suppose Wagoner looked for the letter that afternoon? He desperately needed to talk to somebody about what to do now.

Debbie, he thought.

He'd call Debbie Spindler. She was one of the few people in D.C. in whom he could confide, even though it seemed like their three-month affair was coming to an end. Besides, she had been with the convention from the start, as a member of the Wisconsin delegation. She'd know what he ought to do to get on Wagoner's good side.

She didn't like being pulled out of a Wisconsin caucus but agreed to meet him in the east wing of the National Gallery, by the huge orange-and-black Calder mobile. She could have sounded more enthusiastic, he thought, annoyed. But by the time he walked the six blocks between the convention hall and the gallery, the chill November wind and the slate-gray sky had helped put things in a more cheerful perspective. Wagoner had a full schedule through the afternoon and there were at least three receptions that began at five thirty and stretched on into the evening.

Jerry wouldn't have time to check his desk until the next day. If he got there early and slipped the letter back, Wagoner would never know.

Debbie was waiting for him by the mobile, her short figure almost hidden by her scarf and overcoat. She didn't look delighted to see him and he suddenly had second thoughts.

"You sounded almost incoherent over the phone, Steve—what on earth is wrong?" He started to explain and she interrupted, glancing at her watch. "You have exactly two minutes. I've got a committee meeting right after lunch and I don't intend to miss it."

He couldn't tell her his problems cold-turkey, he thought. He'd sound like a wimp. He'd talk her into lunch and lead up to it gradually, describing everything that had happened since Wagoner had taken over as delegation chairman. Then he'd have to trust to luck that she didn't end up lecturing him like an eighth-grade civics teacher.

But somehow he knew he wasn't going to be that lucky.

They had lunch in the basement of the gallery and he complained about Jerry Wagoner and the changes he had made, especially how Wagoner had isolated him from the rest of the delegation.

Debbie interrupted him with a forkful of chicken salad halfway to her mouth. She had been growing increasingly impatient, frequently glancing at her watch. "Steve, I can't believe I came here just to listen to you complain about how you feel personally slighted. What happened today?"

Suddenly he felt miserable, pushed his plate away and told her about the accident behind Wagoner's desk and Wagoner walking in while he was trying to repair the damage.

The ends of Debbie's mouth curved downward in disapproval. "You took a personal letter," she accused.

He told her how he had tried to return it. As expected, she lectured him. "Being a convention intern isn't all fun and games, Steve—it's a lot of hard work. It's also a splendid opportunity. If you ruin it, you'll regret it the rest of your life." She had puckered up her face while talking and looked remarkably like Mr. Rankin, his home-room teacher in grammar school.

After lunch, she pecked him on the cheek and ran for a cab that had stopped to pick up three other passengers. All Hart could think of was that it was getting near Christmas and time for all good summer affairs to end.

He debated going back to the convention hall, then decided not to. If he did, he'd feel like he was following Debbie's advice to mind his own business, work hard, and consider the convention a learning experience. But he was still smarting from her holier-than-thou attitude and following her advice was the last thing he wanted to do. Besides, he had never really seen the museum before. He'd take the afternoon off, Wagoner would never miss him.

He didn't think of the letter again until he was in his room at the Gramercy Inn that night. He was getting ready for bed and was emptying the pockets of his parka when he ran across it. He studied it a moment, then walked into the bathroom and ran the hot water in the shower until the small room was filled with steam. Back in the bedroom, he worked the flap open and fished out the letter.

He scanned the first page, thinking it was nice to know what was really happening for a change. Halfway through the second page, his pleasure at being on the "inside" faded. He quickly scanned the last page, then went back to the first and read the entire letter again, slowly. He could feel the sweat start to dampen his T-shirt.

He wished to God he had never read it, had been able to put it right back in Wagoner's desk drawer. Then he cursed himself for not having read it earlier when there would have been someplace to go with it, somebody official who would know what to do.

He thought of calling Debbie again, then decided against it. She wouldn't believe him. In any event, it would be unfair to involve her. He opened the phone book on the desk and ran his finger down the listings for "United States Government." He finally found the number and dialed the FBI. The night duty officer on the other end of the line listened politely, then suggested he bring the letter by in the morning.

He'd do that, Hart thought after hanging up. He'd surely do that. He looked around the room for a hiding place, then searched his wallet for a couple of stamps and stuck the three pages of the letter to the back of the dressing table mirror. It wasn't very clever—he'd cribbed the idea from a television movie—but it made more sense than leaving the letter in his coat pocket or on the nightstand.

Just before going to bed, he took three Valiums from the bottle he kept in the bathroom medicine cabinet and washed them down with a glass of water. Then he lay back and forced his mind to blank, letting the Valiums take effect. It was a good half hour before he slipped into a drugged, fitful sleep.

Never once, despite his anxiety, did he consider himself in physical danger.

He never heard the lock being opened with a pass key or the door chain being slipped off with a wire. He didn't hear the intruders until they were halfway across the room and one of them stumbled over a chair. And even when he jerked awake, there was still a split second when he hovered between dreams and wakefulness, trying to make up his mind which was reality.

He decided in favor of reality when the bed lamp was turned on full in his face, blinding him. He was still drugged and confused but sensed that there were three of them. He suddenly realized he was in trouble and started to roll off the bed.

They were all over him then, forcing him back on the mattress. He started to scream and one of them wrapped an arm around his face so tight he could taste the leather of the man's jacket.

"Where's the letter?" somebody asked.

He started to gag and one of the other men said, "Let him talk."

He was terrified. "Back of the mirror," he mumbled, "It's taped to the back of the mirror." And then he was ashamed of himself because he had wet the bed, he was so frightened.

"Got it," a voice said. There was only one man on top of him now and Hart suddenly doubled up, throwing the man off the bed. The others swarmed back, flipping him on his stomach and forcing his head into the pillow. One of them ripped back the blankets and sheet and somebody yanked off his shorts. *My God, what were—*

"Get the restraints," a voice murmured.

He fought silently, possessed of a desperate strength, and heard the bed table go crashing to the floor. Then two of them held him down while the third tied wide leather straps to his wrists and ankles and spread-eagled him on the mattress, pushing his face into the pillow again. His mouth was half open and he could feel his teeth cut the fabric. He started to choke on a mouthful of shredded polyurethane.

His head was swimming and he couldn't feel them on his back anymore. In fact, he couldn't feel the mattress anymore. He couldn't catch his breath, he couldn't breathe. It felt like they were doing something to his back but he couldn't tell what. Then he sensed his muscles weaken, suddenly relax. He heaved convulsively for the last time, his lungs bursting, before losing consciousness.

The last thing he thought of was that it would all be over before New Year's.

December 15
10:00 A.M., *Pacific Time, Tuesday*

"The word is that de Young will announce for the Presidency this morning," Gus Frankel said.

Andrew Livonas stared through the car window at the ten-speeds, the Mopeds and motorcycles that made up the bulk of the morning traffic on Market Street. The last time he had been in San Francisco, it had been Fords and Chevys and Hondas; this morning, there were hardly any cars at all. There had been gas rationing ever since the new Arab oil embargo the year before and now it was so low, most people couldn't drive, period. He wondered if Whitman had squeezed any more oil out of Indonesia—maybe the Vice-President would succeed where lesser envoys had failed. Then he realized Gus was waiting for some kind of comment.

"His office leak it?"

"Yeah," Gus replied. "One of our reporters, a kid named Garber, picked it up."

Except for the traffic, the city looked pretty much the same. The skyline had finally stabilized—no new buildings had gone up in the past few years but then no new buildings had gone up anywhere. And there were a lot more street artists, Powell and Market looked like an Indian bazaar. The latest Labor Department statistics on unemployment automatically popped into his head. Twenty-three percent and that was probably too low.

"You looking for a statement?" Livonas asked.

Frankel shrugged. "You want to make one, I'll see it gets a play."

Livonas ignored the edge in Frankel's voice. Even Gus considered him a member of the enemy camp because he was Whitman's aide. It had been the same everywhere in the West—mention that you worked for the federal government and strangers became actively hostile and friends gave you the cold shoulder. With Gus, it really hurt. Gus was his oldest friend, they even owned a cabin together on the Russian River.

"Maybe later, after the press conference."

But Frankel wasn't ready to let the subject drop. "You still think de Young's a bastard, don't you?"

Livonas squinted at the morning sun shining through a break in the buildings. Vincent de Young. He closed his eyes and saw de Young's smiling face and then Harry Palmer's with his hair hanging over his forehead, still wet from the Bay. Livonas could feel his stomach start to burn with suppressed rage. It had been ten years since Harry had taken his leap. Ten years, one month, and eight days.

"You know, Andy, I think you really blame yourself as much as you blame de Young for Harry Palmer's death," Frankel said gently.

"Spare me, will you, Gus? Save the bullshit for your encounter group." He turned away from Frankel and stared out at the city again.

Frankel's chubby face was suddenly all hard planes and angles. "De Young's popular out here, Andy. To most people in the West, he's a hero." Then, seeing Livonas's expression, he made a conscious effort to change the subject. "How's the convention going?"

For a moment, Livonas didn't know what he was talking about. "The constitutional thing? Who cares?"

Frankel shrugged and pulled into an empty parking space opposite City Hall. "I got the AP summary this morning and it seems to be heating up. It might surprise you, but people out here are pretty interested." He swung his door open, pausing to look back at Livonas. "Just try and listen to de Young with an open mind, Andy, that's all I ask."

They got out of the car and trotted for the City Hall steps, Frankel in the lead. Livonas flipped open his briefcase for the bored cop manning the metal detector, then ran to catch up with Frankel in the rotunda, at the base of the wide Venetian marble staircase. Most of the crowd were state office workers from around the corner—he could see the "brownie" sheet being passed along for them to sign. In front of them were the working journalists and the political groupies who hoped to attach themselves to the governor's campaign in the early stages, when any warm body would be welcome.

There'd be lots of applause, de Young had guaranteed that.

Frankel fished a battered notebook from his pocket. "Bring back old times?"

"Yeah—we covered Jerry Brown announcing for the Presidency from here back in '79."

The governor's aides were trooping down the steps now, waiting to be positioned behind the microphones by de Young's press secretary, Herb Shepherd. Livonas hated Shepherd, from his Pierre Cardin tie to his Bally single-buckle shoes. It was Shepherd who had been de Young's hatchet man in the campaign against Harry Palmer.

He wouldn't forgive himself for that one, Livonas thought. He had convinced Harry to run against de Young in the first place, had volunteered to be his campaign manager.

There was a patter of applause and Livonas felt Frankel nudge him in the ribs. Governor Vincent de Young was at the top of the staircase. He waved to the crowd just long enough for the television cameras to zoom in on him, then led his entourage down the marble steps.

"Great entrance," Livonas muttered. De Young looked good, he couldn't deny that. The governor was a little over six feet, with a ruddy complexion and the trim, tight build of a man who played squash regularly or did a fast five miles every morning. He could turn on the sincerity and confidence at will but most important of all, he possessed an air of command. He would make a great candidate, at least as far as TV and personal appearances went.

Frankel whispered, "Show me the politician who doesn't know the value of an 'up' angle."

Livonas was studying the group around de Young. "You've been suckered, Gus. If de Young was going to announce, he would have brought along the wife and kids."

Following the governor down the staircase were three other governors—Barron of Arizona, Mednick of Utah, Walters of Nevada plus the chief aide to Alaska's Judd. Trailing behind de Young and slightly to his right was a man Livonas didn't recognize. Tall, with sandy hair, his eyes were constantly flickering over the crowd.

"Who's the newcomer?"

Frankel squinted at the man on the staircase. "Buddy of Shepherd's, name's Craig Hewitt. Used to be an instructor with the Army's Special Forces, now he's something with the state police."

Livonas grunted and concentrated on de Young, who grinned and waved to the crowd, then turned to the television mini-cams, his face somber.

"As of eight o'clock this morning, I am mobilizing the National Guard to patrol California highways and protect bulk oil deliveries within the state. The hijacking of fuel trucks has reached catastrophic levels. As governor, it is my duty to see that not one gallon of gasoline intended for our citizens is spirited elsewhere."

"Elsewhere" was the buzz word, Livonas thought. Everyone knew he meant east of the Mississippi.

"What hijackings, Gus? What's going on?"

"Beats me, first I've heard."

De Young waited while a wave of applause swept through the crowd. All he needed was a huge American flag to stand in front of, Livonas thought. Or maybe a state flag, that'd be more appropriate.

". . . dusk-to-dawn curfew on all private vehicular traffic on California freeways . . ."

Livonas shifted uneasily. "What's he trying to do, impose martial law?"

Frankel glanced over, annoyed. "Don't blame him. If your President Massey hadn't fucked up, we wouldn't be in this situation."

"Our President, Gus."

"I didn't vote for him, ol' buddy."

Livonas ignored him and focused on de Young, who had launched into a tirade against the federal government. The Feds were greedy, insensitive, and guilty of everything from rape to incest. When he finally paused for breath, the applause was thunderous. De Young could feel his audience, that had always been one of his strong points. He could even make the bored crowd of state office workers come alive.

". . . make no mistake about it, it's the West against the rest!"

"That his slogan, Gus? 'The West against the rest'?"

"Screw you, Andy."

De Young was standing with his head slightly bowed while the office workers whistled and cheered. All the applause hadn't been bought and paid for, Livonas thought. De Young was popular enough to challenge Massey for the Democratic nomination—depending on the other candidates, he could probably have it for the asking. And if he dropped the West-*über-alles* rhetoric and cut a few deals in the South, there was no telling how well he could do in November.

Strobe lights were twinkling now; de Young was taking questions from the reporters. Livonas edged closer to listen, then looked back at Frankel, disgusted. "You hear what they're asking him? They're nothing but straight men, Gus. He floated that candidacy story to hide the Guard mobilization. Any other politician would have telegraphed it days ahead and the press would have been waiting with some hard questions."

Frankel closed his notebook with a snap, his anger just beneath the surface. "Look, Andy, I didn't ask you to come along, that was your idea. You're out here on a fact-finding mission for Whitman's Energy Task Force—so go out and find some facts. You don't have to hang around and bug me."

"Don't be so touchy, Gus." De Young was brushing up his statesman image now, answering a few planted questions on foreign affairs. Well, Massey was a loser anyway, Livonas thought. If de Young didn't nail him, somebody else would. Whitman should announce this month, no point in letting de Young build up too large a head of steam. By convention time, the governor could be so far ahead even Whitman couldn't catch him.

Then de Young spotted him and shouldered his way through the crowd, his hand outstretched. Shepherd hovered just behind, a tentative smile on his face.

"Goddamn, Andy, it's great to see you." De Young turned to the reporters behind him. "I want you fellows to know that when Andy Livonas went to Washington, California lost the best damn political reporter it ever had." He draped an arm around Livonas's shoulder and flashed a quick smile for the cameras. "When you gonna get your boss to put his ass on the line for the West, Andy?"

Livonas jerked away. "Tell that crap to somebody else, Vince."

But de Young had already stepped into the crowd of reporters, shaking hands and slapping backs. Nobody had heard except de Young, Frankel, and Herb Shepherd. Shepherd would make a note of it. Maybe Gus would, too.

"Harry Palmer was a long time ago," Frankel said. He didn't bother to hide the thread of anger in his voice.

"Politics is politics and friendship is bullshit, is that it, Gus?"

Frankel's lips thinned. "C'mon, let's get out of here." Then, over his shoulder: "A lot's changed since you were here last, Andy."

Livonas glanced back at de Young. The man oozed power, he had a presence that Massey couldn't match.

Frankel was waiting outside and Livonas hurried toward the exit doors. Gus was right. A lot of things had changed since he had been here last, including Gus.

He was almost out the doors before he became aware of the woman arguing with the security guard. Body static had molded her beige crepe dress around a figure that made Livonas pause for a longer look. Thick red hair tumbled down both sides of her face but Livonas could see enough of her features to guess her age at about twenty-five.

"I'm late, goddamnit—I told you they were expecting me!" Her voice was husky, outraged.

The guard was sweating. "Sorry, lady, you've got to go through the detector and have your purse inspected just like everybody else."

She noticed Livonas watching and shrugged helplessly. He'd already guessed what was going on and walked over. She handed him her purse, then stomped through the detector. "How's that? You want me to do it again?" She turned out the pockets of the suede coat she had thrown over her arm. "See? No gun."

The guard turned stubborn, standing up so he was face to face with her. "Lady, I—"

Livonas stepped forward. "She's with our party." He flashed his White House clearance badge so the guard could see the embossed "Secret Service" stamp on it.

"Sorry, sir, it's just that our orders are to inspect all packages and purses."

"That's right, Officer." Livonas took the woman by the arm and walked her back toward the rotunda. She was stunning close up, the faint freckles on either side of her nose adding a mischievous look.

"You really in the Secret Service?" she asked.

"No. That's just a clearance badge, it's not an ID." He handed her back her purse. "What's in it?"

"A gram of coke." She squeezed his arm. "That was a sweet thing to do. Who're you really with?"

"Vice-President Whitman's office—administrative aide." She looked familiar but he had no idea where he might have met her. "How about yourself?"

"The Governor." She glanced around, spotted de Young by one of the pillars and waved.

Livonas smiled uncertainly. "What do you do for him?"

"I sleep with him, hon." She stood on her toes and kissed him on the mouth. "Thanks a heap." She winked, then strode across the rotunda floor to de Young.

Frankel was waiting for him on the steps outside. Livonas said, "Don't keep it a secret, Gus—who's de Young's girl friend?"

"Sally Craft, rock star. She was on the cover of *Time* last month. Six hits in the Top Forty."

Livonas glanced over his shoulder. De Young had his arm around her, his hand resting comfortably just below her waist. Livonas didn't keep up with rock singers but at least he had heard of her.

"I don't know how he does it," Frankel grunted. "He's always got some young broad around."

"Rhino horn, Gus. He puts it in his yogurt." Livonas slipped into his coat. "Sally and the Governor must be quite a scandal."

"Not really, not in this state. I think a lot of people are secretly kind of proud of de Young, like they were about Kennedy. A real stud."

"How about Mrs. de Young? She think he's a real stud, too?"

"Sally never goes to Sacramento, de Young's got a love nest in Nevada City."

Livonas started down the steps. The winter sun had burnt through the morning fog and the city looked crisp and brilliant. But he couldn't say he missed the cable cars or the trendy secretaries in the financial district or the funky little restaurants. As with most cities he had seen lately, he could almost sense the dust settling down. Hardly any traffic, not much business, and a lot of people sitting around with nothing to do.

It had been almost two years since the debacle in Iraq, Livonas thought bitterly. It had started with the takeover of the American embassy in Baghdad, along with twenty-three hostages, by a fanatical Moslem sect. The Pentagon had promptly urged the dropping of a small nuclear device in the desert outside the city as a "demonstration" of what would happen if the hostages weren't released immediately.

Between two and five that morning, President Masscy had changed his mind four times. Finally, despite opposition by Whitman and Al Reynolds of State, he had given the order for the drop.

The device had landed too close to a military airfield and thirty-seven Iraqi air cadets had been killed. Then the prevailing winds had changed and blown the fallout over Baghdad itself instead of the desert.

Within an hour, a mob had stormed the embassy, slaughtering both the hostages and the fanatics who had taken them. And by the next day, riots had engulfed the oil fields of every Moslem state, and exports of crude to the United States were completely embargoed. It had been downhill ever since.

Unfortunately, the synfuels program hadn't been prepared to take up the slack nor would it, Livonas had learned during this trip, for at least two to three more years. Which meant they hadn't touched bottom yet. He sure as hell wasn't looking forward to giving that news to Whitman.

What the hell would San Francisco look like by then? Or by next month?

Frankel's voice cut into his thoughts. "You want to stop off at the M and M for lunch?" The edge had left his voice and he seemed almost apologetic.

They had eaten lunch at the M and M almost every day when Livonas had worked at the *Examiner*. He could almost taste the Polish sausage.

"You're on." He was booked on the red eye for Chicago, he could afford to play tourist for a few hours.

Maybe he could even smooth over his differences with Gus.

December 15

11:00 A.M., *Tuesday*

"Who is he?" the coroner's investigator asked.

The police lieutenant pulled out a small note pad. "The manager identified him as Steven Hart, Anaheim, California. He worked with the convention over in the Pension Building."

"You notify them?"

"Talked to the head of the California delegation—he said Hart was some kind of clerk."

The investigator walked over to the bed. The body lay face down, spread-eagled on the sheets. It was nude, the wrists and ankles attached by leather restraints to the headboard and frame just under the box springs. He lifted the head of the corpse, stared a moment into the lifeless eyes, then let it fall back on the pillow. Slender build, pretty enough if you liked young men. Smooth skin, not much body hair. There was a slight shine on the buttocks. He touched the cold skin, then wiped his fingers on his handkerchief.

He nodded to his junior deputy to start taking notes. "Deceased's age approximately twenty-five—"

"Twenty-six," the lieutenant interrupted. "We got it off his driver's license."

"—twenty-six. Caucasian, five ten, about one hundred fifty pounds." He looked up at the lieutenant. "The photo lab get all their photographs?"

"More'n we need." The lieutenant looked gray. "It's a real mess, isn't it?"

The investigator bent down to pry open the jaws of the corpse and pull out the jockstrap that had been forced between them. "Tentative cause of death: suffocation."

"Hell of a way to go," the lieutenant said.

"The jock's brand-new, it's window dressing," the investigator said dryly. "He suffocated from having his head forced into the pillow. You can see where the fabric's been cut—teeth indentations are still in it." He glanced back at his deputy. "Bruises on the head, back, and buttocks, possibly made by heavy boots. Twelve lash marks on the back at approximate two-inch intervals from the shoulder blades to just above the buttocks." He took out his handkerchief and probed gently. "The victim was probably sodomized. Indications of rectal bleeding"—he hesitated—"put a question mark after that. He may have been dead before then."

He dropped the handkerchief in the wastebasket. "What do you have, Lieutenant?"

"Not much. Stack of porn mags on the nightstand, a jar of lubricant on the floor by the head of the bed. A leather mask, studded paddle, two leather rings—one cock ring, the other looks like a dog collar."

"Where are they?"

"Everything's on top of the bureau."

The investigator rifled through a few of the magazines and casually inspected the leather items. He frowned. "Everything's brand-new." He thought about that for a moment, then said: "Any idea how it happened?"

The lieutenant shrugged. "Sex party. My guess is there were three or four of them. Maybe somebody got carried away. Maybe everybody did."

The investigator lit a cigarette and walked over to the ashtray on the bureau top. It was empty, no butts or crust of ash on the bottom. There were a few crumpled advertising fliers in the wastepaper basket but that was it. No empty beer cans, no indications anybody had been using poppers.

"Pretty neat group for a party, apparently nobody smoked or drank."

He checked out the bathroom. There was a damp washrag and a hand towel wadded up near the basin. The other towels were neatly folded on the chrome rack by the shower stall. Hart hadn't showered beforehand and apparently nobody else had showered afterward or used any of the towels as trick towels. He walked back into the room.

"Any personal effects?"

"Some clothing, a portable typewriter, stack of letters from home, a file of papers from the convention. Hot-plate for coffee, small pot for soup. Wallet, a couple of photographs."

"You take the pictures with you?"

The lieutenant nodded. "They're downtown. Portrait of his mother and father, I'd guess. Two five-by-sevens, one of a boy, the other a girl. Both about twenty. Maybe he went both ways."

The photographs were probably of Hart's brother and sister, the investigator thought. "The wallet still here?" The lieutenant nodded, and he said, "Let me see it."

It was a blue cloth wallet with a Velcro strip to hold it closed. The usual credit cards, a driver's license, health insurance card, a small card saying he was a member of the Smithsonian Institution, and several wallet-sized photographs.

One of them was of a girl on a beach, obviously taken someplace in California. The other was a snapshot taken on the Mall with the Washington Monument in the background. The girl in California was blonde and pretty and had signed the photo, "To Steve with love. Louise." The girl in D.C. was short, almost dumpy, and had black hair. Her photograph was signed, "Love—Debbie."

There were no photographs of any men.

The lieutenant said, "They usually carry pictures of girls as a cover in case they're picked up in a bar for soliciting. Then they flash the photographs and try and play it straight."

The investigator was irritated. Where the hell had the lieutenant been the last twenty years? He stared at the photographs for a long time.

There wouldn't be much of an investigation, he thought. Hart's parents probably wouldn't push for one, even if they had the money to do so; they wouldn't want to risk the scandal being confirmed. The department would consider it open and shut. And Hart himself was from out of town, which meant he had few friends who would raise a stink.

He glanced at the body again. Whoever killed Hart had probably thought of all of that.

He nodded at his deputy. "One prescription bottle of Valium found on premises, no evidence of any recent drinking. No tattoos or other identifying marks on body. Be sure mortician signs for ring, unable to remove from finger . . ."

December 15
3:00 P.M., Pacific Time, Tuesday

It began to fall apart ten minutes after Livonas had settled on a bar stool at the M and M. While Frankel called the office, he worked on a draft beer and flipped through the morning paper, pausing to scan a column in which the writer compared Vincent de Young to Abraham Lincoln, Franklin D. Roosevelt, and Pope John. Livonas wished he had remembered to pick up a *Washington Post* at the hotel.

Frankel finished his call and handed the phone back to the bartender. "Libya and Nigeria just issued communiqués stating they had no intention of relaxing the oil embargo. It doesn't look like your boss did too well with Mexico, either."

Livonas felt a flash of compassion for Whitman. The man had spent the last three years trying to make an incompetent President

look good. It was an impossible task . . . He shook a toothpick from
the empty Tabasco bottle on the bar.

"What they say and what they do might be two different things,
Gus."

Frankel sprayed mustard over his sausage and signaled the bartender for another beer. "Even if he scrounges a few hundred thousand more barrels a day, imports will still be a third lower this
month than last year." He took a bite of the sausage, talking out of
one side of his mouth. "You know who's going to make up the difference? We will."

"Who's 'we,' Gus?"

Frankel waved a hand. "We—California, Colorado, Alaska, the
West. Your national sacrifice area."

The bitter edge was back in his voice. Livonas turned on his bar
stool so he was looking directly at Frankel. "Gus, you're trying to
pick a fight with me."

Frankel's face flushed. "You know what unemployment is in this
state? The Labor Department says it's twenty-three percent. Actually, it's closer to forty. That's because if California is anything,
it's life on wheels. You need a car to get to work, you need it to get
back. And you need the gasoline to run it. It's oil that turns the en-
gines in the lumber mills and it's oil that runs the farmers' tractors.
You know the biggest industry in this state? It's agriculture. Or at
least it used to be. I can take you over to the Valley and show you
farms where half the fields have been left unplowed because the
farmer didn't have the diesel fuel to run his rig."

A pressman at a nearby table glanced over, grinned, and said in an
Australian accent: "That's telling the blighter!"

Livonas drained his glass. "Things are tough all over, Gus, what
makes you think you're the exception?"

Frankel toyed with the last bite of sausage but didn't eat it.
"Thanks a lot from myself and my fellow Californians, your sympathy is touching. The point is, we don't have any gas or oil. Oh, we
pump and refine plenty of it—but we ship it all back East."

"After collecting a healthy severance tax, of course," Livonas said
bitterly. He could feel himself start to lose control. "For Christ's
sake, Gus, do you ever read any papers but your own? Do you know
what it's like in Chicago? Do you know how cold a brick building
can get with only four hours of heat a day? You couldn't piss
enough to melt the ice in the toilet bowl."

He turned back to his new glass of beer. Some of the other customers were staring but he didn't give a damn.

"This 'suffering West' shit is all I've heard since I got here. Twenty people froze to death in a Detroit nursing home last week because the home didn't have enough heating oil. And it's an early winter back East—that's just the beginning."

The red slowly faded from Frankel's face. "Hey, what are we screaming at each other for?" He poured himself another glass from the bottle the bartender had quietly placed in front of him. "I know it's bad in the East. But people out here feel that it's their oil, it's their land, and they're being asked to make all the sacrifices. I'll tell you something else, Andy. We not only have to take care of our own, we have to take care of all the casualties from the East who lose their jobs and wind up out here. It's the Okies all over again."

Livonas looked away. "You sound like de Young."

"Andy, will you listen to me?" Frankel pleaded. "Nobody in Washington seems to give a shit that the coal companies are tearing up the landscape in Wyoming and Colorado, that the synfuel plants are drying up the water we use to irrigate the Imperial Valley, or that people in some of the little towns in the West are dropping like flies because of atomic and germ warfare tests by the federal government thirty years ago or because their town was built on a chemical dumping ground. Come on, when's the last time *you* thought about any of it?"

"The whole country's in a bind, Gus," Livonas said lamely. He stood up and reached for his wallet to pay the bill. "Sorry I blew up—I've been on the road for a week now and I hear this every place I go."

Frankel pushed his money back. "The rhetoric's on me."

Outside in the sunshine, Frankel said: "Is Whitman going to challenge Massey for the nomination?"

"You asking for the record?"

"I was hoping—"

"No way, Gus." The *Examiner* offices were a block north on Fifth and they automatically headed for them.

"Okay, off the record," Frankel said.

"Of course he's going to take on Massey."

"You think Massey will step aside?"

"No, I think he'll be pushed."

"You going to manage Whitman's campaign?"

"Maybe." Livonas allowed himself a small smile. "I wouldn't mind another campaign against de Young."

In Frankel's office just off the city room, Livonas sat on the windowsill and flipped through some snapshots of the land he and Gus owned along the Russian River. He hadn't been there since just before he had gone to Washington.

"Mary and I pooled our gas rations and did some fishing up there two weeks ago," Frankel mused. "Nobody but the locals around. The whole damned area is dying now, no tourists."

Livonas lingered over a shot of Mary Scoma proudly holding up a string of bass. She had been Gus's steady companion for years now. Besides a love of fishing, they shared a mutual dislike for the institution of marriage. That, as Mary had once explained to Livonas, was what kept her and Gus together. Livonas couldn't fault it, he hadn't had much luck with marriage himself.

The last photo in the stack was a snapshot of the redwood cabin with its screened-in porch and lopsided front steps. For the second time in as many hours, Livonas found himself thinking about Ellen ... and Wendy. It seemed more like last month, not nine years ago ...

It had been the Fourth of July weekend, and he, Ellen and Wendy, Mary and Gus had gone up to the cabin. Ellen had dressed Wendy in a flouncy blue pinafore with a string of daisies embroidered on the hem and Wendy had toddled around the cabin, a typical little-girl showoff. Then Livonas had sat on the porch steps and held out a stuffed toy kitten he had bought for her birthday. She had whooped when she saw it and run toward him, laughing, arms outstretched, legs pumping in the awkward gait of a three-year-old.

She was almost in his arms when she collapsed.

Livonas had driven to Marin General Hospital while Ellen held Wendy on her lap, smoothing back the curls from the pale face and desperately repeating, "It's just the heat." Livonas had known instinctively that it was a lot more.

The pediatrician, who wore his black stethoscope like a necklace, told them that Wendy had had a heart attack, that she had suffered from a congenital heart defect. Indeed, it had been a miracle she had lived so long.

A month later, he and Ellen had stood together on a bluff atop the Marin headlands and scattered Wendy's ashes to the Pacific winds. Almost a year to the day later, they had separated.

Gus guessed what he was thinking and said, "You hear anything from Ellen lately?"

Livonas waited for the tightening in his throat to ease. "I got a letter from her last summer."

"Mary and I got a card last Christmas. She still in Geneva?"

Livonas nodded. "She's putting out a newsletter for the World Health Organization."

Gus cleared his throat and shuffled the papers on his desk. After a moment, Livonas looked up, catching Gus in profile. Always a little on the heavy side, Frankel had put on a good twenty pounds, most of it around the waist.

"I see you've got a new addition." Livonas pointed at Frankel's potbelly.

Frankel patted his stomach with mock pride. "Healthiest fat man in the city—pulse seventy and blood pressure one-twenty over eighty." He flipped through a small stack of papers and slid a sheet over to Livonas. "Take a look, it's my physical."

"Pride goeth before a fall, Gus." Livonas went back to the photos, wondering if he'd have a chance to get up to the cabin in the spring.

"Where do you go from here?" Frankel asked.

"Chicago. Whitman wants me to break it to Janice McCall that when it comes to heating oil, the city has all it's going to get." He put down the photos. "I can think of things I'd rather do."

Somebody coughed. "Busy?"

Frankel said, "Come in, Mike" and made the introductions. Mike Garber reminded Livonas of himself ten years before. Medium height, loose build, too much hair, a baggy brown suit, and a skeptical face that believed only a tenth of what it saw. Too thin, too eager, and probably too abrasive for his own good.

Frankel pushed aside his stack of papers. "What've we got?"

"De Young called the shots—Alaska, Colorado, and Arizona have mobilized their own national guards and the governors of five other states are quote studying it unquote." Garber's voice was high, almost squeaky.

"What about the hijackings?"

Garber shook his head. "There've been a few boosts, not many.

Several on Interstate Five plus an isolated tank truck holdup back in
the hills where there was a roadblock and some of the local farmers
drained the tank at gunpoint."

Livonas listened intently. "Any of it cross state lines?"

"If it did, nobody's talking. You'd think the Guv would have
flashed some hard evidence."

Frankel laced his fingers behind his head and looked thoughtful.
"Maybe the Governor's holding the evidence for the Grand Jury."

Livonas caught the skeptical look on Garber's face. "I have to interview Clint Avery at four, after that I'll get back on the hijacking
story. But I can tell you right now I'm not going to find much."

"What's with Avery?" Livonas asked. Clinton Avery had been
speaker of the California state legislature ever since Livonas had
worked for the *Examiner*.

"It's more like what's not with him," Garber quipped. "The Guv
promised to support him for another term as speaker, then knifed
him. He just got voted out this morning. I figure I can get some
choice quotes from him about the Governor."

"Don't make it personal, Mike." Frankel's voice held a note of
warning.

Garber ignored it. "Gus, I keep telling you de Young's full of
shit." He turned to go. "I'll call in from Sacramento."

After Garber had left, Livonas settled back into a chair. "Gus, if
the hijackings are phony, why the hell did de Young call out the
Guard? Grandstand play? Call them out, slap a curfew on civilian
traffic, and blame it all on the Feds?"

"Wake up and smell the coffee, Andy. You used to live out
here—we're dying and the only person who's doing anything about
it is Vincent de Young." The color crept back into Frankel's face.
He leaned across his desk, his voice hard. "Tell you the truth. I
don't know why de Young called out the Guard but I assume he's
got a damned good reason. In any event, he's doing *something*."

So there it was, Livonas thought. Even born cynics like Frankel
were falling in step with de Young. And now it looked as if he and
Gus were saying good-bye.

It had been the same with every friend he'd had in the West.

December 15
  8:30 P.M., Pacific Time, Tuesday

Sally Craft swished the ice around in her glass with her index finger; she had ordered a double Amaretto and now she didn't feel like
drinking it. She settled back in the leather barrel chair and stared
out the window at the Bay below.

It was dusk and Angel and Alcatraz islands were backlit by the
setting sun. Just beyond, billowing banks of Pacific fog filled the Bay
narrows, blanketing the roadway of the Golden Gate Bridge. Above
the top of the fog banks, the slim towers of the bridge shone a brilliant red against the sunset.

It was the right view from the wrong place, Sally thought acidly,
and turned to the husky young man sitting next to her at the bar.
"Who's Vince talking to now?"

"Governor Barron, Miss Craft." He took a sip of beer and smiled
politely. Sally felt a brief twinge of irritation. If there were a duller
collection of ex-jocks than the crew Vince had hired for bodyguards,
she'd like to know where.

She swiveled in her chair so she could see Vince seated at the far
end of the Top of the Mark, the corner nearest the Fairmont Tower
where you could sit and look right down into the hotel rooms. He
had pushed several tables together and was talking quietly to a
dozen well-dressed southwestern types in Neiman Marcus western-
styled suits and hand-tooled calfskin boots.

Two state policemen in mufti rode shotgun at the outboard tables
to see that Vince and his friends weren't disturbed. Governor Barron sat at Vince's right, making notes in a pocket ledger. Sally didn't
like Barron; he was always trying to cop a feel when Vince wasn't
looking. The others she didn't know but knew she wouldn't like
them if she did. They reminded her of the stock her uncle kept in
his feed pens: sleek, overweight, pig-eyed, and bullheaded.

She went back to studying Vince and frowned. What the hell was
she doing here anyway? She wasn't interested in politics and she
didn't care much for politicians. Besides, she could have spent the
evening in Cotati with Rick. They had been on again, off again ever

since their two bands had toured Europe together three years before.

Thinking of Rick made her uneasy. If he had been just a little bit jealous, she wouldn't have gotten involved with Vince. But Rick had thought it was funny. Rick was laid back, northern California style, she had to give him that. Maybe too laid back. She drummed her fingers on the bar and glanced over at the governor's party again. She had once heard hell described as endless boredom and she couldn't agree more.

There was a chorus of squeals from a nearby table. A middle-aged woman with two daughters was pointing at Vince. He looked up at the squeals, then smiled and walked over to sign autographs. The courtly, fatherly governor, Sally thought. She watched him out of the corner of her eye. Christ, he was good in public, he never made a wrong move.

She turned back to the man next to her. "What's your name, hon?"

"Jake Riley, Miss Craft."

He'd been at the bar for more than an hour and he was still hanging onto the same bottle of Michelob. She guessed him to be about thirty-five, a second generation Okie from the Valley who was just starting to thicken around the middle and thin out on top.

"You think a lot of Vince, don't you?" She had yet to run into one of Vince's guards who didn't.

His voice lost its formality and flatness. "There's nobody like him, Miss Craft. Vincent de Young is the best hope the West has." He looked at her expectantly, waiting for an affirmation.

Sally patted him on the hand. "He's sure lucky to have people like you around, Jake." Where *did* Vince get them?

"He's lucky to have your support, too, Miss Craft."

Sally had never really counted herself as one of Vince's supporters. In fact, right now she wasn't even sure she liked him. She didn't understand his politics and she didn't like his friends and recently she had found him boring to be with in bed. Worst of all, she had begun to feel that she was just one of his political props, a link to the younger generation. Not that she minded doing an occasional benefit for him—it was good publicity for her as well. But she'd be damned if she'd become a part of the road show Vince's resident creep, Herb Shepherd, was putting together.

She pushed aside the Amaretto and signaled the Samoan bartender for a Coors.

The truth was, she thought, she didn't like being *alone* with Vince at all.

She liked being with him in public.

Have him touch her when people were around and it was like sticking her fingers in a wall socket. It was a question of power, she thought, not quite understanding it. In public, Vince was somebody else—*really* somebody else. He was ten feet tall, the most dynamic man she had ever met and the most attractive. But turn off the cameras and take away the audience and he was Vince again. Just Vince. Then, with sudden insight: He was a lot like herself. Put her on stage with ten thousand kids out front and the band going like crazy behind her and she was somebody else, too.

"You married, Jake?"

"Yes, ma'am. Three kids, the oldest is six." Sally wasn't sure whether he had smiled or not when he said it. If he had, it was the first expression she'd seen on his face all night. Except when his eyes slid sideways for a peek down the front of her blouse.

"No shit? How old are the other two?"

"The little boy is four, the smallest, Nancy, is one."

Sally felt thin fingers brush her shoulder and smelled the faint odor of Herb Shepherd's mouthwash. "The reception begins in the Governor's suite in five minutes, Sally."

"Why the fuck didn't you tell me that before, Herb?" She slid out of her chair and picked up her purse. "Tell Vince I'll be in my room. And, Herb"—she lowered her voice, biting off the words— "don't touch me, you feel like a goddamned corpse."

Ten minutes, one joint, and two toots of coke later she sat at the small dressing table in her hotel room and stared at her image in the mirror. She'd had it with Vince, it was all over.

Then she couldn't help grinning. A three-month affair with the governor of California. Not bad. And she was dropping *him*. She'd do the concert in San Diego and that would be it. If he needed a hostess, he could always send up to Sacramento and have them take his wife out of mothballs.

She had just finished with her eyebrow pencil when the door

opened and Vince walked in, closing it behind him. He stood with his back against the doorjamb, staring at her. Sally stared back. Vince always managed to project a "home on the range" image—the young California cowboy, full of charm and fight. The poor kid from the run-down ranch who had worked his way to the top, first as a gung-ho military man, then as a successful business executive, and finally governor. Sally was surprised that more people didn't realize the "humble origins" bit was an act. Vince actually came from a three-hundred-acre spread in the Santa Ynez Valley where his father raised prize bulls as a hobby.

She had turned on all the lights in the room to do her face and the glare didn't flatter him. Even from across the room, she could see the small network of wrinkles caused by the California sun. It made her acutely aware that he was twenty years older than she. But it was more than age that had become a barrier between them and it was only during the last few days that she realized what it was.

She had an instinctive feminine fear of him that she couldn't ignore.

"I've been waiting," he said casually. "We're late."

It was the private Vince, the one she could handle.

"Didn't anybody ever tell you you're supposed to knock on a lady's door before entering?" She arranged some strands of hair as she talked, then leaned toward the mirror to check herself out.

"Depends on who the lady is." He walked over and took her chin between his thumb and forefinger, turning her head around so she was looking at him. "And if she's a lady." He looked down at her without smiling. "Some of the biggest power brokers in the Southwest are in my suite—they're dying to meet you. We don't want to stand them up now, do we?"

She tried to shake loose but his fingers felt like pliers.

"You were talking to Andy Livonas in City Hall today," he continued in a monotone. "Stay away from that son-of-a-bitch, understand?"

He let her go and slid his hand around to the nape of her neck and began massaging it. She stared in the mirror at the angry red spots his fingers had left. The touch of his hand on her neck made her flesh crawl.

"I want out, Vince." It was all she could do to keep her voice from shaking.

She could feel him spread his fingers and run them through her hair. "Maybe later but not now, Sally." His voice was pleasant, almost dreamy. "Herb's worked out a two-week schedule for you; he's already cleared it with your manager."

She forgot her fear then, hitting the glass top of the dressing table with the flat of her hand. "Well, fuck him, fuck Shepherd, and fuck you! Nobody's telling me what to do!"

The hand in her hair became a fist and he yanked her to her feet, turning her around so that she was arched backward over the dressing table.

"Nobody's running out now, Sally," he continued in a tight voice. "Not you, not Herb, not Craig, not Bolles, not anybody. After New Year's you can do whatever you want to, but you're going to stick around to sing our national anthem at the convention. Now you'd do that much for me, wouldn't you?"

"God*damn*it, let me go!"

She started to struggle and he playfully held her away from him with one hand. Then the expression on his face melted into something else and he pulled her closer. She brought her knee up to catch him in the groin. He twisted slightly and her knee struck his upper thigh.

"Come on, Sally," he said in a choked, excited voice. He began pulling her over to the quilt-covered queen-sized bed.

"Bastard!" She tried to struggle free and he let go of her unexpectedly, whirling around. His backhanded slap caught her unaware. She was dazed by the shock. He pushed her flat on the bed and straddled her, his hands rough beneath her dress. She twisted away from him and he slapped her again. She could taste the blood from a split lip.

"You're a fighter, Sally, I like that." He grinned at her, fumbling with his belt. "How do you want it?" She desperately searched his face for something familiar. This was a Vince de Young she didn't know.

He yanked up her dress. His fingers scratched painfully against her thighs as he pulled at her panties. "This is the way I've always wanted you, Sally."

She swore and struggled, then remembered when she was seventeen and had made the mistake of going with a biker to Clear Lake for the weekend. She had fought him all the way and it had excited him even more. It was almost a month before the bruises went away.

De Young was lying flat on top of her now, his face next to hers so she could feel his breath on her neck. She forced herself to go limp and lay still on the spread, turning her head away so she didn't have to look at him or smell his breath or feel his tongue on her lips.

Another minute and he rolled off her, pulled up his trousers and walked to the bathroom. Five minutes later she heard the toilet flush. He came out, smoothing back his hair and straightening his coat. His face was the color of clay.

"Pretty yourself up and meet me downstairs," he said in a hoarse voice. He paused at the door. "You can pack up at the end of the month, Sally. But until then, you'll damn well do what I say."

After he had left, she stood in front of the mirror pressing the wrinkles out of her clothes with her hands, fighting back the tears. She fished in her purse for what was left of the coke and a few moments later felt numb if no happier.

She wanted no part of Vince de Young. Not anymore.

She grabbed her purse from the table and ran for the door. She'd catch a cab downstairs and that would be the last Vince would ever see of her.

Jake Riley was waiting for her in the hallway just outside the door.

"Governor de Young said I should see you to his suite, Miss Craft." He was just as polite as he had been at the bar.

Her first reaction was anger—she was nothing but a goddamn prisoner.

Then she was afraid all over again.

December 16
6:00 A.M., Central Time, Wednesday

Livonas was jolted awake by the jet's wheels hitting the icy runway at O'Hare. He yawned and pulled up the small windowshade. He hadn't yet figured out what he was going to tell Janice McCall, Chicago's outspoken—sometimes too outspoken—mayor. It would be a mistake to try and bullshit her. She was tough, smart, partisan, and vindictive, but nobody had ever accused her of being gullible.

He and McCall had been friendly for years, which was why Whitman had asked him to go to Chicago. He knew all the polite ways of saying "no"; he also knew that none of them would work with her.

He was walking through the circular hub of the exit ramp when a policeman inspecting the crowd suddenly stepped forward. "Good to see you, Mr. Livonas."

It took Livonas a moment to place him. Sergeant Max Chernig, Janice McCall's bodyguard and personal sounding board throughout her three terms as mayor.

"Better put on your coat, it's damned cold outside." Chernig pulled open the side door that led directly to the runway below and stepped back to let Livonas go first. The air was so frigid it hurt to breathe. Livonas walked down the icy steps, holding on to the hand rail so he wouldn't slip.

"How's her Honor?" He wasn't prepared, he thought. It was six o'clock in the morning, he hadn't even had breakfast yet. And Janice McCall was all primed to take him apart.

"The Mayor's fine. Except for the cold, of course."

For a moment, Livonas didn't know whether Chernig meant the city or the mayor. The sergeant frequently didn't differentiate between the mayor and the city she ran, an attitude encouraged by McCall.

But the cold must be getting to everybody. One of the few things he had gleaned from reading a copy of the *Chronicle* on board the plane had been the Chicago weather report. The cold snap had lasted for more than two weeks without the temperature once rising above freezing. Snowfall had been heavy until the thermometer had dropped into the low teens. Now a warming trend was on the way and with it, almost a foot of new snow.

He paused at the foot of the stairs, the wind stiffening his hair and numbing his face. The only vehicle around was a nearby police helicopter.

"Where's the Mayor?"

Chernig pointed at the 'copter and raised his voice so he could be heard above the noise of its blades. "She thought you might like an aerial view of the city."

Livonas could make out McCall's perfectly coiffed snow-white hair through one of the helicopter's small side windows. He bent against the wind and walked over.

"Good to see you, Andy." Janice McCall extended a gloved hand from beneath a blue plaid lap robe. Her voice was husky, her hand fragile.

Livonas strapped himself in the bucket seat next to hers while

Chernig climbed in beside the pilot. McCall picked up a thermos and handed Livonas a cup. "Black, with more sugar than is good for you. I knew you wouldn't have time to get any at the airport." She poured from the thermos, her hand shaking slightly. "I'm sorry about the change in schedule but the day is booked with emergency meetings from eight o'clock on."

Livonas sipped his coffee, grateful that she had brought it along. "You're looking well," he said tentatively.

"Don't lie to me, Andy." She tapped Chernig on the shoulder. "Max, ask the pilot to show Mr. Livonas a little of the city." A sideways glance at Livonas, huddled over his coffee. "There's another blanket in the canvas pouch beside you if you need one."

"I'm fine," Livonas said. The inside of the 'copter was cold and he was afraid his teeth were going to chatter. He was well aware that the coffee and the offer of the blanket and the 'copter itself were all part of the staging for their talk.

There was a gentle swaying as the helicopter lifted off the tarmac and turned slightly in the wind. A mumble came from the police radio and Livonas noticed that both Chernig and the pilot were wearing headphones. McCall leaned forward and tapped Chernig on the shoulder again.

"Follow the Desplaines River Road, please, Max—I'd like to show Andy what's left of the forest preserves."

She was all business, Livonas thought. There would be no reminiscing about how he had once covered the police beat for the City News Bureau and she had been a reform alderman. He was sunk in thought for a few minutes, remembering, then glanced up to see McCall studying him. He returned the stare, wondering how he could crack her shell of formality or if he should even try. Only when he was close to her did she look small, hardly more than five feet, with thin Irish features and china-white skin. He decided it was her deep-set eyes that made her seem taller than she was. Janice McCall had a way of looking down at you.

He finished his cup of coffee and leaned back. "We can't do it," he said quietly.

She patted him gently on the arm. "But I haven't asked you to do anything—yet." Nobody was going to disturb Janice McCall's agenda.

"You're playing games, Janice."

Her voice was sharp. "Look out the window, Andy, not at me." Livonas glanced out the side window. They were flying low over what had been the forest preserves, the wooded parklike belt that edged the west side of the city.

"We're selling permits, one tree per household," McCall continued in a quiet voice. "There's no way we can enforce it, of course; people grab whatever they can get."

What he guessed had once been a grove of oak and elm was now a huge vacant lot of hundreds of stumps sticking out of the thick covering of grimy snow. At the far corner of the field, a man in an irridescent down vest and a Navy watch cap exhaled clouds of steam as he struggled with the rip cord of his chain saw. The saw suddenly sputtered into life and the man bent over and pressed the blade against the base of a stump, sending a spray of sawdust into the air.

"That was one of my pet projects in my first term. Restoring the forest preserves. Remember the slogan? 'A city without trees is a city without a heart.' Did I ever thank you for that?"

Livonas wished he had flown directly to D.C. "Janice, I—"

"He'll get five dollars a stump on Lake Shore Drive, maybe more. People in this neighborhood can't afford that. They'll either cut their own stumps or burn their furniture."

Chernig turned in his seat and offered his headset to McCall. She put it on and listened for a minute.

"It's a supermarket looting," she told Livonas. "South Side."

"Does it happen a lot?"

She nodded, her face tight. "Too often. Police Chief Keeney will dispatch some units but the looters will be gone before they get there." She shrugged and handed the headset back to Chernig. "The police are over-extended—the supermarkets and shopping malls are logical targets for looters and there just aren't enough men to guard them and ride shotgun on the coal and oil trucks as well."

She looked out the window at the frozen city below. "The city's starting to feed on itself, Andy, and there's nothing much we can do about it."

"What does Keeney think?"

"He doesn't," she mused. "He bucks the problems up to me." She shifted the collar of her coat away from her mouth so her breath wouldn't freeze on the heavy melton cloth. "Keeney's taught me a great lesson—that there are times when I have to play mother as well as tough broad. He doesn't reassure me, I have to reassure him."

"Why don't you get rid of him?"

She laughed. "You've got a lot to learn about municipal government, Andy. His men think the world of him and I need that more than I need a good administrator."

Chernig turned up the radio. Livonas couldn't quite make out the words, though he sensed the urgency.

Chernig turned to McCall, his face tense. "There's a mob of looters forming west on Lake Street, at the coal yards."

"Tell the pilot to take us there, Max." She poured herself a cup of coffee. When she extended her hand, Livonas could see part of her bare wrist. It was blue with cold.

"I'm not the only one who listens to the weather reports, Andy. There's a warm front moving in and by evening it will be snowing, another ten inches or so on the twelve already here. Then the temperature will drop. There's no relief in sight, there hasn't been for the past two weeks." She shook her head. "I can't blame people."

Livonas spotted them when the 'copter was still blocks away—ants clustering around the coal yard, kept away from the miniature mountains of snow-covered coal by a dozen police in riot gear. More ants were streaming in from the surrounding streets.

The 'copter hovered for a few moments, then set down in a cleared space behind the coal mountains. Livonas handed McCall down to the ground, following her as she picked her way over stray lumps of coal to the front of the yard. He started to shiver and it took an effort of will to stop. With a wind of twenty miles an hour and a temperature of twenty degrees, the wind-chill factor was at least ten below zero. His fingers inside his leather gloves ached.

The riot police were strung out around the perimeter of the coal yard where the cyclone fencing had been, facing a crowd of perhaps three hundred people jeering at them. The police were nervous, the angry crowd was growing larger. If anything was going to be done, it would have to be done in a hurry, Livonas thought. Almost everybody in the mob had buckets and boxes in which to carry the coal; there were even a few kids with wagons waiting on the fringes.

Captain Keeney hurried over, followed by the head of the riot detail, a huge man with a pie-dough face. Keeney was tall, spare, with a Chicago-Irish accent. He looked relieved to see McCall.

"They're getting ugly, your Honor. We fired over their heads once but I think they might try and rush us." He lowered his voice. "Some of the men don't like the duty, they sympathize with the crowd."

McCall listened to him with growing anger, then demanded: "Who has a bullhorn?"

The tac squad commander had been hanging back, ignoring her. Now he pointed to a police car parked at the base of one of the mountains of coal. "We've got one in the car, ma'am." He was studiously polite. He would also be guarding one of the South Side malls before the week was out, Livonas thought.

"Get it for me, Captain—I can't use it over there."

The commander reddened and hurried over to the car. When he brought it back, she took it and walked a few paces to face the mob. Livonas edged after her. The sudden silence was eerie. There was no traffic on the surrounding streets and no sounds from the neighboring stores or factories. The mob had been shouting and cursing, but the moment McCall stepped forward, they shut up as if on cue. It was so quiet Livonas could hear the wind whistle around the corners of the buildings.

McCall braced herself with her feet wide apart and lifted the bullhorn.

"I'm Mayor Janice McCall and I know how cold you must be. But this fuel dump is for all the people of Chicago." She waited a moment, listening to her voice as it echoed back from the empty buildings in front of her. "In my capacity as the mayor of Chicago, I order you to disperse."

There were a few boos and cat-calls from the crowd now but nobody made a move to rush her. She took a few more steps forward, motioning back Livonas and Chernig, who had started to follow her. She was cutting it damned thin, Livonas thought.

"I order you to disperse." McCall's words hung in the cold, still air. She glanced once at the thin line of police behind her, then turned back to face down the would-be looters. Livonas followed her eyes to the front row of the mob: a fat, red-faced woman wearing a purple babushka—a kerchief—around her head and a green scarf tucked into a worn tweed coat; several middle-aged men in fur hats and navy pea coats; some high school kids in brightly colored parkas; a group of housewives so bundled up against the cold you could hardly see their eyes; a scarecrow of a man in a ragged army coat with a thin face made thick by hate. And behind them, more shivering and angry people coming all the time, the pressure of those behind pushing those up front closer to the line of police.

Closer to McCall, Livonas thought.

He remembered a crowded hall during her last campaign with hundreds of voices cheering and shouting "McCall for Mayor!" and wondered if some of the same people were in the mob.

Ten feet in front of him, Janice McCall took a firmer grip on the bullhorn. Her voice was surprisingly harsh for such a frail woman, Livonas thought. "I have given the police orders to shoot all looters on sight!" There was the same eerie silence once again. She repeated the sentence, louder.

The silence broke. Somebody in the back of the mob shouted, "I see you brought along your Gestapo, Janice!" and the red-faced woman in the babushka cried, "She's bluffing!"

But she wasn't bluffing, Livonas thought. She had made the play and there was no stopping it now. That was the horror of it.

There was a sudden movement in the crowd. Several lumps of coal clattered on the frozen ground beside Livonas. The front ranks of the mob surged forward, then just as quickly shrank back. Keeney had snapped out orders and the riot police had brought their guns to ready arms. The crowd was at flash point, Livonas thought. Give an inch now and it would all be over.

In front of him, McCall took another step forward, making the crowd give ground. Livonas caught his breath. She had made a tactical error, she was too close, too tempting for a quick lunge by any of a dozen of them. He felt himself tense. In seconds, one of them would work up the courage—

Then he heard the whine of police sirens a few blocks away. The moment of danger hung in the chill winter air like a balloon, for an instant, popped and vanished. The crowd wavered, a few people turning away at the edges. Then the mob broke completely apart, the remnants drifting up the street, some shaking their fists and cursing McCall and the police, not forgetting President Thomas Massey.

The fat woman in the babushka stayed behind, screaming, "Look at the pig, she's not freezing to death! Look at her coat! They're all roasting in City Hall!" McCall stared at her for a second, then turned away, sagging with fatigue. The thin line of riot police broke up, some of them straggling back to their cars.

Livonas had taken a few steps forward to help McCall and was the first to spot the man. The scarecrow in the ragged army coat had hung around after the rest of the crowd had left. He was running toward McCall, his right arm held away from his side.

"Watch out!" Livonas dove for him, grabbed several handfuls of cloth, then was rolling in the grimy snow, the man pinned beneath him.

Chernig and some of the riot police ran over to help, followed by a calm McCall.

Livonas got to his feet and two of the police hustled the scarecrow away to a squad car. Chernig bent down and picked a bone-handled hunting knife out of the snow. "Close call."

McCall glanced at the knife, dismissed it, and turned to Keeney. Her eyes were dancing with rage. "How many men did you have stationed here to begin with? Two?"

Captain Keeney was white-faced with anger. " 'Shoot to kill' was a dumb order when it came from Mayor Daley. It wasn't any smarter coming from you."

Her breath came out in little puffs of angry vapor. "What would you have done, invited them to help themselves? I'm not fighting for reelection, I'm fighting to keep a city alive. By this afternoon, we would have had anarchy in the city and there'd be nothing you or I or the National Guard could do to stop it. For God's sake, Keeney, use your head!"

She turned away. "Tell your tac squad captain to get off the radio and come here. I want to talk to him. You, too."

Livonas watched as she squared off before the two of them. She had been a mousy alderman, he remembered, but that had been ten years ago. Somewhere along the line she had discovered courage she probably never knew she had.

"Why was it allowed to get out of hand? You should have flooded the area with police the moment the mob started to form."

The dough-faced captain was arrogant. "I didn't feel free to call up more men. There was no way of telling how bad it would get at the start."

"Bullshit!" She spat out the syllables like cherrystones. "The weather forecast has been the top of the six o'clock news for the past two weeks. Everybody in town knows what's coming." Her voice dripped contempt. "The city hospitals switched to coal a year ago. This is their supply yard—or had you forgotten?"

He tried to face her down and failed. "I don't want to hear any more about your men sympathizing with the mobs," she continued. "I don't give a damn if they live in the area or not. They can earn their badge or leave the force."

It had been a gamble Livonas wouldn't have wanted to take. If anybody had been shot, Chicago would have exploded and the country would have had its first civil insurrection of the winter.

Livonas and Chernig walked McCall back to the waiting 'copter. Just before she stepped in, she turned to Livonas. "I know what you're thinking. Go ahead and say it."

Livonas managed a chilled smile. "That you were very brave?"

"No," she said curtly. "That next time I wouldn't be so lucky."

They sat in the cold 'copter in silence, staring out the side windows as they lifted off. Once in the air, McCall poured another cup of coffee from the thermos, tasted it, shivered and poured the cold liquid back in the flask.

"Andy, Chicago's crumbling." She was silent again for a long moment, then abruptly: "I need a favor."

Her support had been the key in overriding Massey's objection and getting Whitman the vice-presidential nomination, Livonas thought. He had been the go-between. Both he and Whitman owed her.

But they couldn't afford to pay up.

She tapped a cigarette out of a pack and let him light it for her. "I want Chicago's fuel allocation increased. I don't mean next quarter or next month or next week. I'd prefer natural gas—most of the homes in the city are hooked up for it—but I'll take oil. Heavy industry can convert to oil in a matter of a few days, which would give us more gas for home heating." She paused for emphasis. "I want a delivery date this afternoon."

"I'll have to check it out," he said without enthusiasm. He had promised himself that he wouldn't bullshit her and he was doing it already.

She spoke concisely and hardly above a whisper, her eyes as hard as agate. "Like you said, no games, Andy—we've known each other too long for that. I want deliveries to start in ten days. I'm not going to preside over the death of Chicago and that's exactly what you're looking at."

She exhaled a thin stream of smoke and waved at the city below. "We're shut down. Half the factories are closed, Inland Steel locked its doors last week. We've had to close down the schools—it was a choice between them or the hospitals. The only thing that's busy in this town is the county morgue. More than a dozen people have frozen to death every day this month."

She pulled the lap robe tighter around her. "I've asked the coroner not to issue reports on cold-related deaths. There'd be riots." She studied him again, trying to read his expression. "I need Bob Whitman's help, Andy."

"No," Livonas said quietly.

"No? Just like that?"

Livonas sighed. "That's right. No. Just like that. There are ten other cities as bad off or worse than Chicago. Detroit for one, Buffalo for another."

"I'm not the mayor of Detroit or Buffalo, Andy. I'm the mayor of Chicago."

Livonas felt tired and miserable. "If we had anything we could give, we would. Maybe a week from now I could dig up reserve supplies."

"Maybe a week from now pigs will grow wings."

"We don't have it," Livonas repeated in a stiff voice. Then he gave up the game completely. "We couldn't afford to play favorites even if we did."

"With an attitude like that, don't ever run for public office, Andy." She scrubbed out the cigarette. "If you won't help me, Vincent de Young will."

Livonas stared. "What do you mean, de Young will help you?"

She leaned forward and tapped Chernig on the shoulder. "Max, let's get Mr. Livonas back to his plane." Then to Livonas, her eyes cold and hooded: "That was his offer. One million barrels of distillate fuel oil for home heating, another two million of residual fuel oil for industrial use, delivery spread over the month of January."

"De Young? How the hell can he get you fuel oil? All domestic supplies are under federal control." Livonas ran over the possibilities in his mind. "Nevada once tried to go into the gasoline business— during the Arab embargo in '74, the casinos were hurting because there were no tourists. California tried it once before and so did Los Angeles. It didn't work then and it's illegal now."

She shook out another cigarette, this time fending off his attempt to light it. "What's your President going to do? Send in the 82nd Airborne to shut off people's furnaces?"

"What's de Young getting from you?" Livonas said bluntly.

"For openers, my support at the Constitutional Convention."

Livonas looked at her, unbelieving. "You're putting me on, Janice. The convention's a sideshow, a sop to a bunch of political hangers-on and small-town blowhards."

Her eyes filmed with frost and her voice became just as chilly. "Governor de Young was quite serious. And I can assure you, Mr. Livonas, so am I."

He'd have to check on it, Livonas thought. When he got back to O'Hare, he'd call his office and ask Julie to find someone to meet him in Georgetown for lunch and brief him on the convention. Maybe there was something going on that he didn't know about. He had a five o'clock meeting scheduled with Whitman and he had to be able to put the whole picture together then. Somehow the convention played a part—Gus had mentioned it and now so had McCall. But exactly where it fit in, he hadn't the foggiest idea.

One thing for sure, Vincent de Young wouldn't waste his time on a sideshow.

The 'copter was flying low, getting ready to settle down on the landing pad at O'Hare. Livonas coughed. Something was tickling his nose and the back of his throat. He looked out the side window to see black smoke drifting up from the chimneys of a cluster of ranch-style homes. Rubber tires, he thought. They were burning old tires . . .

Then they had touched down and Sergeant Chernig had opened the door and was ready to help them out.

"Give my regards to the Vice-President," McCall said in an icy voice.

She didn't offer Livonas her hand.

December 16

Noon, Wednesday

Livonas dropped off his bags at his Georgetown apartment, then walked around the corner to the Big Cheese. The hostess for the second-floor dining room pointed out the corner table that Julie had reserved for him and he headed for it, trying desperately to smother a yawn. A woman was already sitting at the table, engrossed in a cup of coffee and jotting down notes on a small pad. Either he was late or she was early, he thought. He glanced at his watch and decided she was early.

"Hi, I'm Andy Livonas." He shook her hand casually, not really noticing her, searching the room for a waitress to bring him some coffee.

"Kathleen Houseman." Livonas thought she looked vaguely familiar but with three hours' sleep between San Francisco and Chicago and none after that, the whole world looked vaguely familiar. Where the hell was the waitress? Then he spotted the tall blonde who was a fixture in the late mornings sailing across the floor with the coffee pot.

"Thanks a lot for your time." He said it while scanning the menu.

"I'm glad to be of help."

She had a pleasant, husky voice, Livonas noted, concentrating on his coffee. "Julie said you were chairperson of the Washington state delegation."

She brushed a strand of hair out of her eyes. "For the last six months. Before that, I was an elected delegate and before that, I did public interest law in Seattle with Bob Whitman's old firm."

That was the connection, Livonas thought, the reason why Julie had tapped her. Kathleen Houseman, he realized, wasn't quite what he had expected—her voice sounded more matter-of-fact than falsely modest. He set his cup down, for the first time really looking at her. She was in her late twenties or early thirties and quite pretty in a lithe sort of way. She had shoulder-length, wavy brown hair that she wore swept back, fine features with high cheekbones, and almond-shaped eyes that seemed almost Indian. She was wearing a loose-fitting dark blue pullover with a yoke of snowflakes knitted in the wool and the type of faded corduroy knickers favored by cross-country skiers. He knew without asking that they were more than an item of fashion for her.

"Sorry to interrupt your skiing." He felt genuinely apologetic.

"You're not—I brought my skis along. I thought I'd walk over to Rock Creek Park after lunch." She glanced around the dining room. "I've never eaten here, any suggestions?"

"The crab quiche is the best in town and the onion soup's pretty good."

"I'll try the quiche."

He signaled the waitress and ordered the quiche for her and an omelet for himself. Kathleen was studying him over her cup of coffee and he became acutely aware that he had been wearing the same rumpled suit for three days.

Kathleen glanced down at her small pad of notes. "Anything specific you want to know about the convention or should I start from the top?"

"Give me a little of the background, I don't know much about it." He had considered the convention hopeless right from the start.

"I'll keep it brief." She waited while the waitress refilled Livonas's cup. "You probably know the basics—after the last national election the state legislatures petitioned Congress to call a Constitutional Convention to formulate amendments regarding federal taxation. There was a good deal of jockeying for power but eventually Congress did. We're going into our second year now and there hasn't been a substantial piece of anything that's come out of it. Unless you consider a recommended constitutional amendment to reinstate prayers in the public schools as being substantial. I don't. Even on that, New York has petitioned the Supreme Court for an injunction against the convention on the grounds it's exceeded its authority."

The waitress brought their orders and she toyed with a bit of quiche. "At this point, the convention's nothing but a bad joke."

"What happened?"

"The terminal D.C. stall. Congress dragged out the process of assembling the convention long enough to kill the original enthusiasm. Right now the only thing that gets anybody excited down there is a threat to adjourn."

It was about what he had expected. "Why don't they?"

She shrugged. "Congressmen have a hand in appointing acting delegates to replace those who have resigned so it's turned into a congressional pork barrel. For the delegates, of course, it's a power trip. Plus most of them just plain like being in Washington." She looked wistful, remembering. "At one time, it really had potential, some of us really believed we had a chance to make history. Pretty foolish."

Livonas had been watching the emotions flicker across her face as she talked. She hadn't been in Washington long enough to become cynical, he thought. Only dissatisfied.

"I don't know about that. If politics isn't about making history, what is it about? It's just that ninety percent of the time, things get sidetracked."

Livonas didn't want to ask leading questions, but he didn't have that much time before meeting Whitman. "What role has the California delegation been playing at the convention?"

She was obviously curious why he asked. "This month and last they've been the most active delegation at the convention. They've formed a coalition with other western and southwestern delegations—Washington State excepted because of Bob Whitman—plus some of the southern ones. Last week they pushed through a resolution rotating the control of the floor committee, rules committee, and credentials committee by region."

Livonas could guess what was coming. "What's the order of rotation?"

"For the rest of this month, California's in charge of all three—but don't think of it as just California, it's actually the Western Coalition. They caught everybody napping and sneaked it through."

"With California acting as power broker."

She nodded. "I didn't think they'd win in the showdown vote but at the last moment half the Illinois delegation switched sides."

Livonas remembered the 'copter and a fragile-looking woman with bleached-white hair. "The Cook County delegates?"

Kathleen looked surprised. "That's right."

There it was, Livonas thought: a national podium for de Young's presidential ambitions. He'd been right.

He glanced at his watch. Three hours to go before meeting with Whitman. He was looking forward to briefing him on the West and especially on the activities of Vincent de Young. There was nothing Whitman liked more than to talk politics and Livonas could imagine his eyes glow when he told him about de Young and Janice McCall. He signaled for the check, then had another thought.

"How about if I dropped in on the convention tomorrow and you showed me around?"

"Sure. I'll be there for another week."

It was Livonas's turn to look surprised. "Taking a vacation?"

The dissatisfied look returned. "No, I'm quitting. As of the first of the year, I'm going back to Seattle."

That was the problem with D.C., Livonas thought. The people who should stay, left, and those who should leave, stayed. He paid the check and they walked outside, pausing on the brick sidewalk in front of the restaurant. The afternoon air was crisp and he filled his lungs, fully awake for the first time since leaving Chicago. He had missed Georgetown—the streets filled with university students out of classes for the day, the Christmas shoppers struggling from store to store with their bulging shopping bags, the small candles glowing in the Christmas wreaths hanging in store windows . . .

He turned up his collar. "Cold, isn't it?"

"Sure is." Kathleen hugged herself for emphasis. Livonas noted that outdoors her eyes looked more green than hazel.

"Well, listen, thanks a lot. Again." He was surprised at himself. He was stalling, he didn't want to leave her.

"Any time." She returned his smile.

"I guess I'll see you tomorrow then." Shyness, Livonas cursed to himself, was something you seldom overcame, even with age.

"Right." Kathleen pulled off the ski mitten she had just put on and stuck out her hand.

"Kathleen, it's been great. Thanks again." Livonas realized he was still holding her hand. He quickly let it go.

"Katy. My friends call me Katy."

She was stalling, too, he realized.

"Katy, look—how about having dinner with me tonight?" He paused, trying to sound indifferent. "Late notice, I know, you're probably busy."

"I've nothing planned. I'd love to."

He waited until she was a dozen steps away before he shouted, "Hey, you forgot your skis!"

* * *

Livonas shaved and showered back at his apartment, then lay down for an hour's nap. When he woke up, it was four thirty. He dressed hastily and convinced a cabbie it was a matter of life and death, even if he was a single fare. At the Massachusetts Avenue gate of the Naval Observatory grounds, a marine guard waved them through and they drove up to Admiral's House, the white three-story Victorian that was the official residence of the Vice-President.

It was a few minutes after five and what was left of the day was fading fast. Livonas got out of the cab, pausing to stare at the house in front of him. It was a pretty scene, with the deep shadows and the friendly Queen Anne mansion fronted by the rolling, snow-covered lawn. Early evening was always a moody time of day for him, he thought. Most men his age had a wife and children waiting for them when they came home from work. He had an empty apartment or an office or a woman friend willing to tolerate the casualness that had come to characterize his relationships since breaking up with Ellen.

The cabbie coughed. "That'll be ten-fifty, sir."

Livonas fished a ten and three singles out of his pocket and trudged up the icy steps of the porch. The air was fragrant with the smell of burning maple logs and he could hear Ella Fitzgerald singing "I've Got Your Love To Keep Me Warm" on the upstairs stereo. Vivian was the Fitzgerald fan; Whitman himself didn't care much for music.

It was Vivian who answered the door, beaming when she recognized him. "Andy, what a pleasure. Let me take your coat."

He stepped inside, brushing past the big Christmas wreath on the door, and hugged her briefly. "It's great to see you, Viv. Where's Larry?" The huge ex-marine sergeant had been Whitman's personal valet and bodyguard since he had become Vice-President.

"We knew you were coming and I thought I'd answer the door myself." She stepped back to admire him as fondly as she might have her own son. "How was your trip?"

"Good enough, I guess."

She picked up on his lack of enthusiasm and looked sympathetic. "Last time I was in Seattle, it seemed like all I did was fight with my old friends." There was sudden silence from the stereo and she smiled. "I'm afraid Ella's run out. Bob's in the study, he's expecting you. Can you stay for supper?"

"I'd love to, but I've got a dinner engagement."

"I'll bet she's beautiful." She paused on the stairs, her face shadowed with worry. "Bob's been a little under the weather lately, Andy. I don't think it's anything serious but . . . well, you know, don't let him overdo it. Given half a chance, I know he would."

Livonas assured her that he wouldn't. He walked down the hall to the study, tapped once on the door, and let himself in. Whitman was already getting up from behind the huge Chippendale desk that dominated the mahogany-paneled study. He clapped Livonas on the back, then gestured to the lounger at one side of the desk. "Welcome back to wintry Washington."

He returned to the green leather swivel chair behind his desk and studied Livonas with a fatherly expression. "You're looking good, Andy, really good."

"So are you," Livonas lied. Whitman was a huge bear of a man with craggy features, thick snow-white hair, and a slow, almost shuffling gait. He had lost weight and his face was creased by a few more lines since Livonas had seen him last.

Whitman opened up his right-hand desk drawer and took out two shot glasses and a bottle of Scotch. He poured a shot in each, then handed Livonas one and raised his own in a toast. "To all of us, Andy."

Livonas let the Scotch burn its way down, then settled back on the lounger. Bob Whitman was the reason why he had thrown over a newspaper career for politics. Whitman was living proof that politics and integrity were not a contradiction in terms. He hadn't found many others.

He studied Whitman while the big man filled his briar pipe with a special blend of Turkish and Virginia tobaccos from a teakwood humidor on his desk. A maple log crackled in the fireplace on the other side of the desk and through the windows Livonas could see the central tower of the National Cathedral on Mount St. Albans, outlined against the darkening sky.

"You read my report?" Whitman asked as he reached in the pocket of his plaid shirt for his silver pipe lighter.

"It wasn't very optimistic," Livonas said. "I wouldn't say Libya and Nigeria showed much flexibility."

"They're both Islamic countries, Andy." Whitman took a puff on his pipe and for a moment smoke screened his features. "They're not willing to forget the desert bombing—except for a price. Certainly Libya isn't."

Livonas cocked his head. "That wasn't in your report."

"They asked a price they knew we wouldn't pay. Abandon Israel, abandon Egypt, abandon all our allies in the Near East."

Livonas said automatically, "We can't do that."

Whitman took another drag on his pipe. "It might be a popular move in some quarters."

"What about other oil sources?"

Whitman turned so he was facing the fire. For a moment he was profiled against the leaping flames, his white hair a sudden golden color. "Venezuela has increased its quota and we've got an under-the-table agreement with Indonesia that we don't dare publicize." His voice reflected his weariness. "I'm afraid that's about it. I pretty much came up empty-handed."

"You knew it would be a bust before you went." Livonas hated to see Whitman look defeated. "There's no immediate solution. I know it, you know it, even Massey must know it."

"Massey." Whitman was lost in thought for a moment. "How was it on the West Coast?"

"You want the oil figures first or a rundown on the political situation?"

"Oil first."

Livonas opened his briefcase and handed Whitman a three-page statistical abstract.

"The figures are for the amounts of crude arriving at West Coast ports, the amounts going through the refineries, and the final shipping figures, including the amounts of crude sent through the East-West pipeline."

Whitman didn't look at it. "Tell me what it says, Andy; you wrote it."

"Some supplies are probably being diverted," Livonas said slowly.

"Who's the villain, or is there more than one?"

"My favorite choice is Vincent de Young."

Whitman looked interested. "Why de Young—aside from the fact that you two don't get along."

"He promised one million barrels of home heating oil to Janice McCall. Plus two million of residual fuel oil, delivery guaranteed through January."

Whitman put on his reading glasses. "Let's see this." He was silent for a moment, then: "You're off base, Andy. The amount of diversion you show here could be accounted for by personal usage, siphoning off by employees along the way, and the black market. There's nothing here that would even come close to amounting to three million barrels."

"That's what de Young promised McCall," Livonas said stubbornly.

Whitman ran a stubby finger down the columns of figures again. "Then he must be getting it from someplace else. And the only countries he could get oil from in that quantity would be Canada or Mexico, probably the latter. But Mexican production was allocated worldwide months ago—they couldn't supply de Young without taking it away from somebody else and that's not only bad business, it's bad politics."

"What about reserve production capacity?"

"Maybe—every country has reserve production capacity." He looked up, curious. "What's he getting from Janice?"

"Her support at the Constitutional Convention."

Whitman looked puzzled. "That doesn't make any sense at all, Andy, why the hell would he be interested in the convention? It hasn't done anything, it's not about to."

"I just had lunch with Katy Houseman," Livonas said, trying to tone down the intensity in his voice. "For the rest of this month, at least, California's running the convention."

Whitman settled back in his swivel chair. "You're about to give me a lecture on the political situation."

Livonas shifted the lounger closer to the fire. It was chilly in the house; the formal dining room and the huge main-floor living room had been closed off but Whitman still kept the thermostat low. "I think de Young plans to use the convention as a forum for his bid for the Presidency."

Whitman shrugged and went back to re-stoking his pipe. "How? And what happens next month when, presumably, another state is running the convention? Besides, I'm not all that sure de Young will try for it. He'll have trouble without eastern electoral votes and there's no state east of the Mississippi that he could carry. A few of the southern states, maybe, but that would be it."

Livonas felt uneasy. "De Young's well liked throughout the West, Bob. Everybody hates Massey." He hesitated. "I can't think of any other reason why he would offer McCall the oil except to use the convention."

Whitman steepled his fingers under his chin and stared at Livonas. "What makes Janice think de Young intends to deliver the oil at all? He probably figured she would do exactly what she's done—use his offer to blackmail us. The Justice Department will prohibit the deal, he'll blame the federal government, and everybody will end up hating us and loving him for at least trying. Everybody except his fellow westerners, who will wonder why, if he can get oil for Chicago, he can't get it for them." He shook his head. "If it's true, he's offering too much for too short a gain. The whole deal sounds harebrained to me."

Livonas didn't say anything. Whitman studied him for a long moment. "All right, you won't buy it. Why not?"

"I think Janice McCall has more brains than you're giving her credit for," Livonas said bluntly. "She's getting a lot for what she considers very little—you're right on that score. What worries me is that de Young obviously thinks it's a good deal, too."

"They really like de Young that much out there?" Whitman asked, curious.

"They hate Massey that much." Livonas couldn't help it then, it had been building up ever since he had walked into the house. "Thomas Massey is dangerous. He's dangerous to the party and he's dangerous to the country. We both know it, why don't we talk about it?"

Whitman didn't meet Livonas's eyes. "Dangerous is a pretty strong word, Andy. Incompetent, perhaps—I'd go along with that. But a man learns in office, he grows in office."

It wasn't what Whitman was saying so much as how he was saying it. Where was the snap, where was the fire? Where, for that matter, was the sheer pleasure of debate? Whitman had never needed others to convince him of what to think or what to do.

"Bob, Massey can't get reelected, you know that. You could have the nomination for the asking and there's nobody better equipped for it. You were the most powerful man in the Congress and right now you're the only man in the entire Massey Administration that the country at large respects."

"You want me to run, is that it?"

"It's either you or Vincent de Young."

Whitman's voice was chilly. "Tell me, Andy, what motivates you the most—your admiration of my so-called political talents or your hatred for Vincent de Young?"

Livonas went white. "That's below the belt."

Whitman sighed. "You're right, Andy. And I'm more than sorry. But consider it in political terms. Dumping an incumbent isn't easy, particularly if he's a member of your own party. It's been tried often enough but the only time it succeeded was with Franklin Pierce." He laced his fingers behind his head and stared thoughtfully at the ceiling. "President Massey is a man of many weaknesses, Andy. Most politicians are. I've often thought of politics as a profession for insecure men, small-town boys who never stop trying to make it in the big city. Sometimes they get their priorities confused. Massey fears unpopularity more than failure and the result is that he's both."

"So what are we going to do about it? We need a Roosevelt and you're willing to settle for a reject from the Philadelphia Main Line."

"Andy." Whitman hesitated. He looked exhausted. He still hadn't recovered from his trip overseas, Livonas thought. "I think the problems of the country are such that it wouldn't make too much difference who was in charge. I can't see Vincent de Young doing much different—or much better."

Livonas couldn't believe what he was hearing. He stood up and leaned his knuckles on Whitman's desk.

"We're not talking about de Young now, we're talking about you. Bob, the country's in trouble, deep trouble, and everybody knows it. Almost all our oil imports have been cut off, we don't have enough national energy resources to go around, and there's sectional rivalry for what's left. Without oil, you don't stay warm, you don't work, you're immobilized. The West has most of the nation's resources and wants to hang on to them. The East desperately needs its fair share. Massey hasn't the power or the prestige to mediate between them—the Cudahy bill is one of the few opportunities this Administration has, and western congressmen won't even let it out of committee. It's still there, isn't it?"

Whitman grimaced. "Probably until hell freezes over."

Cudahy's bill was one of the cornerstones in Administration energy policy. It proposed a federal surcharge on the severance tax that states charged corporations for the coal they mined and the oil and gas they pumped. It was an attempt to even things out between states that were rich because of their energy resources—and getting richer from state-levied severance taxes—and states that were poor. Despite the fact that the bite was on the energy companies, the western and Gulf Coast states had fought the bill bitterly.

Livonas helped himself to half a shot of Scotch and knocked it back. "We need a President that both West and East respect, one who's lived in the West and understands the East." He paused to let that sink in. "I must have talked to fifty state chairmen, local club leaders, and elected officials, and you know the first question at the top of everybody's list? How do we get rid of Thomas Massey? Their next question is, when is Bob Whitman going to make himself available for his party's nomination."

Whitman stood up and came out from behind the desk to put his arm on Livonas's shoulder and walk toward the study door. "Nice try, Andy. But even though Tom Massey has his problems, he's basically a good man and I'm not going to run out on him now just because the sledding's a little rough. I've also got to be practical. If Vincent de Young would have difficulty getting easterners to vote for him because he's from the West, then so would I. I'm a westerner, too."

Whitman was almost leaning on him as they walked across the study and Livonas remembered Viv's warning not to push him too hard. Well, he had pushed but he wasn't sorry. What he was sorry about was that he had misjudged Whitman so badly.

"The only thing in Chicago that was colder than the weather was Janice McCall's voice when she told me to give you her regards."

"That's because she's blaming me for something over which I have no control." Whitman's voice became harder, more remote. "We're friends, Andy, lifelong friends I hope. But if you're looking for someone to run for President, you're going to have to look somewhere else."

They shook hands, then Whitman said goodnight and quietly closed the study door. Livonas walked back to the hall closet to pick up his coat and hat.

He couldn't get over the change in Whitman, a change that left him more depressed than anything that had happened to him in the West. The country desperately needed Robert Whitman.

But Robert Whitman had given up.

December 16
7:00 P.M., *Wednesday*

Kathleen Houseman strode down the path alongside her landlord's house with her Trak skis balanced on her shoulder, picking her way over the flagstones that led to the two-room cottage she had rented from the Emersons ever since coming to Washington. She could see Mr. Emerson silhouetted on the living room shade, mixing the evening cocktails for himself and his wife. She'd miss them both, she thought, and she'd miss Stu Lambert, but that was it.

Which, all in all, was a rather sad commentary on the last two years of her life.

She'd just stomped the snow and ice off her boots and put the tea kettle on the stove when the phone rang with Andy Livonas announcing that he wouldn't be free until nine or nine thirty that night. He was really sorry . . . She said "*Shit!*" under her breath and then it occurred to her that maybe he really was tied up. She could be vague about maybe making it again next week and let the situation drift, which was what she usually did in similar circumstances, then abruptly decided against it. If he didn't mind eggs twice in one day, she said, she could make an omelet. He sounded pleased and offered to bring some wine. She said that she'd see him around ten.

The kettle was whistling when she hung up. Andy Livonas. Preoccupied and not too friendly at the start of lunch, relaxed and . . . interesting . . . at the end of it. She hadn't noticed a ring but couldn't imagine he hadn't tried marriage at—what, forty?—which would make him either a widower or divorced.

She hesitated, questioning herself for one brief moment. She could keep the evening cool. Then she shrugged. Livonas was attractive, friendly, and unless she misread all the signs, he was interested in something more than her mind.

She turned on the rest of the lights in the tiny cottage. The place was a wreck, it would take at least an hour or two to clean it up. She considered herself something of a maladjusted slob—not compulsive enough to keep a place neat but never able to resign herself to just letting things slide.

The cottage had been a real find, the nicest place she had ever lived. After the Emersons had sold their car, Lee had converted the garage himself, putting in wide pine planking for the floor and building a brick fireplace in the central area that was now the living room. Then he had turned the toolshed with its slanted ceiling into a bedroom with a row of casement windows looking out on Martha's flower garden. On a spring morning, she could wake up to the sight of the red and blue morning glory vines that covered the trellises alongside the Emersons' house.

She had scoured auctions and estate sales for the three small antique Persian prayer rugs for the pine floor, bought the tufted loveseat at a garage sale on Rio Road, and scavenged the ancient reading chair by the fireplace from the Emersons' basement, covering it in a deep blue-and-white floral-patterned cotton fabric.

She had made the white cotton curtains in the living room and bedroom herself and bought the red-and-white checkerboards for her pullman kitchen for five dollars at Raleighs. She had spent one whole weekend hanging and rehanging her collection of pen-and-ink drawings and black-and-white photographs. And then she had stopped. The old steamer trunk meant to be a temporary coffee table had become permanent, serving as her desk and dining table as well. And the days set aside to repaint the kitchen a more cheery color than its chocolate brown had come and gone.

She took another, less critical look around. It needed more of a picking-up than a cleaning, a half-hour's work at most. And a fresh fire would take the dampness out. After a hot bath, she'd check the fridge and dash down to the corner if there was anything she desperately needed. She speculated once again on how the evening would end. She liked his looks and, best of all, in ten days or so there would be a continent between them.

She went to draw her bath, placing the telephone with its long extension cord on the floor nearby in case one of her fellow delegates called.

There was enough hot water in the tank for a full tub and she sank down into it until only her nose, mouth, and eyes were above the surface. She turned off the procelain hot water knob with her foot. Sheer comfort, she thought, almost buoyant in the old-fashioned claw-foot tub. She closed her eyes and let the heat soak into the muscles of her calves, thighs, and buttocks. She knew she had pushed herself too hard the first time out, had warned herself that she'd regret it later just before going beneath the Dumbarton bridge at a racing run.

But then, she always pushed herself, she thought. She had pushed herself to make a three point eight in college so she'd be assured of law school. And she pushed herself there, *had* to push herself. She wondered for a moment what life would have been like if she had specialized in tax law instead of public interest. It was her fascination with politics that had decided her. On campus, she had gotten involved with the Young Democrats and after graduation sought a job with Bob Whitman's law firm. And when the chance came to run for delegate to the Constitutional Convention, she had jumped at it, despite her father's warnings.

Edward Houseman was a cautious, plodding man, a bookkeeper by profession, whose life was full of dire forebodings. In Seattle, Washington, Kathleen's life had all the predictability of the totals at the bottom of his neat rows of figures. Washington, D.C. and the Constitutional Convention meant uncertainty, precisely what Edward Houseman had spent a lifetime avoiding. During Kathleen's regular Sunday dinner visit, he would lean over his plate of roast chicken and ask her, "Why do you want to go off to a city you've never seen and give up a good-paying job in Seattle's best law firm? Do you know how many unemployed lawyers there are these days?"

It was her mother who had surprised her. Julia Houseman, a secretive, overweight woman who always dieted during mealtimes and sucked continuously on hard candies in between, had cornered her one day and asked her into the kitchen for a "little talk." "You go to Washington," she had ordered, gripping Kathleen by the arm so hard it hurt. "Don't let him scare you, that's what he's done to me all my life."

It was a unique moment in her life, one where her world had turned upside down and she had reversed her opinion of her mother by a hundred and eighty degrees.

She left for Washington at the end of the month.

She was half dozing in the tub when the phone rang. It was Debbie Spindler in need of sympathy. Considering the circumstances, Kathleen did her best to provide it. She hung up feeling drained and depressed.

She climbed out of the tub, grabbed the oversized bath towel and began drying herself in front of the full-length mirror attached to the back of the bathroom door. Debbie was a bitch. She had sounded far more concerned with her reputation than with the death of her boyfriend. What would people think when they discovered she had been going out with someone the police had said was—as Debbie indignantly put it—"perverted."

Finished, Kathleen spread the damp towel over the shower rod to dry. Debbie had said she'd seen Steven for lunch the afternoon before he was murdered. That he'd said he was in some kind of trouble but had glossed over it.

Just what the hell had he done, anyway?

Kathleen poured a Scotch and water for herself and a bourbon for Livonas, balancing them precariously on a plate already loaded with English biscuits and a wedge of Bel Paese cheese that she'd found in the back of the refrigerator. She carried them into the living room where Livonas sat on the end of the loveseat, watching the flames leap and dance in the fireplace.

"I hope the cheese is all right," she said. "I can't remember when I bought it."

Livonas tried some on a cracker. "It's fine."

She picked up the poker and played with the fire. The silence was the awkward one of a man and woman who haven't figured out what, if anything, they have in common. Kathleen watched Livonas nibble on the cracker, stretching out the process as long as possible. She had pulled the same trick herself. You can't talk with your mouth full so keep it that way as long as possible.

It occurred to her that he looked more handsome in sport clothes than a suit. He had changed from his rumpled pinstripe into a pair of brown cords, along with a forest-green chamois cloth shirt and a pair of dark brown walking boots with salt marks around the sides.

His face had what her grandmother would have called character. A broad forehead with brown eyes that looked straight at you from beneath bushy eyebrows that almost met at the bridge of a decidedly Roman nose. A strong chin with a mouth of slightly uneven teeth containing more than their share of gold and silver, and thick black hair that was turning gray at the sideburns and above the ears. He was muscular, with exceptionally broad shoulders for a man of average height, and not even a hint of a tire around his waist.

"That's a pretty dress," Livonas said, tentative.

"Thanks. It comes in handy in the cold weather." After deliberation, she had put on her brown knit sweater dress along with her one heirloom, a single strand of natural pearls left her by her grandmother.

Her mind, she realized, was a hopeless blank. The witty remarks that she had thought up while cleaning the house had vanished with Livonas's first knock on the door. Suddenly she was sorry she had gotten herself into this.

"Does it itch?" Livonas asked.

She looked blank. "What?"

"Does your dress itch?"

"Not if you wear a slip underneath." What a dumb question, she thought, then realized he was having as tough a time as she was.

"What are you going to do back in Seattle?"

She was thankful for another question. "I don't know. But it might be nice to do something physical for a change. Maybe I should get a job as a ski instructor in Sun Valley. I worked there the winter after college."

Livonas helped himself to another cracker. "They closed it down after we cut off the gasoline for the ski lifts. I was just up in that area and got told all about it—in great detail." He concentrated on the cracker for a moment and Kathleen was afraid the long drawn-out silence would return. "Maybe you could teach cross-country skiing. That's all that's going to be happening this winter—if anybody can get the gas to drive up there."

"You don't need an instructor for cross-country, just big thighs," Kathleen said, patting hers to illustrate the point. They both laughed and she felt herself sinking back into the contours of the chair, relaxing.

She began to have a rough idea of what it must have been like for him out West. Anybody from the federal government had to put up with a lot of hostility these days. The last time she'd called home, her father had told her about a Bureau of Land Management supervisor who had been run out of Auburn, a town not far from Seattle. He'd told the story with far more relish than regret.

"What do you do when you're not working for Bob Whitman?"

"Not much—that takes up all my time. I used to play racquet ball, I used to go sailing, I used to go to the movies. The only thing I get in now is an occasional workout at the gym." He shrugged as if to apologize. "This is actually my first evening out in several months."

So that accounted for his lack of bureaucratic spread. "I'd think you'd be on everybody's list of eligible bachelors." She sounded more flirtatious than she intended.

Livonas's eyes wandered over to the photograph on the wall of the fog-enshrouded Portland fishing docks, then back to her. He smiled. "I wasn't counting official functions. I used to have some friends outside of government, but after a while they got tired of me ruining their dinner plans and I got tired of their complaints about all the things the Administration had fucked up."

She noticed his glass was empty and stood up. "Let me refill that and I'll start dinner." She walked into the kitchen and poured him another. Livonas followed her, leaning against the kitchen door-jamb.

"You know, you could always be a cook," he said, watching her chop the onions, zucchini, and tomatoes and shovel them into the sizzling skillet.

"That's a thought. Maybe I'll ask for a letter of recommendation after dinner." She cracked five eggs one-handed and dropped them expertly into a copper bowl, then beat them to a froth with a whisk. "You used to be a newspaperman, right?"

He nodded. "Before that I was a lineman for Ma Bell."

"Did you like it?"

"At first. My route was along the northern California coast. Spent the day driving my truck around and ate lunch under the trees. The pay was actually more than I needed. But after six months I'd be at the top of a pole and I'd say to myself, this is it, Livonas, so you better get used to it. Twenty years from now the chances are you'll still be right here hanging by your safety belt. I must have sent résumés to twenty newspapers, and then a friend of mine got me a job with Chicago's City News Bureau as a reporter. They offered me half what I was getting at the phone company but I was packed and gone the next morning."

"How did you get from being a reporter to special assistant to the Vice-President?"

"Thrift, hard work, and bribes in high places."

"Don't let that get around—about hard work—or you'll be brought up before the Civil Service Commission."

He rapped the kitchen wall with his knuckles. "This place bugged?"

"Only with a stray cockroach or two." He laughed. She poured the eggs into the pan. "People give you credit for getting Whitman the nomination."

"Or the blame, if you talk to Tom Massey." He watched her ladle the mixed vegetables onto the eggs, now set. "I was working in Seattle for the *Post-Intelligencer*, met Bob, and wrote a few speeches for him. After that, I couldn't keep away from the political scene. I got married and managed to get a job as political reporter with the *San Francisco Examiner*. Wrote a series on the Endicott Gas bribery case, the wire services picked it up, and Bob offered me a job as his aide on his Senate investigating committee. By then my marriage had broken up and there was nothing holding me in San Francisco; I've worked for Bob in one capacity or another ever since coming to Washington."

He helped himself to a slice of raw zucchini and she pushed another piece toward him with her spatula. She wanted to ask him about his marriage but thought better of it.

"I read the stories but didn't remember the by-line."

He looked around for the bottle of Scotch, found it and poured her a refill. "How about yourself? How'd you wind up in this town?"

She paused as she took a sip of her drink. "I guess I've been in politics all my life. I even ran for president of my high school senior class. Maybe I had always planned on coming here." What she hadn't planned on was leaving so quickly.

"Did you win?" He opened the bottle of wine. Thank God he didn't sniff the cork, Kathleen thought.

"No, I lost to the quarterback of the football team. He was kind enough to offer himself as the consolation prize."

Livonas laughed. "And you accepted?"

"Of course—he *was* the quarterback. I lost my first election and my virginity on the same day."

"Which hurt worse?"

"The election, definitely. The other, not at all—except for a bump on the back of my head from the car door handle."

She turned up the sides of the omelet, slid it out of the pan onto a serving dish, and handed it to him.

He looked blank. "Where's the table?"

"The steamer trunk in the other room."

"Where'd you go to school?" His voice sounded slightly muffled by the wall.

She raised her voice. "I went to Stanford, then to law school at the University of Washington. I worked for Bob Whitman's old firm, public interest, some of it pro bono. I liked it."

"You going back there?"

That was a possibility, but she'd had a job offer as an executive administrator of a regional solar energy project in the desert area of eastern Oregon. Getting the program on its feet would be a challenge, and after a year with the Constitutional Convention, she could use one. She thought of asking Livonas his opinion about it, then decided not to.

"Hey, when do we eat?" Livonas was back in the doorway.

She picked up the wine bottle and two long-stemmed crystal glasses from the cupboard. "Right now."

"Need some help?"

"Sure—grab a couple of plates from the counter cabinets. The salad's in the fridge." Livonas slipped behind her to get at the cabinets. His back touched hers and she leaned against him slightly. He reached for the plates and she followed him into the living room with the wine and the glasses.

She wondered what it would be like to sleep with him.

After dinner, she poured him the last of the wine and sat next to him on the couch. The fire had burnt down to its embers and Livonas yawned and stretched. For a moment, Kathleen was afraid the evening was about to end.

Then Livonas said, "Want to take a walk? There's a great sky tonight—I caught a glimpse of it coming over."

"Why not? I'll get our coats."

The temperature must have dropped twenty degrees since she had come home and the puddles of slush along the path were now frozen and slippery. Livonas was waiting for her at the end of the path, his mackinaw wide open. Clouds of frozen breath had formed around his head, thrown back as he stared at the sky. He waved a hand toward the north.

"That's the Seven Sisters and over there are Orion and the Big Dipper."

She looked up. The Milky Way arced across the center of the sky, a carpet of crystal brighter than the moon. They started walking up the flagstone path to Rio Road.

"Wait a minute." She turned and zipped up his mackinaw. "You'll catch cold like that."

Hands in his pockets, Livonas bent down and kissed her. "Thanks." He slipped his arm around her waist. Halfway down the street, she stopped and pointed to a sled half hidden in a snowbank. "Let's take it."

They dug it out. "The best hill's at the corner of Quebec and Wisconsin," she said. Livonas put his arm around her waist again, his hand resting on her hip, and they walked down the street, the sled bumping along behind them. She felt comfortable, relaxed.

Then they were on the lip of a hill that started as a steep slope and after fifty feet leveled out into an open space between some tennis courts on one side and a playground on the other.

"Dibs on top," she laughed.

The air was cold, the stars a brilliant dust in the night sky. Livonas lay down on the sled, totally dwarfing it. He pushed himself far enough back to grip the handles.

"If you're going my way, lady, you better climb on."

She crouched down behind him, then jumped on his back, the motion sending the sled flying down the hill. She held onto Livonas's shoulders, started to slip sideways and clutched his legs between her own to right herself. Banks of white streaked past them as they flew over the snow. Livonas leaned right and Kathleen followed his lead. A rock flashed by on her left and she shouted, "Nice miss!" in his ear. She flattened her body against his, letting him shelter her from the chill wind that increased with the speed of the sled.

"Lean!" She shifted her weight to the uphill side, at the same time dragging her foot in the snow. Livonas leaned with her. The sled shuddered, bounced once, tilted on its uphill runner, then slid completely around to come to a stop pointing back up the hill.

Livonas's cheeks were flushed, his breath warm against her face. He turned around and they kissed gently, rolling onto the snow, soft and squeaky cold beneath them. They lay there for a moment, then Livonas pulled his hand from underneath her and traced the line of her lips with his forefinger.

"We better get up or I'll get an embarrassing frostbite."

"I know a great place to get warm," she said.

"Where's that?"

"My bed."

He kissed her again, their lips parting. "I was hoping for an invitation."

She threw the latch on the front door as his arms encircled her from behind. She turned to him and they kissed. She ran her hands up his back and through his hair, cold and frozen at the tip ends. Then she felt him unbuttoning her coat, his hands going inside to touch her breasts. She could sense her breasts grow taut under his fingers, even through the thickness of her woolen dress. She reached down and put her hand on him and he pressed between her legs with his thigh.

"Where's that bed you were talking about?" Their foreheads were touching and his voice was husky, almost a whisper.

She nibbled at his lower lip. "I thought maybe you wanted to make love right here."

Livonas looked at her as if he was considering the possibility and she moved her arms around his back, then let him go. "It's in here." She pushed him in front of her.

She lit two candles on her bureau and walked over to Livonas, who stood by the side of her bed, waiting. She put her arms around his neck, then carried him down with her onto the bed. The shadows cast by the candle flames danced behind them on the wall. They tugged each other's clothes off and Kathleen reached over and turned the covers back.

It was as easy as she had imagined it would be with him. She hugged him to her with both arms, opening her mouth to his, feeling his tongue against her own. She ran her hand down his back and thighs, then to the length of him, feeling his contours. He pressed toward her, kissing her neck, touching her breasts. She shivered and felt herself opening up as his hand moved downward through her hair. She lifted toward him. The sensation of his sex inside her spread in waves throughout her body. Time flowed, slowly at first, gradually building up until she cried out with the pleasure of him. Then she felt his orgasm begin.

Later, in the quiet of the bed, she listened to his steady breathing, then ran a hand gently along his side, taking care not to awaken him. By the first of the year she would be back in Seattle and Andy Livonas would be a pleasant memory—more pleasant than she had imagined. She felt vaguely depressed, wondering if the relationship might have had a future. But her plans had been made for several months now and she wasn't about to change them on whim or for a short-term Washington affair. She'd had enough of D.C., especially in the past few months. The city and the people in it had struck her as having little connection with the real world, a world she desperately wanted to get back to.

No Andy Livonas was going to change that.

December 16
11:30 P.M., Pacific Time, Wednesday

They'd been laying five-card draw steadily since ten o'clock and Fred Schwarting had retreated into his usual role of sullen loser. Rossi, the little bastard, had a way with cards. He also had a flair for playing above his head, like a weightlifter who psyched himself up before making a lift or a basketball player who couldn't miss a free throw. Rossi was always sublimely confident that he couldn't lose, and as a result he seldom did.

Schwarting was of the-cards-call-themselves school. *That* had been a mistake. When Rossi dealt, he couldn't draw flies.

"I miss them," Rossi said.

Schwarting looked up from his hand. Rossi had tilted his chair back against the guard shack wall and was studying his cards. He was wearing his self-confident look that never failed to infuriate Schwarting. Rossi was not only smaller than he was, the little man was half his age, which didn't help things a bit.

"Miss who?"

Rossi waved a hand in the vague direction of the refinery behind them. "The guys. How long's it been since they had a night shift?"

Schwarting thought for a moment. How long had it been since Chevron had dropped the lobster shift? A year? A year and a half? At night now, it was only them and a maintenance crew.

He glanced at his hand. Crap, as usual. He discarded a seven and a three, saving a pair of sixes and a queen kicker. "Gimme two."

Rossi slid two cards across the table and Schwarting picked them up. Another three and a king. Why had he saved the kicker? Because Rossi had been winning all night, that was why. He had to do something to break the little prick's luck.

He yawned. "I'm folding, it's all yours." It was no great loss. At a quarter ante, seventy-five cents limit, the pot was only a few bucks. "Remind me to pick up another cake on the way home."

Rossi looked surprised. "I thought you were dieting?"

Schwarting stifled another yawn. "It's Jenny's birthday party. She went up and down the block and invited every six-year-old in the neighborhood. The wife says we'll need another cake."

There was the sound of a truck outside—several of them judging by the noise their tires made on the gravel—and Schwarting shoved back from the card table. "We got company."

"So somebody took the wrong turn-off. Lemme take a leak and I'll be right with you."

Schwarting took a last look at the bank of TV surveillance screens that filled the far wall, then stepped outside the guard shack. He blinked for a moment in the bright spotlights and shivered slightly. It was a nippy night out and overcast; you could really feel the fog off San Francisco Bay. The acrid odor of gas and crude still hung in the air and the cold made him miss the occasional wave of warmth when the plant was working full blast and they burned off the excess gases.

It took him a moment to focus his eyes—the guard shack was outlined in the spotlights and the cylindrical cracking towers themselves were a brilliant maze of lights. The trucks were outside the cyclone fence a dozen yards away. They weren't exactly trucks, more like camouflaged troop carriers of some sort. Furthermore, they had shielded headlights, which made them a little difficult to see; they tended to fade into the darkness of the hills on the other side of the asphalt road.

He walked over, regretting that he had left his pistol back in the

shack. Who the hell was it at this time of night? There'd been a lot
of rumors about hijackers lately but he couldn't recall any reports of
them hitting a refinery.

A few yards on the inside of the fencing, he stopped, cupped his
hands, and shouted: "The freeway's to your left!" A man climbed
out of the cab and walked over, followed by several others who
dropped off the back. Schwarting felt a little easier. They were
wearing California state police uniforms.

The first man in uniform, not much older than Rossi but obviously the man in charge, said brusquely: "Open the gates. We've
been assigned to guard the refinery."

The guy looked official and he was wearing the uniform but
Schwarting hesitated. "You got papers? I don't know a damn thing
about this, nobody's told me anything." He felt stupid when he said
it. Some goddamned clerk had been too lazy to pick up the phone
and call him.

The man's eyes were shadowed by the brim of his hat and
Schwarting couldn't read his expression. "I don't need any goddamned papers. Open up."

Why the hell was the guy coming on so hard? Schwarting
frowned. "Look, Officer, this refinery's under the jurisdiction of the
federal government, not Standard Oil. The State of California
doesn't have any authority over us. If you haven't any authorization
on you, I can call the company security office but that's the best I
can do."

Somebody hollered, "We can't wait all night, fatty!" and there
was laughter from both trucks.

Schwarting felt another flash of uneasiness. What was going on?
He was acutely aware now of the lights and the chill air and the
smell of oil and the faint murmur of the wind in the brush along the
roadway. Where the hell was Rossi? On the phone, he hoped; he
must've heard most of what had been said.

He squinted at the tall man on the other side of the cyclone
fence. "Mister, you got any ID? I can call the office and—"

"Watch it! He's got a gun!"

It took Schwarting a second to realize they didn't mean him and
he whirled to see Rossi lope out of the guard shack cradling a rifle.
Jesus, the dumb kid was going to do something stupid—

There was a *crack!* from one of the trucks and Rossi staggered.
Another shot and the little man was jolted backward, the rifle flying

from his hands. The front of his shirt was suddenly sopping wet with a spreading chocolate-colored stain.

He hadn't even had time to scream, Schwarting thought blankly. It was all in slow motion now and even turning back to the fence seemed to take minutes.

"What the *fuck* do you think you're—"

Then something sliced his leg and something else hit him in the chest. It felt like somebody had hit him with a hammer. He crumpled to the ground as the first of the trucks whirred into motion and crunched through the fencing. The strands of snapping wire sounded like corn popping.

He started crawling toward the darkness of a bush. Men were dropping off the backs of the troop carriers now and running toward the storage tanks and the cracking towers. *Jesus*, the pain in his chest was terrible . . .

The lead man, the officer who had demanded entry, pulled a pistol from his belt, waved it toward the refinery, and was running with the others when he suddenly remembered Schwarting and whirled around, dropping to one knee.

Schwarting's last impression was of the gravel on the ground cutting into his left cheek, the soft sound of the wind drowned out by the rattle of gunfire around the cracking towers, and the California state policeman holding the pistol with both hands as he took aim and fired.

December 17
                    8:00 A.M., Thursday

Major General Charles Rudd, President Massey's military advisor, straightened his shoulders to ease the growing pain in his back, then sank farther down into his overstuffed chair and watched the snow falling outside the windows behind Massey's desk. The windows in the Trophy Room opened onto the balcony, which in turn overlooked the huge expanse of the Ellipse. He could barely see the Washington Monument beyond, almost hidden by the drifting flakes. The second blizzard of the season and it was still only December.

He looked away from the windows and leafed through the folder holding the reports to be given at the meeting. They summarized in cold, hard facts the growing national catastrophe. He read a page, felt more depressed than usual, then closed the folder and turned to study the President.

Massey was in his shirt sleeves, leaning back in his swivel chair and playing with an ivory letter opener, one of a collection he kept on the cluttered desk top. Rudd was fascinated by Massey's hands. They toyed a moment with the ivory opener, put it down, picked up another, then sought out the ivory one again. These days, Massey's hands were more of a window on his soul than his eyes . . .

Rudd smothered a cough and tried to focus on Whitman's report, then his attention strayed back to Massey. In his three years in office, he had aged visibly. His shoulders had developed a slump, his skin color was bad, and his face reminded Rudd of the slow softening of a scoop of ice cream—the crisp, hard edges had gone first and now the soft peaks were starting to droop . . .

Whitman finished his report. Massey nervously cleared his throat. "Nigeria, too? I thought we had indications . . ." His voice trailed off.

Whitman was obviously irritated. "It would be political suicide for any Islamic government or for any country with a sizable Islamic population to break the oil embargo. Most of the governments are fragile and preoccupied with keeping the internal opposition at bay."

"And the Saudis? I thought the Yamani faction was regaining its influence?" Massey sounded plaintive.

Al Reynolds interrupted to say, "Five key members were arrested this morning by the Royal Family. Yamani fled to Switzerland."

Rudd switched his attention. Aside from Whitman, Albert Reynolds, the Secretary of State, was the only man of real stature present. Something of a gnomish misanthrope, he had been a career diplomat all his life and could be a latter-day Metternich if Massey didn't constantly undercut him.

"If you've got any good news, Bob, don't hold it back." Massey's attempt at banter came out with a cutting edge of sarcasm.

Whitman's smile was chilly. "There's a possibility of Venezuela increasing its allocation, and commercial contacts in Indonesia have indicated the government will overlook transshipments of crude from Japan." He glanced at Rudd. "There's a military string at-

tached to that; the government's interested in bartering oil for
F-18's but can't do so directly. It will increase Japan's oil quota and
allow the Japanese to reship part of it here, strictly under the table,
of course."

Whitman's trip had turned out exactly as Rudd had predicted.
The Vice-President had come back virtually empty-handed. The
deal with Indonesia had been his only real success and that was for a
scant 50,000 barrels of crude per day.

"Your trip to Beijing," somebody said. "There's nothing about it
in the summaries."

Rudd turned his head. Hugh Ramsay was one of Massey's better
choices for an advisor. A black, he had been a young executive with
Conn Oil before making a name for himself with the Department of
Energy. But Massey still deferred to Jess Kearns, president of Gulf
Coast Oil, a pale man with thinning reddish hair and a tendency to
skin cancer, who never sat in direct sunlight, preferring the shadows
of the room. In all the meetings he had attended, Rudd had never
heard Kearns offer a constructive suggestion.

"That's because nothing panned out, Hugh." Whitman sounded
tired. "The new off-shore wells in the Yellow Sea show promise, but
so far China's oil production is just managing to keep pace with its
own economy."

Whitman was a large, shambling man who reminded Rudd of
Lyndon Johnson without the crudeness. He was the most politically
astute member of Massey's Administration; Massey couldn't have
won the election three years ago without Whitman as his running
mate. He had been far more popular than Massey, especially with
the Congress. He knew it inside and out, there was hardly a member
who didn't owe him a favor or who wouldn't do him one if asked.
And perhaps most important of all, he was respected overseas. The
Russians took him at his word, the highest compliment they had
paid an American official in years.

Roger Anderson, the Secretary of the Department of Energy, now
had the floor and Rudd's eyelids lowered. It was too warm in the
room as it was and Anderson was anything but a dynamic speaker. A
moon-faced man who floated through Washington on a personal
cloud of optimism, he had been with the President when Massey
was mayor of Philadelphia. He was the media expert and Pollyanna
of the group. If Armageddon were announced for tomorrow, Anderson would remind them all to be grateful that it wasn't today.

"... gasoline stocks fell ten million barrels to one forty point two, distillate fuels totaled one ten. Strategic oil reserve stocks remain at seventy-five million barrels ..."

Rudd was fully awake now, feeling the familiar rush of anger. For minimal home heating during the winter, distillate fuel stocks should have been two hundred or more. The country would be bone dry by February despite rationing. The Strategic Reserve didn't really count, it had been earmarked for the military by the last Congress; it couldn't be tapped for civilian use.

The only difficulty was that it actually totaled less than the seventy-five million Anderson claimed.

"... production from Alaska's North Slope continues to decline while off-shore discoveries in the Baltimore Canyon area have been disappointing and oil in the western overthrust belt has been more difficult to extract than anticipated ... shale oil projects in the Four Corners country are behind schedule and operations at several Colorado strip mines have been curtailed by sniper fire ..."

Rudd felt jolted. That hadn't been in the summaries, either. And he had received no word of it through official channels, which was something he'd have to look into. Everybody in the room was alert now, looking not so much at Anderson as Massey. The mining companies had requested federal marshals two months ago.

Massey seemed surprised at the sudden show of interest. "I'm sure local authorities can take care of it, it hasn't been entirely unexpected."

The man wasn't going to do anything, Rudd thought, feeling another surge of anger. Not a goddamned thing.

Anderson droned on and Rudd dropped his eyes to the folder to scan the figures that Anderson was talking about with all the proper pauses and flourishes. It was the same optimistic crap he'd heard last month.

He looked around the room, despairing. Whitman was the only one who really commanded any popular respect and he had knuckled under to Massey.

"General Rudd?" Whitman was chairing the meeting now.

It took Rudd a moment to recall what he had just been asked. Military stocks of oil ...

"They're adequate within the continental United States, though diesel fuel for the Navy is running low. Additional guards have been posted at all military supply dumps as a precautionary measure."

Livonas was the last to give a report, a somewhat personal recital of moods and conditions throughout the West. Livonas was a good deal more than just Whitman's aide, Rudd thought. He was more like an alter-ego, though Livonas lacked Whitman's experience. But then again, you couldn't tell what was beneath the surface. He had never gotten to know Livonas and momentarily regretted it. The report sounded slanted, but then Livonas came from that neck of the woods.

When Livonas had finished with his description of Governor de Young's offer to Janice McCall, there was a long silence in the room. Rudd had met de Young once and hadn't liked the man; Livonas confirmed his assessment. De Young was dangerous and unprincipled but what the governor's motives might be, Rudd wasn't sure. De Young's interest in the Constitutional Convention was probably some sort of media ploy.

Massey stood up and walked around to the front of his desk, his face set and determined. Maybe they had gotten through at last, Rudd thought cynically. Maybe Massey had finally grasped the situation the country was in, that it needed leadership. In the first and final analysis, that was the real duty of a President.

"De Young is popular, he's got clout—it's obvious he's going to run against me." A glance at Whitman: "You agree?" Without waiting for an answer: "He'll be tough—he's strongest in the West and Southwest but there'll probably be some defections from the South, too."

Rudd sat there in cold shock, fighting to shift gears. The election. He hadn't thought about it in weeks. Massey would fight any attempts to dump him, of course, he wasn't the type to go quietly.

Massey pointed to Anderson. "Rog, de Young is your responsibility. I want to know what kind of national organization he's building, where the funds are coming from. Have a team monitor the network newscasts, see what kind of coverage they're giving him, how much time he might have bought under the table."

Livonas was staring at Massey as if he didn't believe what he was hearing. "What are we going to do about de Young's promise of oil to McCall—"

Massey tried to sound patronizing, then grew red because his voice betrayed him and crept up a register. "What are we going to do? That's what we've been discussing all morning, Mr. Livonas—weren't you listening?"

They were all looking at Massey now, who had turned away from Livonas in an attempt to ignore him. There was a false heartiness to his voice. "I remember campaigning against Ross Hubeck in Philadelphia—in his way, Governor de Young reminds me a lot of Hubeck. He had what you call electoral flash, the sort of thing that fades in the stretch . . ."

Only Roger Anderson was hanging on his words. The others were listening in a embarrassed silence. Massey sensed the embarrassment and trailed off. Whitman took pity on him and stood up, the signal that the meeting was over.

"Thank you, Mr. President."

A servant turned up the lights as they filed out. Rudd picked up the folder from beside his chair and walked to the door where Massey was shaking hands. When it came his turn, he said automatically, "Mr. President, if there's anything I can do . . ."

Massey looked remote and Rudd wasn't sure he was seeing him. "If I need you, General, I'll call."

He turned away and the butler closed the door. The last glimpse Rudd had of Massey was the President walking over to his desk where the butler had placed a silver tray holding a highball glass with the presidential seal on it, a small silver ice bucket, and an unopened bottle of twenty-one-year-old Chivas Regal Royal Salute, all arranged in a neat triangle.

"I wouldn't want his problems."

Al Reynolds had been standing behind him, watching.

"They're not just his problems, they're ours, too."

Reynolds's face looked pinched and birdlike. "I understand you're not as close as you once were, Charles."

Rudd wasn't sure whether it was a political dig or a try for information. He tried to keep the sarcasm out of his voice. "When's the last time you had a private talk with him."

"I haven't. Not for months." A slight hesitation. "And you?"

Rudd started for the staircase just off the center hall. "Last week. I gave him a look at the down side and he hasn't talked to me since. I'm surprised it hasn't made the rumor mills by now."

On the landing, Reynolds reached out a thin hand and touched him lightly on the shoulder. "I'm not so sure any of us could do a better job—under the circumstances."

"You could have cut the gloom in there with a knife," Rudd said curtly. "And he did absolutely nothing."

"There's probably not much that can be done."

"You're defending him, Al."

"Sympathizing is more like it."

"Al." Rudd hesitated. "This used to be a great country. I think it still can be. But I sat in there for an hour and listened to it go down the drain."

They were on the walk outside now, waiting for their cars to be brought around. The snowflakes were thick and wet, and a block away the city had vanished completely behind a veil of white.

Reynolds's car arrived first. He paused at the door, looking back at Rudd. "The country's in difficult straits, Charles—but please don't think you're the only patriot among us."

December 17
11:00 A.M., *Thursday*

Livonas had never been inside the old Pension Building, though he had passed by it often enough. Dating from just after the Civil War, it was one of those government buildings that had survived in downtown Washington because no one was sure who had the authority to tear it down.

It was late morning and the cold snap had abated just enough for the snow to turn to slush and soak through his shoes. He hunched his shoulders inside his overcoat and joined the long line of delegates waiting to get in.

One of the guards at the door with a bullhorn warned those in line to have their identification ready. From the complaints around him, Livonas guessed that the ID check was a new policy. On impulse, he pulled out his old *Examiner* press card when he got up to the door. The sergeant-at-arms glanced at it and flashed him a quick smile.

"You're a long way from home, Mr. Livonas. You must miss California as much as I do."

Livonas shoved the card back in his wallet, thankful the guard hadn't noticed the date on it. "Sure do—where you from?"

The guard ignored his question. "You'll have to move on, sir, you're holding up the line." Livonas walked on in, feeling that the guard was staring at his back.

He paused for a moment at the rear of the hall. It didn't look quite as run-down as Katy had described. A crew of janitors were sweeping the aisles; from the size of the mound of trash to his right, it had been a long time between sweepings. There was the usual convention hubbub on the floor itself but he couldn't help noticing two sign painters moving down the center aisle, repairing the state standards that were not too tattered and lettering new ones for those beyond repair.

Livonas spotted the Washington state standard and threaded his way over. Katy was talking to a thin young man with a large adam's apple, a beak of a nose, and straight black hair that kept falling over his steel-rimmed glasses. Livonas waited quietly behind her, absorbing the action on the floor. He was going to touch her on the arm, then thought better of it.

"Will the Wyoming delegation please approach the platform and present their credentials?"

"They're pulling everything in the book, Katy, they're—" The young man noticed Livonas and stopped in mid-sentence.

Katy turned to Livonas. "I'll be with you in a minute. The Credentials Committee has decided to review delegate credentials and we're in the middle of a recertification fight." She sounded cool but then this wasn't a social occasion. She turned back to the young man. "When will the first challenge come to the floor?"

"With Connecticut—they'll insist on appealing the Credentials Committee's ruling to the floor."

"How soon?"

"Ten, fifteen minutes."

She cocked her head. "Well, at least we'll get an idea of their support." She moved back slightly to include Livonas in their conversation. "Stu, I want you to meet Andy Livonas. Andy, Stu Lambert." She suddenly made up her mind. "As soon as it comes to the floor, I want to call for debate, Stu. How many challenges so far?"

Lambert consulted his note pad. "A hundred and fifty challenges, a hundred and twenty-five of them delegates who voted against the resolution putting the California coalition in control." He hesitated. "Let me check, I may be off by a few."

He disappeared into the crowd and Katy picked up her clipboard from a folding chair. "Why don't you come with me," she said to Livonas. "I'm going to check in with the Connecticut people. California's trying to get a two-thirds majority by challenging our delegates' credentials."

She strode across the floor and Livonas hurried to keep up with her. "I should have been able to see this coming," she said over her shoulder. "But I was concentrating on getting out of town."

For a moment he almost lost her in the maze of folding chairs which had been shifted so often most of the aisles had vanished. He was pushing past the California delegation when a man in front of him turned and Livonas found himself face-to-face with Jerry Wagoner.

Wagoner stared at Livonas, his eyes hostile. "So the Massey Administration has decided us little people deserve some notice?"

Wagoner and de Young had worked together for years. Livonas had disliked him from the start. "If I'd known little Jerry Wagoner had come here all the way from Beverly Hills, I'd have dropped in sooner. Good seeing you, Jerry."

Katy was a dozen rows away now and he hurried to catch up with her. If Jerry Wagoner had been brought in, it meant that, from de Young's point of view, the stakes at the convention were damned high. Wagoner was a key man in de Young's clique and the governor wouldn't be wasting his time or his ability.

Katy was talking to a man and a woman standing beneath the Connecticut state standard; Livonas thought they could have posed for Grant Wood's *American Gothic*. Katy was explaining his presence as he walked up. "Andy Livonas is here as an observer from the Vice-President's office. Andy, Sara and Tom Evarts."

Sara ignored him. "They're holding back two thirds of our delegates' credentials," she said, indignant.

Katy frowned. "How many challenges will hold up?"

Tom Evarts shook his head, his face splotched with anger. "It's all a subterfuge. They're trying to guarantee their majority."

"How many will really hold up, Tom?"

Evarts shrugged. "Maybe a third, the rest can be cleared by the end of the week." He spoke with a clipped New England accent.

Sara said, "We could challenge some of their delegates from the floor. California has at least twenty delegates who don't have legitimate credentials."

"Everybody knows they were appointed directly out of the governor's office," Evarts said, angry.

" 'Everybody knows' is not good enough for a credentials challenge," Katy said. "We missed our chance when we didn't get anybody on the Credentials Committee. Connecticut's going to be the first challenge, that right?"

Sara nodded. Katy turned back to Evarts. "Tom, try and get the floor and stall. Ask for debate, then insist that each challenge be considered separately. Then ask for a division of the house. And keep appealing rulings of the Chair to the convention floor—we'll wear them out."

Evarts seemed reluctant. "I don't want to argue, Katy, but they're going to win anyway. They've got the votes." He didn't want to take orders from Katy, Livonas thought; that was his real objection.

Katy suppressed her irritation. "Tom, if you can get the microphone and keep shouting challenges, it'll take them from now until next Friday to get through the first round. And if we can put off the credentials report for a few days, it will give us enough time to get our own credentials in order."

Evarts nodded. "Okay, I'll do what I can."

A gavel was pounding methodically over the din and Livonas turned to watch the chairman, a Job-like look of patience on his face, calling the convention to order. Katy started pushing down the aisle. "I'm spotting in the Washington section, we'd better get over there."

"I thought you told me nothing was happening," Livonas said.

She looked strained. "It wasn't—until today. And then all hell broke loose and I haven't yet figured out why. You see the painters and the janitors around? They even had a television crew in this morning."

California certainly wasn't wasting any time, Livonas thought. He settled back in his chair as the chairwoman of the Credentials Committee took the floor, listening attentively as she recited the committee's report.

"Alabama, ten delegates approved, two challenged pending arrival of proper credentials. Alaska, five delegates approved. Arizona, seven delegates approved. Arkansas, fourteen delegates approved. California, forty-nine delegates, forty approved, nine challenged pending arrival of proper credentials."

"You can bet all those challenged are from northern California," Katy whispered.

"Connecticut, twenty-five delegates, nineteen suspended pending arrival of proper credentials."

"Madame Chairman, Madame Chairman!" Evarts was at the microphone in the center aisle. "Connecticut demands to be heard on the challenge to its credentials!" Somebody had cut the microphone, Livonas noted, but Evarts's bellow could be heard throughout the hall.

Two other members of the Credentials Committee joined their chairlady and the convention's chairman on the podium. After a hurried consultation, the chairman took over the microphone.

"The gentleman from Connecticut may speak on a point of personal privilege."

"The sovereign State of Connecticut moves that the challenge to its nineteen delegates be set aside."

"So moved!" The seconds came from various spots in the hall.

The chairman looked bored. "The question will come to an immediate vote."

Katy lunged to her feet, her hands cupped around her mouth as she pushed toward the speaker's platform. "Debate! Debate!" The rest of the Washington state delegation picked it up and were joined by allies throughout the hall until all Livonas could hear was "Debate! Debate!" Katy had planned it well, he thought, watching Evarts striding back and forth, shaking his fist at the podium, leading the chant for debate.

On the podium, the chairman, his face a dark crimson, was shouting into the microphone.

"Will the sergeant-at-arms please remove the Connecticut delegate!"

Three monitors moved out from the back of the hall and headed for Evarts. They were almost up to him when Katy and Sara pushed in front of him, locking arms and barring the guards. One of them made a grab for Evarts over the women's heads but was fended off.

The chairman gaveled for order as cries of "Shame!" filled the hall. Giving up, he left the podium. He walked to the edge of the platform and squatted down to confer with Katy and the two Evarts. A moment later, they were joined by the chairlady of the Credentials Committee. The chanting in the hall faded to a buzz of conversation.

"Will the convention please come to order." Another rapping of the gavel. "The chair recognizes Madame Chairman of the Credentials Committee."

The chairlady looked unhappy. "I move that the credentials report be tabled until Friday morning."

"So moved!" somebody in the hall shouted. There was a voice vote, carried by the "ayes." There was only a sprinkling of "nays," most of them, Livonas noted, from California. The chairman now announced that they would hear a report from the Housekeeping and Maintenance Committee. A young man with glasses two rows over shouted, "Fuck housework!" and a wave of laughter broke the tension.

Katy came back to sit down beside Livonas. She was sweating despite the chilly hall.

"Pretty good," Livonas said.

She shook her head. "It was Tom, really. He's got a built-in PA system." Lambert came over and gave her a congratulatory peck on the cheek. Livonas felt vaguely jealous.

Lambert grinned. "I heard from a Massachusetts delegate that you kicked a guard in the balls."

She laughed. "No, but Sara got one in the shins with those wooden clogs of hers."

"She really kicked him, huh?" Lambert's admiration was complete.

Livonas reached out and lightly touched a growing bruise on her cheekbone. "Looks like you took a whack yourself."

She took a compact from her purse and examined the bruise in the mirror. "Think it'll be a black eye?"

"Guaranteed." It was a fiery inch-wide welt.

"Mr. Chairman." A voice came from the other side of the hall. "California wishes to be recognized."

Livonas half stood up to see what was going on. Wagoner pushed his way to the aisle microphone. A hush swept the hall.

"The chair recognizes the chairman of the California state delegation."

"The Supreme Court has just announced that it will rule on the New York state petition for an injunction against the Constitutional Convention." Wagoner paused every few words to give them time to sink in. "This is an attack on our very existence." Another pause. "An attack on the only institution in Washington, D.C., that truly represents the will of the people. I move to cancel our Christmas recess and ask that a sense-of-the-body resolution be drafted immediately stating that the Constitutional Convention is a separate and independent body." A final pause. "That the United States Supreme Court has no authority over the will of the people!"

"So moved!" The shouts came from all over the hall, followed by calls for the question.

Livonas turned to Katy. "Aren't you going to do something?"

She looked grim. "I couldn't do anything—even if I knew what to do. The Supreme Court has started something it might not be able to stop."

"What do you mean?"

"If the Court rules that the Constitutional Convention has violated its charter and the convention decides to defy it, we may be right in the middle of a constitutional crisis."

Livonas looked blank. "I don't get it."

"We could end up with a runaway convention," she said patiently. "It happened with the first Constitutional Convention in 1787. It was originally convened simply to amend the Articles of Confederation. It ended up by throwing them out and writing the present Constitution of the United States."

"You mean they might write a new Constitution and then ratify it as well?"

She hesitated. "If you throw out the old Constitution, there's nothing that says you have to follow the former ratification process. In the final analysis, constitutional legitimacy rests on the consent of the governed."

"You think they'll defy the Court?"

She shrugged. "Listen."

Half the delegates were standing now and a chorus of "ayes" filled the hall. There were almost no "nays."

"You've just heard what they'll do."

Livonas stared at her, then at the delegates around them. They'd defy the Court, he thought, and California would lead them. The convention might be far more important than just as a launching pad for a de Young Presidency.

A new chant had broken out in the California section and now filled the hall.

"Time for the West! Time for the West! Time for the West!"

The chant was raw, angry emotion and it occurred to Livonas that the anger went far beyond the constitutional questions being debated at the convention itself.

It wasn't really a chant, he thought. It was a rallying cry.

December 17

1:45 P.M., *Thursday*

They were out in the crowded corridor after the luncheon recess when somebody called, "Katy! Katy!"

Livonas turned to see a short, slightly plump young woman in a brown coat and crimson scarf hurrying over, her cheeks still red from the cold outside.

"Wait up, Katy!" They stopped and a moment later the woman joined them. Katy said formally, "Debbie Spindler, Andy Livonas. Andy's with Vice-President Whitman's office."

"I was with the police all morning," Debbie said, out of breath. "What's happened so far?"

"We lost," Katy said dryly.

Debbie wasn't listening. "They had me going over mug shots. To see if I recognized any of them. Can you imagine? Why should I know any sex offenders? I certainly don't think Steve knew any of them."

"Steven Hart was with the convention," Katy said in an aside to Livonas. "He was the aide from California who was murdered. He and Debbie were ... friends." She sounded distant and Livonas guessed she didn't care for Debbie.

Livonas took another look at Debbie. She was about twenty-two, a little on the dumpy side, with brown hair and too much makeup. Livonas remembered seeing the story in the newspaper. Hart had apparently been a participant in an S&M gang bang that had gotten out of hand.

"I'm very sorry," he murmured.

Debbie ignored him. "Nobody can tell me Steve was a pervert, Katy. If anything, he was oversexed."

"What do you think really happened to Steve, Debbie?" Livonas said.

She looked directly at him for the first time, realizing she had a new audience. "I think he was involved in something. I think somebody wanted to make it look like that kind of murder." She faltered. "He demanded to have lunch that afternoon, he told me he had gotten in some kind of trouble."

Livonas was suddenly alert. "What sort of trouble?"

She looked as if she were going to cry and suddenly seemed more human. "He had an argument with Jerry Wagoner, the chairman of the California delegation. He said Jerry had been picking on him. Wagoner thought Steve wasn't paying enough attention to convention business."

The standard difficulty that a young aide might have with the head of a delegation, Livonas thought. Except Hart had made a luncheon date with Debbie to complain about it, which might mean that something had brought it to a head.

"What did he talk about, Debbie? Something that happened that day?"

The tears were starting to leak through her lashes now. She told him how Hart had accidentally broken the latch on Wagoner's desk drawer, spilling the contents on the floor, and had just gotten everything back in when Wagoner had walked in.

Gotten everything back in, that is, except for one letter which he'd stuffed in his pocket.

Livonas frowned. "Did he read it?"

She shook her heard. "It was marked 'Confidential.' He was going to put it back early the next morning."

It was like looking through a crack in a door and trying to construct the whole scene from the slight sliver that you saw, Livonas thought. Wagoner would hardly leave important mail around, unopened and unread. Which meant it was probably some mimeographed handout; "Confidential" stamps meant less than nothing these days.

And then again, he could be wrong. But you'd still have to strain to tie the two events together. Debbie Spindler wasn't the first woman to have a boyfriend who led a double life.

"Did you talk about anything else, Debbie?"

"Politics," she said plaintively. "Just politics."

December 17
    3:30 P.M., Pacific Time, Thursday

"What's happening, Gus?"

Frankel didn't look up. "Don't you ever knock, Garber?" He kept making small initials on the assignment sheet in front of him. "Locally we've got a hot story about an ambulance running out of gas on its way to Mt. Zion Hospital. If that doesn't strike you as page one news, there's the bust of a black market in gas rationing coupons in Pacific Heights, or the Muni announcement of the elimination of bus service between one and five in the morning—which shouldn't hurt the local drinkers because the Alcoholic Beverage Control Board has just hung a midnight closing on all bars to give everybody time to get home."

He pushed back in his chair. "The big one down south is that they're closing Disneyland, not enough tourists. Anything more on the Chevron refinery?"

Garber shook his head and slipped into the chair in front of the desk, hooking a leg over the arm. "The captain in charge didn't want to talk. I pushed and he said the two guards were killed by hijackers." He tapped his pencil against his teeth. "First time hijackers have hit a refinery."

"How'd they know it was hijackers?"

"The captain said they had plenty of evidence, that there were indications a tank truck had been there. Myself, I think the whole thing stinks. Did you ever take a good look at that refinery? It's enormous—it'd be like a flea attacking an elephant. I think we ought to go out there, talk to some of the employees. In any event, it's given the Guv a great excuse to assign the state police to supplement civilian guards at the refineries."

Garber lived in a paranoid world filled with villains and evil plots, Frankel thought. "So check it out."

"You said you were going to call Livonas about it," Garber prompted.

"I don't have to. I talked to General Bolles at Sixth Army Headquarters in the Presidio. He said the state police acted at the Army's request, that under the circumstances Washington thought it best there should be state guards rather than federal troops."

Garber rubbed his chin. "Score one for Washington, I didn't think they were that sensitive to how people felt out here." He hesitated. "That puts de Young in charge of all the refineries and the pipelines."

"He's the Governor, for chrissakes."

Garber shrugged. "How's the rest of the country doing?"

Frankel keyed the visual display terminal next to his desk and called up the directory of news stories on the national scene. He watched a moment while the headlines scrolled past on the green screen.

"If I can believe the wires, shitty. U. S. Steel is closing down its mills in Gary and there's the usual story about people freezing to death—Pittsburgh this time."

"You don't really believe them, do you, Gus? I mean the stories about people freezing to death back East."

Frankel felt defensive. "I'd be less than human if I didn't believe them—but they're also used to justify increased oil allotments for the East." He thought about it a moment. "If you want to accuse me of losing my objectivity, Mike, go ahead. Just remember that nobody back East believes we're walking instead of driving out here—or that we've got a helluva lot longer way to walk than they do."

He wasn't sure whether Garber had been baiting him or not. So he was a California Firster, he didn't owe anybody any apologies for that. He never claimed he was nonpartisan, only that he tried to be.

"You didn't come in here to argue politics, Mike. What's up?"

Garber dropped a sheet of paper on his desk. "The Guv is throwing a party but he was real careful not to invite the press. The Airport Hilton. He's reserved the main conference room and made arrangements to have a buffet supper catered. Don't ask me who'll be there, I couldn't find out—except a lot of them are supposed to be from out-of-state. Super hush-hush, they're bringing in G-Troop for security."

The governor's special guard, Frankel thought. He glanced over the notes. "Who told you?"

Garber counted off the sources on his fingers. "One, a friend of mine in Sacramento who works a paper shredder. Two, my waitress friend at the Torch who said that G-Troop would be handling security. And three, the night manager of the Airport Hilton who's had a crush on me ever since we both went to San Francisco State and who confirmed everything."

"How many will be there?"

"A hundred fifty, maybe two hundred."

Frankel felt dubious. "You try and get Shepherd to confirm any of this?"

Garber looked disgusted. "If it's super-secret, Gus, it's because Shepherd doesn't want anybody to know it. If I let anything leak, the meeting will be canceled or they'll sit around and talk about the weather."

"Wrong. He might increase security but he couldn't afford to cancel the meeting or change the agenda. If you had pinned him, you might have gotten something out of him." He paused, realizing he had to make up his mind about something. "You asking for the story?"

"Sure. It's right up my alley."

"I'm sorry to disappoint you," Frankel said reluctantly, "but you can't have it."

It was the first time he'd ever seen Garber get angry. "What the hell you talking about, Gus? I developed the leads, they're all my sources."

Frankel folded the sheet of notes and stuck it in his pocket. "You can't have it because I'm taking it."

Garber opened and closed his mouth like a dying fish. "That isn't fair, Gus. Besides, you don't have the time."

"It sure as hell isn't fair," Frankel admitted, "but I do have the time—we're down to less than thirty pages a day now." He paused. "You hate the Governor too much, Mike."

"And you're neutral, that it?"

"More so than you, Mike."

It was dusk when he arrived at the motel and drove into a parking lot that was almost filled for the first time in a year. He went to the coffee shop first and sat at the counter by the door so he could keep an eye on the lobby. It was a strange mix, he thought after a few minutes. A lot of Texans, judging by the way they dressed, and a number of Japanese and Mexicans. He listened hard for accents and finally decided there was a contingent of Canadians as well.

He should've brought Garber along; Mike knew more of the wheelers and dealers on sight than he did. But that would've had its drawbacks—they knew him, too. He finished his coffee and walked out to the lobby, taking up a station by the magazine counter. He recognized some checkbook politicians and a few corporate lobbyists from Sacramento. It was probably a meeting where de Young was going to turn the financial screws . . .

Still, there were a lot of state police around, enough to make him feel uneasy. Then he spotted Governor Barron of Arizona talking with an older man who had the bearing of an army officer in mufti. Barron was one of de Young's strongest political supporters, which would make sense if it was money-raising time. Craig Hewitt was standing by the cigarette machine, watching the crowd, which meant the governor couldn't be far away.

"Who was the leak, Frankel?"

He hadn't heard anybody walk up behind him but he recognized the voice. He turned around. "Hi, Herb. Quite a little wing-ding you've put together."

Shepherd's smile never made it as far as his eyes. "It's a closed meeting, Frankel, it's not open to reporters."

Frankel glanced around the lobby. "Judging by the dignitaries, it's a pretty important one."

"How'd you hear about it?"

Shepherd had been born suspicious, Frankel thought. "I didn't. I was on my way to the airport to pick up a friend and stopped to eat. All the restaurants in the airport were closed months ago." He glanced at his watch. "I've got about ten minutes, you wouldn't want to fill me in, would you? Off the record?"

Shepherd hesitated, then decided to play it friendly.

"Actually, it has nothing to do with any possible presidential campaign on Governor de Young's part. It's a meeting of western governors to deal with the energy shortage. We didn't notify the press—there's some confidential material from the federal government we have to go over—but I'll be glad to send you a press release." He tried the smile again. "Exclusive. You'll get it before anybody else."

The funny thing was, he didn't think Shepherd was lying; it rang true. Shepherd hadn't told him everything but then he'd admitted he was holding something back. There was just the glint of wariness in Shepherd's eyes, a trace of suspicion . . . and something else, something that told Frankel to play along and get the hell out.

"Thanks a lot, Herb—appreciate it." He looked at his watch once more. "I better get going."

And then he couldn't help it.

"You have many of these private meetings?" He said it with as much innocence as he could.

In a flat voice: "Not many."

What the hell was wrong with Shepherd? The man had handled bigger meetings than this. Frankel nodded and walked back into the lobby, heading for the doors, feeling Shepherd's eyes on his back all the way.

Once outside, he took a moment to let the tight feeling around his chest drain away. He had time, Garber had said there would be a buffet supper first and that would take an hour. He couldn't go back into the lobby, Shepherd might still be there, or if he wasn't, another member of the governor's staff would. And there would be no getting into the conference room in any event; G-Troop would see to that.

He hesitated, then sauntered around to the back of the building. There was a small light above the delivery entrance and he slipped in and walked back along a quiet, deserted hallway. He guessed he was directly behind the main conference room. Now he'd have to get lucky . . .

He stopped by one door, listened a moment, then turned the knob and pushed the door open a few inches. A deserted meeting room. He was about to shut it again, then paused for another look. The far wall was actually a huge folding partition. The room was part of the main conference room which the hotel had cut down by a third. Beyond the partition came the faint buzz of conversation.

He stepped inside, easing the door shut behind him. He stood for a long moment, listening, then walked over and inspected the partition. It didn't quite meet the wall at the far end, leaving a two-inch gap. He held his breath and edged closer to peer in. The room beyond had been set banquet style with liquor setups on each table and steam tables along one wall. The tables were filling up and he glanced over at the table on the dais. De Young, Shepherd, Barron, the military man that Barron had been talking to—he looked familiar but Frankel still didn't recognize the face—and several others whom he couldn't place at all.

There was a stack of chairs in the corner of the room he was in, and Frankel walked over and carried one of them back to his peephole, sat down and looked through into the room again. There was an enormous map of the western United States, including a large chunk of the Pacific Ocean, behind the dais. De Young might not be making a pitch for money after all, Frankel thought. He might be talking about trade, that would account for some of the faces in the lobby.

But still, why the security?

From the room beyond came the sounds of laughter, the clink of silverware against plates, and the muted hum of a hundred different conversations. It would take an hour for them to eat, an hour before the speeches started.

Frankel felt in his pocket for his small notebook and leaned comfortably back in his chair. He could wait, he had all night.

It was almost nine o'clock by the time the busboys had cleared the tables. Frankel noted that none of the busboys were allowed to remain in the room and that the state police now guarded all the doors through which they had wheeled the serving carts. The security was foolish in one sense, he thought; anything this size, there had to be leaks.

But that was one of the more unsettling points. Garber's contacts had merely said that something big was up; none of them had indicated that they knew what it was.

He concentrated on the head table, catching his breath when the military type who had been talking to Governor Barron turned his face in profile. Frankel recognized him from a television newscast. General Earl Bolles.

But Bolles was on active duty; he was prohibited by law from taking part in a political campaign.

What the hell was going on?

Governor Barron was acting as toastmaster and clinked his knife against his glass to call the meeting to order. He introduced everybody on the platform and Frankel hastily jotted down names—he could check out the ones he didn't know in the newspaper's library.

He yawned a few times as Barron began a typical "the man who" speech.

They gave de Young a standing ovation and Frankel himself felt a thrill. If it came to a campaign between de Young and Massey, he didn't see how Massey stood a chance. Granted that de Young would have problems with the East, but given the population shift to the West and the South in the last twenty years, a presidential candidate could lose the East and most of the Midwest and still have enough electoral votes to win.

The speech itself was vintage de Young, a stirring indictment of the federal government, the manifest destiny of the states that made up the American West, the ties with neighboring countries, the future that was speeding down on them ...

He finished to more ringing applause and Frankel sat there, his pen poised over his pad of paper, still waiting for the punchline. But there was no mention of the upcoming presidential campaign, there was no appeal for funds, there was no castigation of President Massey as a candidate, there was no discussion of the energy shortage.

It didn't make sense.

The last speaker was Herb Shepherd and there was a curious tension in the room now. De Young was the man of the hour, but it was Shepherd who would give them their marching orders. There was a roll of applause, then Shepherd stepped up to the microphone and flashed a smile.

"All of you will be delighted to know that the government of Indonesia has accepted Governor de Young's offer and exercised its option to cancel the oil agreement recently made with the United States ..."

Frankel almost snapped his pencil. He couldn't have heard correctly. De Young had sabotaged an oil agreement that Whitman must have made with Indonesia. But that was against the law. De Young was, in effect, conducting foreign policy and just incidentally sabotaging the whole country, including the West.

He could guess at the follow-up. De Young would step in personally a week later and revive the deal. He'd be the hero and the federal government would have egg on its face. Or was that it? What the hell were the Indonesians getting out of it? In any event, it was dirty politics on a massive scale.

Ten minutes later, he knew what was going on and was so scared he thought he was going to wet his pants.

"Hey, you—what the hell you think you're doing?"

Frankel kept his eye to the sliver of light showing through from the next room. "Security," he said in a voice he hoped wasn't shaking. "Dockstader assigned me."

"Who's Dockstader?"

Frankel turned to look up at the young member of G-Troop standing behind him, his hand on his holster.

"Internal security," he grunted. "You don't think we trust everybody in that room, do you?" He stood up and moved away from the crack. "The guy at the third table to your right—he's had that briefcase on his lap during all the speeches. I think he's carrying something."

The trooper looked dubious and moved up to the slit. He stared for a moment. "I don't see anybody with a briefcase on his lap."

Frankel picked up the pedestal ashtray standing on the floor a few feet away. He started to swing it and the glass dish in the top slid off and shattered on the floor. The trooper swung around.

"What the hell you—"

Frankel brought it down with all his might, catching the trooper at the base of the neck. The young man fell to his knees and Frankel hurried out of the room. He avoided the lobby, going out the delivery entrance. Once outside, he leaned against the side of the building and caught his breath, thanking God it was a cold, misty night. He would have bet he had lost five pounds in sweat just running down that one short corridor.

He found his car in the parking lot and sat in the dark for a moment, trying to make sense out of what he had seen and heard. He ought to call Livonas, he thought bitterly, tell him that he had been right all along.

But first he'd write the story for tomorrow's edition. Then he'd call Livonas.

He drove out of the parking lot with his lights off, afraid he might be followed.

The newsroom was deserted when he got back. Some of the sports reporters worked late but it was close to midnight, too late even for them. He got a candy bar and a cup of black coffee with double sugar from the vending machines in the hall, then walked back to his office just off the newsroom, switched on the desk lamp and turned on his VDT. The familiar green screen was the first cheerful thing he had seen all night.

He ate half the candy bar and finished a second cup of coffee before slugging the story "governor" and typing in "garber/frankel" as the by-line. Mike deserved the lead credit, it was really his story. He had been suspicious all along.

His fingers hesitated over the keys. This was obviously just the first story in a series; a lot of people were involved—almost all of them high up in state and national governments. De Young's interference with the Indonesian oil deal was only the tip of the iceberg.

But he felt more depressed than elated about the story. He had been counting on de Young, had wanted to believe in him, *had* believed in him. So he had been a fool.

He started typing, watching the letters as they appeared on the screen and mouthing the words under his breath. He felt better when he had finished the first graph. By the third graph, the story was writing itself. The governor and Shepherd would deny it all, of course, and the Indonesian government would be smart enough to cover itself. They'd have to do a lot of digging, lean on Garber's contacts, try to find a source in Sacramento . . .

He lost himself in the words on the screen, then suddenly glanced up at the wall clock. There had been a noise in the darkened newsroom. Somebody had come in, probably the first of the skeleton crew that showed up early in the morning. But it was only one thirty and they didn't come on until five.

Maybe Sanders, one of the sports reporters, had dropped by to file his story. He might have been late, gone out with the coaches or the players after the game and hung one on. Or maybe one of the drama critics had stopped by after a cast party to get his impressions of the show down while they were still warm. No, it was probably Sanders.

He sat there for a long moment, listening, then got up and stepped out of the door of his office. He felt sweaty. It had to be Sanders, he'd have a cup of coffee with him and take five.

"Hey, Ed—"

The words died in his throat. There was nobody there. Nobody's desk lamp was on, there was nobody hunched over a typewriter, there was no greenish glow from any of the other VDTs in the room. Just the hulking shadows of desks, piles of books and papers, the faint outlines of a stack of spare swivel chairs against the far wall. And a brooding quiet.

But somebody sure as hell *was* there, he could feel it. He edged back into his office. He'd better call the security desk downstairs, have a man come up and check it out.

It sounded like mice scurrying in the corners of the room behind him. He looked up from the phone just in time to see two men in ski masks leap from the shadows into his office.

"*What the fuck—*"

Neither one of them said a word. He desperately tried to shake them off while he punched at his VDT. They pulled him from the small office, holding his arms tight against his body as they rushed him toward the windows overlooking the street.

A third man by the windows yanked one wide open. Frankel tried to scream, clutching frantically at the desks and chairs in his path. He grabbed at a nearby partition, kicked out with a foot and felt it sink into something soft. There was a sharp "oof" of breath from the man he had kicked in the stomach and Frankel tore himself free. He picked up an old-fashioned lead-weighted paper spike from a nearby desk, whirled and threw it at the two men clawing for him, then turned and ran for the elevator. He was breathing hard, his sides aching, spinning swivel chairs into the aisle as he ran up it. He was going to make it, he thought, panting. If he could get to the elevator.

He was up to the second partition when they tackled him, smashing his face into the floor. They yanked him to his feet, the blood streaming from his nose and mouth, and ran him back down the aisle again. His legs were wobbling; if they had let him go, he would have fallen. He grabbed feebly at the last partition and one of the men hit him in the stomach, hard. When he doubled over, they thrust him through the open window.

He hung over the sill for a moment, a cold wind blowing in his face, still fighting for something to hold onto. He was trying to twist back into the room when somebody kicked his legs out from under him and shoved him the rest of the way through the window. He grabbed at the sill and one of them jammed the sash down to break his fingers, then threw it open again and he slid out. He heard a voice scream from a great distance away and the window abruptly vanished above him.

He clutched at the wind and twisted frantically in the chill night air, turning just in time to see the sidewalk exploding up at him.

December 18

6:00 A.M., *Friday*

There was a loud buzzing in the background, like a lumberjack's chainsaw, that Whitman finally recognized as the alarm clock. He'd been dreaming—God, what had he been dreaming?—something terrifying, he couldn't remember the details. He had been trying to get away—from what?—and hadn't been able to. He lay in bed, aware of the dampness of the sheets and the warmth of Vivian lying beside him. He was still half-smothered by sleep. And too warm, he thought. There were too many blankets on the bed, especially for a man who had nightmares.

Then he became more conscious of the fact that it wasn't the nightmare that had woken him up. He swung his feet over the side, feeling for his slippers, and sat there in the darkness. Beside him, he could feel Vivian moving around in bed. She clicked on the bed-table lamp and looked up at him, her face apprehensive.

"What's wrong?"

"It was just a nightmare."

Vivian got up and slipped into her robe, then padded into the bathroom. He could hear the water faucet running and she returned with a damp, ice-cold washrag. She laid it across the back of his neck. It was hardly therapeutic but it felt good. Reassuring. Like having somebody take your temperature. He was absurdly glad that she was there, that he wasn't alone.

"It was the nightmare," he repeated, the panic retreating, leaving behind a residue of depression. "I'll be okay in a few minutes."

She stroked his forehead. "I'm worried about you."

"Nightmares do that to me," he said. He felt more comfortable now. "I'm surprised I haven't had more lately."

"Try and get some sleep."

"It's not worth it for half an hour."

She went into the bathroom again and turned on the shower, adjusting the temperature for him. A lukewarm shower would help, would wash away the sweat and the fear, Whitman thought. He lay on the mattress a moment longer, aware of the chill in the room. The furnace hadn't come on yet and it was another cold morning.

He got up and shuffled over to the window, pulling aside the lace curtains and the shade to look out. The moon was still up, it wouldn't be dawn for a while yet. He could sense the silence of a winter morning and stared at the snow-covered lawn lit by the moon and the small bulb in the guard shack at the entrance. It would make a perfect scene for a Christmas card: the snow mounded on the branches of the blackened tree limbs, the lonely guard shack with the small wreath in its one window, the black, wrought-iron fencing with the ribbon of white on top that ringed the Observatory grounds, isolating them from the rest of the city. But they weren't as isolated from Washington as the White House now was.

He let the shade flap back and walked into the bathroom. He stepped into the shower stall and let the water splash over his face and back, then slowly soaped down, tired of the day before it had even begun. He had a good idea of what was waiting for him at the Executive Office Building. It was now public knowledge that Massey was gradually freezing out Charles Rudd as his military advisor and special aide, which meant that all of Rudd's supporters on the Hill—and the general had been assiduous in courting Congress— would be on the horn demanding that he intervene. As if he had ever had any real influence on Massey. And Rudd wasn't the only advisor that Massey was in danger of losing—although the others would probably leave of their own volition.

Massey had never learned how to use the levers of power. His relations with Congress were bad, those with his Cabinet officers and department heads even worse. He favored incompetents like Anderson who vacillated, afraid to offend; unable to make up their own minds, they seldom offered dissenting views. Or else he appointed department heads who "married the natives" as soon as they were confirmed, siding with their department's entrenched bureaucracy against the President. Massey never asked the men he appointed to argue the issues in his presence, then decide for himself what the wisest course of action would be. He made up his mind in private and sought confirmation after the fact.

President Kennedy had learned from his mistakes. Whitman had been on the Senate Foreign Relations Committee then and remembered it well. After the Bay of Pigs fiasco, Kennedy had invited dissenting views, insisted his advisors debate the issues in open forum.

The process had proved invaluable later, during the Cuban missile crisis. Unfortunately, Tom Massey was no Kennedy. He was a second-rate President who preferred the counsel of third-rate advisors.

And somewhere along the misty path that Massey was traveling, the country was heading for the brink.

It was a little after seven when he sat down to breakfast in the kitchen. The early morning sun was streaming through the windows. Vivian had chosen bright yellow curtains and a yellow tile to go with the light pine cabinets. It was the most cheerful room in the house and had the best view of the grounds outside. Occasionally he'd desert the study to spread papers and reports out on the kitchen table, the tea kettle whistling in the background. Somehow it lent perspective to the problems spelled out before him.

Vivian was at the stove fixing breakfast, the one meal of the day that she never failed to prepare herself, jealously reserving this hour for the two of them. She watched him while he drank his orange juice and buttered his toast.

"I thought Andy would be over for dinner by now."

Whitman neatly took the top off his soft-boiled egg. "He's been busy; a lot of work piled up for him. For God's sake, Viv, he just got back."

She looked at him shrewdly. "The other night he seemed depressed about his trip."

"He went out there and discovered most of his old friends had become enemies. I was afraid he might."

She poured herself a cup of coffee and sat down at the table. "You two have an argument?"

She'd worm it out of him eventually, he thought. She took an even more proprietary interest in Andy Livonas than he did.

"Yes, Viv, we had an argument."

He adjusted his glasses and picked up the paper again. He seldom bothered with the news—briefings kept him ahead of the papers—but the columnists were breathing fire as usual. There weren't many cheap shots, these days the Administration was a sitting duck for honest criticism, but he still wondered how many reporters had ever run for public office or held a government job.

Vivian was silent, waiting for him to continue, and he sighed and put down the paper. "He wanted me to knife Tom Massey."

He waited for her to say something. She must have guessed what Andy had suggested, what he had wanted. But she merely nodded and said, "That doesn't sound like Andy," and let it go at that. Now it was his turn to study her, to try and figure out what was going on behind that face he had loved for so long. She didn't meet his eyes and he wondered how much she knew or guessed.

As they had promised each other in the marriage ceremony thirty years before, she had been with him in sickness and in health and especially in the disappointments. He had lost his very first campaign for state representative and had reluctantly decided to spend the rest of his life in Edmonds, just outside Seattle, as a small-town attorney specializing in real estate law. It was Vivian who had persuaded him he could win if he based his second campaign on his principles and the supporters he had won in his first.

He hadn't involved her in that first campaign; he did in the next. And she had served as his sounding board ever since. Most important of all, she had been as much good friend as wife. When he had lost in the bruising primaries to Massey, Vivian had salved the disappointment and later counseled him to follow Livonas's advice and accept second place on the ticket.

There was a knock on the kitchen door and Larry inched it open. "General Rudd to see you, sir."

Vivian finished her coffee and took the cup over to the sink. "It'll be cold in the study, Bob. Why not talk to him out here?"

He nodded to Larry and finished his toast while Vivian reset the table with a clean cup and saucer. A few minutes later Larry ushered Rudd in. Vivian held out her hand while Whitman got to his feet. "It's good to see you, General. Coffee?" She poured him a cup, kissed Whitman lightly on the cheek, and then vanished through the kitchen doors. Whitman felt grumpy; he didn't know if he was up to handling Major General Charles Rudd at seven thirty in the goddamn morning.

Rudd took a sip of his coffee and settled back in his chair, staring out the window. "It's going to be a cold morning."

Whitman felt uneasy; Rudd *always* made him feel uneasy. Even though he was in mufti, Rudd wore his suit like a uniform, you could almost see the stars glittering on his shoulders. Why the hell did he feel nervous? Whitman wondered. World War II and Staff Sergeant Robert Whitman were more than forty years in the past.

He pushed over the sugar bowl. "The cold snap's supposed to last for a week, but I guess if I had to choose between snow or rain, I'd take snow."

He could see Rudd marshaling his thoughts as if he were marshaling troops. The general had something important on his mind, Whitman thought. Ordinarily Rudd would have faced him instead of looking out the window; his briefcase would be on the table, a sheaf of papers to his right, and he would lose little time in explaining why he was there and what had to be done. Whitman had never shared Massey's and Reynolds's enthusiasm for the general, but he acknowledged Rudd's intelligence and dedication. The fact that Rudd had lost Massey's confidence was hardly good news; the general had been half the brains and a good deal of the energy of the President's staff.

Whitman wondered again what Massey had first seen in Rudd. The general didn't look the part. He was small, slightly built— Maxine Chesire of the *Post* had dubbed him the "jockey general"—with somewhat thick features and coarse black hair. It was the eyes, he thought. Dark, piercing, the "look of eagles" to go with his hawkish personality. Massey would consider Rudd competition, of course, but then that was one of Massey's major failings. Almost anybody was competition.

"Something's on your mind, Charlie."

Rudd shrugged. "The energy meeting yesterday. I had the feeling that a hundred serious problems were facing us and none of them were solved."

"Such as?"

"Sniper fire at the strip mines in Colorado for one. De Young's call-up of the National Guard for another." He had trouble suppressing his anger. "I can't believe it, I didn't know anything about the snipers until the meeting. I heard about half the Guard call-ups on television before I got an official report."

Whitman dropped another slice of bread in the toaster. "Looks like the chain-of-command has developed a few rusty links, Charlie. You want anything besides that coffee?"

"No, this'll be fine." Rudd looked irritated. "Goddamnit, did you listen to Anderson? Any clerk in the DOE could have given a better report, he could have read it out of the Lundberg Letter—it probably would have been more accurate if he had."

Whitman stared down at his coffee cup. Rudd was feeling the isolation from the Presidency.

Rudd turned away from the window. "Did you ever suggest to Massey that Anderson should be replaced?"

Whitman grew cautious. "Massey's pretty loyal; I don't think anybody would get very far suggesting he dump Anderson."

Rudd looked satisfied. "Meaning you tried and he didn't buy it. Did you listen to Anderson's recommendations? Cut back on mail deliveries, cut back on gasoline rations? *Jesus H. Christ!*" He slammed his fist on the table. "The last will be easy—come February or March, people will kill for a gallon of gas."

"I don't think it will be quite that bad."

"Bad enough." Rudd shook his head. "Did you watch Kearns? What's the old saying—'as useless as tits on a boar hog'? I've never heard him say a goddamn thing in a meeting. He just sits there, taking it all in. He's the liaison with the industry, why doesn't Massey do some arm-twisting?" He reached for half a slice of toast and started to nibble at it.

What's your real gripe?"

Rudd looked back at the window. "Massey. He can't do the job, he's never been able to do the job."

Whitman was curious. "What really happened between you and Tom?"

"Maybe I was too positive when he asked for an opinion." Rudd was pensive. "Given a certain set of facts, I tend to think there's a minimum number of logical responses that can be made. We don't think alike—that was obvious from the start." He hesitated. "For an advisor, I'm afraid he picked the wrong man. We developed an adversary relationship almost immediately."

He picked up his cup and walked over to the window to stare out at the lawn. This can't go on. I've worked with Massey too long, I know him too well. The only thing he really worries about is how he looks on the six o'clock news and if tomorrow's story in the *Post* will be above the fold. His attention is riveted on the domestic situation, he doesn't have a world view. If we had to take any kind of normal military action, we just wouldn't have the reserves to last it. And the Soviets know it."

"You have any suggestions?"

"The President . . . lacks decisiveness." Whitman could sense Rudd searching for the right words. "I don't think he's going to develop it in time." He looked back at the windows a moment, then mustered up the courage to spell it out. "I think you ought to play a more active role. You've got the moral authority if not the actual position. I think a number of the Cabinet officers and White House staff would be willing to hold meetings with you, figure out a plan of action, and then present a united front when we meet with the President." His words were tumbling out now. "I think he'd go along, I think he's too sharp a politician not to."

"You mean I should undercut the President," Whitman said dryly. "Hold parallel meetings and then present him with ultimatums, threatening him with leaks if he doesn't go along with the presidential decisions that we were never elected to make." He cocked his head. "Is that what you had in mind, General?"

Rudd's voice was as cold as his own. "That's exactly what I had in mind. If it's necessary. And I think it's necessary. I think you think so, too."

Whitman turned away and stared out at the lawn, at the guard house and the guard in front, flapping his arms to keep warm. "I'll not sabotage the Presidency," he said quietly.

December 18

10:00 A.M., Friday

There was an air of excitement in the convention hall that Livonas sensed as soon as he walked in. The difference in the appearance of the hall was startling—they must have had crews working all night, he thought. Broad strips of new red, white, and blue bunting were draped from the railings of the galleries that ran around the interior of the Pension Building. Hung between them were the flags of the fifty states, staggered so that they repeated themselves diagonally. The effect was similar to a catchy three-line melody that kept repeating itself over and over in your head.

The pounding of the speaker's gavel caught his ear and he turned to see that the decorators hadn't neglected the speaker's platform. Yesterday, it had been a battleship gray. It was now a shiny enamel blue with "Constitutional Convention II" painted on the front apron in fire-engine red. Banks of portable theatrical lights had been rigged around the platform and an elaborate free-floating three-sided canopy had been suspended from the ceiling by guy wires. It was six feet on a side and painted the same blue as the speaker's platform.

"Sir, would you please take a seat?" The young deputy sergeant-at-arms was dressed in a new red blazer with the blue-and-gold convention seal embroidered on his left breast pocket.

They even had new clothes for the help. Livonas took a seat at the back, glanced around with interest at the delegates, then looked toward the speaker's platform. The chairman had just relinquished the podium to the next speaker. Well over six feet tall, he had thick silver hair and a weathered, handsome face that managed to look both gentle and stern at the same time.

He stared out at the convention hall and the delegates gradually quieted down.

"Let me share with you a little story, my friends," the speaker began. "Many generations ago, three brothers and their older sister inherited a large tract of land from their daddy, who had taken sick and died of the fever." His Texas accent was thick, with the resonance of an old-fashioned circuit preacher. "Soon after their mourning, the children met in solemn convocation and agreed to hold their daddy's land in common but grant to each other those separate rights that each requested."

Livonas had seen him somewhere before but couldn't place him.

"Now the first brother requested the right to raise cattle, the second brother asked for the right to raise sheep, and the third brother the right to hew timber. When the sister's turn came to make her request, she said her only interest was in future generations, so she reserved the right for their children and their children's children to convene another convocation if and when it ever became necessary. The three brothers promptly wrote that right into the sacred covenant that they drew up among themselves.

"Over the years their families prospered and multiplied. They tamed the virgin land, built cities, damned rivers, and constructed railroads. Then trouble came." The speaker shook his silver-thatched head in disapproval. "Those descendants who lived in the eastern portion of the land began to exploit their brothers and sisters who lived in the western. So the people called their second convocation to redress their grievances. And do you know what those descendants who lived in the eastern part of the land said?"

The speaker paused for dramatic effect.

"They said you can have your convocation, we'll even give you a hall"—he waved his arm to include the hall in front of him—"but we reserve the right to pass on anything you might decide, and unless we go along with it, you can't do a damned thing." He looked scandalized. "Now, do you know what the people in the story did?" He paused again before answering himself. "They told their brothers and sisters in the East to take another look at the sacred covenant that bound them together. And then they went right ahead and held their convocation anyway."

The speaker lowered his voice to a conspiratorial level. "Now, isn't that just what the Supreme Court, with the urging of our brothers and sisters from New York State, is about to do?" He raised his voice to a gravelly roar. "Isn't the Supreme Court about to tell us that even though we, the people, have believed for two hundred years that we were guaranteed the right through our Constitution to come together in a solemn conclave for a redress of our grievances, that such a convention has no power? No power to right wrongs? No power to adjust inequities? No power to relieve ourselves of the burden of an oppressive federal government?"

The speaker smiled and chuckled softly. "You know what I say to my eastern brothers and sisters and their Supreme Court? I say, 'I'm sorry but a long time ago our daddies made an agreement together. And please remember just who our daddies were: Thomas Jefferson, Alexander Hamilton, James Monroe, Benjamin Franklin, John Hancock, and John Quincy Adams. They made an agreement that if their descendants decided it was time once again to convene a Constitutional Convention, why, they had a right to do so. And you, honorable members of the Court, whose authority is also prescribed by that very same document, have *no* right to interfere with those separate powers granted to this body by our Constitution!' "

The applause started then and the speaker put up his hand to stop it. "And further, I would warn my brothers on the Supreme Court to tread lightly because if this body"—he waved his hand at the delegates in the hall—"should decide that the Supreme Court no longer serves its function as the supreme arbiter of the law, then this body has a right, nay, a duty, to do whatever is necessary to preserve our rights. And that includes changing, reconstituting, or amending the functions which were envisioned for it by our forefathers!"

The speaker stood with bowed head as the applause from the convention floor washed over him. Livonas found the speaker's allegory chilling. It was an open invitation for the delegates to thumb their nose at the Supreme Court, and judging from the applause, the delegates were prepared to do just that.

He found Katy standing next to Stu Lambert, both of them looking grim.

"Who's Uncle Remus?"

"Carl Baxter. Ever hear of him?"

The face was familiar then. "The brilliant Texas criminal lawyer with a reputation as an outstanding political crackpot. He's always been good for at least one story during the Silly Season."

"You think he's a crackpot," Lambert said. "I think he's a crackpot. But most of the people here think he's a constitutional genius."

"In Texas," Katy added, "they say that if you have enough money to hire Carl Baxter as your attorney, you can kill anybody you want."

Back on the podium, the chairman was pounding his gavel. "The convention will come to order!"

Lambert grabbed Katy's arm. "The dumb shits! They said they were going to get somebody else besides Goodwell to speak against the resolution and now he's up there."

Livonas looked back at the podium. The man standing next to the chairman was twenty years younger than Baxter and fifty pounds lighter, dressed in a black three-piece suit. Baxter had projected a friendly, rumpled father image with a "down home" style. The new man looked like a smart-ass New York lawyer who favored European suits and referred to crowds as "mobs" and "rabble."

"Maybe they couldn't find anybody else on short notice." Katy looked at Livonas, worried. "Jonathan Goodwell's one of the top constitutional lawyers in the country—and he's a delegate. That'll make a difference." She was trying to cheer herself up, without too much success, Livonas thought.

"We're cutting our own throats," Lambert griped. "Goodwell's got all the warmth of a garter snake."

On the podium, Goodwell stepped briskly over to the microphone, holding up his right hand like a traffic cop to silence the spattering of applause from his supporters around the hall.

"Ladies and gentlemen." Goodwell said the words as only a man could who didn't really believe them. "I see no reason to talk to you in homily as Mr. Baxter has done. I assume as delegates to this

Constitutional Convention that you have a layman's understanding of the law." Goodwell pursed his lips and looked around the hall with a false benevolence.

"What's a homily, chief?" The man who had broken the silence was dressed in a cowboy hat and camel's hair sportscoat and was sitting with the North Dakota delegation.

Goodwell hesitated, blank-faced, then said: "A homily's a tedious exhortation. The purpose of this convention—"

"What's a tedious exhortation?" somebody shouted from the other side of the hall.

California this time. It wouldn't have mattered how good an orator Goodwell was, they weren't going to let him finish.

Goodwell decided to make a joke of it. "Let's say I am exhorting you, sir, to observe proper decorum."

The half of the hall where the western delegations sat promptly erupted with laughter and boos.

"Let me rephrase it." Goodwell was angry now and his words had a clarity that surprised Livonas.

"What we have here is a constitutional question whose kernel is this: The doctrine of separation of powers reserves exclusive powers for the legislative, executive, and judicial branches of the government. This Constitutional Convention was called by the state legislatures for the purpose of regulating taxation. But it's now gone beyond that, it's taken up the question of the separation of church and state by proposing a constitutional amendment regarding prayer in public schools. By doing so, the convention has raised the question of whether it can take up subjects outside its prescribed agenda. That is a constitutional question. And if the Supreme Court isn't supposed to decide constitutional questions, who is?" He peered through his glasses at the audience, satisfied that he had finally made his point.

"What they're supposed to do is stay out of our hair," somebody shouted.

Goodwell stiffened and leaned into the microphone. "May I call the body's attention to 'Marbury versus Madison,'" he snapped. "In constitutional issues, the Supreme Court is the final arbiter—"

"Marbury versus who, chief?"

Goodwell ignored the shout. "As a duly constituted body of the Republic, we must abide by the decision of the Supreme Court.

The resolution before us implies that the Court has no right to rule on the constitutionality of our actions." Goodwell paused, his face tight. "That's utter nonsense. This convention is guided by law, we can't allow it to be swayed by emotions."

There was a rising chorus of boos. Goodwell looked puzzled as he left the podium. Livonas noticed that even the members of the New York delegation, after a few desultory handclaps, sat silently on their folding chairs.

The secretary of the convention, a small woman in a dark blue pants suit, now came to the microphone. "The motion is: 'The Second Constitutional Convention strongly urges that the United States Supreme Court cease and desist from interfering in its sovereign affairs.'" She retreated to the table to the left of the podium and the chairman took over.

"All those in favor?"

A roar of "ayes" flooded the hall.

"All opposed."

There was a strong chorus of "nays." Livonas was surprised. Even with the disastrous argument by Goodwell, his position had a solid core of support. At least there would be something for Katy to work with.

That is, if she didn't go back to Seattle.

Lambert had disappeared on an errand and Livonas turned to Katy. "Have time for lunch? I've got a table at Ebbitt's."

She looked worried. "Sure, but I've got to be back by two."

December 18

12:45 P.M., *Friday*

Ebbitt's was an old-time bar and grill midway between the White House and the Pension Building. Livonas liked the way they served their draft beer in frosted mugs; it also had one of the best grills in town.

They pushed their way through the crowded foyer and were seated by the maître d' at one of the small varnished tables along the wall opposite the bar.

"Your convention's turning into page one news," Livonas said.

Katy shrugged out of her coat, folding it over the back of her chair. "California's taken control. I thought when we stopped them during the credentials fight, they'd back off a little."

Livonas glanced at the menu. "Who brought Baxter in?"

"It was California's idea."

"You mean Jerry Wagoner's."

"He's running the show over there." She waved away the menu when the waiter came. "I'll have artichoke salad and coffee."

"A few more days," Livonas said, watching her face, "and you won't have to worry about it."

She looked blank. "Why not?"

"You're going back to Seattle, remember?"

"I'm looking forward to it." There wasn't much conviction in her voice.

"Any idea why California is so dead set on running things?"

"It's not California, Andy, it's the entire West."

"All right. So why?"

"What Baxter said summed it up. The whole West was hanging on his words. It's regional differences, we can't ignore them any more. It's not just the energy thing—the East and the West don't think alike, don't act alike, don't share the same values."

"But California picks up a lot of brownie points for making it possible," Livonas said. "California pays for the sprucing up of the hall, California leads the opposition, California imports Carl Baxter. You make a lot of friends that way. Pardon me, Vincent de Young makes a lot of friends that way."

"If he's behind it, he's sure going to a lot of effort."

"Over the weekend, the convention picked up a lot of ink and air-time. Believe me, somebody in Sacramento was counting the number of times de Young's name was mentioned."

She looked thoughtful. "You've really got a thing about him, don't you."

Livonas was slower in responding. "I happen to think de Young would be a disaster as President."

She glanced at her watch. "What do you want me to do about it? Not that I'm in love with the man myself."

"Reconsider your decision to resign."

"There are plenty of other delegates opposed to what California is doing, they'd be as effective as I would." He didn't look convinced. "All right, tell me why you think I should stay."

"Because I think the country needs a better President than de Young. Because I think you'd want another candidate to win. Because I think de Young should be opposed on all levels. And because I don't think anybody else would be as good as you."

"Appealing to my competitive instincts, huh?" Katy smiled.

Livonas kept a poker face. "You struck me as the type who likes a good fight."

"Now and again."

The waiter arrived with his beer and chops and Katy's salad and coffee. Livonas said, "So, what are you going to do?"

"You haven't mentioned a name yet. On whose behalf am I supposed to lead the opposition to de Young?" He knew she was thinking of Whitman.

"We'd be a committee of two," he said. "At this point, Bob Whitman isn't running."

She looked stunned. "Bob's not going to challenge Massey for the nomination?"

He shook his head. "I spent an hour with Whitman before I saw you the other night. I tried to persuade him to run. He threw me out of his office."

"So what's the point?" she asked after a moment. "Not that I have anything against hopeless causes—except losing them."

"I'm going to try again tomorrow morning. I'll either leave his office with his okay to build his candidacy or I'll resign."

There it was, he thought. It was the first time he had articulated it, but he had known it would come down to this ever since the argument with Whitman on his return.

"Then what?" She seemed genuinely concerned.

"I'll work for anybody willing to go up against de Young."

She was puzzled. "What is there about de Young and you?"

"I don't like his politics." He tried to leave it at that but she wouldn't let him.

"I don't like the politics of a lot of people but I don't make a personal crusade of it."

"I managed a campaign against de Young once. I convinced a friend of mine, Harry Palmer, to run against de Young for state attorney general. It took a week of arm-twisting but I finally persuaded him."

She said, "And he didn't win."

Livonas nodded. "About ten years previous, Harry had financial problems and tried to kill himself. He spent a few months in a mental hospital. De Young found out and used it. I had ten shrinks lined up ready and willing to swear to Harry's stability. What de Young did was launch a campaign to drive Harry over the edge again. They phoned him at all hours, circulated obscene letters in his name, planted rumors and outright lies with the columnists, had people follow him with cameras. It worked—they drove him crazy. A week before the elections, Harry stopped his car in the middle of the Golden Gate Bridge and went over the side."

She stared at him for a moment, shocked, then said: "Couldn't anything be done about it?"

Livonas felt drained. In talking about the incident, he had relived it. "Oh, sure, I fired up the Fair Political Practices Commission. After three months of investigation, they fined Herb Shepherd, de Young's campaign manager, a hundred dollars for circulating unsigned campaign literature."

He finished his beer and leaned back in his chair. "What do you think would happen if Vincent de Young were elected President with the Constitutional Convention in his hip pocket?"

"I don't like to think of it," Katy said. "There's no precedent."

"I'm afraid a lot of things would happen during a de Young Presidency for which there would be no precedents," Livonas said. "That's what scared the shit out of me this morning. De Young's well on the way to taking over the Constitutional Convention for his personal use."

"Then I guess we're a committee of two."

Livonas felt relieved. "There won't be any trouble with you withdrawing your resignation?"

She smiled. "I already did. First thing this morning."

"You really put me through the wringer." She looked contrite and he added without thinking, "How about dinner tomorrow?"

The faint smile froze on her face. She shook her head, covering his hand with hers. "Andy, the other night was great—but I really didn't want to get involved then and I still don't. All right?"

He withdrew his hand from beneath hers. "If that's the way you want it." He meant it to sound adult but knew he sounded hurt. After Wednesday night, he had fantasized about having an affair with Katy Houseman.

She finished her coffee, avoiding Livonas's eyes. "Still friends?"

"Of course." He managed a smile, then said, "We'd better get back to the convention."

They didn't talk on their way back to the convention hall. Why was it, Livonas wondered, that ever since his marriage, his relationships with women had always been so casual and passing? The answer was obvious: because that was the way he wanted them to be. Now he wondered if his feelings about Katy signified some major shift.

He glanced over at her. She seemed to be lost in thought.

Livonas stayed at the convention for another hour, listening to a committee-of-the-whole debate a constitutional amendment that would ban abortions. It was a volatile issue but it was also only the opening round; the heavy hitters of Carl Baxter's caliber would be saved until later. He checked his watch; there was too much waiting for him back at the office to hang around the convention any longer.

He said good-bye to Katy, then looked for a washroom. He found one near the main exit and was about to go in when he heard the shrill bleep of a police whistle behind the door. He listened, surprised, then dropped his coat on the floor and hurriedly pushed through.

Inside, a slender man in brown cords and black leather jacket was backed up against one of the urinals. He was holding a whistle in one hand and with the other was trying to protect his face. There was an ugly bruise under his left eye and his moustache dripped blood.

Facing him were two men, one in his early forties, burly, well over six feet with his bulk in his chest and stomach. The other was younger, maybe thirty, a dirty blond with a linebacker's build and heft.

The fat man growled, "Get the fuck out of here, buddy, this doesn't concern you." He was closest to the door, obviously acting as backup in case they were interrupted.

Livonas nodded, turned as if he were going to leave, then whirled. He stiffened his fingers and drove them deep into the fat man's stomach, then opened his hand and brought it sharply upward, catching the fat man under the chin with the heel of his palm.

The fat man staggered and went down, hitting his head on one of the tiled urinals. He sat on the floor, dazed, blood seeping from his scalp.

It had happened too fast for the blond to come to the fat man's aid. Now he lunged for Livonas, who backed away, grabbing a nearby broom and dropping into a crouch, fending off the blond with the broom handle.

"The convention's just recessed," he lied. "This place is going to be mobbed."

The blond hesitated, then ignored Livonas and yanked the fat man to his feet. He turned at the door to glare at the man in the leather jacket still holding the whistle. "Not a smart move, fruit." And to Livonas: "See you around, asshole."

After they had left, the slender man said in a shaky voice: "Thanks a lot."

Livonas's hand hurt and he was breathing hard. "Both of us were lucky." The slender man was still trembling. "You okay?"

"Yeah, sure."

"Why the whistle?"

The man shoved it in his pocket. "The faggot's friend in need; it started on the coast."

"What'd you do, proposition the blond?"

The slender man looked angry. "Not my type." Then he paled, turned and vomited into the urinal, holding onto the sides with both hands. When his gagging had stopped, he walked over to a washbowl and sloshed cold water on his face.

"They got me a few times in the stomach—if you hadn't walked in, I probably would've lost my teeth." He held out a wet hand. "Paul Harris."

"Andy Livonas. What the hell'd they want?"

Harris was calmer now, wiping his face with a paper towel and dabbing at some bloodstains on his jacket. "They're part of the enforcement squad; I think they wanted to make an example of me."

Livonas said, "I don't get it."

"I'm a delegate from California." Harris gave up on his jacket. "I didn't vote right on the last motion."

"So they worked you over? That's hard to believe."

Harris shrugged. "There's a lot that's hard to believe."

"I'd like to hear more about it," Livonas said slowly. And so, he thought, would Katy and Stu.

Harris shook his head. "Not from me, mister. They made their point."

Livonas fished a card out of his wallet and handed it over. "I'd really like to hear about it," he repeated.

Harris studied the card, nervous. "I guess I owe you," he said reluctantly. "But not here. There's a restaurant—The Three Chefs—across from an apartment complex in Silver Springs; we won't bump into any other delegates out there."

He handed the card back and Livonas said, "What would be a good time?"

Harris's face had started to swell but he managed another painful smile. "Tonight, while I'm still feeling brave. Around eight. I'll try to get Hank Miller to come, too—he's my roommate, another delegate. They tried to nail him ten days ago but he got away."

After Harris had left, Livonas soaked his hand in cold water and flexed the fingers. They would ache for a week. He wiped his hands and slipped into his coat, smiling slightly.

De Young's ship of state had just sprung a leak.

December 18

4:00 P.M., Friday

Livonas sprawled back in his swivel chair and stared glumly at the stack of paperwork that had accumulated in the ten days he'd been away. In between visits to the convention and everything else, he hadn't made a dent in it. In fact, just looking at the lopsided pile was enough to inflict him with paralysis.

He shivered. The heavy snows and rains had brought with them a damp cold that seeped through the red granite walls of the Executive Office Building. It made his office about as comfortable to work in as an abandoned boxcar.

He had just summoned up enough courage to tug at a sheet of paper sticking out of the middle of the pile when Julie, his executive secretary, swept into his office.

"Saved," she said, looking critically at the stack. She placed a memo on his desk. "The Vice-President's gone home for the day, you can reach him there."

He let go of the sheet of paper and sprawled back in his chair again to read the memo she had given him.

It was from Congressman Cudahy, chairman of the House Energy Committee. The bill he was sponsoring, the Severance Surcharge Tax bill, expected to be voted out of committee during the morning session, hadn't been. A freshman congressman—van Delph, from Michigan's lower peninsula—had switched sides, joining the bloc of western and gulf coast committee members opposing it. Cudahy had been forced to table the vote until Monday morning or risk seeing it defeated. He wanted Whitman's help.

At the top of the memo, Whitman had scrawled: "*Andy, see what you can do.*"

Julie had been waiting in the doorway while he read the memo, which meant she had read it, too.

"Julie, get Fran Murphy on the phone and tell him to stick around, I'll be right over."

"Right," Julie said, then added: "You have a reminder on the calendar to pick up your tux for Elizabeth Packard's party tomorrow night. Should I have it delivered?"

"Please." Livonas tugged off his ancient wool pullover, grabbed his suit jacket and briefcase, and ran to catch the four o'clock shuttle bus for the Hill. Things had been bad enough in Washington before he'd left; since coming back, they had gotten even worse. More and more it seemed to Livonas that he was on the losing side of a battle he didn't understand, being fought on a battlefield so obscured by smoke that he couldn't distinguish friend from foe. It was not a nice feeling.

Francis Murphy, Cudahy's administrative aide, was a slender, curly black-haired Irishman who had spent all his adult life in politics, starting as a page in the New York state legislature. He had worked his way up to Governor Hugh Carey's chief legislative aide and for the last ten years had worked for Congressman Cudahy. Livonas considered him the smartest legislative aide on the Hill.

"I thought Manny was going to throttle the son-of-a-bitch." The immaculate Murphy crossed his legs, taking care not to muss the crease in his trousers, and started picking bits of lint off the top trouser leg.

"Got any ideas why the sudden switch?"

Livonas was leafing through a slim file that Murphy had handed him on Congressman van Delph—a few clips from local papers, a

"Man in the News" profile in the *Grand Rapids Press*, and an embossed announcement from the law firm of Bunker, Workman, and Spirotta of Grand Rapids welcoming their new partner, the Hon. Congressman Jerry van Delph, to their firm.

Murphy recrossed his legs and started working on the other pants leg. "Oh, I've got an idea. Last weekend Congressman van Delph was invited on a fact-finding junket to inspect the energy resources of the West, including those of Las Vegas. Governor Walters of Nevada threw a little dinner in the committee's honor. Among the other dignitaries present were Governor Barron of Arizona and Vince de Young's man, Herb Shepherd."

Everywhere he turned, there was Vince de Young, Livonas thought, blocking bills he didn't like, subverting the Constitutional Convention . . . What the hell was he after?

"I don't know if they took pictures of Jerry with some Las Vegas ladies that he doesn't want passed out at Sunday services back home," Murphy continued. "My guess, though, is that it's the old retainer-at-a-later-date flim-flam."

He leaned over and tapped the announcement card in the folder Livonas was holding.

"Next summer, I suspect that any of the umpteen utility companies who've been lobbying their collective asses off trying to defeat the bill will discover they just can't do without the services of Bunker, Workman, and Spirotta. At this point, I couldn't care if they caught Jerry pulling his pecker at Sunday Mass but we've got to try and find another vote by Monday morning."

Livonas guessed from the flatness of Murphy's voice that he didn't hold out much hope.

"How about his district? Any place where he's vulnerable?"

Murphy shook his head. "Blueberries, gravel, and local tourism is about it. I don't think there's a federal contract in the whole damned district."

He took a pack of wintergreen Lifesavers from his coat pocket and popped one in his mouth. "I told Manny we might as well kiss it off for this session. But you know Manny . . ." He sucked thoughtfully on his Lifesaver. "I went ahead and set up a meeting for you with van Delph at five. If you want my personal opinion, I think it's a waste of time."

Livonas leafed through the folder again, picked out the newspaper profile and read through it. It was the usual small-town-boy-makes-good article, with a picture at the bottom showing the blond-haired, fleshy-faced congressman standing on a riverside boardwalk flanked by a pleasant-looking older man and woman—probably Mr. and Mrs. van Delph, senior.

He was about to return the clip to the folder, then took another look at it. The photo showed a large bargelike boat in the river behind the figures. A dredge. He squinted, trying to make out the insignia on the ensign flying from her stern.

"You got something?" Murphy asked.

Livonas looked at his watch. He was already ten minutes late. No time to check, he'd have to wing it. "A dinner at the Sans Souci says Congressman van Delph sees the light."

At the door, Murphy said: "I hope I'm lucky enough to lose. Remember, Andy, van Delph might look like one but he's really no dummy. He just hasn't had his cherry popped."

Van Delph's office was one floor down and around the south side of the Rayburn Building. Livonas was told the congressman was on the phone and while he waited, he studied the framed black-and-white glossies that covered three walls of the outer office. He amused himself by searching for a picture that didn't include the congressman's own broad, smiling face. He had gone through two entire walls without any luck when the door opened and Congressman van Delph stood beaming at him.

"Mr. Livonas, what a pleasure!"

Livonas returned the hearty grip and the warm, radiant smile. The black-and-whites didn't do van Delph justice, he thought.

"Good to meet you in the flesh, Congressman." Livonas nodded at the photographs.

Van Delph smiled modestly. "I must have a picture of everybody who ever voted for me. My constituents really like to see themselves up there when they come for a visit." Livonas caught a quick, appraising glance as van Delph draped a soft arm around his shoulder and ushered him into the inner office.

Livonas eased into one of the comfortable armchairs in front of the desk while van Delph lowered his bulk into the swivel chair behind it. The desk top was covered with neatly arranged stacks of bulging manila files—the no-nonsense working congressman image.

Van Delph had probably pulled them out especially for the meeting with him.

Van Delph was fidgeting, trying to hide his apprehension. Livonas decided to throw him off balance. If the congressman had guessed why he was there, then he'd probably also prepared a little speech on why he had changed his vote.

"Bob wanted me to tell you how pleased he was to have your support over the past year on behalf of H.B. 520. He wanted you to know if there was anything you needed, all you had to do was ask."

Van Delph's face reddened.

"I . . . ah . . . I thought you knew about the vote—"

Livonas held up his hand. "No need to apologize, Jerry. That's why the Vice-President thought it important that I see you now. In the final analysis, we all have to vote our consciences." Livonas exchanged a look of pure sincerity with van Delph. "The Vice-President wants you to know he understands."

Van Delph had a face you could read like a map. Right now it showed a little guilt but mostly relief. Livonas's tone became matter-of-fact, as if the vote were now a dead issue.

"Your district includes Grand Haven, doesn't it?"

Van Delph's expression became wary. "That's right, I was born in Grand Haven."

Livonas glanced away to smother a yawn. He could sense van Delph watching him, trying to figure out what he had, if anything. Murphy was right, the man wasn't stupid. He just hadn't been around very long.

He looked up at van Delph and smiled. "I thought I recognized it from that picture of you with your folks." A print of the newspaper photo was among those in the outer office. He stood up. "Nice country, my parents used to take me there for vacations when we lived in Chicago." He tucked his briefcase under his arm. "Pleasure to have met you, Jerry."

Van Delph scurried out from behind his desk. "I'm glad you dropped by, Mr. Livonas, first chance I've had to really talk to you." He wrapped a meaty arm around Livonas's shoulder once again as he escorted him to the door. "Please tell the Vice-President . . ." Van Delph paused as if overcome by emotion. "If there's anything I can do for him, just anything . . ." He trailed off, misty-eyed.

Livonas stopped at the door. "Why, that's very nice of you, Jerry. I'm sure the Vice-President will appreciate it." Then, as if the thought had just occurred to him: "Say, you know that picture I mentioned? Isn't that an Army Corps of Engineers dredge in the background? I bet they have to go in there pretty regularly to keep the river from silting up."

Van Delph's ruddy complexion faded to a chalky white. "That's right," he said slowly. "They have to go in there every June."

Livonas turned free of the congressman's arm and patted him cheerfully on the back.

"The Vice-President is having lunch with Senator Downey next week—he's been chairman of the Armed Services Committee ever since Bob was in the Senate. Matter of fact, I think it was Bob who arranged for him to get the chairmanship."

The game was over now and he and van Delph stared grimly at each other. "I imagine those dredges are in high demand," he continued in a soft voice. "The municipalities get them pretty much for free, don't they?"

Van Delph nodded. The son-of-a bitch is figuring how much it's going to cost him, Livonas thought.

"I'll see you on Monday, Congressman. Fran Murphy told me he's discovered some new arguments for the Severance Surcharge Tax bill and he wants to present them to the committee in hopes of switching some votes."

Livonas opened the office door. "He only needs one vote so I guess he's got a pretty good chance."

He stood there with the door open, waiting.

"I suppose he does," van Delph said stiffly. He made no attempt to hide his distress.

Livonas smiled. He was tempted to continue the conversation. There were a lot of things he wanted to tell van Delph, who now looked like some college sophomore caught in a fraternity prank. It was hard to believe he was thirty-four. Unfortunately, it wasn't as hard to believe he was a United States congressman.

"See you Monday," Livonas repeated cheerfully.

He called Murphy up on the hall phone with the good news, then headed for the shuttle bus outside. He was almost to the elevators when he remembered he was supposed to meet Jeff Saunders for a drink at the Class Reunion at 6:00 P.M. He looked at his watch. It was already six-fifteen.

He ran back to the phone. There was no way he could cancel.

The young deputy FBI director had gone out of his way to get the coroner's report on Steven Hart and wanted to deliver it personally. And after meeting Saunders he'd have to pick up Katy and Stu and drive to Silver Springs for the meeting with the two dissidents from the California delegation.

He was beat already but there was no hope at all of getting home before midnight.

December 18
8:15 P.M., Friday

Livonas drove while Stu Lambert dozed next to him and Kathleen curled up on the back seat, trying to catch up on the sleep she had missed the previous night. It had taken his secretary all afternoon to wrangle the car and six gallons of gas from the White House motor pool, and the car wasn't worth a damn. The engine pinged, the speedometer dropped below thirty-five going up the slightest grade, the seats were as uncomfortable as a park bench, and the heater didn't work.

But as Lambert said, "At least it looks like a car." Livonas shivered and stared out at the dark, deserted highway. Silver Springs wasn't that far from Washington and traffic was almost nonexistent, but they were running half an hour behind schedule. If Harris, the California delegate, were as skittish as he seemed, he might not wait.

Ten minutes later, he dropped off Kathleen and Stu on the corner opposite the restaurant and parked the car a block away. The parking lot behind The Three Chefs was almost empty but he passed it up. The cream-colored car with the White House sticker would attract as much attention as a priest at a bachelor party. He smiled, then sobered. He was getting as paranoid as Stu, who'd been jumpy ever since he'd heard about the two delegates and the enforcement squad.

The inside of the restaurant was hot and steamy and smelled of cheap chili and hamburgers; it was crowded with young singles and couples. Livonas guessed they were residents of the housing complex across the street. The restaurant had been designed as a half-hearted imitation of an Englishman's supper club. The walls were lined with reproductions of red-coated gentry chasing foxes and scenes from the Battle of Trafalgar. The red hunting jackets were now spotted with grease and the sea off Cape Trafalgar looked like pea soup.

Jutting off the large cocktail lounge and bar were the smaller dining rooms. Livonas quickly checked them. Harris and another man—probably his roommate, Miller—were sitting in "Ye Olde Coach Room," a shadowy alcove furnished with several red naugahyde booths.

Kathleen and Stu slid into the booth first and Livonas followed. Both Harris and Miller looked twenty-seven or twenty-eight. Both had short, sandy hair and well-trimmed moustaches and when the swelling in Harris's face went down, both would look remarkably alike. Each was wearing jeans and a leather jacket and had the kind of physique that Livonas associated with gyms. They were Californians, all right, he thought, and wondered if regional looks were starting to predominate over ethnic.

Everybody at the table seemed slightly uneasy. Livonas said, "Katy, Stu, I'd like you to meet Paul Harris and Hank Miller."

They shook hands and Kathleen murmured something about seeing them around at the convention. Then Livonas said to Harris, "Whereabouts in California are you from?"

"Los Gatos, Hank's from Pleasanton." He seemed nervous. Miller, who sat on the outside of the booth wasn't looking at Livonas at all. He was facing the door, checking everybody who came into the restaurant.

Livonas picked up the menu. "Anybody hungry? It's on the house."

Miller glanced away from the door, a look of exasperation on his face. "C'mon, Paul, let's get this over with, I keep worrying we're being watched."

Livonas looked at Kathleen. She hadn't been willing to believe his story about the enforced discipline in the California delegation. She did now.

"When did California first start making moves to take over the convention?" Livonas asked.

Harris took a sip of his beer, nervously wiping away the suds that clung to his moustache. "Right after Jerry Wagoner arrived from

Sacramento. He was a special appointment by Governor de Young. Two days after he settled in, he started weeding out all the delegates who weren't one hundred percent de Young supporters."

"How?"

"He'd make you feel you weren't wanted, he'd exclude you from caucus meetings. There was an inner circle and an outer circle and then the rest of us. Pretty soon there were no invitations, no receptions, and no parties. He'd spread, you know, rumors. Then he'd say the budget had been cut and we'd have to double up in a hotel." He smiled slightly. "Hank and I moved out here then—we had our own resources. The others just quit in disgust. Right now we're nonpersons, the rest of the delegates won't speak to us."

Miller looked away from the door again. "Tell him what happened the night before last."

Harris exchanged a private glance with his friend. "Hank and I . . . had a fight so I went into town for the evening and dropped in at Wylie's." He hesitated. "Do you know it?"

Livonas nodded. "Yeah, on Wisconsin. Who'd you see, Governor de Young running around in his Judy Garland drag?"

Harris and Miller looked blank, then laughed. "I was standing at the bar," Harris said, "and this guy—a real hunk—came up to me and says, 'Don't I know you?' I said, 'Well, you do now' and then I recognized him. When I was living in San Francisco, he was the afternoon bartender at the Brig, where I used to hang out. It was old-home week, you know—small-world time. So I said, 'What're you doing here?' And he says, 'I'm here with my troupe.' 'I didn't know you were a dancer,' I said. Christ, he was built like a fullback, not a Nureyev."

Harris paused for dramatic effect and took another sip of his beer. " 'Not that kind of troupe,' he said. 'Gee T-r-o-o-p, as in state police.' " He looked questioningly at Livonas. "You know what G-Troop is?"

Livonas had read about it a few years back. It had been one of those paramilitary stories that hit the news and then vanish. De Young had reorganized the state police and highway patrol and formed a special strike force to deal with everything from marijuana growers to terrorists. The "G," he recalled, stood for "Governor."

"G-Troop is de Young's secret police," Miller cut in. "They were brought to D.C. to act as floor marshals at the convention."

"You don't need a special police squad to muscle people on a convention floor," Livonas said.

Miller looked disgusted. "Go ahead, Paul, you tell him." He turned back to inspect the people entering the restaurant.

Harris's lips thinned. "De Young uses G-Troop for a lot of things. Like blackmail. You know what that asshole was doing in Wylie's? Trying to entrap a delegate. A closet queen, you know the type— wife and three kids in the suburbs but likes an occasional night out with the boys. My friend from the Brig told me he was supposed to meet the delegate for a date, even boasted how they had set up a suite at the Four Seasons for secret filming so they could blackmail delegates into voting with the Western Coalition."

"Why'd he tell you?" Livonas asked, suspicious.

"Because he thought I was still a de Young supporter." He looked thoughtful. "I started out that way. I guess we both did."

Livonas took an envelope out of his coat pocket. "What do you know about Steven Hart?"

Harris played nervously with his beer, looked at Livonas, then glanced away. "Not much. Like us, he didn't get along with Jerry Wagoner."

"How badly didn't he get along?"

"Jerry never liked him, right from the start. The feeling was mutual. Earlier, on the day Hart was murdered, Wagoner was really pissed at him."

"What about?"

"We never found out. Hart had gone to lunch and never came back."

"Was Steven Hart gay?" Livonas asked.

Harris and Miller exchanged looks and Harris said in a distant voice, "Hank, the man wants to know about Steven Hart."

Miller shrugged. "I tried to score on him at a party a couple of months ago and he threatened to punch me out." He looked humiliated. "As far as I could tell, Hart was Mr. Straight."

Livonas opened up the envelope and took out the report Jeff Saunders had given him. "I want to read you the coroner's report." When he finished, he said: "Does that make sense to you, knowing Hart?"

Harris glanced at Miller. "You're the one who's into leather."

"I think somebody set him up." Miller hesitated, trying to think of a way to phrase it. "Any leather scene is actually a ritual. The slave sets limits and everybody observes them. Murders occur when some idiot tricks out with a stranger and lets himself be tied up so he's helpless. Then he's an easy mark for robbery—or worse. But a group scene is usually an organized one. Limits would have been observed, he wouldn't have been hurt." He shook his head. "I think somebody wanted to make it look like an S and M murder. The police don't really get excited about finding the killer, the relatives don't like the notoriety and don't push it." He looked uneasy. "From the coroner's report it sounds like they probably—" He stopped in mid-sentence.

"Like they probably what?" Livonas prompted.

"Like they probably screwed him after he was dead."

Livonas glanced at Katy and Stu. The loose ends were being tied up. De Young had done a lot more than cut deals and rely on regionalism to capture the convention. He had used blackmail and intimidation and now . . .

Murder?

The longer he thought about it, the more he was convinced. Debbie Spindler had said Hart had taken a "Confidential" letter from Wagoner's office. But the coroner hadn't listed such a letter in Hart's personal effects.

Whoever wanted the letter now had it. And had killed Hart so he couldn't talk about its contents.

December 19

9:15 A.M., *Saturday*

The small talk around the conference table had flagged and Livonas glanced again at his watch and wondered when President Massey would arrive. The meeting of the Energy Task Force had been called for eight thirty sharp and only Roger Anderson didn't seem concerned. But then all Roger had to do when the meeting was over was to keep the President company, laugh at all the jokes he had heard a dozen times before, reminisce about the good old days in Philadelphia and, if the rumors were true, keep the President's glass filled.

Hugh Ramsay leaned over and whispered, "Maybe we should start a pool on when he'll get here."

Livonas said, "I'll take ten o'clock" and then there were voices in the hallway and Massey walked in. Livonas started to get to his feet, then relaxed when Massey waved his hand. The President wasn't in his shirt sleeves this time but was impeccably dressed in a dark three-piece worsted suit. He was freshly shaven—Livonas could smell the lemon-scented cologne clear at his end of the twenty-foot table—and carrying a cup of coffee and a saucer.

"Good morning, gentlemen." Massey set the coffee cup on the table and flashed the smile that three years before had won him the election. Livonas chorused, "Good morning, Mr. President" along with the others and Massey settled into the swivel chair at the head of the table. He took a single sheet of paper from the folder in front of him, glanced at it, tapped his pencil, and looked around the table. The smile faded and Livonas realized that for once Massey had something important to say but couldn't think of a way to begin.

Massey finally nodded to Anderson and said in a husky voice, "You tell them, Rog. I guess there's no sense in beating around the bush."

"No point at all, Mr. President."

Anderson's voice never seemed to lose its cheery tone, though this morning Livonas thought he sounded a little more self-important than usual. He rustled some papers in front of him while Massey took a sip from his coffee cup. "Cables last night from our contact in Jakarta, Mr. Fahmy, report that contrary to the agreement reached with Vice-President Whitman two weeks ago, the government—"

"They japped us!" Massey interrupted, slapping the table with the palm of his hand. "There'll be no shipments of crude. None!"

Livonas shot a glance at Whitman. The Vice-President, as usual, looked impassive. Whitman's day was getting off to a bad start, Livonas thought, and it wasn't going to get any better when he had it out with Whitman at their noon appointment.

Massey glanced around the table again and Livonas wondered if he were looking for someone to blame. He stopped at Whitman and Livonas waited for the sparks to fly. Then he suppressed a smile. Massey had changed his mind and retreated to the safety of his coffee cup.

"I don't need to tell you what a heavy blow this is to the country, to this Administration, to my Presidency." Livonas thought he sounded more self-pitying than angry. "The real problem, of course, is what are we going to do about it? This has started out to be the worst winter in thirty years and right now we're faced with an additional shortfall of fifty thousand barrels of oil per day."

The shadows under Massey's eyes were more pronounced and he was slurring his words, Livonas noted, but it sounded like a new Massey. He was getting directly to the point.

"I was hoping you gentlemen might have some suggestions." Massey's voice was stained with sarcasm. He looked at Al Reynolds. "Al, am I being presumptuous when I say State ought to have had some inkling of what's going on over there, why the Indonesians decided to shaft us?"

Reynolds spread his gnarled hands. "Working through a commercial contact like Mr. Fahmy is a lot different than working through our embassy. We've queried the Swiss embassy and the CIA as to why the Indonesians pulled the rug, but so far nobody's come up with an answer."

"Couldn't Fahmy shed any light?"

Reynolds looked unhappy. "This time, the Indonesian authorities wouldn't even talk to him. All we have is the two-line message from their energy ministry saying the agreement has been canceled."

Abdel Fahmy was an Egyptian journalist and a friend of Livonas—one of the reasons Livonas had been invited to sit in on the energy meetings. Fahmy had access to all the officials in Jakarta but unfortunately lacked decision-making authority.

Massey hunched over his coffee cup, glaring across the table at Reynolds. "Follow it up, there's got to be a reason." He didn't wait for Reynolds to offer anything more. "We need some coffee here," he said abruptly. "Help us all wake up."

He walked back to his desk, flipped a switch on the intercom and ordered coffee to be brought up, then returned to the conference table. "Mr. Kearns, Indonesia used to be a heavy supplier for Gulf Coast Oil, didn't it? Why do you think the deal went sour?"

Massey wasn't taking charge so much as he was trying to place the blame, Livonas realized. Maybe nobody there could tell him why the Indonesians had pulled out but somebody sure as hell should have been able to warn him . . .

Kearns cleared his throat, his expression one of apology. "We've done our damndest to negotiate on our own, Mr. President, we've even violated the law." He nodded self-righteously. "I don't mind admitting it, I'd defend it in any court of the land as an act of patriotism. We've offered substantial personal remuneration, but we can't move any of the officials there. Frankly, I was surprised that our Vice-President"—he nodded at Whitman sitting across from him—"had any luck at all, temporary as it was."

The meeting was interrupted by a White House butler who came in with a tray holding two pots of coffee and cups, a cream pitcher and sugar bowl. He had a fresh cup already poured for Massey.

"Thanks, Malcolm." The butler took up a position against the wall. Massey turned back to Kearns. "If it were Gulf Coast Oil, Mr. Kearns, I think you might have succeeded," he said in a thick voice.

"How about you, General?" Massey had found a new target. "I realize civilian solutions aren't your specialty, of course."

Rudd looked grim. He had been waiting for this, Livonas thought. Massey usually avoided discussing the military option, which was Rudd's bailiwick. After the Iraqi debacle, Massey distrusted his military advisors, although Rudd himself had been against the Iraqi plan from the start, arguing that military power should be used, not just demonstrated.

"I wasn't going to suggest one, Mr. President. I think we've tried every possible civilian solution for almost a year now with no luck whatsoever."

He worked the small combination lock of his briefcase and took out a folder stamped "Top Secret," placing it on the table in front of him.

"All of you know we have several updated contingency plans regarding events in the Persian Gulf that would cut us off from its oil. Any one of them could become operational within hours."

"You talking about an invasion, General?"

Massey sounded irritated and Livonas guessed the rumored friction between him and Rudd had gone past the point of no return. By the end of next week, Massey would probably have appointed somebody else as his military advisor.

Rudd nodded. "That's right, Mr. President. We've had two carriers and a dozen other warships plus several dozen support ships on station in the Indian Ocean for the past several years. We have a Rapid Development Force, which now numbers close to a hundred thousand men, and we have a dozen high-speed SL-7 cargo ships that could bring in backup supplies within fifteen days."

Rudd tapped the folder in front of him. "The preferred plan involves a quick surgical strike to occupy the United Arab Emirates, Qatar, and parts of Oman at the mouths of the Persian Gulf and the Gulf of Oman. Once those areas are secure, we'd have the option of extending our control up the gulf coast to Kuwait."

"Don't you think the people living in those countries might object, General?" Al Reynolds's voice was soft.

Rudd leaned back in his chair, completely at ease. Livonas thought he looked in his element.

"I don't think it would matter much. All three countries border the gulfs; they can be easily invaded from the sea. Their combined population is approximately two million, about that of Philadelphia. The degree of military resistance they could offer would be minimal. The amount of oil production we would gain, however, would be major—especially if we occupied Kuwait as well. It would total more than four million barrels of crude a day. Even considering production inevitably lost in the course of occupation, that's more than enough to ease the shortage."

"I can't understand why you've left out the Saudis," Reynolds said sarcastically. "That would add another ten million barrels."

Rudd smiled at the sarcasm. "The Saudis are capable of more resistance and we would also run into obvious logistical problems because of the size of the country. From a diplomatic point of view, the Saudis have been friendly in the past and presumably might be friendly again in the future."

"Wouldn't the Arabs in the region combine against us?" Ramsay objected.

Rudd shook his head. "The operation would be over in a matter of a day or two, long before effective opposition could be organized. And I can't imagine Iran and Iraq cooperating. They might try to land troops in the Emirates by sea but I think we could control the gulf. Their other alternative would be to march through Saudi territory to reach the Emirates and I'm sure the Saudis would object. Iraq, of course, borders on Kuwait and could defend it directly—if they wanted to risk it. But don't forget, while we'd be in the south, Egypt and Israel would be effective counterweights in the north. In any event, attempts at assistance by land or by the sea could be interdicted from the air—which we would control."

Massey ran his finger around the rim of his coffee cup and shot Rudd a sly look. "What about the Russians, General? Are you going to interdict them, too?"

By the look on his face, Rudd didn't think that the Soviets were a major problem.

"I think we would have to tell the Soviets at the very start exactly what was happening. I don't think they would object, at least privately, if we let them know we understood their desire to protect the Kurdish minorities on the other side of their border with Iran."

Livonas couldn't resist saying, "You mean you're planning to give the Soviets the northern half of Iran."

Rudd hesitated just long enough to let Livonas know he was an outsider.

"If the Soviets want it, there's little we could do to stop them."

Reynolds had moved from outrage to open contempt. "In the long run, I'm not so sure the prize would be worth the winning, General. The United States would be forever branded an aggressor in the eyes of the world community."

"Forever is a long time," Rudd said, equally contemptuous. "And I doubt the people freezing in New York and Chicago and our other northern cities would lose much sleep about what the world community thought."

Livonas caught Whitman's eye. Rudd's plan was exactly the one he and Whitman had thought Rudd would propose and it was the one plan that Livonas had researched at length before going West.

"What are we supposed to do now?" Reynolds asked, his voice shaking with anger. "Vote on it?"

"Only one man here is the Commander-in-Chief," Rudd said softly.

There was sudden silence in the room. Rudd had had his chance at bat and come very close to hitting a home run using a fine combination of logic and flattery. Livonas could feel the sweat gather in his armpits. He stared at Whitman. Why the hell was Bob waiting?

Massey stood up. His tie was loose and it looked to Livonas like he had trouble focussing his eyes. "Then let's do it, General," he growled. "I've had it up to here with studies."

Livonas was stunned. Even Rudd seemed shocked by Massey's decisiveness. Did Massey realize he was committing the United States to war, declared or otherwise?

Whitman cleared his throat to get the attention of those around the table, then fumbled for his pipe and made a show of filling it and tamping down the tobacco.

"If I may say something, Mr. President." He took a slow, relaxed puff. "Sometimes I'm amazed at the short-term memories of our military. In recent years we've seen two attempts by the military to release hostages held in that part of the world. The first ended in complete failure." He paused, his eyes on Massey. "The second was a catastrophe. Now General Rudd has proposed invading no less than four countries bordering the gulfs."

Rudd started to protest. Whitman held up his hand. "You're about to accuse me of comparing apples and oranges, General, I realize that. I mention the hostage rescue attempts only to point out the frequent failure of the 'best-laid' plans. I think we ought to examine such possibilities in your proposed invasion. We would have to have complete surprise, which I doubt we could achieve, given the press in this country and elsewhere. Lacking such surprise, I think we would find the Straits of Hormuz and other choke points to be blockaded or mined. Granted, the Navy could take care of those difficulties in short order."

His pipe had gone out and Whitman took the time to relight it. Livonas knew it was a bit of business to give his argument time to sink in.

"But I suspect the major oil fields in the Emirates, as well as those of Kuwait and Saudi Arabia, are also mined and the same is undoubtedly true of off-shore oil rigs. I can't think of any strike that would be so swift the nations involved wouldn't have time to destroy their refineries and drilling rigs."

"That's a gross misrep——" Rudd began.

"In good time, General. When you say 'quick, surgical strike' you make it sound relatively bloodless. But what we're really talking about is a war in the Persian Gulf that could be very bloody, that could easily spread, and which might end up depriving us of the very oil we seek. Perhaps for as long as two or three years. We could repair the refineries and oil rigs, of course, but this would have to be accomplished in the midst of a hostile population."

Whitman fumbled for his tobacco pouch. "Two more points and then I'll be through, General. I have a question about the Soviet response to our little adventure. I can't quite see them being satisfied with a nibble of Iran when they might benefit by our example and swallow the whole thing. But I'll grant that if they're willing to trade the entire Persian Gulf for a little piece of that country, it would be some horse trade."

Livonas felt a twinge of pity for Rudd, who was looking increasingly uncomfortable.

"There's also the problem of Western Europe and Japan," Whitman continued, his voice harsher. "The United States is embargoed, but Germany, France, Italy, and Japan are not. We start a war in the Persian Gulf and we run the risk not only of failing to gain any oil for ourselves but of depriving our allies of it. I'm afraid we wouldn't have them as allies for very long. With the collapse of NATO, I'll leave it to your imagination as to what the Soviets might be tempted to do."

There was a long, uncomfortable silence. Massey turned to Rudd, his voice tentative. "I guess that pretty well demolishes your plan, General."

Rudd's eyes lidded with disgust. "There are a lot of 'coulds' and 'mights' and 'suspects' in Mr. Whitman's argument. Of course there are risks—you can't make an omelet without breaking eggs. As a military man, I wouldn't suggest any venture that didn't stand a good chance of success. The Joint Chiefs and I have been over this plan a dozen times."

He leaned across the table, pushing the folder toward Massey. "Just five minutes ago, you approved the military option, Mr. President." He paused. "The biggest risk of all is to do nothing."

Massey took another sip of coffee, trying to ignore the collective embarrassment of those around the table. Then he regained a smug composure. "It's true I initially agreed, General. For the sake of argument."

Rudd's expression came close to hatred. "The continued shortage of energy—specifically oil—is endangering the security of the United States. Unless something is done, and done soon, I couldn't guarantee the loyalty of the military. You can't expect men to try and defend the country if lack of decisiveness on the part of the Chief Executive makes it impossible in advance."

Whitman was on his feet now, his own face tinged with anger. "I think you ought to enlarge on that, General. What do you mean, you can't guarantee the loyalty of the military?"

Rudd froze. "Any officer can resign his commission, including the Joint Chiefs of Staff," he said. "If they disagree too deeply with policy, they have the same option as their civilian counterparts."

Livonas wasn't sure the general had meant that at all, and judging from the expressions of the others around the table, he guessed they weren't sure, either.

Massey signaled the butler to refill his coffee cup. "I would never sacrifice our military preparedness," he mumbled. His brief moment of decisiveness had passed. Then his eyes fixed on Anderson as if there might be help from that quarter. Anderson suddenly found it necessary to bury his face in his handkerchief.

"Rog, didn't you say there were four nuclear plants in the Midwest that are supposed to be shut down because of radiation leaks?"

Anderson hastily pawed through the contents of his briefcase, looking relieved when he found the sheet he was searching for. "Yes, sir, those are Zion One and Dresden Two in Illinois, Cook Two in Michigan, and Monticello One in Minnesota. They're all scheduled to go off stream the first of January for inspection of hairline cracks—"

"Unless the plant managers are willing to certify that they're too dangerous to continue operation, cancel the shutdowns." Massey glanced around the table, daring anybody to disagree with him. Livonas found it hard to look at him; the President couldn't hide his air of defeat, his own awareness that once again he had been too weak to make an important decision or to offer alternatives.

"Some calculated risks have to be taken, you do that every time you light a match. This Administration is willing to take those risks." Massey finished his coffee and put the empty cup on the table. "Rog, ask the Advertising Council for a new campaign built around the theme of voluntary conservation of energy. It might be a good idea if I gave the pitch; we'll need all the TV exposure we can get prior to the election."

He stood up to leave, holding on to the back of his chair for support. "Sometimes I wonder if there's any point in continuing these meetings. Good morning, gentlemen."

The butler opened the door and Massey left the room, steadying himself on the butler's arm. Massey had been jaunty enough when he had come in, Livonas thought. He stopped at the end of the table as the others were leaving and casually stuck his finger in the bottom of Massey's coffee cup, then tasted it.

"It's vodka." General Rudd was at his elbow. "He breaks open his second liter by six and passes out by eight."

December 19
Noon, Saturday

"How's it going, Andy?" Whitman swiveled around in his desk chair to face Livonas, who made himself comfortable on the leather couch to the right of Whitman's oversized desk. The large bay windows behind Whitman's head were fogged over and Livonas could barely separate the outline of the West Wing of the White House from the grayness around it. The Executive Office Building was only a few hundred yards away, which meant the fog was one of the worst of the season.

"You been following the Constitutional Convention lately?" Livonas slouched down on the couch, jamming his hands in his pockets and stretching his legs out in front of him.

"Sounds like it's blowing up a little tempest over there." Whitman had leaned back in his chair and was concentrating on twisting a stray pipe cleaner into a circle.

"I've spent the better part of two days at the convention. Katy Houseman showed me the ropes."

"Nice girl, Katy," Whitman said paternally. For some reason, the pipe cleaner seemed to be defying his efforts to twist it into a perfect oval.

"What's going on is more than just a 'little tempest'—you should have heard them go at it yesterday. There's a constitutional crisis developing and furthermore it has 'Made by Vincent de Young' stenciled all over it." Livonas stood up and started to pace the floor. "My first assumption was that de Young was out to use the convention as a national forum for his presidential campaign. I think I underestimated the scope of his ambitions."

"How so?" Whitman sat up in his chair and pulled a yellow legal pad from his desk drawer, ready to scribble notes.

Livonas stopped in front of the desk, his hands clasped behind his back. "The California delegation—led, staffed, and directed by de Young people—is organizing a bloc of western and southwestern delegates to take over the convention. Most of the westerners have a lot in common so that's not too difficult. But they're also picking up delegates from other areas than just Chicago. They're cutting deals and using bribery, physical intimidation, parliamentary ploys, and good old-fashioned demagoguery. And I can quote you chapter and verse on any of that."

He walked back to the couch, took a manila folder from his briefcase, and handed it to Whitman.

Whitman took out his reading glasses. "What's this?"

"It's a copy of the voting breakdowns at the Constitutional Convention, I got them from Katy. I think we can assume that Janice McCall is not the only one benefitting from Vince's generosity."

Livonas walked over to stand behind Whitman. He pointed at the bottom of the page. "That's a list of the delegates who have broken with their region or state and voted with the Western Coalition on the motions that gave them control of the convention apparatus—the motions upholding the credential committee challenges and the motion censuring the Supreme Court for interfering with the affairs of the convention."

He walked back to his chair. "I've sent a copy over to Hugh Ramsay—I thought he might be able to find out if there are any unauthorized fuel oil shipments to various cities or states or if their reserves are above their quota."

Whitman took off his glasses, then laced his fingers behind his head, and leaned back, relaxed.

"Hugh won't be able to find anything solid for weeks, maybe a month. Perhaps longer. And if everything you say about de Young is true, I can hardly see him overlooking a few well-placed bribes in the Customs Service or the DOE for that matter—the bureaucracy is riddled with de Young partisans as it is. Even without them, it would be a good month before anything unusual showed up." He went back to the pipe cleaner. "You're not the type to play Don Quixote, Andy, but you're coming dangerously close to it."

Livonas reddened and started to object. Whitman held up his hand, his voice harsher this time. "What you're charging—and I use the word advisedly—is that de Young is bribing blocs of delegates at the Constitutional Convention with promises of illegally obtained foreign oil. You are, in effect, accusing the governor of California of bribery and criminal conspiracy."

"In the case of Janice McCall, the evidence is pretty hard," Livonas said, grim-faced. "You realize that once the Western Coalition nails down control of the convention, de Young can use it to bypass the Congress. It isn't the Congress that has to ratify the amendments proposed by a Constitutional Convention, it's the state legislatures." He waited for it to sink in. "That's a whole new ball game. With the convention locked up and the power of the Presidency behind him, de Young could be the most powerful President this country has ever had. You just said the bureaucracy was riddled by de Young partisans. What makes you think the Congress isn't? Yesterday I went round and round with Congressman van Delph on the Cudahy bill. De Young had bought him—ask Francis Murphy about it."

Whitman turned his chair so he was staring out the window. "I could have gotten that bill through months ago," he growled.

"That's right," Livonas said with emphasis. "*You* could have." He let the conversation hang there, wanting to tell Whitman about Hart's death and his own suspicions and not sure how to bring it up.

"What'd you leave out, Andy?"

Livonas hesitated, then told him about Hart's murder and what Harris and Miller had told him about G-Troop and Jerry Wagoner's enforcement squad. When he had finished, he stood there feeling foolish. There was damned little to support the shadowy premise he was building; he knew it and he also knew Whitman could pick it apart.

But in the telling, he had convinced himself even more.

Whitman sighed. "Andy, it's a good thing you're not a lawyer." He waved his hand at the folder on his desk top. "What you've brought me are conclusions drawn from delegate voting patterns on three votes at the Constitutional Convention, some stalled bills in Congress, a private talk with Janice McCall, the tragic death of an aide with the California delegation, rumors of an 'enforcement squad' by disaffected delegates—and a lot of personal paranoia probably motivated by your hatred for de Young." He held up a hand. "I'm sorry, Andy, I have to consider that as a possibility—de Young's a subject on which you're not completely rational. What you've done is come to me with a lot of supposition and not much proof. What do you expect me to do with it?"

"There's such a thing as being too much of a lawyer," Livonas said, flushed, then choked back his anger. He had come to convince Whitman, not to argue with him.

"Bob." He took a deep breath, sorting out his thoughts so he

would sound as dispassionate as possible. "The country's turning
into a battleground. In the last week there have been fuel riots in ten
cities and it's still December. The Congress is split down the middle
and the executive branch is at a standstill—the President knows
more about makeup and lighting than he does about running the
damn country."

He stood up and paced the room, turning to face an impassive
Whitman. "I don't know what de Young is up to but it's more than
just guaranteeing himself the presidential nomination. Right now
he's taking over the Constitutional Convention. That's no joke—I
don't care what the convention started out as. He can use it to bypass the Congress and effectively change the structure of the government. Reread Article Five of the Constitution. Constitutional lawyers might debate it, but de Young's pulling it off. And with the
situation in the country as it is, he'll succeed. He stands a good
chance of becoming this country's first Imperial President."

Whitman didn't say anything and Livonas sat down, deflated.
Whitman had once been so strong, so powerful. Now the man
seemed dwarfed by his surroundings.

"I'm not asking you to have de Young arrested, just for you to
provide some goddamn leadership for the country. For God's sake,
you wanted the nomination once. Why not now?"

Whitman looked at the pipe cleaner with quiet satisfaction, then
glanced up at Livonas. "You ought to see yourself, Andy—you look
like you want to tear me apart."

Livonas laughed and the tension was broken.

Whitman continued gently. "We've spent most of the morning
talking about me, Andy. Let's talk about you for a change."

Livonas leaned back. "All right, it's your turn."

"How long have you been in Washington now, Andy?"

"Roughly eight years, give or take a few months."

"And you were in politics—along with being a reporter—for how
long before that?"

That would include both California and Chicago, Livonas
thought. "Another eight minus the year in Cambridge on a Neiman
Fellowship."

"And you're now how old?"

Livonas felt uncomfortable; he had a sudden idea what Whitman
was driving at. "Forty-two."

"What about your personal life, Andy? You haven't had much of one for a number of years now. Am I right?"

"I don't see—"

Whitman held up his hand again. "Yes, you do. I'm not picking on you, Andy, just pointing out something. You've given up your whole life for politics and yet you've never even run for public office. If I asked you about your personal life—I don't mean your sex life—you couldn't tell me about one woman with whom you've developed any kind of on-going relationship since Ellen. If I pressed you, you'd tell me you didn't have the time. That's what you'd say, isn't it?" He didn't wait for an answer. "Why did you do it, Andy?"

Livonas sat there, mute.

"You don't have to answer me," Whitman said. "I already know the answers. One of them is that politics is a great game, a lot of fun, though it's the most fun for people like me. Another answer is that a lot of people need a cause and politics gives them one. A lot of times, it doesn't particularly matter what the cause is. And there's an altruistic answer. People with causes are people who care a lot. About other people." He paused. "And about their country. One of the greatest shames these days is that most patriots are afraid to admit it. Somehow it's corny or naive. But we wouldn't have a country at all if it wasn't for the people who cared. Right from the grass roots up to the President—I've known some incompetent and mediocre Presidents but I've never known one who wasn't a patriot."

He studied the pipe cleaner for a moment, then dropped it in the wastepaper basket. "You're a patriot, too, Andy."

Livonas wanted to protest. Why the hell was Whitman telling him this? What was the point?

Whitman looked sad and tired. He took his time lighting his pipe. "I know damned well that for the past six months, you've made me your cause. You've been pushing me to run for the Presidency. You've been talking me up among your friends, among the party heads out in the country, among all the people both of us know are important. All by yourself, you've been responsible for a remarkable little boomlet. You've also gotten me in dutch with Massey, but that hardly matters. You're a damned good friend, you think a lot of me, I know you admire me. I probably flatter both of us when I say I think you've pushed me because you honestly felt it was best for the country."

Livonas grabbed wildly at the opportunity. "You're necessary, there's no other choice—"

"Andy, for God's sake, stop it!" Whitman's anger faded almost immediately. His voice was flat. "You've been devoted to me, which is what it makes it so hard for me to tell you this."

Livonas didn't want to hear what he knew Whitman was going to tell him.

"The ticker's shot," Whitman said, taking a slow puff on his pipe. "Before I went to Africa, I had a checkup at Walter Reed. The doctors say the left ventricular wall is nearly destroyed. I had a severe infarction—heart attack to you, Andy—a year ago and walked through it. I never knew it. It happens; the doctors call them 'silent heart attacks.'"

Livonas sat there in silence, stunned.

Whitman smiled. "Cheer up, it's my heart, not yours. They say if I take it easy, I have one, maybe two years. If I don't . . . Any 'undue stress' is the way the doctors put it."

"I wish you had told me before," Livonas said, agonized.

Whitman's voice was rough with emotion. "I'm not sure what your plans will be now, Andy. My hope is that, whatever you do, you do something for yourself."

Livonas only half heard Whitman's last few comments. The doctors could be wrong, he thought defiantly. And then: They were right. Bob Whitman had aged ten years in the last few months.

The last real hope for the country was gone.

December 19

2:45 P.M., *Saturday*

"Katy!" Stu was struggling up the aisle toward her, pushing his way through the tide of delegates heading for the exits in anticipation of the afternoon recess. "Something's up—they've doubled the floor marshals. They've got four on each mike and two at each exit."

Kathleen stood on one of the folding chairs for a look, using Stu's shoulder for balance. The hard core of the Western Coalition were still in their seats, while her own people were leaving the hall. On the speaker's platform, Jerry Wagoner's protégé, Ray Griffin, Frank Spinella, the chairman pro tem, and the chief sergeant-at-arms had their heads together in a tight little circle.

"*Shit!* Stu, get our people back in here—they're the only ones leaving for recess." What the hell was the West up to now?

She watched Stu hurry through the hall, buttonholing three or four familiar faces for a quick huddle and then moving on to another group while the first few delegates spread throughout the hall bearing the word. One of the smartest things she had ever done was to back Stu Lambert as a delegate when all she had known about him at the time were his politics and his sense of humor. His organizational abilities had come as a complete surprise.

On the speaker's platform, the huddle broke up and the chairman reached for his gavel. He'd have to call for a vote to set aside the recess, Kathleen thought, checking her watch. Then she could call for a quorum and by the time they had untangled that, Stu would have everybody back inside. Her panic eased and she slipped into an aisle chair to wait for Jerry Wagoner to make a move. She didn't have long to wait.

Wagoner climbed the steps to the podium while several technicians adjusted the small spots to give him some subtle back-lighting.

"Fellow delegates, what we've all been dreading has just occurred." Wagoner stared somberly out at the hall, giving the delegates time to quiet down once again. "This afternoon, after a hot lunch in a well-heated building, the Supreme Court announced that by a *majority of one* we, the Second Constitutional Convention of the United States, have no constitutional authority to propose amendments except on federal taxation.

"By a *majority of one*, the Court has usurped the rights of this Constitutional Convention.

"By a *majority of one*, the Court has usurped the very Constitution they took an oath to uphold!"

Shouts of "Shame! Shame!" rippled through the hall, turning into a rhythmic chant of outrage. Kathleen sat in shocked silence, waiting for the anger of the delegates to subside. She hardly noticed Jonathan Goodwell when he took the seat beside her, looking up only when he jogged her elbow and handed her a copy of the Supreme Court decision.

"It's a good legal document," he said, satisfied.

She thumbed through the four separate opinions that made up the majority decision, then looked up at Goodwell, incredulous. "A good decision? If they were going to uphold the injunction, it should have been unanimous and only one opinion, the way they did with school desegregation and the Nixon tapes."

She handed the copy back to him. "Five–four with four separate majority opinions?" She felt disgusted and betrayed. "This has no authority at all!"

"I wouldn't say that," Goodwell protested. He paged through the decision. "There's some fine legal thinking in here, Kathleen. Any constitutional lawyer would find it hard to ignore."

Kathleen wanted to grab him by the lapels of his Harris tweed jacket and shake him. "Jonathan, this isn't a goddamn *Yale Law Review* debate, this is a political convention. Look around, for God's sake!"

A mass of delegates were now parading down the center aisle and around the perimeter of the hall. The cries of "Shame! Shame!" had dissolved into a more ominous chant: "Hey, hey, what do you say? The Supreme Court has had its day!"

Kathleen watched the group behind them snake down the aisle and parade before the speaker's platform: angry, red-faced, arms locked, fists punching the air. The delegates marching with them weren't only the younger radicals. The Iowa delegates who had been talking with Sara Evarts just minutes before were with them, and so was a group of middle-aged women holding up hastily scrawled poster-board signs for the TV cameramen who flanked them on either side. One sign said: "Prayers Yes—Supreme Court No" and another: "The Supreme Court Will Go to *Hell!*"

"My God, what should we do?" The combination of Kathleen's outrage and that of the delegates had finally gotten through to Goodwell.

Despite his faults, Goodwell was, after all, on her side. Kathleen's anger cooled. "There's nothing we can do until the demonstration dies down. Then we'll see what Wagoner does." Wagoner was standing on the podium with Griffin and the chairman pro tem beside him, watching the demonstration.

"My guess," Kathleen continued, "is that they'll table the motion to replace the Chair and then put a motion on the floor declaring the convention independent of the Supreme Court's authority."

Goodwell was horrified. "They can't do that!"

Kathleen couldn't help smiling. "I wish Jerry Wagoner agreed with you."

Ten minutes later, Jerry Wagoner resumed his position behind the podium.

"I move the adoption of the following resolution: 'The Second

Constitutional Convention duly constituted under Article V of the Constitution of the United States of America is a free and separate body, independent of the authority of the Supreme Court, Congress, and the executive branch of the government, responsible only to the will of the people and their sovereign states.' "

Kathleen glanced over at Stu. "The Court played right into their hands."

"Sure did." Lambert looked disgusted.

"Why didn't they just decline to rule under the principle of separation of powers?"

Stu shrugged and Kathleen went back to studying the action in the hall. There would be one speaker for the Wagoner resolution and one against—herself. She'd have to try and protect a Court that for years had ignored warnings from constitutional lawyers and congressional critics that it was operating as a super-legislative body. The critics had warned that the Court was becoming political and now the gauntlet had been thrown down and de Young's Western Coalition was successfully organizing the widespread resentment that had been simmering against the Court.

"The Chair recognizes Kathleen Houseman, who will speak for five minutes against the resolution."

Stu gave her a good-luck pat as she walked back to the microphone in front of the hall. She felt like she was about to go off a diving board.

"It's a legitimate question to ask whether or not the Supreme Court exceeded its authority in ruling on the New York petition. Whether or not it overstepped its own separate and unique powers granted to it by the Constitution."

She paused to gauge the audience, gratified that the earlier smirks and bored expressions had disappeared and the buzz of private conversation had ceased. She relaxed her grip on the mike and moved back a few inches so her voice would sound more natural.

"When the Supreme Court oversteps itself, there are legal and constitutional remedies that can be sought." There was some activity going on in the back of the hall; for a moment, she couldn't figure out what it was. "There is the ultimate remedy of impeachment by Congress of the justices of the Court. And there is the simpler initial step of filing a petition for a rehearing. Before we as a body take a position we might later regret, we should at least consider such a petition for a rehearing."

The activity in the back of the hall had become a carefully organized "spontaneous" demonstration, with marchers snaking down both aisles, delegates from California in the lead. She hurried to finish. "I offer a substitute motion as follows: that the Constitutional Convention II as a body first petition the United States Supreme Court for a rehearing before taking any further action."

She had been so intent on introducing the substitute motion that it was a few seconds before she realized the mike had been turned off and the only thing the delegates could hear was the chant: "Hey, hey, whaddya say—Supreme Court get out of our way!"

The demonstrators streamed out in front of the speaker's platform, surrounding it as well as Kathleen and waving their signs. Kathleen held her ground. Eventually the chanting would have to stop and then she'd make damn sure the chairman put her substitute motion on the floor. A dozen rows in front of her, she saw Stu Lambert edge toward one of the microphones halfway down the left-hand aisle. Sara Evarts had already reached the other.

They want to play rough, we'll play rough, she muttered to herself. In a few minutes the chants began to falter and the chairman gaveled the demonstration to an end.

"The motion on the floor is: 'The Second Constitutional Convention of the United States duly constituted under Article V of—"

"Point of order, Mr. Chairman!" Kathleen shouted, ignoring her dead microphone. A demonstrator standing next to her, a fat, redfaced man, caught her in the ribs with his elbow. She elbowed him back and shouted: "The substitute motion takes precedence!"

The chairman avoided looking in her direction. Now Sara Evarts at one aisle microphone and Stu Lambert at another pointed at Kathleen, shouting for the chairman to recognize her point of order.

Kathleen glared at the Chair, who still ignored her. There were more shouts from the floor and she whirled to see Stu and Sara struggling as they were half carried and half shoved out of the hall by a phalanx of marshals. The demonstrators now pushed between her and the Chair and resumed their chanting. She tried to bull her way through but the demonstrators hemmed her in. As the chanting faded, Kathleen heard the Chair announcing over the loudspeaker: ". . . those in favor of the California resolution signify by saying Yea." There was a roar of "yeas" from all over the hall. He called for the "nays" next and there was a half-hearted volley of responses.

She could stage a walkout, Kathleen thought. But the moment

passed as the chairman entertained a motion for adjournment and called for the question and the vote in the same breath. The crush around her thinned as the delegates streamed from the hall.

Kathleen swore, then sat down in an empty aisle chair and tried to make sense of the turn of events. Jerry Wagoner must have had advance notice of the Supreme Court decision and had his plans ready when the time came. He had been swift, cool, and ruthless, and if she didn't know it before, she now knew it would be an open convention where anything and everything went.

The hall was almost empty now and she walked toward an exit. She had a meeting with Andy Livonas scheduled for later, but right now she needed a drink. She had a rule against drinking alone, but that afternoon she was willing to make an exception.

Just outside the hall somebody behind her said, "Katy, wait a minute." She hardly recognized Stu. His nose was swollen and both the nostrils were packed with cotton. "One of those assholes popped me one."

"Those bastards aren't floor marshals, they're bouncers." Harris and Miller's enforcement squad was branching out, she thought acidly. Then she noticed Stu was weaving. She grabbed him by the arm. "You all right?"

"Yeah, I've already fainted. I'm just a little rubbery."

"You better sit down." She tightened her grip on his arm and walked him over to a bench by the water fountain. He sat with his head back until his color returned and his eyes lost their dazed look.

Kathleen stood up. "I've got to meet Andy Livonas." She was reluctant to leave him.

Stu inspected the blood on his handkerchief, then held it up to his nose again. "I'll be okay. Joanie Spero said she'd take me back to her place. She's a nurse."

She was also built like a Barbie doll, which seemed to be Stu's taste, Kathleen thought.

It was barely five o'clock but it was almost dark. She spotted Livonas standing under a streetlight, his collar turned up and his hands in his pockets, watching the delegates stream by.

"Livonas!" She hurried over.

He turned, his face breaking into a smile. "How about a drink?"

"I could use one." They fell in step, Kathleen matching her stride to his. She wanted to tell him how pleasant it felt to have a friendly face waiting for her, then decided not to.

They caught the subway and half an hour later were huddled over drinks in the Georgetown Inn's lounge. Behind them, a piano player tinkled his way through a Cole Porter tune. She told Livonas about the vote to defy the Supreme Court. He seemed moody, then gulped his drink and told her about his meeting with Whitman. She wanted to know the details and he didn't spare her.

"Poor Bob." Kathleen looked down at her half-finished Scotch and water and wondered what else there was to say. She had a mental image of a healthy, vigorous Bob Whitman greeting her with a bear hug at his Labor Day barbecue. She hadn't seen him since and had difficulty picturing him as the old, sick man Livonas described.

"The doctors say he'll be an invalid in a year and dead in two— that is, if he cuts his schedule back. If he doesn't, it's just a matter of time until the stress gets to be too much."

"How's he taking it?"

"He's pissed off, he doesn't want anybody to know. I think it's the first thing he's run up against in his entire life that he doesn't know how to fight." Livonas looked unhappy. "He thinks we should get a campaign going around Senator James Hartwell."

She looked blank. "I don't really know him. What do you think of him?"

"Not much. But we need somebody to challenge Massey in the primaries."

Livonas leaned back in his chair and signaled the waitress for another round. He was ugly-handsome, Kathleen decided; maybe that's what made him so sexy.

"I heard they turned off the microphones on you," Livonas said.

She nodded. "We've got a potential runaway convention and the West's playing hardball. Stu got slugged this afternoon."

"Is he all right?"

"He was when I left him." She took a sip from her glass. "I keep thinking about the convention," she said slowly. "It's like being drawn into a whirlpool. You keep going around faster and faster."

"And de Young's at the bottom of the pool," Livonas said. He took a handful of nuts from the small dish in front of him and leaned back in his chair. "What you need is a break. I've been invited to a party tonight—want to come along?"

She felt instantly distant and cursed herself for it. "I've got a party I'm supposed to be at, too. Special guest of the hostess type thing."

Livonas looked disappointed and changed the subject, talking about the pros and cons of Hartwell as a presidential candidate.

She was only half listening, wondering again if a relationship with Andy Livonas could have a future.

December 19

9:15 P.M., *Saturday*

For a Christmas party, Livonas thought, the only thing lacking was the Christmas spirit. He stood just inside the doorway to the baronial living room of Elizabeth Packard's Chevy Chase mansion, nursing a drink and idly studying the guests. Ordinarily laughter and the buzz of conversation would have drowned out the quartet playing Mozart in the far corner. But tonight the collection of Washington's social and political elite seemed curiously subdued. Livonas watched them chatting quietly by the windows or huddled in little groups of three or four on the elegantly upholstered sofas. A larger but only slightly more animated group had taken over the conversation pit in front of the black marble fireplace while a few strays kept to themselves, occasionally ambushing a passing waiter for a glass of champagne.

Uniforms must be back in fashion, Livonas thought, studying General Rudd, who was standing just in front of the young woman cellist. He was talking with three other military men in dress uniforms, their chests carpeted with campaign ribbons. They reminded Livonas of the World War II movies he used to watch as a kid, except none of the quartet looked like William Holden or even Audie Murphy.

It had taken an act of will and a shot of Jack Daniels at the Hay-Adams bar to convince himself that after a thirteen-hour day he was still up for Elizabeth's annual Christmas bash. He had begged off dinner, but Elizabeth had insisted he drop by afterward, there was somebody she wanted him to meet.

Livonas felt like meeting one of Elizabeth Packard's eligible young women about as much as he felt like leaving the Hay-Adams but reasoned both would be better for his health. Besides, the afternoon paper had reported that Governor de Young was in town to testify before the Senate Committee on Federal Land Use and knowing Elizabeth Packard, she would have corraled the governor for her party. There was always the chance he might learn something.

"Andy, there you are." Livonas turned to see Elizabeth sweeping across the main hallway with Katy in tow. "I'd like you to meet Katy Houseman." She beamed as Livonas kissed her on the cheek. "I think the two of you should get to know each other."

"We've met," he said, trying to sound casual. Elizabeth smiled knowingly and said, "Well, then, I'll just leave the two of you to chat." She disappeared through the sliding doors into the huge marble-floored dining room where a buffet was being served by candlelight. A handsome gray-haired man in tux and black tie met her in the middle of the room and escorted her over to the table.

"She likes Senator Hartwell a lot," Katy said, "and I think he has a crush on her." And then they were staring at each other and Livonas found himself fumbling for conversation. "You didn't tell me you were going to the same party."

"I didn't know." She laughed. "Were you aware that Elizabeth Packard thinks you're the 'most divine,' single forty-year-old male in Washington?" She was wearing a full-length forest-green skirt with a white blouse open at the neck showing off her string of pearls. Livonas remembered the pearls.

"Washington hostesses love me," he said. He changed the subject. "What do you think of the party?"

Katy looked amused. "Everybody wants to know about the Constitutional Convention. Mention it a month ago and you were instantly *bor*-ing. Incidentally, I was talking with Congressman Valdez—he's a great admirer of Governor de Young and can't understand why I don't get 'on board.' "

Livonas was surprised. Arizona congressman Dan Valdez was one of the senior members of Congress, representing a district that relied heavily on federal contracts. Because of that, the Administration had been counting on him as a strong supporter.

Katy waved the highball glass she was holding. "I was just on my way to get ol' Dan a refill. Want to walk me over?"

They drifted toward the bar and he said, offhand, "How's Debbie Spindler?"

"Recovering, I guess. We're really not that close." She put the highball glass on the bar and nodded to the young bartender for a refill. "See you later, Livonas."

She gave Livonas a friendly nudge with her free hand and started back toward the living room. Livonas followed her with his eyes, wondering what she meant by the nudge, if anything. Then he dismissed the thought. It would probably be best for both of them if they just drifted into a casual friendship.

He took his highball glass and wandered into the library, a room of dark wood paneling and leather chairs and couches that had become a male sanctuary at Elizabeth Packard's parties; a place where cigars could be smoked and politics discussed without apology.

For a moment Livonas thought the room had been redecorated. The walls were lined floor to ceiling with decorator-bought, leather-bound volumes, the carpets were a plush chocolate-brown pile, and there were pairs of red-leather easy chairs angled toward each other in every corner. Then he realized that it wasn't the furniture or its arrangement that seemed different, it was the guests. He was expecting to hear the usual banter of conversation, the laughter at an off-color joke, the heated but friendly arguments about the latest appointments or policies of the Adminstration and what hotshot back in the home district was turning out to be a real threat.

Tonight, instead of being scattered around the room in congenial groups, the guests had congregated primarily at the opposite ends, with the tea cart that held after-dinner liqueurs and cognac occupying the middle.

Livonas set his glass on a bookshelf ledge and watched as Senator Lovejoy of Montana and Robert Bellamy, a former congressman from Maryland and a current Undersecretary of State, approached the tea cart from either end, poured themselves a cordial, and then retreated to their respective corners without exchanging a word or even a glance.

Lovejoy and Bellamy had been friends at one time, Livonas knew. But their behavior now mirrored the attitudes of the others in the room—westerners at one end and easterners at the other with mid-westerners and southerners scattered in between.

There was a minor commotion in the hallway and the quiet buzz of conversation in the library stopped. Livonas filed out with the others to see what was happening.

Vincent de Young stood by the outer door in the hallway, brushing the snow off the collar of his coat and handing his hat to the butler. Crowding in behind him were Herb Shepherd, Craig Hewitt, and half a dozen others in the governor's retinue. Shepherd was helping de Young shed his three-quarter-length sheepskin coat when Elizabeth Packard hurried over. He turned to greet her, saw Livonas standing in the library doorway, stared for a second, then reached out with both arms for Packard.·

"Elizabeth, every time I see you, you've grown prettier. Hope you don't mind my dropping in so late?"

She neatly slipped out of his embrace. "Always an honor to have you, Governor." She turned to the man behind her. "You know Senator Hartwell, of course."

De Young pumped the senator's hand. "Of course, delighted to see you again, Jim—been following your Lands and Fisheries bill." A final slap on the back for Hartwell, then de Young stepped past him to grab the hand of Carl Baxter, resplendent in a red velvet tuxedo jacket, standing in the center of the arched doorway to the living room. "How are you, Carl?"

Baxter smiled broadly. "Couldn't be better 'less I was in Texas, Vince."

De Young was already reaching for still another hand. He glanced at Baxter over his shoulder. "Jerry tells me you gave quite a speech the other day."

"Just told 'em a little ol' parable is all I did."

De Young was working his way down what had become an informal receiving line. "I heard it was one hell of a parable . . . good to see you, Sam . . . hello, Dan, didn't know you'd be here . . ."

Still at the door, Livonas watched Packard signal Jamie, her social secretary, a look of displeasure on her face—her Christmas soiree was turning into a reception for Governor de Young. A moment later, Jamie was pushing waiters armed with trays of champagne through the crowd. The group around de Young began to break up as guests filtered back into the living room and library.

Livonas glanced back at the door, wondering if the governor had brought along his favorite pop singer, but Sally Craft was nowhere in sight. He started for the living room, then spotted Katy by the grand piano, surrounded by three young State Department types exuding diplomatic charm. Her face was set in a soft, easy smile and she seemed intent on their conversation. Livonas resisted the urge to join them and retreated to the library.

"Governor, what would be your strategy for economic recovery?"

De Young was standing in the center of the room, pouring himself a brandy at the tea cart and fielding questions from either end. The contrast between the tanned, obviously fit, confident de Young and the aging, ineffectual man in the White House was almost overwhelming.

The man who had asked the question was Congressman Valdez, an elderly, stoop-shouldered man who wore a bollo tie with a turquoise clasp that matched the color of his eyes.

De Young looked up from his brandy and flashed him a smile. "Dan, the time has come for the political leaders of this country to frankly admit that the health of the whole depends on the health of the various parts. The only real strategy for recovery is a regional one. In my own particular case, a strategy of recovery for the West."

Livonas hung back in one corner of the library, shaking his head. He had heard de Young imply as much in the West, but to say the same thing in Washington while trying for national exposure was political suicide.

He looked over at Herb Shepherd, expecting him to step in and correct the governor's gaffe. But Shepherd stood with his back to the bookcases, a bemused smile on his face, not moving.

". . . while the East, of course," de Young continued, "has its unique problems of urban decay, outmoded industrial plants, lack of natural resources. Frankly, its continued reliance on the federal government to bail it out and its colonial treatment of the natural resources of the West has to end. The East should rely on its own ingenuity and resources, not use political clout to exploit the other regions of the country."

It was rhetoric specifically designed for the West, Livonas thought. In this part of the country, it was insulting. De Young had to be a smarter politician than this.

"Excuse me, Governor, but I don't know when I've heard such crap."

Livonas turned, surprised. He had assumed the little group in the library were all de Young supporters. He hadn't noticed Manny Cudahy, the diminutive senior congressman from Brooklyn who had served his first term the year Livonas was born. The congressman's face was the color of roast beef.

Cudahy stepped up to de Young and waved his finger beneath his nose.

"This is one country, the United States of America, one country under God, indivisible, and don't you forget it." Cudahy shook his head. "You, an ex-Army officer, saying what you have said in these times, you should be ashamed of yourself."

Livonas could see de Young redden, start to say something, then bite it off and look helplessly around. The sincerity of the old man's indignation was obvious. So was the fact of his limp, caused by a shrapnel wound in his right leg. And so was the Bronze Star from World War II that he wore in his right lapel. Nobody in the room would applaud de Young for verbally flattening Cudahy.

"Manny, don't get so excited." Congressman Valdez had come to de Young's aid. He and Cudahy, Livonas recalled, had been allies in Congress for more than twenty years. Valdez put his arm around Cudahy's shoulder. "Manny, let's not let politics ruin a fine evening." Behind them, Shepherd had stepped over and tapped de Young on the shoulder, nodding for him to leave the study.

Cudahy shook off Valdez's arm, his voice trembling with anger. The room was quiet, with everybody staring at the two men, uncertain of what they would do. "Representative Valdez, what Governor de Young said was not politics, it was demagogic filth!" He stepped closer to Valdez and Livonas couldn't help but smile. Two elderly fighting cocks, neither of them much over five feet tall.

Valdez lost his stoop as he drew himself up his full height, his face its own particular shade of crimson. "Congressman Cudahy, on behalf of Governor de Young I demand an apology!"

"*Kishmir tuchas,*" Cudahy sneered. He reached around and patted his backside so there would be no confusion as to what he meant.

Valdez needed no translation. He picked up his glass of cognac and splashed it in Cudahy's face.

Livonas stepped forward to push between the two men. He was a moment too late. Cudahy's arching roundhouse right landed on Valdez's lower lip. Livonas had forgotten how much split lips gushed. He caught the elderly Valdez, holding the enraged man away from Cudahy. The blood flowed down Valdez's chin onto his white dinner jacket, glistening in bright red droplets before it soaked into the cloth.

Behind him, somebody said, "Oh, my God" and Livonas looked over his shoulder to see Cudahy crumpled on the floor. Cudahy's swing had knocked him off balance and he had fallen, gashing his head on the corner of the tea cart.

There were now a dozen guests around them trying to help the congressmen. Livonas let Valdez go and watched as the two men were half-carried out of opposite library doors, staring at each other in disbelief. Valdez's chin and shirt were deeply splashed with red while Cudahy's face was the color of parchment as he gasped frantically for breath.

Livonas walked swiftly out of the library, slipping out a side door into the chill night air. Violence was always ugly but between two seventy-year-old men, it was obscene. It has been unreal at first and almost comic, like the violence in a Punch and Judy show. But it wasn't funny when you saw it close up, when you saw the withered, split skin, the dripping blood, the breathless gasps.

He'd had enough of the party. He didn't know where Katy was, but at the moment he didn't feel like tracking her down to say good night. All he wanted to do was to get out, go back to his apartment, and have a nightcap. Or maybe three.

Through the windows, he could see the party had come alive but for all the wrong reasons. The guests in the living room were recounting the details of the fight in low tones while Elizabeth Packard circulated, soothing nerves, calming injured feelings, and motioning Jamie to have the waiters bring more champagne.

Livonas walked back inside to get his coat and spotted de Young surrounded by the trio of military officers who had been in the company of General Rudd earlier in the evening. Livonas couldn't resist. He walked over. "Hi, Vince."

"Hello, Andy." De Young was wearing an easy smile but didn't bother hiding his distaste, and Livonas was mildly pleased. "What can I do for you?"

"I hope I'm not interrupting anything?" The military men detected the edge in his voice, mumbled assurances that he really hadn't, and faded back into the party. Livonas slipped his arm around de Young's back, cupping him firmly by the shoulder. "I just wanted to ask what you're pulling at the Constitutional Convention, Vince." He felt de Young try to break free, held him for an instant, then let him go.

De Young whirled, his easy smile gone, his eyes hard. "You're out of line Livonas. For somebody's foot-rubber, you're very much out of line."

Livonas laughed, watching de Young's face flush. Behind the governor, he could see Herb Shepherd hurry over from the other side of the room.

"Vince, I don't know where *your* foot-rubber was tonight but he sure didn't help you keep your foot out of your mouth. You know the papers are going to pick up on the bullshit you told Valdez and they'll crucify you. Not smart, Vince."

De Young looked puzzled. Herb Shepherd knew the press but de Young didn't, and Livonas knew he had him worried. "East of the Mississippi, you won't even win the primaries in your own—"

"Governor!" Shepherd had finally caught up with them.

De Young immediately eased back into his public role, the smile returning around the corners of his mouth, his voice loud and friendly. "Great to see you, Andy, real pleasure. I'm sorry to hear about your friend, a real loss to the state." Shepherd touched him lightly on the arm and de Young started for the foyer.

Livonas felt something cold in his stomach. "What friend, Vince?"

De Young turned. He looked faintly surprised. Whatever else he felt was immediately masked.

"Gus Frankel—the media in California will be the less without him."

Livonas felt like his face was frozen.

"What happened?" His voice was emotionless.

"I thought you knew. Suicide—the papers said he was in bad health. I understand he left a note. He was a great loss to the state, a great loss."

De Young left and Livonas got his own coat and walked outside on the balcony, letting the drifting flakes of snow settle and melt on his face. Below, Senator Hartwell was escorting de Young and his retinue down the walk to a waiting fleet of limousines. Livonas watched Hartwell and Shepherd shake hands and then de Young took Hartwell's hand in both of his and clapped the senator on the back . . .

The tears came slowly to Livonas and then were replaced by a dull rage. Gus a suicide because of bad health? For Christ's sake, just a few days ago he had listened to Gus boast about how healthy he was.

Then he thought of Mary Scoma and checked his watch. He still had time to call Whitman and catch the red-eye to San Francisco. He owed it to Mary to be there. And he owed it to Gus.

He went to get his overcoat. He'd talk to Garber, the political reporter, too. Garber had worked with Gus every day. Maybe Garber knew something that he didn't.

Maybe.

December 20
                   8:00 A.M., *Pacific Time, Sunday*

"We sent you a telegram Friday morning," Garber said. "We thought Gus would have wanted you to know."

They were alone in Frankel's office, though most of the evidence of Gus's tenure had already disappeared. There was a large carton in the corner and Livonas guessed it held the photographs that had decorated the walls and the desk top as well as the framed diploma from Northwestern University's Medill School of Journalism and the one from the Universal Life Church attesting that Gus Frankel was a bona fide minister of the Gospel.

"How's Mary taking it?"

"Better than any of us expected; she's one strong lady."

Livonas walked over to the window and looked out. It had been raining ever since he had arrived and Mission Street and the adjoining sidewalk were glistening with small torrents of water funneling into the sewer on the corner. He wondered if it had been raining early Friday morning when Gus had smashed into the concrete below.

He turned away from the window and walked over to sit in Gus's chair behind the now-cleared desk. Garber was standing by the door, nervous, deferential, not experienced enough with tragedy to know the proper things to say or do.

That's what death really amounted to, Livonas thought—an embarrassment for all concerned.

He cleared his throat. "I didn't get to my office until Friday afternoon; there was a lot of stuff on my desk—the telegram was probably right on top. I never saw it." He shook his head in wonderment at it all. "Vince de Young told me at a party last night."

"Jesus," Garber said.

Livonas was silent for a moment, remembering the cabin up at the Russian River and Mary and Ellen cleaning and frying up the trout that he and Gus had caught. It seemed like it had all happened twenty years ago.

"Did he leave a note?"

Garber nodded, opened a thin file folder on the desk, and pulled out a sheet of ordinary typing paper. "It was addressed to Mary but the cops opened it."

Livonas took the sheet and read it. "Dearest Mary," it began. "The medical records at Kaiser will explain everything. It just seems better to get it over with now and spare myself the pain and both of us the misery. I love you. Gus."

He reread it a second and a third time, then put it down on the desk. "What'd the doctors say?" he asked, still thinking about the note.

"Spinal cancer. Apparently the specialists had told him he'd be a vegetable in a matter of months and dead within the year."

Garber sat down in the small wooden chair opposite the desk and inspected his fingernails. "I thought Mary would want to know everything firsthand so I tried to get through to the doctors at Kaiser. The medical report was two weeks' old, the doctor who had written it was in the Midwest at a convention. He won't be back until next week."

Livonas fingered the note again and tried to imagine Gus writing it. "If you didn't talk to the doctor, how'd you find out?"

"I got it off the state police report."

Livonas glanced up. "Why not the city cops? Don't they have jurisdiction?"

Garber shook his head. "New law. State police now have jurisdiction over local authorities when it's suspected that a political murder might be involved."

"Who does the suspecting?"

"The state's attorney general." Garber locked his hands behind his head and leaned back. "I guess he thought there might be some doubt as to whether Gus jumped or was pushed."

Livonas fingered the note again. "This stinks," he said quietly.
Garber nodded. "Yeah, I know."

Livonas leaned back in his chair. "How do you know, Mike?"

"He was a two-fingered typist and a lousy one at that. He couldn't
have typed his own name without making a mistake. That note
looks like it was worked over by a business school graduate." Garber
cocked his head. "How'd you spot it as a phony?"

"Gus was of the old school," Livonas said, staring at the note and
frowning. "You never type a letter to somebody you love, you always write it by hand. Plus his personal name for Mary was 'kid.' He
would've written, 'Hey, kid, I've got problems.' And personally, I
think Gus would've hung in there as long as he could've. He also
showed me his latest medical report a few days ago— it said he was
the healthiest fat man in the city."

Garber looked faintly cheered and Livonas felt somewhat that
way himself. There wasn't much you could do if Gus had really
been suffering from cancer. But there was a lot you could do if Gus
had been pushed. Revenge wasn't nearly as good as resurrection, but
it was something.

"What was he working on last?"

Garber's smile was a faint shadow of his usual cynical grin. "De
Young had set up some kind of secret meeting at the Airport Hilton.
Gus covered it, then came back here to write it up and ..." He
shrugged.

"How come Gus was covering it? I thought you were the political
reporter?"

"He said I had a hard-on for the Governor. Myself, I think he just
wanted to keep a hand in."

"You follow it up?"

Garber looked angry. "I asked for the assignment and Petris, the
new city editor, said forget it. They rewrote a press release from
Shepherd's office and ran that."

Livonas put on his coat and hat. "Gus write anything about the
meeting at all?"

Garber shook his head. "We checked the computer, he didn't
write anything that night."

"What about his notebook? He always carried one with him."

"I looked all over for it. I couldn't find it."

Whoever had pushed Gus must have taken it, Livonas thought.

He started for the elevator, Garber trailing after him. Just before the doors opened, Livonas said, "This might get hairy."

Garber shrugged. "Gus was a good friend of mine."

From a distance, the Airport Hilton looked like a chrome-plated cereal box with a blue "H" on top. Livonas took a left into the parking lot, stopping between a diesel Mercedes shuttle bus and a battery-powered red laundry truck.

The front lobby was filled with people sitting forlornly amid mounds of luggage waiting for word about their standby on the day's flights. A number of them would stay through the night.

Garber looked at Livonas, curious. "What are you trying to find out?"

"Same thing Gus was," Livonas said quietly. "Who was here and what'd they talk about. Gus didn't have any personal enemies; if somebody helped him out that window it had to have been because of what he found out." Livonas glanced around the lobby. "See if you can get a look at the hotel register. I want to see the meeting rooms."

Garber looked at the desk and the bored young girl behind it. "It shouldn't be too difficult."

Mr. Frederick Barrish, the manager, confirmed Livonas's opinion that as a group, hotel managers could be described as "pleasant-looking." Barrish was no exception. A black man in his mid-forties with modest Afro, warm brown eyes, and smooth, milk-chocolate complexion, Barrish had a permanent "May I help you" expression on his face. His office was small and crowded with filing cabinets. Barrish had been working on a small stack of bills when his secretary showed Livonas in.

Barrish looked momentarily unhappy and frustrated, mumbled something about constant interruptions, then remembered his role and stood up, holding out his hand. Livonas took his card from his wallet and gave it to him.

"We're planning on holding a fund-raising dinner for Vice-President Whitman shortly after the first of the year, Mr. Barrish."

Still holding the card, Barrish came out from behind the small desk and pumped his hand. "Pleasure, Mr Livonas—we've already had local fund raisers out here and everybody seemed happy with the facilities; I'm sure you will, too."

Livonas couldn't be sure but he thought Barrish's smile had drooped slightly around the edges when he had first noted Livonas's connection with the federal government. He leaned over and pressed the intercom button on the desk. "I'll be showing a client the banquet facilities, Hilda. Take all my calls."

Barrish took a ring of keys off a peg on the wall and ushered Livonas back into the hallway. At the end of the corridor, he unlocked a pair of double doors. "This is the International Ballroom, the largest of our banquet rooms."

The huge room was fully carpeted in a royal-blue and had dark wood paneling with three gaudy, cut-glass chandeliers hanging from the ceiling. At the far end of the room were stacks of folding chairs and knock-down banquet tables.

Barrish reached behind some drapes and the chandeliers glowed with a soft light, suffusing the room with a sparkling irridescence.

"We can serve a sit-down dinner for eight hundred people," Barrish began, reciting the familiar figures. "The room can also be subdivided, through the use of partitions, into three smaller rooms for groups of two hundred or so."

Livonas strolled over to the collection of tables and chairs against the far wall. Apparently the motel had hosted a party a few days ago and hadn't yet cleaned it up. There were trash cans full of empty bottles, half a dozen deflated balloons, and what looked like a huge rolled-up map. Above, near the ceiling, a few more balloons swayed lazily in the air currents.

"You have banquets here often?" Livonas asked.

Barrish looked unhappy. "Not nearly as many as we used to, of course. This last week, we had quite a successful one." He gestured casually at the litter on the floor, almost proud that the proof of actual business was still at hand.

"Sizable meeting?" Livonas asked politely.

Barrish made a gesture with his hands. "Small—not more than three hundred—but it presented problems in its own way. Primarily for the kitchen."

"For the kitchen?"

"You know, different dietary requirements depending on your country of origin, your religious outlook, that sort of thing. We need at least forty-eight hours' advance warning if there's to be a departure from the preselected banquet menu."

"I can understand that," Livonas said, and wondered who the

foreigners were who had put such demands on Mr. Barrish's kitchen.

"Is there anything else I can show you?"

Livonas turned and looked at the huge room again, imagining it partitioned in two so de Young's banquet would have been in one room and the other would have been deserted, ideal as a room in which someone could have watched and listened.

Gus might have done it, probably had. But apparently nobody had caught him at it since he had made it back to the office. Unless, of course, somebody had tailed him. Or had spotted him and known who he was.

Back in the office, Barrish squeezed in behind his desk and started tapping out figures on his desk calculator. "The International Room can be rented by itself, though rental is usually determined by the number of sleeping rooms your group takes." He fished out a small folder. "Here's a floor layout so you can see the location of the other conference rooms and the various dining facilities."

Livonas sat there sweating, desperately trying to think of ways of decoying Barrish out of his office, when the intercom chirped: "Front desk, Mr. Barrish—an argument over billing for a checkout. It's the Costanzas, they had the Presidential Suite." Barrish sighed and stood up, ready to usher Livonas out.

"I can wait," Livonas offered hastily. "There're a few more questions I'd like to ask."

A moment later, he was alone. He knew what he was looking for, had known it the moment he walked into the room and watched Barrish working the calculator with the stack of bills on the desk to his left. They would have been the previous week's billing, the ones that de Young's banquet had run up.

He walked quietly over to the desk and thumbed quickly through them. Several for the governor's office, attention Herb Shepherd, for the International Ballroom and two floors of hotel rooms. Plus bills from suppliers for the dining rooms, a laundry bill, a bill from Bernie's Limousine and Shuttle Service . . .

There were no individual bills for rooms. Small details like that didn't concern Mr. Barrish.

Garber was waiting for him in the lunchroom, sitting in a corner with a stack of reservation cards beside him. "Find what you were looking for?"

Livonas shook his head. "Not really. It could have been a meet-

ing plugging de Young for President. Judging from the leftover bottles every table must have had a liquor setup. Shepherd reserved the
rooms, made all the arrangements—not exactly news. What about
you?"

Garber pushed the cards at him. "See for yourself." He sounded
frustrated. Livonas frowned and picked up the cards.

"I didn't know there were so many Smiths and Joneses in the
world," Garber said. "You would've thought this was Caesar's Pal-
ace instead of the Airport Hilton."

Garber was right. A half dozen or so Japanese names but the rest
of the more than two hundred were all too common, not one of
which struck a chord. A top-level secret meeting of strangers? Not
bloody likely. Livonas handed the cards back.

"What did you find out?" Garber asked.

"A couple of things. The manager complained about having to
fix different dinners for a number of those present because of reli-
gion or the countries they were from."

Garber stared. "What's he talking about? Ninety-nine percent of
these guys are as American as apple pie."

"All those Smiths and Joneses," Livonas said dryly.

"You mentioned something else," Garber said.

Livonas shook his head. "Probably not much. Barrish had been
going through the bills for de Young's party and there was a large
one for Bernie's Limousine Service. That didn't make sense."

"Bernie's is a shuttle service between the airport and here, especially the International Terminal and Butler Aviation—foreign businessmen and corporate heavies who fly into Butler in their own
planes."

"Put them together," Livonas said slowly, "and it means some
pretty exotic strangers were around who didn't want to give their
real names. Who would know?"

Garber drained his coffee and stood up. "Customs, who else?"

Livonas parked in front of a rain-washed brick building with a
sign saying BUTLER indented in the concrete above the main doors.
It was part of San Francisco's International Airport and Livonas's
first stop before the International Terminal itself.

The small reception area was dark and nearly deserted. The windows opposite the entrance overlooked a small section of tarmac

empty except for a lone Lear jet with MYLO SEMICONDUCTOR emblazoned on its tail.

To one side of the reception area was a narrow oak table where three well-dressed middle-aged men had opened their attaché cases for the blue-uniformed customs inspector. The inspector glanced through each case, then gathered up the passports and retreated to a chair at the end of the table where he copied the appropriate information into a ledger, then returned the passports without a word.

The customs agent himself was in his early sixties, close to retirement, Livonas thought, with a full head of white hair and the reddish, heavily veined face of a full-time boozer.

He started to pack up his ledger. Livonas guessed he dropped down from the International Terminal whenever Butler had any business that required a customs agent.

Livonas walked over and the inspector looked up, slightly annoyed. "I was told only three planes had come in—you file a flight plan?"

"Just looking for information," Livonas said. He pulled over a nearby chair and sat down. Garber stayed behind by the doors, watching. "I didn't get your name, Inspector."

"Meehan. Inspector Patrick Meehan and as of January one I'll have my thirty years in and it will be *Ex*-Inspector Meehan." He slowly shook his head. "And I don't give out information to strangers, in fact I don't give out information, period." His breath smelled of Listerine and bourbon. Meehan folded his arms across his chest and leaned back in his chair. He stared at Livonas, confident in his power as a civil servant.

Livonas reached into his wallet and handed over a card. Meehan read the card, raised an eyebrow, glanced at Livonas, and read the card again. There was something in the back of his eyes and Livonas had a pretty good idea of what it was.

"You said you had a question, Mr. Livonas?" Meehan desperately tried to sound polite but he lost the battle to his Saturday night hangover.

Livonas kept his face impassive. "Is it true a customs inspector can be fired for drinking on duty?"

The something in the back of Meehan's eyes turned to terror. "I don't drink on duty, sir; I nip other times but not on duty."

Livonas smiled. "I do believe you, Pat. Believe me. You've been working here long?"

"Almost all those thirty years." Meehan's eyes were pleading.

"Thursday night," Livonas said. "Was there a lot of activity here at Butler?"

"Thursday night," Meehan repeated. "Yes, there was, sir. Quite a bit. Mostly corporate planes from Canada and Mexico."

Livonas pointed at the ledger. "May I?"

Meehan hesitated, then closed his eyes briefly, mumbled something, opened the ledger to the appropriate page and shoved it over. Livonas quickly copied down the entries. Two planes and ten names, point of origin: Mexico City. Two planes and eight names from Edmonton, Alberta; still another plane and five names from Calgary.

He stood up and pocketed the sheet of paper. "You've been very cooperative, Mr. Meehan, thank you."

"There was a lot of activity at the International Terminal that night, too," Meehan offered, anxious to please. "The limo driver told me—the one who drives for Bernie's. He was taking them all down to the Airport Hilton."

Garber had walked over and was standing by Livonas, listening.

"Where were they from?"

Meehan screwed up his face, doing his best to remember. "Japan, I think he said. A half dozen Japanese. And some Indonesians. I remember that pretty well; we don't get many Indonesians these days."

Livonas looked pleased. "Why, thank you, Mr. Meehan—thank you very much."

Outside, he showed his list to Garber. "You recognize any of these names?"

Garber ran his eyes down the sheet of paper as they walked to the car. "They're all with big oil companies. The Canadians are with Edmonton Energy, Hidalgo Rivera is executive secretary of Petrolema S.A., the Latin American oil consortium."

"They were probably a lot of the John Does at the hotel," Livonas said. Five minutes later, on the freeway, he asked: "Gus didn't leave any notes on this meeting at all?"

"None except the note you read," Garber said.

Livonas stared out the window at the lengthening shadows creeping across the concrete. "So during his last day on earth, Gus Frankel traveled out to the Airport Hilton to cover a story, then drove back to his office and, instead of writing that story, jumped out of the window. Why'd he bother going there in the first place?"

"He didn't jump," Garber said evenly. "I thought we'd decided that he was pushed." He was quiet for a long moment, then hit the steering wheel in frustration. "I should've gone, damnit, it was my story—he pulled me off it."

An idea wriggled through the back of Livonas's mind, vanished for a second, and then he had it.

"What'd you look under in the computer?"

"Hijackings first, I thought he might have had an angle on that. Then de Young, then for anything by-lined Frankel. Nothing."

"Did you think of looking under your own name?"

Garber looked blank. "No. Why?"

"Gus did that to me a couple of times, pulled me off stories where I had developed all the leads but, for one reason or another, he wanted to cover the story himself. But he always did a split by-line and always gave me top billing—it was his way of apologizing."

Garber stared for a second, then floored the accelerator. Livonas watched the speedometer needle struggle past sixty-five and stop. Fast, for a government car. He relaxed, watching the scenery as it flew past. The police didn't hand out tickets for speeding any more; burning up your precious gas rations doing something as ridiculous as speeding was considered its own punishment.

Ten minutes later, they were alone in Garber's cubicle, watching the "garber/frankel" story scroll past on the green screen of the VDT. The first paragraph was full of sardonic praise for de Young.

"I knew he liked the prick but I didn't think he liked him that much," Garber said.

Livonas shook his head, intent on the words on the small TV screen. "He's setting him up."

Garber stopped the scrolling for a minute. "Read that."

On the screen, the line read: "*Governor Vincent de Young's state police Wednesday night relieved the federal government of control of the oil refineries and fuel dumps in the State of California.*"

"We checked it out with General Bolles, the Sixth Army Commander," Garber continued. "He confirmed that he had asked Governor de Young to assign the state police to the refineries." He studied Livonas. "You didn't know that, did you?"

"It's news to me," Livonas said, surprised. "It's probably news to everybody else in Washington, too."

Rudd should have known, he thought to himself. And Kearns. Certainly the FBI should have.

Garber yelped and stopped the scrolling. "That's as far as Gus got, take a look."

"In a secret meeting tonight at the Airport Hilton, Governor de Young took credit for the recent cancellation by Indonesia of a projected oil contract with the United States. Among the business, political, and military leaders who applauded de Young wildly for his action were Governor Barron of Arizona, General Herman Bolles, Commanding General, U.S. Sixth Ar—"

There was nothing more. Gus had been interrupted in the middle of the last word.

"I hate the bastard but I still can't believe that." Garber glanced around at Livonas. "Why the fuck would he do that?"

"The CIA calls it destabilization." Livonas reread the final paragraph, memorizing it. "It makes it easier for a government to fall or a strong man to take over—in this case, de Young."

He could go back to Washington now and feed de Young to the FBI, or he could spend another day here and try and find out more.

He pushed the "print" button and the printer in the corner spit out a copy of Frankel's unfinished article. He tore it off and put it in his pocket, then pressed the "kill" key on the terminal. "I don't think it would be too good to leave the story around for the state police to find, Garber. If they did, you might end up sharing more than a by-line with Gus."

There wasn't any doubt that de Young was involved in Gus's death, though proof would be hard to come by. And there were still a few things that didn't make sense. He could understand why Gus had been killed—but Gus's story didn't explain de Young's interest in the Constitutional Convention. Nor did it explain why Steven Hart had been murdered.

He decided to send the names he had picked off the hotel and customs registries to Jeff Saunders, his friend in the FBI, then see what else he might be able to discover.

He shivered, feeling like a small boy who had just opened the door to the cellar, knowing beyond all doubt that something was moving around in the darkness down below and terrified because he didn't know what it was.

December 20

11:00 A.M., *Sunday*

It seemed to Whitman that he had just lain down for a Sunday nap when Viv roused him.

"Bob, wake up. You've got a visitor."

He tried to focus his eyes in the dim light from the study lamp. "Who is it, Viv?"

"Babs Massey."

He swung his legs off the couch, leaning his elbows on his knees while the last touch of sleep drained away. He turned up the study lamp and blinked, reaching for his glasses on the end table. "Show her in, Viv. You want to stay?"

She shook her head. "I'm sure she wants to see you alone."

She left and he straightened his tie and ran his fingers through his hair, brushing it down around the sides. He and Babs had campaigned together, but despite two months on the road, he had never gotten to know her very well. Nobody had.

During the past year, she had played such an active role in Massey's Presidency that one columnist had suggested the country would be better off with Babs as President and Tom Massey as house husband.

"Bob, I hope I'm not disturbing you."

He got up from the couch and walked to the door of the library. "You're not disturbing me, Babs—you're welcome any time." He motioned to one of the chairs by his desk and poured her a glass of sherry from the decanter on the library shelf.

Back in his chair he studied her while her gray eyes returned his gaze. She was there for a reason; Babs Massey seldom did anything that was strictly social. She was a stunning woman, he thought. In her early fifties, she looked more in her early forties. Auburn hair that she wore in graceful waves, a slender neck, broad-shouldered for a woman, tall, trim-waisted. More striking than pretty, more dignified than either. Her strength showed in her face and the way she carried herself. The comparison that always came to Whitman's mind was that of a woman executive, though she was far more brittle and remote. The attacks by the *Washington Post* on Massey and sometimes on herself had made her even more so.

She was wearing a brown tweed suit and a light blue mohair scarf and looked more comfortable in the library right then than he did. Babs liked to play at being the power behind the throne, Whitman thought, and she played it passably well.

She glanced at her watch. "I know it must be close to lunch for you and Viv. But I"—uncharacteristically, she fumbled for words—"need advice. It's about Tom." She managed a wry smile. "I'm sure you suspected."

Whitman took his time lighting his pipe, watching her through the smoke. He had a hunch she had something other than advice in mind.

"Tom isn't well." She hesitated, testing the waters, then took the plunge. "You've seen him in meetings, you must have come to the same conclusion." It wasn't confession time, Whitman thought, she was laying out the facts as she saw them. "He drinks continuously these days."

"Everybody drinks in Washington, Babs, you know that. It's an occupational hazard for politicians. And when things aren't going right, they drink more than usual. But I've seldom seen Tom drunk."

"I've seldom seen him sober," she answered tartly.

"Babs." Whitman hesitated, wondering how he could phrase it. "Tom faces one of the most difficult crises that any President has had to confront. I think he should realize that the problems are not his alone." He was thoughtful for a moment. "Or yours. You should try to influence him to rely more on his advisors."

She took a sip of sherry, her face a mask. "Do you have a cigarette?" He shook one out of a pack and lit it for her, then left the pack on the desk near her chair. She said, "Unfortunately, he won't accept advice any more. Not from anybody. Not even from me."

The flames from the fireplace danced over her cheekbones, making her look almost Egyptian. "Tom has withdrawn. From his advisors, from his staff, from me. He seems incapable of making decisions, even the most minor ones. And he doesn't trust anyone, especially General Rudd." She smiled slightly. ' He's the only one with backbone, you know that. I think the General is a very competent man. But I also think he could be more tactful."

Whitman was curious. "How do you mean?"

"General Rudd's very much a competitor. At least, he gives advice like one. He's very quick and proud of it. In many ways, he's quicker than Tom. He doesn't bother to hide it."

"General Rudd is very bright," Whitman said diplomatically.

"I'm aware of that. He's also goddamned insensitive." She scrubbed out the half-smoked cigarette in the ashtray and promptly reached for another. Her voice was jumpy. "Tom's coming apart. He's paranoid—there's no other word for it."

Whitman stood up and walked over to the library shelf and poured himself a small bourbon from the bottle next to the sherry decanter. "I should think that handling Charlie Rudd would be the least of Tom's problems." He glanced at her over his shoulder. "More sherry?"

She shook her head, lost in thought. "No, thank you." She was sitting dead center in the big wingback easy chair, her legs crossed at just the proper angle. Whitman tried to imagine her as a young girl, very prim, very proper, with a carefully calculated reserve. A reserve that had, with time, become a shell.

She leaned forward in the chair. Whitman had the impression that having come this far, she was now willing to abandon caution altogether.

"Tom can no longer cope. Not just with the Presidency. He can no longer cope, period. He lives in the past. Last night he rambled on for an hour about when the Phillies won the World Series. He was a big fan of the players and they liked him, they cut some TV spots for his campaign for mayor. He wanted me to look up the tape he had made of them." She paused, looking wry. "I didn't have to. His memory was very good."

She moved her head slightly and the light from the study lamp made her look her age. Her voice was harsher now. Her face twisted and for a moment Whitman thought she was going to cry. "Tom has to face his failures every day and he can't. He's reminded of them every time he reads a paper, when he watches the news on television, even in his staff meetings." She sounded wistful. "With good luck he could have served two terms as President and gone down in the history books as well-meaning but mediocre. But even that's an opportunity he's not going to have."

The picture was bleaker than Whitman had suspected.

She said, "I know what you're thinking. That I'm his wife and shouldn't say these things. But I'm not married to just an ordinary man, I'm married to the President of the United States." She leaned back and blew thin streams of smoke through her nostrils. "Tom needs help. He still likes you, still respects you." She hesitated again. "Tom can't make decisions, not really. You could make them for him. I would see to it that he would accept them." Her voice was emotionless.

Whitman didn't say anything.

"You could move your office into the West Wing, like Mondale did," she continued. "We could work together, we have before."

It wasn't possible, Whitman thought. Not with the Thomas Massey who had presided over the energy meeting he had attended earlier. Within two days, Massey would hate him. Whatever the solution might be, what Babs was proposing wasn't it—and not just because of his own health.

"He won't be running again," she said in a decisive voice. "I'll see to that, too. He won't announce it until a few weeks into the primaries. That will leave the convention open for you and, of course, you'll be nominated. In effect, you'd be serving as President a year ahead of time."

Whitman reacted then, had to. "You're offering me something I don't want and don't think would work," he said slowly. "Tom still has his pride."

She stared, then said in an icy voice: "I don't believe you. You ran for it once, you tried very hard for it at one time."

"You're upset, Babs." He didn't know what to say.

"Tom can't run the country," she said in a brittle voice. "But he's got another year in which he has to try. That year will be disastrous. And you know it. I've seen him sit in the Oval Office for hours, just staring out the window."

Whitman stood up and took his glass over to the library shelf. He made a show of stoppering the sherry decanter to give her time to recover. When he turned around, she was getting ready to leave.

"He'll never resign," she said in a bitter voice. "That's the one thing he will ask my advice about and I'll never approve." She pulled on her gloves, looking at him coldly. "That's what you really want him to do, isn't it?"

December 20
12:00 *Noon, Pacific Time, Sunday*

Livonas jockeyed the car out of its parking space in front of the
Chronicle-Examiner building and limped across Fifth Street just
ahead of the light. It was a bright, warm Sunday—the rain had
stopped and the cloud cover had burned off—and the downtown
streets would be crowded. He could smell the food from the ven-
dors' stalls in Union Square. A generation of Southeast Asian refugees had established commercial squatter's rights in the square and
gradually taken over the nearby Tenderloin. It reminded Livonas of
the Saigon slums, only worse.

He turned up Bush Street and parked in a lot near Le Central, a
small, chic restaurant where San Franciscans with a lot of money
and not much to do liked to take long lunches. For years, whenever
he was in town, Clinton Avery had held court at the corner table in
front. Avery, the personable former Speaker of the Assembly, had
been one of the most prominent black political figures in the state.
When Livonas called him at home, Avery sounded less than enthusiastic about meeting him but then suggested they get together at
Le Central.

He strolled inside, ignoring the haughty maître d' who hurried
over. "A table will be open in just a minute, sir."

There were at least three open that Livonas could see but he
didn't argue the point. It was difficult to maintain an image of chic
elegance when few people could afford to spend fifty dollars for
lunch.

Avery was sitting at his old table along with his law partner, his
haberdasher, a local columnist, and a man whom Livonas didn't recognize. Avery was heavier than Livonas remembered, and older—
the hair that fringed his balding scalp was almost white. But the sar-
torial splendor hadn't changed much. He was wearing a three-piece
charcoal-colored worsted suit and a hand-painted designer tie—this
season's male fashion item.

The maître d' noticed the direction of Livonas's glance and announced a table was available after all. Livonas shook his head.
"Thanks, I'll sit at the bar."

He took a seat on one of the high oak stools and continued to study Avery while he sipped an ale. If there was anybody in California who should bear a grudge against de Young, it was Clinton Avery. Avery had been speaker for ten years, the second most powerful man in the state government after the governor. According to Garber, Avery had jumped party lines a few months back to support de Young on one of the few unpopular bills the governor had ever backed. But de Young hadn't rallied the promised Republican support to make up for the damage Avery had done within his own party and Avery had lost the speakership. Garber had said Avery was bitter and from what Livonas knew of the ex-speaker, he was probably vindictive as well.

Avery glanced up, saw Livonas, then excused himself to the others at the table and strolled over to the bar. He ignored Livonas's hand and nodded at the bartender. "A coffee, please, Joe." He turned slightly in Livonas's direction. "You still Whitman's A.A.?" His eyes weren't on Livonas at all but were checking out the room.

"That's right, Clint, I still got my job. Sorry to hear about yours."

A sardonic smile flickered over Avery's face. "You gots to roll with the punches, mah man, you gots to roll with the punches," he mimicked.

Livonas took another sip of his ale. "You must have learned a new way to roll."

Avery shot him a quick glance. "How's that?"

"With a sucker punch."

"It's an art, Livonas. You come in for Gus Frankel's funeral?"

"I was a day too late."

"Sorry to hear about Gus." Avery was studying the room again. "I'll miss him." His voice was so low nobody could possibly have overheard him. "You didn't want to see me just to sympathize."

"But I did," Livonas said casually. "You've been one of the mainstays of the party in the Bay Area, we don't like to see one of our own get turned out on the street because of a little bad luck. Your talents are too valuable, Clint, you're too well known, too widely respected."

"And you're too full of shit, Livonas." Avery's eyes suddenly registered mild surprise. "You're going to offer me something."

Livonas nodded. "We'd like to help out, Clint."

Avery's face was a mask. "A federal judgeship, perhaps? Something to keep me off the welfare rolls in my old age?" His voice turned cynical. "Come on, Livonas, what do you want?"

"Why'd the Governor screw you, Clint?"

Avery looked down at his coffee cup, then picked up the spoon and swirled it around in the dark-brown liquid. "Why don't we just say personal differences and let it go at that."

"Because the Governor's been screwing too many people lately," Livonas said. "He's also being a little too nice to others—people who don't even live in the state. We were wondering why." He emphasized the collective pronoun. "He's running so hard for the Presidency some people are being trampled in the rush."

"I hadn't heard," Avery murmured.

"We thought we ought to find out what the Governor's up to," Livonas continued. "So I said to Bob Whitman, I think we might have a real friend out there who could help us."

"And I was the lucky winner." Avery drained his coffee. "If you'll excuse me, I have to get back to my table."

Avery should be jumping at a chance to nail de Young but he didn't even seem interested, Livonas thought.

"I didn't realize you were that loyal to the Governor."

"Did I say that?"

Livonas touched him lightly on the shoulder before he could turn away. "I'm serious, Clint. We'd like to see you play an active role on the federal level."

Avery looked bemused. "You're better than I thought, Livonas. That's a good pitch. Simple but flattering, vague but specific at the same time. For that you deserve something." He hesitated, then said smoothly: "The Governor wanted a younger man as speaker. Nothing complicated. It isn't his fault that I was naive, I just outmatched myself."

Avery turned to leave but Livonas reached out and took hold of his arm. "The Governor's been playing fast and loose with the election laws, Clint, along with a few others. The son-of-a-bitch is up to his neck—you know it, we know it—and we're going after him with everything we've got." He hesitated. "You need us. We can be good friends, Clint, and we're not asking for all that much." His voice cooled a little. "You've got to take sides on this one."

For the first time Avery met his eyes. "Take sides against de Young? I'll tell you something about Vincent de Young, Livonas.

While you're worrying about him stepping on your toes, de Young's already got a steel-tipped shoe planted in your crotch. You and me, we're just small fry. If I were you, I'd drop a wreath on Frankel's grave and catch the first plane back to D.C."

"What happened between you and the Governor, Clint?"

Avery shook off his arm. "Why should I tell you? For promises, for something you won't be able to deliver? For old times' sake? We never had any old times, Livonas. You wore dirty shirts and ran around playing Front Page for the *Examiner*. I didn't like you then and we haven't gotten any closer since."

He brushed some lint off his suit jacket, then, without moving his lips, said, "Professor Charles Yates is the Governor's biographer, you can reach him at the Hoover Institution down at Stanford." He shifted his shoulder slightly. "You know the two gentlemen who just came in?"

Livonas followed the movement with his eyes. Once you knew, they were hard to miss. Two stocky men, both with sandy hair, one with a moustache, one without, dressed in J. C. Penney suits. They looked like they ought to be in a gym working out, not sitting in one of San Francisco's more expensive restaurants pretending they were interested in the menu.

Avery was all smiles now. "Good seeing you again, Andy. Take care of yourself."

He was already heading back to his table, stopping at two or three along the way to shake a few hands. Anyone watching would've thought he'd had a casual conversation with an old acquaintance.

Livonas paid his tab and left, wondering who had tipped off the governor's men. He got into his car and turned the key a dozen times before the engine kicked over. He looked in his rear-view mirror.

The two men in the J. C. Penney suits were across the street a few cars down in a blue Plymouth sedan. They didn't pull out of their parking spot until he was halfway down the block, then they followed him over to the St. Francis, keeping a discreet distance.

Unlike the airport hotel, the St. Francis was deserted. The three bellhops on duty looked drowsy and the desk clerk gave the impression he resented anybody checking in. Once he had the room key, Livonas stopped at the American Airlines counter and used his federal priority to book a six o'clock flight back to D.C.

On the way to the elevator, he passed one of the plainclothes cops sitting on the end of a lobby couch, his face buried in the Sunday comics. Livonas recognized him by the cut of his suit and his scuffed cordovan shoes.

The bellhop ushered him into the outside elevator and Livonas watched the colorful stalls and waving pennants of Union Square recede beneath him. They stopped on the twenty-third floor and the bellhop opened the door to his room and made the ritualistic circuit, dropping his suitcase on the webbed holder and flicking on the lights in the john. Livonas took a sportcoat from his suitcase and handed it to the bellhop along with a five-dollar bill. "Have it back by five and leave a call at the desk for an airport cab, same time."

The bellhop took the jacket and pocketed the bill, smiling for the first time. "Anything else, sir?"

Livonas plucked the "Do Not Disturb" sign off the doorknob. "Hang this on the outside when you leave."

After the bellhop left, he lay down on the bed and stared at the ceiling. The state police would question the bellhop when he got downstairs and soon they'd have to decide whether to let him fly back to D.C. or kill him. Somebody else would make that decision, of course, along with where and when and how. But that could be settled by a phone call.

What the hell was de Young hiding that was worth murder?

And then he caught himself thinking of Gus Frankel, one of the few people he had ever met who seemed incapable of malice. They had caught Gus alone and thrown him out an open window . . . He forced the image from his mind and thought of calling Mary Scoma again—he'd tried to see her earlier but had run out of time—then decided against it. Any calls from his room would be monitored and he didn't want to put Mary in danger as well.

He glanced at his watch. Fifteen minutes; he was cutting it thin. He slipped on his suit coat and opened the door slightly. Nobody was in the hall. He made sure the "Do Not Disturb" sign was still on the door, then walked quickly down the carpeted corridor to the fire stairs.

Ten minutes later, he slipped out from behind two garbage dumpsters in the alley and joined a group of middle-aged businessmen walking up Geary Street, eating from small containers of Laotian finger food they had bought in the square. He'd catch the Airporter at Ellis and Taylor and once at San Francisco International, he'd switch to another Airporter going down the peninsula.

Avery had handed him too good a lead in Yates. He couldn't go back to D.C. without checking it out . . .

At the airport, some flights had just come in and Livonas joined the double line of people waiting for the bus going south to Santa Clara and silicon valley.

"Takes me longer to get from here to Santa Clara than it does from here to L.A." The man behind him was in his early forties, wearing a plaid cap pulled down tight over his head. A matching scarf was tucked under the collar of his Burberry.

"Yeah, sure does," Livonas mumbled.

The man smiled broadly. "How'd you like the game?"

"I thought it stank," Livonas muttered.

"I'm a Stanford man myself but I gotta admit you're right . . ."

The line started to move and Livonas shuffled forward with the others. A few steps more and he felt an aggressive tap on his shoulder. He turned.

"Didn't they give you one of these in the terminal? I noticed you weren't wearing one." The man in the plaid cap was pointing to a cheap enamel stickpin of the California state flag on the lapel of his raincoat.

"They missed me." The space in front of him had widened and Livonas hurried to close the gap.

"Christ, I thought they got everybody." The man held out a handful of flag pins. "I got some extras for the guys at the office. Here, it's on me."

He chuckled at his pun. Livonas grabbed a pin and stabbed his coat with it. Almost everybody in line was wearing one and those who weren't wore flag pins of the other western states. Then he was at the door to the bus. He paid the driver and climbed on, taking the first single seat he found.

The man in the plaid cap walked past him along the narrow center aisle without a glance. Livonas studied him in the driver's mirror and wondered why the hell the man had picked him to talk to of all those waiting for the bus.

He shrugged it off and stared out the window. He was getting paranoid . . .

* * *

The bus let him out on El Camino Real, directly in front of the main gate to the Stanford campus. He found a phone booth across the street and three calls later knew Charles Yates's home number, along with the information that Yates was a professor emeritus at the Hoover Institution. Livonas dialed him at home and introduced himself as a free-lance writer based in Washington. Would Professor Yates mind being interviewed about his biography of Governor de Young? The professor asked his name twice, then gave him directions to his home. Two miles, he said. Easy walking distance.

Half an hour later, Livonas turned down a loose gravel driveway that curved through an evergreen hedge and then opened onto a landscaped lawn. Professor Yates's ranch house was behind a kidney-shaped swimming pool that curved around the front of it like a moat. Livonas followed the flagstone steps up to the door and pressed the buzzer. Chimes tinkled through the recesses of the house.

The man who answered the door was in his mid-seventies with a deeply lined hawkish face and a salt-and-pepper moustache trimmed with Prussian precision. He was dressed in a yellow turtleneck and charcoal-gray slacks. Well over six feet tall, he had only a slight hint of a stoop.

"You must be the writer chap." The professor held the door open with one hand and drew Livonas inside with the other. His grip was firm enough to suggest it had been viselike when he was younger.

"Professor Yates, it's very kind of you."

"I enjoy talking about California's most distinguished citizen, Mr. Livonas. It's a pleasure. My study's right this way."

Livonas followed him down a beige-carpeted hallway, one side of which looked out over the swimming pool. Yates did all right for himself, he thought.

The study was a large book-filled room with a long, inlaid flat-topped desk at one end and a large stone-and-mortar fireplace at the other. A huge charred log smoldered behind a fire screen. In back of the desk were thick ochre drapes; Livonas guessed the windows overlooked the front lawn.

Yates bent down by the fireplace and shoved rolled newspapers and kindling beneath the log. "Not quite dry, but it'll burn in time." He sat down in a hard wood rocker angled to face the fire-place and motioned to a brown-leather easy chair beside it. "Usually people want to interview the subject, not the biographer, Mr. Livonas. You've got quite an unusual approach." He started rocking, a few inches forward and a few inches back. His eyes were wide and speculative and not very friendly.

Livonas dropped his overcoat on one end of the desk and eased into the chair. He flashed a smile. "Actually who but a biographer would know the subject best?"

"Perhaps, perhaps." A slight narrowing of the eyes. "I'm a little at a loss, Mr. . . . ah . . . Livonas? Just exactly what can I tell you?"

Livonas settled his notebook on his knee and held his ball point pen at the ready.

"Primarily I'm interested in how you met the Governor, what you think of his career so far, and where you think he's going."

Yates chuckled. "What you want is a synopsis of my book and I won't give you that."

"Your timing's just right," Livonas said smoothly. "You'll be published . . . when, early fall, just before the election?"

Yates stared. "The election? Oh, yes, yes, of course. It's been a tremendous effort on my part, taken all of my time for the past three years." He became expansive. "As you can guess, a difficult sub-ject—"

"You first met the Governor . . . ?" Livonas asked.

"Vincent used to be a student of mine here at Stanford." Yates smiled proudly. "He had an intuitive grasp of history, you could see the formation of a natural leader even at that age." Another chuckle. "A straight-A student, I can assure you."

"You think he'll win the election?"

Yates looked blank again. "Oh yes, of course."

What the hell was wrong? Livonas thought, uneasy. Yates didn't seem interested in the election, didn't take advantage of the oppor-tunity to enlarge on de Young as a candidate.

"His approach to politics, Professor, would you say that de Young was pragmatic or idealistic—"

"A visionary." Yates's eyes lit up. "But a pragmatic one." The professor smiled slightly. "Certainly he's one of the few American politicians to realize the ramifications of the westward thrust of the United States. To give myself credit, I emphasized that in my books. But it was Vincent who expanded on it, who grasped the practical, the political essence of it."

Behind the professor, hanging on the walls of the study, were dozens of photographs, all of them of de Young, including a large photomontage of incidents in de Young's career. Some of the photographs were large portraits, one or two hand-tinted. De Young had the light blond hair of a surfer then. He was almost pretty, Livonas thought, with the type of looks that broke women's hearts on the morning soaps.

"You're not putting words in the Governor's mouth, are you, Professor?"

Yates stammered to a halt. "Oh, my, no. Vincent has read and approved of every word I've written."

Livonas raised an eyebrow. "That's a little unusual, isn't it?"

Yates frowned. "No, of course not. It helps eliminate errors of fact. And, of course, he commissioned it, he found a western publisher for it, he has every right to read and correct it."

Time to squeeze, Livonas thought. All he'd gotten so far was a simplistic rehash of turn-of-the-century historian Frederick Jackson Turner.

"So what you've really written, Professor, is not a scholarly work at all but actually more a piece of political propaganda."

Yates stood up and stalked over to his desk. He lifted a petrified wood paperweight off a set of galley proofs and picked them up.

"Political propaganda?" He waved the galleys, then slammed them back down on the desk top. "That's what the people in Washington would call it." His face was marbled pink with anger. "Washington has raped, pillaged, and plundered the West. It's deliberately passed laws, played with economics, and throttled its own sense of ethics to help one region of this nation exploit another." The professor straightened up, his eyes shining with rage and conviction. "Vincent de Young is a visionary, Mr. Livonas. The country should be proud of him, *will* be proud of him!"

Chimes sounded and Yates walked to the doorway. "In the next week, you'll learn everything you want to know about Governor de Young's vision of the future." He paused. His words were measured, filled with pride. "I know Vincent's mind as well as I know my own. I'm probably one of the few political scientists in the nation who understands his genius."

He disappeared down the hall. There was the low murmur of conversation outside and Livonas walked over and parted the drapes slightly. A green sedan was parked in the driveway, its engine running. The driver stood by the hood of the car, lighting a cigarillo. Two men in raincoats were waiting by the side of the house for the professor to open the door. One of them was the man with the flag pins and the plaid cap.

The door opened and he could hear Yates say, "Mr. Livonas? He's in my study."

Livonas turned and grabbed his coat off the desk. Next to it was the set of galleys, along with a folder marked, "Maps, Charts and Graphs—de Young." He grabbed the petrified wood paperweight for a club. Then he picked up the galleys along with the folder.

There were voices in the hallway and he tucked the galleys and the folder under his arm and tugged at the sliding glass doors, quietly slipping outside. The driver of the car stood with his back toward him, puffing on his cigarillo and watching some fat sparrows foraging on the lawn. Livonas charged across the gravel. The driver heard him and turned, surprised.

"Hey, what the—"

Livonas caught him with the paperweight along the side of his head. The man went down, clawing inside his coat for a gun. Livonas yanked open the car door, knocking aside the gun arm at the same time. He jumped in, felt somebody catch his leg, and sprawled across the front seat. The galleys spilled out of his arm and onto the driveway.

He doubled back, grabbing for the folder and found himself staring into a .45 automatic. The man on the ground was blinking blood out of his eyes and trying to aim the gun with one hand while holding onto Livonas's leg with the other.

Livonas kicked back, smashing the bridge of the man's nose with the heel of his shoe. The man let go with a scream and Livonas pulled himself back behind the wheel, slammed the car into drive, and jammed his foot down on the accelerator. The car jerked, then skidded and fishtailed. For a moment, Livonas thought he was going to lose it.

It took all of his self-control to keep his foot off the brake as he skidded the length of the driveway. He didn't realize they were shooting at him until a hole appeared in the windshield just below the rear-view mirror.

His eyes jerked upward. In the mirror he could see the man in the plaid cap holding a gun with both hands, his feet spread wide. A sheet of paper suddenly blew in front of his face, then other pages of Yates's book fluttered across the driveway and into the pool.

A few feet more and he was out on the street. He swung the car toward Stevens Creek Boulevard, two miles away. He could probably get that far before they set up roadblocks, then he'd have to abandon the car and try hitching a ride. And that wouldn't be easy. It was getting toward dusk and the only traffic on the freeways would be trucks. And state police.

He was six blocks away now and forced himself to loosen his grip on the steering wheel and ease up on the accelerator. He took a deep breath. He was safe for five minutes. Maybe ten.

He glanced over at the folder, whose contents had slid out over the seat. Some Xerox copies of maps and what looked like textbook graphs. On top was a large map showing the western half of the United States along with western Canada and Mexico and the Pacific Ocean and the countries surrounding it.

The caption at the bottom of it caught his eye. "The West, unshackled from the moribund East, is destined to be the leading power of the twenty-first century."

Livonas swore and yanked the steering wheel to the left to keep from swerving off the road. He concentrated on the semi-deserted freeway, wishing he'd held onto the galleys.

Then he remembered the one person who just might be willing to fill in the missing pieces for him.

Sally Craft.

There had been a short mention of her in a gossip column he'd read on the plane coming in from D.C. Sally was staying up at Nevada City for the holidays. What was more interesting was the columnist's comment that ". . . the Governor and the gorgeous rock star are headed for splitsville . . ."

Livonas fervently hoped so.

He left the car a few hundred yards from a truck stop and caught a lift with the driver of a semi hauling groceries to Reno. The driver was about thirty with sandy hair, thick arms, sleeves rolled almost to his shoulders, and tattoos of eagles on his biceps. He was strictly monosyllabic while he played with the rig's elaborate C-B system.

Half an hour later, he got tired of the chatter on the shortwave and glanced over at Livonas.

"Where exactly did you say you were going?"

"Grass Valley," Livonas lied. "You can drop me off at Auburn." He would try and catch a ride at one of the hamburger joints along the intersection of Route 49 and Interstate 80. Nevada City was just a little beyond Grass Valley.

"What the hell's up there?"

"My brother—only way I can get to see him is to hitchhike up."

The driver fingered a small tin of chewing tobacco. "That's the only way you can get into the small towns these days. Most rigs will pick you up if you look harmless."

He gave a sideways glance and Livonas could feel the sweat start. The state police could have used the C-B band to issue a bulletin— and a reward. The driver could also be a de Young sympathizer, probably was.

"Where you from, Buddy?"

Livonas almost said D.C., then caught himself. "Chicago."

"No shit?" The driver grinned and thrust out a thick hand. "Shake—all this time I was thinking you were a California weirdo."

"How about yourself?"

"Cleveland. Not the garden spot of the universe but good enough for me." Livonas felt the tension drain out of him for the first time in two days. "Great town," he said.

December 20

8:30 P.M., *Pacific Time, Sunday*

At the A&W root beer stand in Auburn, Livonas was picked up by three young loggers who had rebuilt their old pickup truck to run on pure alcohol. They dropped him off in front of the National House on Broad Street, Nevada City's main street. The oldest of the three boys had sized him up, suspicious, and then confided that the city crowd and the local pot dealers hung out there.

The town was almost deserted—it was Sunday night and only the bars were open. The rest of the quaint Victorian shops that lined the street were either closed for the evening or shuttered permanently.

The National House, which billed itself as the longest contin-uously functioning hotel in California, was still open, though the travel agency next to it was boarded up. Livonas walked through the double doors into the red-wallpapered lobby, past the red loveseats that had once belonged to Lola Montez, and into the bar.

He stood in the entrance for a moment until his eyes adjusted to the flickering candlelight. The bar was busy but not crowded. From their looks, most of the customers were part of that community of wealthy urban refugees who made Nevada City their home and drinking their avocation. The natives, if they had the money to drink in public, hung out at the roadhouses between Nevada City and the smaller backwoods logging towns with Gold Rush names like "Rough and Ready" and "Dutch Flat." It had been that way ten years ago when he was there last and from what he could see, it hadn't changed much.

He made himself comfortable on a stool at the short side of the L-shaped bar, ordered an ale, and settled back to watch the action. If Sally Craft made Nevada City her second home, odds were she had a candyman in town and the National House bar would be his hangout. It was a long shot but the only one he had.

It took him about fifteen minutes to pick out the candyman and then it turned out to be a her and not a him.

She was at the extreme other end of the bar, in the center of a lit-tle group of three to four men, the members of which were con-stantly changing. She was about twenty-three, dressed in a green plaid wool shirt, jeans, and with her light-brown hair cut in a short, stylish bob. She could have been a model in a granola ad except for her eyes. Her eyes were street-wise, flitting from one friend to an-other, then taking in the rest of the bar or glancing over at the doors whenever she heard them swing open.

Livonas almost missed it when she made a sale. A man in a puffy down parka and a black goatee wandered up to the bar, ordered a shot of bourbon, downed it, and was gone. Livonas looked around for the granola girl. She had disappeared as well. She must have slipped out the back, he thought. The bartender wouldn't want the exchange on the premises even if he was cut in.

Fifteen minutes later, the process was repeated. A small, fiftyish man wrapped in a sheepskin coat pushed through the double doors and strolled up to the bar. He made momentary eye contact with the girl, then ignored her. She took her purse off the bar, gave the heavyset man in the embroidered work shirt sitting next to her a hug, and left through a rear doorway marked "Exit." Livonas guessed that the man in the embroidered shirt did her holding.

He put a five-dollar bill on the bar and walked outside, stepping into the doorway of the travel agency to wait.

In minutes, the man in the sheepskin coat strode past him. Livonas followed him around the corner, watching him get into the passenger side of a black-and-red land cruiser. In less than two minutes he got out of the car, loudly sniffing the free taste up his nose.

Livonas opened the land cruiser's door and slid inside. He closed the door, then froze. The dealer was pointing a revolver midway between his stomach and his heart.

"I've never seen you before," she said quietly. "Everybody in town would believe me if I said you were a rapist."

He shook his head. "I'm not."

"Narcs are second on the list," she said, holding the pistol stready. "Nobody likes them, either."

"I'm looking for somebody," he said.

Her eyes were very bright, even in the darkness. "If I said you were a rapist, nobody would blame me if I shot you," she repeated.

Girls who looked like they stepped out of granola ads didn't shoot people, he thought, but the nervous tic that fluttered just above the dimple in her cheek wasn't reassuring.

"I'm not a narc, I'm not a rapist. I want to talk to one of your customers."

"Who are you?"

She sounded plaintive and he realized he wasn't the only one in the car who was scared. He started to reach for his wallet and she jerked backward, pressing herself against the driver's door. He held up both his hands to show her they were empty.

"Maybe we shouldn't trade names," he said easily. He hesitated, studying her. "I want to talk to Sally Craft."

Her eyes narrowed. "You're one of the creeps from the governor's office."

He shook his head. "I'm with the federal government."

She waved the pistol. "Get the hell out of my car, I'm not setting up Sally."

"I want you to call her." He was careful not to make any sudden move. "I want you to tell her that the man with the Secret Service pass is in town to see her, that he's still holding her purse."

She shook her head. "Why should I tell her that?"

"You don't know me but I can find out who you are," he said quietly. "My guess is that this is a one-bust town. Agents from the Drug Enforcement Agency could be up here tomorrow."

It was an empty threat, the DEA hardly operated at all in the western states now. But the chances were she wasn't aware of that. Nevada City existed in its own little time and place.

The dealer was more calculating now, less nervous. "She won't come back to town today, she's been in once already."

"Why don't we ask her?"

She thought it over, then slipped the pistol back in her purse and slid out of the car. They walked in silence back to the National House. Livonas sat at a rear table while she talked briefly to the heavy in the embroidered shirt, then walked to the phone booth and made a short call. When she came back, she ignored Livonas altogether and sat down next to her friend at the bar. She wasn't casing the room now and didn't look up at the new arrivals; she had closed up shop for the night.

He sat there watching the long hand on the wall clock lurch ahead minute by minute. It had been a dumb move. There was no guarantee the dealer had called Sally but a lot of reasons to think she might have called for help. She might have protection.

Fifteen minutes later Sally Craft breezed through the doors, spotted him at the table, and sauntered over, smiling.

"I'll be goddamned, I knew it had to be you. Livonas, right? Vince told me you were a son-of-a-bitch and these days any enemy of Vince is a friend of mine."

She put her arms around him and kissed him on the lips. Her face was flushed from the cold and her auburn hair tumbled from beneath her knit wool cap and cascaded down the back of her waist-length fur jacket. He had almost forgotten how pretty she was.

"I've got a little biz to take care of at the bar, hon, then let me buy you a drink and fix you up with something else that's bad for you if you're in the mood."

She walked over to the bar and chatted a minute with the dealer, then returned with another ale for him and a Coors for herself. She poured the beer into her glass and took a long swallow. Livonas stared at her, wondering how he could draw her out.

"I appreciate the interest, but what'd you really drop by for?"

"Is Vince around?"

She shook her head. "He's in Houston—some big party."

"How come you didn't go?"

"Vince's parties bore me." Her mood abruptly changed. "I'm finished with Vince. It was pretty romantic for a while but you know how those things go . . ." She glanced down at her hands, drumming out a silent melody on the table top, then back up at Livonas. "The only problem is that he isn't finished with me." She smiled faintly. "Where you headed after here?"

"Back to Washington."

"The Vice-President's office, right?" She brushed her hand across her face. Livonas noticed that her nose had begun to run and guessed it wasn't from a cold. "I think I'll take a trip to the little girl's room."

She got up, nodded to the dealer, and both of them made the trek to the ladies room. After a few minutes, she came out of the washroom and returned to the table with a new case of the sniffles. "I don't know why I do it to myself," she said, staring at him intently. Her pupils were hardly bigger than pinheads. "Yes, I do," she amended. "Boredom."

Livonas felt something congeal inside him. Sally Craft was coked to the gills. Coming up to Nevada City had been a waste of time.

"I mean, you can see that, can't you?" She leaned across the table, anxious for his confirmation.

"I should think hanging around Vince would be a lot of laughs," he said sarcastically.

"Horse . . . shit." She pursed her lips at the end of each syllable.

"Then why the hell don't you leave him? Is he such a big help to your career?"

She looked offended. "Hey, don't get nasty with me, man. Your fight's with Vince, right?"

"Right," Livonas said heavily. He started to slip on his coat.

"Vince won't let me leave for one more week," she protested. "The only way I got out tonight is because my watchdog thinks we're going to run away together and I told him I was out of K-Y jelly."

He sat back down. "They keep you locked up?"

"More or less." Sally took another sip of her Coors. For a moment her eyes were vacant and wandering, her voice tinged with self-pity. "Vince thinks I'm a real asset with the kids." Then she grimaced, as angry at herself as she was at de Young. "Vince is a fucking freak—he gets his jollies raping women."

"Why don't you leave the son-of-a-bitch?"

She started tracing the beer rings on the table top with her forefinger. "I pulled train for the Hell's Angels when I was seventeen. The one thing I learned is that sometimes you don't leave when you want to. You leave when they get tired of you." She looked up at Livonas with sudden resolve. "I'll leave after I sing the national anthem for him at the Constitutional Convention."

He stared. "Why is it so important to de Young that you sing 'The Star-Spangled Banner'?"

Sally blinked, confused for a second. "You got the wrong song, hon. This is the national anthem for the Western States of America." She began to drift off, then brought her eyes back to him. Her mouth turned down at the corners. "I hope he gets his ass handed to him."

Livonas remembered the folder with the charts and graphs for Professor Yates's book. The caption at the bottom of the map leaped to mind. *The West, unshackled by the moribund East, is destined to be a leading power in the twenty-first century.*

Unshackled.

There were no more loose ends. He took the map from his pocket and spread it out on the table. Vincent de Young was at the center of a secessionist plot that included every state west of the hundredth meridian, as well as Louisiana and Oklahoma. The plot must have been brewing for years—the country itself had been coming apart for decades. The western states had become rich and powerful, while the eastern half of the nation had dwindled in population and importance, becoming more and more a poor, provincial backwater, its industrial system antiquated, its cities dying, its people without hope.

De Young's biggest asset had been the state of the country itself. East–West tensions had been building for a quarter century. People in the western states had been primed to accept secession as the logical consequence of what seemed like irreconcilable differences between East and West.

De Young must have co-conspirators throughout the West, in the Congress, in the Pentagon, in the intelligence services, probably in the executive branch itself. Steven Hart had found out about the role the Constitutional Convention was to play—and had been murdered. Gus Frankel had stumbled across it and they had shoved him out a window. Livonas wondered how many others there had been.

Yates had said a week and Sally had just confirmed it. In a week, Vincent de Young would announce the secession of the western states at a Constitutional Convention which had been stacked to legitimize his actions. And at the moment, there wasn't a damned thing the federal government could do. Nobody else in the government even knew about it—or was talking about it.

He had to get back to D.C. immediately, he had to tell Whitman about it. . .

He glanced over at the doors, half-expecting de Young's state police to come bursting through. But it was just another quiet Sunday evening in the small Sierra town; nobody was intent on anything more than their beer and their drinking companions.

He turned back to Sally. "How long has Vince been planning this?"

She shrugged. "You got me, hon. He told me I was going to sing just a few nights ago." She made a face. "They're really terrible lyrics."

"I'll bet they are," Livonas murmured. "And I haven't even heard them yet."

December 20

9:00 P.M., Central Time, Sunday

The ballroom was crowded, the air heavy with the cloying scents of a hundred expensive perfumes. De Young guided Gwen Beaumont effortlessly across the terra cotta floor to the brass rhythms of the Tex-Mex band. With the exception of Louisiana's governor Charlie Long, everybody they wanted had lined up on their side and a lot of them were here tonight. Shepherd had counted a dozen governors and close personal friends of a dozen more circulating through the rooms of the Big House, Ed Teillberg's Spanish-style mansion.

Ed had done one helluva job, de Young thought. So far he had shaken hands with the presidents of three Houston banks, the chairman of the board of Houston Data Systems, the president of Lone

Star Steel, and the chief executive officer of Brownsville Natural Gas, a conglomerate that held leases on eighty percent of the rigs in Galveston Bay. All of them had been brought on board by Ed.

"You're a superb dancer, Governor." Gwen Beaumont's somewhat out-of-breath flattery broke through his euphoria.

"It's because I have such an accomplished partner," he said, smiling down at her. He rather liked the old lady, admired her spunk. Fifteen years ago she had inherited Denver's only afternoon newspaper from her husband and had turned it into a chain of forty spread throughout the West. Her daily editorial, "Voice of the West," ran in each of the papers and referred to him as "the Savior of the West."

They glided past the bandstand, close enough to the watching crowd that he could sense the undercurrent of tension. He was being studied and analyzed and knew perfectly well what the whispers of the crowd were about. Was tonight the night? Too bad they were going to be disappointed. The key word was "secession" and it would have to wait until the convention when the television cameras were on him and he had an audience of millions.

The music drifted to a close and he bowed to Gwen, then turned to face the entire length of the ballroom. It was a vaulted two-story room with a bedroom balcony at the far end and Confederate and Texas flags crossed overhead. A dozen colorful piñatas dangled from the ceiling and along the sides of the room were tubs holding huge cacti, shimmering with hundreds of Christmas ornaments.

It had been an enormous living room before the rugs had been rolled back and the heavy Mexican-style furniture shifted into the corners. At the bar along one wall, men in expensive leather boots and suits by Pierre Cardin and Bill Blass chatted with elegant women wearing the latest by Givenchy and Yves St. Laurent and Dior.

At the far end of the bar, a group of military men, looking somewhat out of place in all the high-fashion elegance, were holding a reunion. De Young recognized Tom Teillberg, Ed's kid brother, who had been two years behind him at Stanford and was now the commanding general at Fort Hood, and Rear Admiral Richard Thompson. He'd meet the others later.

As he strolled off the ballroom floor, he worked the crowd, shaking hands and slapping backs, effortlessly remembering the names and anecdotes that Shepherd had supplied during the briefing on

the plane. At the doorway, he turned and held up his arms to acknowledge the applause, then hurried toward the study, trailed by
well-wishers eager to be recognized, to have a private word with
him, to share a confidence.

There was a burst of applause when he walked into the luxurious
study. He smiled and waved, glancing quickly around the room. He
remembered the Catlin portrait of Sitting Bull and the Remington
painting of Cabezo de Vaca that stared at each other from opposite
walls and the teakwood table holding the ivory inlaid Pente board.
But mostly he recalled the rich smell of the library of books bound
in Moroccan leather. Years ago, he'd spent a spring vacation on the
ranch with Ed. Most of the ten days had been spent right in this
room smoking the old man's cigars and sampling his liquor while he
and Ed debated Mill's *Principles of Political Economy.*

The men in the study crowded around him, their hands and faces
swirling in front of him in a sort of smoky kaleidoscope.

"Hello, Casey, great to see you, boy . . . glad you could make it,
Hal, been looking forward to it . . . Fahd, I can't say how much it
means to me that you're here . . . Goddamn, Lloyd, didn't think
you'd be here, pleased, really pleased . . ."

His mind quickly leafed through their dossiers. Casey Roberts
commanded the SAC base in Colorado Springs. He had gone to
college with Hal Stein, who now owned System Electronics, the
largest computer firm in the Santa Clara valley. Fahd Haddad was
the key economic advisor on whom the Saudi royal family relied. He
had been responsible for Sheik Yamani's fall from grace, thereby
squelching an impending rapprochement with the federal government. Lloyd Smith, the governor of Colorado, had fallen in line the
day before yesterday after a prolonged period of fence-sitting.

More people pressed forward. He shook more hands, winked at
some, slapped others on the back. He had never worked a crowd
better, or for that matter, a better crowd. He grinned at his private
word play.

Then General Bolles, in full uniform and looking remarkably like
General MacArthur, was pumping his hand. During the evening,
Bolles had made sure to introduce the various generals and admirals
to him. Following him now was Rear Admiral Thompson, whose
name had almost slipped his mind but not quite . . . and Governor
Riley of Kansas, another fence-sitter coming down on their side . . .

The library was jammed, mostly with people he'd talked with privately during the day. The words ran through his mind ... A new country, one with friendly relations with the old but also with a frank understanding between them of their basic differences in outlook and life-styles. Secession was the only solution ... Now was the time to act, he told them, to get on board or be left behind.

Somebody started a chant for him in the ballroom and the crowd swirled around him, half-carrying him out to the hallway. By God, they could do it! he thought jubilantly. Ed Teillberg pushed through the crowd and they locked arms. It was the right time in history, de Young thought, and he was the right man.

At the arched entrance to the ballroom the band struck up a medley of "Yellow Rose of Texas" and "Calilfornia Here I Come" and the cheering dancers cleared a path to the microphone. It didn't matter what he said, he thought. Everybody there knew what was really going on.

The band fell silent and he waited for the tension to build. The bandleader lifted the microphone from its stand to hand him and he brushed it away, taking a few steps forward so everybody could see him. "I have a few remarks to make but first I'd like to introduce some new friends."

He spotted Rear Admiral Thompson easing his way back through the crowd toward the veranda. "I'd like everybody to meet Rear Admiral Thompson." He waved a hand to indicate Thompson, a thin, nervous man in a poplin suit. "The Admiral has come all the way from the headquarters of the Pacific Fleet in Hawaii to be with us tonight."

He led the heavy round of applause. The admiral, he thought, looked a little like a dog who had just been caught nosing through the family garbage.

It took ten minutes to introduce the rest. He concentrated on the military; it was smart to pin them down, and their presence bolstered everyone's confidence—all you had to do was listen to the applause swell when another general or admiral took his bow.

When he had finished, he let his smile fade and lowered his eyes, waiting until he heard the first nervous rustle before looking back up at his audience.

"The twenty-first century is almost upon us and I want to underline what most of you already realize—that it's the destiny of the West to lead the countries of the Pacific Rim into the new century."

The only sounds in the room were the quiet clink of glasses and the occasional smothered cough.

"The western states have sustained the rest of the nation with food. With technological marvels. With all that has graced this country for the past fifty years. But the eastern states have a natural allegiance with the countries of the Atlantic Rim. They look to the East, not to the West. They have taken . . . and taken . . . and taken . . . our blood, our sweat and, yes, our tears . . . and will continue to do so for a hundred years to come. Unless"—he paused—"unless we take our destiny into our own hands!"

The applause thundered across the ballroom floor, interrupted by the *whopping* sound of helicopter blades settling toward the lawn outside. Shepherd drifted over with a glass of brandy and whispered, "That's got to be Northrup." Northrup, the goddamned governor of Texas, de Young thought; he should have been there hours ago.

He drained the brandy and, flanked by Wagoner, Shepherd, and Bolles, waited by the bandstand so Northrup would have to walk the full length of the room to reach him. A moment later, the band struck up "Texas, Our Texas" and Northrup strode in, his arm draped around Charlie Long, the governor of Louisiana, trailed by a dozen officers of the Texas National Guard. Northrup must have waited at the air base for Long to show up so they could make an appearance together. He'd have to keep an eye on the shrewd, old bastard.

Then the flashbulbs started going off and people were chanting "Time for the West! Time for the West!" and his euphoria returned with a rush. He greeted Northrup and Long with bear hugs, then stepped between them and raised their hands.

There was another torrent of applause. He smiled, gave a final wave to the crowd, then hurried back to the library with Shepherd. It was a far smaller group this time—himself, General Bolles, Jerry Wagoner and Shepherd. He walked over to the burnished-leather couch facing the sliding glass doors that overlooked the wide field-stone veranda. The doors were slightly open and he could hear Barron's nasal twang off to the right.

". . . so the Nigra says, 'This parrot's the dumbest damn bird I ever see'd. It don't even talk—I'll show you.' Then the Nigra sticks his nose up to the cage and says, 'Polly want a cracker?' and the goddamned parrot takes off his spectacles and puts down his little book and chirps. 'Nigger want a watermelon?' "

The joke was followed by an embarrassed silence. De Young grimaced.

"Herb, would you close those damn doors."

After he slid the doors shut, Shepherd pulled up a nearby chair and took a list from his briefcase, handing it to him. "These are the latest," he said in a low voice.

De Young took a pair of reading glasses from his pocket and scanned the sheets of paper. Some of the names he knew but most of them were unfamiliar. They went as low as major in rank with duty stations spread along the coast and in the Rocky Mountain area. He noted that the Commandant of the Air Force Academy in Colorado Springs was on the list and guessed he was a friend of Casey's.

He looked over at Bolles. "What about Admiral Marshall? His flunky, Thompson, looked like he was going to wet his pants when I introduced him."

"I've talked to Marshall." Bolles sucked on his ever-present pipe. "There won't be any problem."

De Young handed the papers back to Shepherd and turned to Wagoner. "What about the convention, Jerry?"

"The West is solid except for Washington State—Whitman will keep it from falling in line. Most of the Gulf Coast states will go along, with the exception of Florida. And the votes we dealt for in the Midwest are holding." Wagoner hesitated. "The East has begun to organize an opposition led by Kathleen Houseman, a delegate from Washington State. But it's too late for her to be effective."

There was a knock on the library door. Shepherd answered it, then motioned de Young over. Craig Hewitt, the head of G-Troop, was in the hallway. De Young's eyes narrowed. What the hell was Hewitt doing here? He poured himself another brandy and nodded for Hewitt and Shepherd to join him in a far corner of the room.

"What's up?" He looked from one to the other.

Shepherd cleared his throat. "We lost Livonas." He shot an accusing glance at Hewitt.

"I take full responsibility, Governor." Hewitt's voice was a soft rasp.

De Young fought to control his anger. "Did he find out anything?"

Hewitt shook his head. "He tried to steal a copy of the old man's book but dropped it getting away."

Maybe he found out something, maybe he didn't, de Young thought. In any case, nothing could be done about it now. He motioned to Hewitt and walked back to open the library door. Hewitt was necessary but, just the same, there were times when the man made his flesh crawl. "We'll get together later in the evening, Craig."

Hewitt looked as if he wanted to salute. "I want you to know that the men involved will be disciplined."

"Just tell them to keep trying." De Young eased him back into the hallway, pulling the door closed. It didn't matter what Livonas had found out, it was too late to do anything.

Time had run out for the East.

December 21

5:30 A.M., *Monday*

"The Vice-President's in the study, sir." Larry closed the door quickly behind Livonas, cutting off the blast of frigid early morning air. Livonas handed over his coat, then followed the ex-marine sergeant through the darkened foyer toward the light fanning out from beneath the study door.

Larry knocked once, then pushed the door open, standing to one side to let Livonas past. Whitman was sitting at his desk, dressed in his favorite ratty bathrobe, reading. A small log blazed in the fireplace behind him. He glanced up and put down the book.

"Larry, bring us a pot of coffee, will you?" He motioned to a chair. "Have a seat, Andy, you look a little ragged."

Livonas pulled over a chair and straddled it, leaning his elbows on the back. Captain Asten's F-18 had been built for speed, not for comfort.

"Any further trouble getting out of Beale?"

Livonas shook his head. "Your phone call did it." Beale Air Force Base was thirty miles away from Nevada City on Route 20 and the dealer had driven him there as a favor to Sally. Colonel Waters, the officer of the day, had been unfriendly from the moment he had shown the colonel his White House ID. "After your call, they didn't want to force what could have developed into a sticky situation." He paused. "But I don't think there'll be any other planes leaving Beale for the East."

Whitman looked surprised. "I don't follow you."

Livonas took Professor Yates's map from his coat pocket and dropped it on the desk. Whitman unfolded it and spread it out, glancing at it casually.

"I was wrong about de Young," Livonas said. "He's not interested in becoming President of the United States. He's not going to run. He's not even going to declare. Read the caption."

Whitman studied the map again, then read the caption aloud. " 'The West, unshackled by the moribund East, is destined to be a leading power in the twenty-first century.' "

There was a light tap on the door and Larry came back in with a tray holding a pot of coffee, cups, cream, sugar, and a small plate of toast. Whitman poured two cups of coffee, letting Livonas add his own sugar and cream.

Livonas waited until Larry had left, then said, "Next Sunday, California will introduce a resolution at the Constitutional Convention calling for the right of the states, individually or severally, to secede from the Union. With the West now in control of the convention, my guess is the resolution will pass by a large majority."

He took a sip of coffee that burned his throat. Whitman was staring at him, his face registering shock.

"Once the resolution passes, Governor Vincent de Young is planning to announce the secession of the Western States and the formation of the Western States of America." He pointed at the map in front of Whitman. "The states involved are shaded in blue—what's popularly known as the West plus Texas, Oklahoma, and Louisiana. Washington State might hold out as sort of an East Prussia."

Whitman hunched over the map. Livonas watched him run his finger down the ragged edge of blue, along the borders of Montana and Wyoming and Colorado, then along the northern edge of Oklahoma, down to Louisiana and over to the Mississippi River.

"You better back up to where we left it on Saturday, Andy. I gather the Governor didn't tell you this himself." Whitman leaned back in his chair, drumming his fingers on the desk top.

Livonas's voice was so tight he was afraid it was going to crack. "A week ago, de Young mobilized California's National Guard—

were you aware, incidentally, that the California Guard has been actively recruiting for the past three years? All the other western states followed suit with the exception of Washington. De Young then took over control of all the oil refineries and tank farms in the state, along with the pipelines and the hydroelectric plants. Gus Frankel, at the *San Francisco Examiner,* checked with General Bolles of the Sixth Army and Bolles said Washington had okayed it—that the takeover by the state had been arranged to relieve the federal government of the burden."

Whitman sat up straighter in his chair. "He's lying."

"That's right," Livonas said. "General Bolles is a traitor. He's at the top of what will probably be a very long list. Gus did some more investigating and found out that de Young was also responsible for the torpedoeing of our oil agreement with Indonesia."

"How the hell did Frankel find out about all this?"

"There was a meeting at the Airport Hilton near San Francisco Thursday night. Apparently everybody was there, including representatives from Mexico, Canada, Japan, Indonesia, the Philippines—every major economic power of the Pacific Rim—all wanting to cement relations with the new country. General Bolles booked half a floor to accommodate like-minded members of the military."

Livonas hesitated. "They filled out registration cards under names like Smith, Jones, Brown, and Riley, but the bill went to Bolles at Sixth Army headquarters." His voice became softer. "Gus went back to the office directly from the hotel to write it up. It was late at night and he was alone. He got through three paragraphs and then he went out a window. The police said he came down with a sudden case of suicide."

He stood up, took a crumpled sheet of computer print-out paper from his coat pocket, and handed it to Whitman. "That's the first three paragraphs of Gus's story. That's as far as he got before they threw him out the window. They didn't find the story in the computer because Gus had filed it under the name of the reporter who developed the lead."

Whitman read the short article through once, then again.

Livonas poured himself another cup of coffee. "The timing is important. Gus started to write his story twenty-four hours before we found out about the cancellation of the Indonesian deal. De Young knew about it a day before we did."

He studied Whitman, who was staring at the map again, lost in thought. "I called Jeff Saunders from San Francisco and gave him a list of the few foreign nationals we could identify at de Young's meeting. He was going to check them out and send what he found over to you."

Whitman looked tired, his face lined from the strain. "He did. Four of the Japanese were from the Trade Ministry, two from the Defense Ministry, and the other three from the private sector, including the president of Mitsubishi. Three of the Canadians are leaders in the western Canada secessionist movement." He shrugged. "I didn't know what to make of it."

He reached for the coffee pot and refilled his cup with a shaking hand. "You said you stole the map?"

"I looked up Clinton Avery. When I was on the Coast last week, I'd heard he was on the outs with de Young. He was too scared to tell me anything directly but steered me to a Professor Yates at the Hoover Institution. De Young studied under Yates when he was a graduate student and Yates has been working on his biography. He showed me the galleys. I needled him some and he got angry and told me that in a week everyone would know what a visionary political leader de Young really is."

Livonas rubbed his eyes. "Somebody tipped off de Young's hit squad that I was there. When the Professor went to let them in, I grabbed the galleys and a folder of illustrations and ran. I dropped the manuscript when they started shooting at me."

Whitman's voice was like dry silk. "So after talking with the Professor and looking at the map, you concluded that de Young was involved in a secessionist plot."

"No," Livonas said, thoughtful. "Maybe in retrospect I should have. Sally Craft, de Young's mistress, told me. She said de Young asked her to sing the national anthem of the Western States of America for him after his speech at the convention."

Whitman closed his eyes a moment. "We should have heard about this months ago."

"We better find out why we didn't." Livonas felt like he was suffocating. They were running out of time. "Bob, six days from now, de Young will announce the secession of California and the other western states will follow. The formation of the Western States of America will be blessed by the convention, supported by the populace, and backed by what amounts to a standing army."

He desperately searched Whitman's face for some other reaction than what seemed to be one of overwhelming sadness. "Massey will be confronted by a *fait accompli*. What's left of the United States will become a second-rate power overnight, no stronger than Great Britain and with just about as few prospects."

There was a long silence and he could feel the tension grow between them. Whitman got up from behind his desk and opened the window blinds, letting the pale winter sun throw weak shadows across the floor.

Livonas started to pace in front of his desk. "De Young's a traitor, a murderer. He's the leader of a secret rebellion, he's done his best to destabilize the federal government. What are you going to do when he asks the Constitutional Convention to legitimize the secession of the western states?"

"First of all, I'm going to notify President Massey," Whitman said in a strangled voice.

"And what the hell do you think he'll do?"

"I've no idea," Whitman whispered. "It's up to him. He's the President."

"He'll sit around with his thumb up his ass like he always does!" Livonas shouted.

Whitman glared, then ignored him as he angrily punched the buttons on his phone. Livonas could hear it ring on the other end of the line. Whitman identified himself and asked for the President. He waited a moment, then said, "I don't give a damn what he's doing, Mrs. Massey. I want to talk to him." He listened a moment longer, then softened his voice. "How long?"

There was a pause. Then he said quietly, "I'm sorry, Babs." He put the phone back in its cradle and looked up at Livonas. "Tom's drunk. He's been on a bender since yesterday morning. He hasn't even been to bed."

"You don't have a choice, Bob," Livonas said slowly. "You have to force him to resign. Under the Twenty-Fifth Amendment, you have the authority to take over as the Acting President. If he doesn't resign voluntarily, then you'll have to convince the heads of the executive departments that Massey can't fulfill the duties of the Presidency."

Whitman stared at him, mute, his face ashen.

"I know what I'm asking!" Livonas burst out. "For you to kill yourself. Don't you think I've thought about it? I've tried to figure out some al——"

Whitman cut him off. "Andy," he said in a husky voice, "it's not your fault. I know what I have to do." He reached for the phone again. "I've got to talk to Vivian, but first we have to get General Rudd over here."

"Rudd?" Livonas looked blank.

"We have to control the military," Whitman said.

December 21
8:15 A.M., *Monday*

It had started to sleet and Livonas could feel the temperature dropping. A gloomy day for one of the gloomiest occasions in the country's history. He turned slightly in the jump seat to glance at the grim faces behind him. Whitman was sitting at the left, staring somberly out the window, flanked by Ted Kennedy, finishing his first term as Speaker Pro Tem of the Senate, and Ralph Gorman, the Speaker of the House. Chief Justice Burger was on the right, trading an occasional comment with Kennedy.

General Rudd shared the lead limousine with Paul Nash, the Secretary of Defense, Attorney General Bob Knox, two generals from the Joint Chiefs, and the Secretaries of the Army and the Air Force. The Secretary of the Navy, Richard Foster, had left Washington for Hawaii on Saturday. And just before they started for the White House, a worried Rudd told Livonas that Governor Inouye had declared martial law in the Islands. Additionally, and more worrisome, a portion of the Pacific Fleet had sailed from Pearl Harbor under the command of Admiral Marshall. But nobody knew who had given Marshall orders to go to sea.

Rudd was doing better than Livonas had expected. He'd been the first to show up at the Vice-President's house where Whitman had quickly sketched in the situation, then told him that he was to be head of the National Security Council and chairman of the Joint Chiefs. Rudd had at first looked enormously relieved, then recovered and insisted on direct access to Whitman.

Rudd didn't want to go through him, Livonas thought. He could understand that. Besides, as Whitman's White House Chief of Staff, he'd have enough to do.

The limousine slowed and he glanced out the tinted side windows as they circled Farragut Square. Six more limousines followed them in the procession, carrying the heads of the various executive departments, their key aides, and a dozen hand-picked congressmen. If Massey refused to relieve himself as President, then they'd have to depend on the heads of the executive departments to support Whitman's request that Massey be relieved.

For what it was worth, and Livonas wasn't sure it was worth much, Whitman had received pledges from a majority of them that they would back him. However, Roger Anderson had opposed the removal and had some support. Whitman had also asked Rudd to poll the Joint Chiefs to verify their support. Word would leak out, of course, and it wouldn't take much imagination to deduce that removing Massey wasn't the only alternative on the Washington drawing boards, particularly for those just the other side of the Potomac.

A dozen camouflaged army jeeps joined the motorcade as it reached Pennsylvania Avenue. Everybody in the limousine craned their necks to look out the windows. Livonas felt a momentary chill. Up to now, the situation had seemed almost dreamlike. The flight in from California, the early morning meeting with Whitman, the phone calls and the assembling of the motorcade, the almost deserted, rain-swept streets . . .

The jeeps and the grim-faced men in them were sudden, crushing reality.

"That's the Black Beret battalion from Fort Meade," Whitman murmured to the others.

Rudd had insisted on the presence of the Berets, the special internal antiterrorist troops. He felt responsible for the protection of the future Acting President and his staff. And until there was time to screen the Secret Service he wanted to bypass them.

The military would be assuming unprecedented power during the next few weeks, Livonas thought. It was unavoidable, but it worried him. Most of the military would look upon the present situation as a calamity; a few would consider it an opportunity. He had yet to make up his mind just how Rudd considered it.

The motorcade slowed to a stop at the West Gate. Livonas twisted around to peer out the front window. Rudd was shaking hands with stocky, moon-faced Jack Mahon, the special agent in charge of the White House Secret Service force. The conversation was brief, Mahon occasionally glancing over at the Black Berets, who had lined up in formation on the outside of the iron picket fence, their snub-nosed Ingram Mac-10 machine guns at their sides.

Rudd returned to his limousine and Mahon waved the motorcade through the gates. The Black Berets remained outside and Livonas wondered if Mahon had insisted on that. He started to sweat a little. Babs had agreed to meet them in the foyer of the West Wing and escort Whitman and himself to the Oval Office where Massey was waiting for them.

A White House guard opened the car door and Livonas climbed out into the chill, damp air. He hurried to the portico to wait for Whitman, then turned to watch the ABC and NBC television vans pull up. Rumors had already leaked out that something was up. He would have to handle the press afterward. He wasn't looking forward to it.

He shivered while Whitman helped Chief Justice Burger from the car. The sky was a nasty, overcast gray and probably as light as it would get. It was the winter solstice—the shortest day of the year.

Whitman and Rudd arrived at the portico at the same time. Whitman motioned Rudd in through the doors, then fell in step with Livonas. "It's best I go in first, Andy. Give me three minutes alone, then you come in." He lowered his voice. "Keep the others in the anteroom until we need them."

Babs was waiting for them in the foyer wearing a wide-shouldered black dress, her hair drawn back in a severe bun. She ignored Livonas and looked directly at Whitman.

"The President asked me to escort you to the Oval Office." She was formal and distant. Livonas felt another twinge of worry. Massey could have sobered up and decided to fight them.

Then Babs noticed the entourage behind him. Livonas caught a hardening around the corners of her mouth. She shot an accusing glance at Whitman, then turned on her heel. Whitman hurried to catch up with her while Livonas dropped back with the others, who had slowed their pace to match that of the Chief Justice. Burger was recovering from his second stroke in as many years and now walked with the aid of a thick ebony cane.

He offered Burger his arm, wincing as he felt the justice's fingers dig into his biceps.

"Just precisely what is this incapacity the Vice-President has alluded to Mr. Livonas?"

Livonas chose his words carefully. "Extreme exhaustion, brought on by acute alcoholism."

The Chief Justice peered at him from beneath his bushy eyebrows. "And if the President refuses to step aside?"

"Then Vice-President Whitman will have to invoke section four of the Twenty-Fifth Amendment. The heads of the various executive departments are here if that becomes necessary."

Burger halted for a moment in the hallway, leaning with both hands on his cane, his face stern.

"You understand that my interest lies in upholding the Constitution, not in the exigencies of the present political situation, no matter how grave."

Livonas was solemn. "It's because of Vice-President Whitman's concern for the Constitution that he thought it imperative the Chief Justice be present." Burger nodded, squared his shoulders, and resumed his slow shuffle toward the Oval Office.

Now Kennedy and Gorman dropped slightly behind. "Mr. Livonas," Kennedy said, "what if the 'principal officers of the executive departments' don't agree with Bob?" They were now in the anteroom. Burger heaved a sigh as he made himself comfortable on a nearby couch.

Kennedy was thinking exactly what he was, Livonas thought. Most of the department heads were loyal to Massey; some of them went as far back as Philadelphia. They could stonewall it if Massey chose to fight, and then Whitman might have no recourse but to resign himself. All things were possible, he thought; there was no way he could reassure Kennedy.

"Then we're in trouble, Senator. We're facing a second Civil War. I don't think the country can either avert it or win it with President Massey in office."

Both Kennedy and Gorman went pale. Livonas glanced at his watch. Eight thirty-seven. Whitman had been with Massey long enough. "Bob wants me in there alone for a while. I'll come and get you when . . . we've reached a decision."

Kennedy managed a faint smile. "Good luck, Andy." It struck Livonas that in the ten years he had known him, it was the only time Kennedy had called him by his first name.

* * *

Inside the Oval Office, Massey was laughing. He stood with his back against the front of the oversized desk, studying Whitman through the side of a silver-rimmed Old Fashioned glass. He was wearing a green velour pullover and charcoal gray slacks marbled with wrinkles—Livonas guessed he had fallen asleep in them.

Babs sat stiffly on the couch, studying both men with bitter detachment.

Massey turned the glass so that he was looking at Whitman through the blue presidential seal. "Wanna drink?" Whitman shook his head, his face registering a faint anger. Massey waved the glass at Livonas, the Scotch sloshing over the rim and onto the blue carpet. "How about you?"

"No, thank you, Mr. President," Livonas said evenly.

Massey shrugged and walked carefully around the desk, holding onto the edges for support, then collapsed into his green-leather swivel chair. He glowered at Whitman.

"Rumors, that's all they are, rumors." He waved a hand, just missing the crystal Scotch decanter that stood between the two banks of phones on the nearby side table. "When I ran Philly, I even had to hire some son-of-a-bitch just to deal with 'em."

He refilled his glass and turned to Livonas. "How'd you like to be in charge of rumors, Livonas?" Massey chuckled, then took another gulp from his glass. His eyes narrowed. "Relieving me was your idea, wasn't it?"

"I'm sorry, Mr. President," Livonas said bluntly. "I don't think you're capable of fulfilling the functions of your office any longer."

Massey fumbled for the decanter again. "You don't have a vote, m'boy," he said thickly, "it's not up to you."

Babs got up from her chair and walked swiftly over to him. She shot a defiant look at Whitman, then reached out to help Massey to his feet. "This discussion has gone far enough, there's no point in continuing it."

Massey shrugged her off and leaned forward, palms down on the desk, glaring at Whitman.

"What you told me about de Young has got to be the biggest cock-and-bull story I've ever heard. An insurrection! I wouldn't be surprised if de Young planted the story himself. So I come out crying wolf and make a fool of myself. You'd like that, wouldn't you?"

Babs started to interrupt. "Tom——"

Whitman cut her off. "For the record, Mr. President. We have reason to believe that in a matter of days the Constitutional Convention, controlled by Governor de Young, will legitimize the right of secession. Once it does, California and the other western states will secede and Vincent de Young will form the Western States of America."

Livonas watched, fascinated, as the President's expression changed. His face reddened, his lips thinned, the muscles in his jaw formed tight little knots. "He won't get away with it. I'll send a planeload of U.S. marshals out there and we'll arrest him for treason. The whole damn plot will go poof!"

His anger subsided. He looked shyly at Whitman, then at Livonas. He was searching for some sign of approval, Livonas thought. Then even that vague look of hope faded.

"You don't think I can handle it, do you?" Massey sat back down in his chair, reached for the tumbler of Scotch, took a few quick swallows, and then unconsciously struck a pose with his back straight, his jaw thrust out at a slight upward angle in imitation of Franklin D. Roosevelt. A week ago it would have been pitiful. Now it was frightening.

Livonas decided to cut in and increase the pressure. If Massey wouldn't relinquish power voluntarily, then they'd have to rely on the heads of departments and the risks immediately became greater.

"Mr. President, the national guards of the western states are now fully mobilized; for all practical purposes, they constitute a western army. General Bolles of the Sixth Army as well as others have gone over to de Young, have been working with him for months. The oil refineries, the pipelines, the hydroelectric plants are all in the hands of the western governors. And we've just heard that a portion of the Pacific Fleet may have defected."

He watched while Massey splashed another refill into his glass. Massey recapped the decanter and sat back in his chair, frowning at the amber liquid.

Whitman cleared his throat. "Mr. President, the situation requires that something be done immediately. We can't let it drift."

Massey didn't answer but continued to concentrate on his drink.

"I'm not talking for my own benefit, Mr. President." Whitman's voice now had a dangerous bite to it.

Livonas shot a glance at Babs, who had gone back to sit quietly in her chair. She was trying to hold back tears.

Massey took a swallow from his glass, set it down on the desk blotter, and stared blankly at Whitman. "You wanna call a meeting?" He turned the word over in his mouth. "Meetings are for politicians, what Philadelphia needs is action." Massey looked sternly at Whitman, unaware of his slip.

Whitman was openly angry now and Massey's expression changed to a sullen pout. He reached again for the Old Fashioned glass but Whitman got to it first.

"Tom, I think you should step down temporarily from office. Considering your health, your condition . . ."

Massey drummed his fingers on the desk top. "Surprise. Bob Whitman wants to be President." For a moment he almost sounded sober. "It's not the country that can't wait . . . it's you that can't wait." He leaned across the desk, squinting up at Whitman. "You think you could have done better than me?"

"I'm going to have to, Tom," Whitman said. He put the glass back down on the table, directly in front of Massey.

Babs walked over to the desk again. "You have no authority to force the President to resign." She sounded almost shrill. She put her hand on Massey's shoulder. He looked up at her, uncertain.

Livonas interrupted again, worried how Whitman was taking the strain. "You're mistaken, Mrs. Massey. It's possible for the Vice-President and the heads of the executive departments to relieve the President if, in their opinion, he can't perform the duties of his office." He paused. "General Rudd is now briefing the department heads in the Cabinet Room."

Massey came to life, his face a mottled red. "You son-of-a-bitch!" he shouted at Whitman. "You're the goddamned plotter!" He jabbed angrily at a row of buttons on his desk.

Livonas heard the faint ringing of an alarm just before the first wave of Secret Service agents, pistols drawn, burst into the Oval Office. He was pushed roughly against the desk by the agents, who formed a shield around the President with their bodies. Behind him, something crashed to the floor followed by the faint, smoky odor of Scotch.

"Arrest him!" Livonas turned to see Massey hysterically waving his finger at Whitman. The two agents closest to Whitman reluctantly aimed their guns at him. White-faced, Whitman opened his jacket to show he wasn't armed.

There was silence for a long moment, then Livonas nodded to Jack Mahon, who had followed the agents into the room. "Nobody's armed, Jack. The President rang by mistake."

Mahon hesitated, then lowered his revolver. The other agents moved away. Massey stood alone by his desk and slowly upended the Scotch decanter. The last few drops trickled down the side and onto the desk blotter. He didn't look up to meet their eyes.

Mahon glanced at Whitman and Livonas, then back to the President. He stared for a moment, then looked away. "Let's go, men. I'm afraid the President's a bit under the weather."

In the open doorway, Senator Kennedy and Congressman Gorman huddled together with an ashen-faced Chief Justice. After the agents left, Livonas beckoned them to come into the room.

Whitman turned to Massey, still staring at the damp spots on the blotter. "Mr. President, I'm now going to the Cabinet Room to ask the principal officers of the executive departments that you be relieved pursuant to Section Four, Amendment Twenty-Five of the Constitution, and that I be designated Acting President until such time as you can discharge the duties of your office."

Massey lifted his head and stared at Whitman. Livonas wasn't sure he had actually heard, or even understood, what Whitman had said. Then Massey slowly turned and buried his head in his wife's shoulder. Babs put her arms around him and pressed him to her, murmuring to him as she might have to a small boy.

Livonas gave him a moment, then unzipped his briefcase and took out two copies of the two-sentence letter acknowledging that the President could not fulfill his duties. He gave one copy to Whitman and quietly laid the other on the desk. Massey glanced at it, then looked up at Whitman. To Livonas, he sounded like a child asking a question of his parents.

"Should I prepare a speech?"

Whitman smiled gently. "No need to, Mr. President. Besides, you'll be back at your desk in no time. Right, Andy?"

Livonas nodded, overwhelmed with pity for the man. "No time at all, Mr. President. The job could have gotten to anybody."

Massey was still staring at Whitman, his face full of loneliness and desperation. "The pressure," he repeated dumbly.

Whitman nodded, handing the letter to the Chief Justice. Burger fumbled a pair of black-rimmed reading glasses out of his breast pocket, put them on, and slowly read the letter aloud.

"I, Thomas H. Massey, finding myself unable to discharge my duties as President of the United States, hereby relieve myself of the powers and duties of the office until such time as I am able to resume them. Vice-President Robert Whitman will serve as Acting President. Signed, Thomas H. Massey."

Burger handed the letter back to Whitman. "It looks in proper order." Whitman put it on the desk in front of Massey, next to the other copy.

"I'm still the President, aren't I?" Massey asked hopefully.

Whitman said in a husky voice, "That's right, Mr. President. This is just a temporary arrangement."

Massey reached for the pen Livonas held out to him and scrawled his name at the bottom of both copies, then pushed his chair away from the desk and hid his face in his hands.

Whitman picked up the letters from the desk and handed one to Kennedy and the other to Gorman. Kennedy held his copy gingerly in one hand and clasped Whitman's hand with the other. "God bless," he said hoarsely. "God bless."

Babs Massey was the first to break the silence that followed. She touched her husband gently on the shoulder. "It's time to go now, Tom."

They weren't through yet, Livonas thought, grim. Now he had to play bad guy. "Mrs. Massey, before you go . . . We have to release a statement to the press. I think it would help if you were along—it would stop any hard questions about the President's health as well as any questioning of the transition."

Whitman looked surprised. "Andy, I don't think—"

"We have to do it," Livonas insisted. "The first thing de Young will attempt to do is subvert your authority as Acting President. Mrs. Massey publicly supporting you in front of the media will undercut that." He turned to Babs. "I realize I'm asking a lot of you. I wouldn't do it if the future of the country didn't depend on it."

Babs glanced at the frightened butler in the doorway and said quietly, "Please stay with the President while I'm gone." She turned back to Livonas.

"It's my country, too, Mr. Livonas. I love it as much as you do."

December 21
10 A.M., Pacific Time, Monday

". . . the Lord maketh his face shine upon thee, and be gracious unto thee . . ."

De Young tilted his head, savoring the strong ocean breeze as the last words of his mother's favorite biblical quotation ran through his mind. He couldn't see the edges of the crowd and worried for a moment that those in the back wouldn't be able to hear. It was a warm day for December, even in Los Angeles, with a stiff breeze that tousled his hair and feathered the mayor's words.

". . . even this federal office building behind me is a symbol of the federal oppression of the West. Uncle Sam owns half of our sovereign State of California, two thirds of the great State of Utah and ninety percent of Nevada—but he owns less than one percent of New York and less than two percent of Illinois and Pennsylvania—"

A roar of protest filled the plaza and volleyed off the sides of the surrounding buildings. Mayor Holland was doing a skillful job, de Young thought. They'd be screaming for blood by the time it was his turn to speak.

"We're prisoners in our own backyards! It used to be the westerner's dream that someday he could own a little spread of his own, raise a few head of cattle. That dream's now become a nightmare. We can't establish ranches on our own lands, we can't mine our own lands, we can't even fish our own rivers without the federal government telling us how to do it! It's like having the federal government tell you when you can mow your lawn, what flowers you can plant in front and what vegetables you can grow out back, and when you have to paint the porch. We're not going to stand for that!"

Mayor Holland, a short, balding man with heavy jowls and thinning reddish hair, gripped the sides of the podium and stared somberly out at the crowd as it roared its approval. De Young smiled. Not one in a thousand had ever owned a ranch, or wanted to, but Holland had tied it back to the little white house with the picket fence that everybody *did* want to own. The audience had heard the speech a dozen times before but loved it anyway.

There had to be a quarter of a million people in the plaza, he thought, glancing around. Shepherd had told him the crowds were building but this was the first time in a month he had spoken at an open-air rally and he was surprised.

"I have the great privilege . . . and honor . . . to introduce the man who is leading us forward in our fight for justice and equality . . ." Just in front of the speaker's platform, a man in a blue short-sleeved shirt was pointing him out to his son sitting on his shoulders. De Young smiled and waved, making sure the press down in front noticed. ". . . a man who has given us new dignity, new hope—Governor Vincent de Young!"

Another round of shouts and whistles and de Young stood up and clasped his hands over his head. He suffered through the traditional bear hug from the mayor, then strode over to a podium studded with a dozen microphones. He stood there for a moment looking out over the acres of faces and letting the chant of "De Young! De Young!" build to a crescendo. This was power, power you could feel.

He grinned at those in front of the speaker's stand, noticing that almost everyone had California state flag pins in their lapels or pinned to their shirts and blouses, then looked down at his watch. Just a few words, he reminded himself. It was only ten o'clock and already they were running an hour behind Shepherd's schedule.

He waved a hand and the chanting dwindled and stopped. Then he let righteous anger furrow his brow.

"We *demand* the return of our lands. We *demand* the right to conduct our own foreign trade and conclude those treaties regarding that trade. We *demand* the right to control our own revenues. And we *demand* the right to control our own government!"

He lowered his head as if in prayer, glancing at the rows of reporters and photographers below him, furiously scribbling notes or clicking away with cameras. They had damned well better be, he thought. They had just heard his first call for sovereignty in everything but name.

The cheering had begun to die and he threw up his hands. Silence swept the plaza.

"But to demand is no longer enough. We must act! Yesterday, the California delegation at the Second Constitutional Convention placed four amendments before that convention for consideration.

The first of them reads ... 'the fifty sovereign states are hereby granted the right of eminent domain over all federal lands within their borders.' "

He paused to let the tension build. Then he gripped the podium and leaned toward the microphones. "We have just received word that this morning that amendment was passed overwhelmingly by the convention!"

The cheering rolled across the plaza like a tide. He waited another moment, then launched into the brief wrap-up.

"We have now taken our destiny into our own hands! It's—time for the West!"

He waved once in response to the cheers, then began shaking the hands of the local politicians clustered around him. A state policeman tugged at his arm and he turned for a last wave at the crowd and hurried off the platform.

A platoon of police cleared a path for him from the speaker's platform to the black limousine parked nearby. Herb Shepherd was already in it, staring glumly at the crowd behind the wooden barricades. De Young slipped in beside him, yanking his sport jacket out of the way as a state trooper slammed the door.

Shepherd took out a small note pad and glanced at it. "You've got a rally in Portland at three and a rubber-chicken fund-raiser in Las Vegas at seven. There's a midnight meeting in Phoenix but we'll have to hump to make it."

It was a killing schedule, de Young thought. He watched the sunwashed buildings through the car windows for a minute, then turned back to Shepherd, faintly irritated by his moodiness. "You look like you lost your only friend, Herb."

"Burton's coming unstuck." Shepherd handed him a black briefing folder. "He's meeting us at the airport."

De Young opened the folder, pausing at the photograph mounted on the first page. George Burton looked sternly out at him in a three-quarter profile view that looked like it had been culled from an annual report. A grim, narrow face with obsidian banker's eyes.

Burton's list of vital statistics was in keeping with the photo. Current position: Chief Operating Officer of the California National Bank, San Francisco. Age: Fifty-three. Three children, two in college, the third retarded at birth. Wife: Penelope Pemberton, nickname, Penny. Former member President's Council of Economic Advisors, Foreign Affairs Council, Board of Directors, World

Bank—and on the boards of directors of fifteen different corporations. Likes: French-vanilla ice cream, pilsner beers. Dislikes: Rich foods. Hobbies: Philatelics and yachting.

Next to Walter Wriston of Citibank, George Burton was the country's most powerful banker.

"The General on the plane?"

Shepherd nodded. "He's flying with us to Portland."

De Young relaxed and yawned. Having Bolles around would reassure Burton. Besides, they weren't asking him for much right now—just that he use his influence to make sure his eastern financial friends remained neutral during the next six days. With rumors of secession, capital would start to flee the country and make it all the more difficult for Massey to maintain a stable government. With pessimistic reports from the bankers, the flight of capital would increase . . .

De Young turned to stare out the tinted windows. The crowds lined Century Boulevard for blocks, waving state flags and chanting "Time for the West! Time for the West!" as they drove by. Just before reaching the airport, the motorcade veered off onto an emergency access road and they sped across the tarmac toward a 727 waiting in a far corner.

De Young took the time to shake hands with the maintenance crew, then followed Shepherd up the portable steps. Over the 727's tail, he noticed a Lear jet rolling toward them. Burton, he thought, smiling—being super cautious and making sure that only those present knew of the meeting.

Inside the cabin, General Bolles and a ruddy-faced Carl Baxter were waiting for him at the bar that had been set up in the first-class cabin. Suspended from the overhead was a small color television set showing panoramic shots of the crowds along the boulevard.

Baxter grabbed his hand. "I watched your speech, Vince—you really had 'em going."

"I took a leaf from your book, Carl." He clapped Baxter on the back and turned to Bolles and Shepherd. "George Burton will be coming on board in a few minutes. I'd like you to sit in at the start of the meeting, General." He grinned at Shepherd. "Nothing like a general's uniform to help a banker find his backbone, right, Herb?"

He and Bolles had barely squeezed past the small galley into the conference room in back when Ray, the black security officer, pushed aside the curtains to announce Burton's arrival.

De Young strode to the doorway, grabbed Burton's right hand in both of his, and drew him into the compartment. "Herb told me you were coming, George—it's really great to see you."

Burton was taller than he looked in the photograph and thinner. The narrow face and the hard eyes were the same, however. Burton was the type who seldom smiled and never laughed.

"Good to see you, too, Vince. Penny sends her best—she's a great fan of yours." Burton was friendly but carefully distant.

De Young slipped an arm around Burton's shoulders and ushered him over to a group of royal blue lounge chairs at the rear of the cabin where General Bolles stood.

"General, I'd like you to meet George Burton, one of our most important supporters." De Young watched Burton's face carefully while they shook hands. "General Bolles is chairman of our Joint Chiefs, George—we've just been reviewing the military situation."

Bolles reached for his briar and lit it, smiling briefly. "Pleasure to have you aboard, Mr. Burton." It was just the right touch, de Young thought, approvingly.

He eased into one of the chairs and motioned for Burton to take one across from him, then pressed the button on the table console. He nodded at Bolles, who left at the same time that one of the state cops assigned to the flight came in.

"Two bottles of beer and some of that ham, Harry."

The state cop came back with a tray of food and beer. De Young made an open-faced sandwich of a slice of pumpernickel and ham and took a bite. Burton held his bottle of beer but didn't take a sip. He was too smart a man not to realize it was much too late to back out now, de Young thought.

He assembled another sandwich and said quietly, "George, what is it you'd like to talk about?"

"I'm not sure that I'm ... that *we* are doing the right thing. Frankly, Governor, I feel like a traitor."

De Young let a slight coldness creep into his voice. "Traitor to whom, George? I was elected to lead the people of my state. They're westerners and so am I. My loyalty is to them, not to some moribund geopolitical unit." De Young leaned across the table. "If I were to desert them now, when we are on the brink of the future, when they are filled with hope for the first time in years, I would feel like a traitor, too—to them."

He bit into his sandwich and poured the beer into a tall, frosted glass. "What about the people you represent, George? The businesses you've nurtured? Can they survive under the policies of the federal government? You don't have to tell me—I know they can't. Do you think it's going to get any better for them? You don't have to answer that, either. We both know it won't. Not under the present system."

Burton now poured his own beer and took a sip.

De Young decided all Burton needed was a little reassurance. " 'Any people anywhere being inclined and having the power have the right to rise up and shake off the existing government, and form a new one that suits them better.' Do you know who said that, George? Abraham Lincoln. In 1846."

De Young paused.

"You run the biggest bank in the West, George. You actually have a fiduciary relationship with millions of people. I think you owe it to them to ask yourself a question: Would they be better off with the United States of America guiding their destiny from Washington or with the Western States of America, a new country in which they would have vastly greater opportunity to determine their own future?"

He stared into Burton's eyes. "Your country needs you, George. And your country is the Western States of America."

Burton nodded, but his face remained impassive. "Exactly what do you want me to do, Vince?"

"George, I'm going to shock you. I don't want you to do a damned thing—except tell the truth. And prevail upon your eastern banking friends to tell the truth."

Burton looked blank. "I don't follow you."

De Young leaned closer. "When rumors of secession leak out, bankers and investors in the international community are going to be concerned about the financial stability of the United States. The Administration will want you to lie, to say the country is sound." He shrugged. "I think you ought to tell the truth, George. I think you ought to say you lack confidence in the financial policies of the United States Government."

Burton was nodding more enthusiastically now and he looked relieved. De Young got to his feet. Burton stood up and pumped his hand, smiling. "I think you can count on me, Governor—you have my word on it."

De Young smiled, lowering his voice to a confidential tone. "You know, the Western States of America is going to need a Secretary of Commerce, George. It should be someone with your connections in the international financial community, your outlook, your sense of patriotism."

He held up his hand. "You don't have to give me an answer now but I wanted you to know that we want you or somebody you can recommend."

They walked to the front cabin where Baxter was still glued to the television set, watching some footage that had been shot at the convention. Bolles was sitting quietly in the corner, going over reports. He glanced up at them, then stood up to shake hands with Burton. De Young gave the banker an affectionate clap on the shoulder.

"Wonderful to see you again, George. Give my best to Penny."

He was about to go back to the conference table with Bolles and Shepherd when the announcer's voice on the television set caught his attention.

"We rejoin the ABC network for a news bulletin from Washington, D.C." De Young turned just in time to see the network logo replace the blue-jacketed anchor man. Shepherd and Bolles pushed up to the bar to watch, as did the two state police who had been working in the galley.

A voice from the television set said, "We now take you to the White House briefing room." The logo faded and the outlines of the briefing room faded in. De Young caught his breath. Andy Livonas was standing next to Babs Massey in front of a forest of microphones.

The camera moved in for a close-up. Babs Massey's eyes were red, as if she had been crying. She looked straight into the cameras, making an obvious effort to control her voice.

"My husband, President Massey, suffered a physical collapse early this morning and is now under intensive care at Walter Reed Medical Center. He has asked Vice-President Whitman to assume the post of Acting President." Her voice cracked and she paused a moment to regain her composure. "Mr. Andrew Livonas, Acting President Whitman's aide, will answer your questions. I am sure that all of you will join me in praying for the President's recovery."

In the briefing room on the screen, the press corps stood up as Mrs. Massey left the room. De Young stared at the set. It was a brand-new ball game. Whitman wasn't about to make the same mistakes that Massey had. He swore to himself. Livonas was smart. With Babs announcing the replacement of Massey, nobody was going to ask embarrassing questions. Not right away.

"Brief me on the rest later, will you, Carl?" He nodded to Shepherd and Bolles. "General, Herb, could I see you in the conference room?"

He watched them while they sat down, sizing them up once again as he had a dozen times before. Shepherd had been with him for close to eight years now, the sharpest political strategist in the West, as a reporter had once called him. Bolles, with his military bearing, thin, aquiline face, and ever-present Dunhill briar, made the perfect general. It wasn't hard to imagine him inspiring confidence in the troops. The general was also acutely aware of the political cross-currents in the country.

Neither of them showed any hesitation or uncertainty now.

"I think we ought to assume that the federal government has learned of the secessionist movement," he began. They had agreed weeks ago that it was inevitable Washington would find out. The gamble had only been when.

Shepherd said, "I'll radio Hewitt to double your personal security. They'll probably try to arrest you."

"Do it later, Herb." He doubted that Whitman would send marshals after him and chance a provocation. Whitman would probably work around their perimeter, probing for weak spots, before he decided to come at them. One thing for sure, the Constitutional Convention would get rougher. He'd have to get in touch with Wagoner as soon as possible.

The word came over the intercom that they were about to take off and he buckled up. Once they were airborne, he moved over to the conference table. Shepherd took three yellow note pads from his briefcase and slid one over to him. De Young took out a silver fountain pen to make notes.

"The pluses for us are that Congress is in adjournment and it's going to take a few days to get everybody back to Washington. Whitman will find it difficult to move very fast. His first option, as Herb suggested, will be to send federal marshals to arrest us. He'll scope that out and reject it. The only real worry we have is the federal military."

He looked over at Bolles, who cleared his throat. His voice was patient, precise—the voice of the classroom instructor.

"I don't think that's a very real worry at all. Federal forces will be hamstrung, by and large, because there'll be opposing loyalties down to the platoon level at almost every military base and on every Navy ship. It will take time for personnel to jump one way or the other. On the other hand, I would say that our own state national guards and air national guard units are completely reliable, as are various ships and bases where we've been able to transfer in loyal personnel and transfer out those who might not go along."

Bolles fumbled for his pipe again. "By the time things start to sort themselves out, the Western States of America will have been recognized by a number of nations—all those along the Pacific Rim, the Soviets, Eastern Europe, probably a half dozen African countries."

Shepherd was staring at the general with narrowed eyes. He and Bolles had never seen eye to eye, de Young thought, one of the virtues of having them both on the team. Each could play devil's advocate for the other.

"If it comes right down to it, General, how do we fight a civil war?"

"Military action?" Bolles seemed reluctant to use the word "war." "I think by tomorrow night various guard units will be in a position to establish roadblocks at the vital mountain passes in the Rockies. We should also be in a position to secure all civilian airports with runways long enough to land jets. Military air bases might be more of a problem, but I doubt it; I've already mentioned split loyalties at most bases and I imagine conditions will be pretty chaotic in case of any . . . action."

He tamped down the tobacco in his pipe and took his time lighting it. "We're self-sufficient as far as food and energy go. There may be an attempt to blockade West Coast ports but it'd be difficult to mount, especially when the command infrastructure of a large part of the Pacific Fleet is loyal to the West."

Bolles, like Wagoner, was too confident, de Young thought. But then, perhaps he had a right to be. He had been working on the problems of the federal military for more than a year.

"What about the Air Force?"

Bolles shrugged. "That's the quickest and the easiest service to sort itself out, in one sense. We have the air national guards in the western states. General Casey can probably hamstring SAC, if not control it." He smiled at Shepherd. "I rather doubt that Americans are going to nuke each other, but we'd be quite capable of strafing invading troops or bombing supply lines."

"There's got to be a down side," Shepherd insisted. "It's not going to be a piece of cake."

Bolles looked thoughtful. "I didn't mean to imply it was. Given the long haul, it would be difficult for us to hang onto Louisiana and parts of Texas and Oklahoma. The terrain's hardly in our favor. On the other hand, federal troops would have to take territory. All we have to do is keep it."

De Young tried to fight his own feelings of elation. After Burton, it was refreshing to hear someone who was sure of himself, who was confident. The federal government's hands were tied, politically and militarily, and in the short time before the convention he didn't see anything that even Bob Whitman could do to change that.

But they weren't out of the woods yet and he didn't quite trust military men, not even Bolles. They had a tendency to want to play with their toys.

"I can't stress too much that this is a political problem," he said. "If it comes down to civil war, whichever side fires the first shot is at a great disadvantage. That shot will determine who the underdog is—with everything that implies for public opinion both here and abroad. Martyrdom has always been a great rallying point." He looked at Bolles while he talked, watching for a reaction.

Bolles leaned back in his chair. For one of the few times since de Young had known him, he looked completely relaxed. "The breakup of the United States is inevitable, Vincent. If not this year, then definitely the next or the year after that. We're not talking about just the secession of the West. We're talking about the fragmentation of the United States in the face of the collapse of the authority of the central government."

"That's pretty theoretical," Shepherd objected.

Bolles puffed on his pipe and laced his fingers behind his head. "Is it? The ties that bind the states have been unraveling for a long time. The economies are too different, so are the life-styles. Choosing between the East and the West is like choosing between living in the nineteenth century or the twenty-first. It's no contest."

After Bolles had gone up front, de Young said, "He sounds pretty confident."

"Too confident." Shepherd looked unhappy.

"What's your complaint?"

Shepherd glanced at the curtains. Behind them there was the sound of the television set and occasional laughter at something Baxter had said in his loud Texas twang.

"He's a rear-echelon general," he said glumly.

For Shepherd, every silver lining had a cloud, de Young thought. He pressed the table button and asked the state policeman to bring another pot of coffee.

"One last thing," Shepherd said. He was smiling now and de Young knew he had been saving something.

"It's not Christmas yet, Herb—what's the surprise?"

"Anthony Cabot will be in Seattle. He wants to talk to you."

Cabot. The Secretary of the Treasury in Massey's Administration. Ex-chairman of the Securities and Exchange Commission. One of the East's own.

He leaned back and stared at Shepherd for a long moment, then murmured, "Nice job, Herb." Shepherd looked like he had just been scratched behind the ears. "Nice job," de Young repeated.

The coffee came and he poured himself a cup and turned to gaze out the window at the billowing bed of white clouds below. What a strange and marvelous feeling to know your destiny is at hand, he thought.

December 21

7:45 P.M., *Monday*

"At this time, the Chair will entertain a motion to permit Andrew Livonas, Chief of the White House Staff, to read a short statement from Acting President Robert Whitman."

"So moved!" Livonas recognized Wagoner's bellow, silencing the rumble of boos from the right side of the hall. Wagoner was dusting off his fair-minded image, he thought cynically. The chairman called for a voice vote, then turned the podium over to him.

Looking out over the rows of sullen faces, Livonas spotted Wagoner in an aisle seat just beneath the California standard. He sat with his arms folded, his face expressionless. Rudd had wanted to arrest Wagoner and the top leadership of the Western Coalition. He had argued against Rudd, urging that Whitman send a statement to the convention instead. Whitman had sided with him against the general.

There was going to be trouble from Rudd. He and the general disagreed on almost every issue. Earlier in the day, they had discussed how to respond to de Young's address at a convention of the Sagebrush Rebellion in Ogden, Utah. The governor hadn't called for secession but he had come close. Whitman had decided that to accuse de Young of plotting it would give the governor an advantage. "Let the bastard figure out how to float that one himself."

Livonas unfolded the paper he had taken from his pocket and fought back last-minute nervousness. "Ladies and gentlemen, President Whitman regrets that he's unable to be here with you this evening. In his stead, he's asked me to read a short message to the convention."

He waited a moment for the flashes from the photographers' strobes to die down. Whitman had wanted to address the convention himself but Rudd had vetoed it on the grounds of security, and Dr. Mills, the heart specialist from Walter Reed, had warned it would be too strenuous.

Livonas cleared his throat and concentrated on the paper in front of him. " 'Fellow delegates, in my unique position as our country's first Acting President, I want to share with you my profound belief in your historic role as delegates to the Second Constitutional Convention. It is my fervent hope that each of us, in our own way, occupying unusual positions in our still young Republic, can work together in the spirit of cooperation and find the remedies for the grievous and difficult situation in which we find our country. I extend to you my best wishes. Signed, Robert Whitman, Acting President of the United States of America.' "

The applause was polite if not prolonged. Livonas threaded his way off the stage and back to where Katy sat. He had just sat down when there were cries and shouts in the back of the hall. He glanced around. Reporters were streaming up the center aisle to where a group of burly monitors and members of the Western Coalition had gathered in an angry knot just inside the main doors.

Other delegates climbed on their chairs to see what was happening. Across the aisle a woman in her mid-twenties with a mane of ash-blond hair and wearing a Pennsylvania State sweater two sizes too large was saying to nobody in particular, "They tried to arrest Allen—the assholes tried to arrest Allen!"

Katy looked up, alarmed. "Who?" Stu Lambert hurried over and the four of them stood facing the back of the hall.

"Federal marshals," the girl said. "The Supreme Court issued bench warrants for the convention leadership."

Katy turned to Livonas. "Those stupid shits."

Livonas shook his head. "It's a setup. Burger gave me his word no warrants would be issued. The *Washington Post* ran an interview with Burger this morning in which he said the same thing."

Stu Lambert pushed into the aisle for a better view. The growing knot of people by the main doors had turned into a procession moving down the aisle with the solemnity of a funeral cortege. Allen, a tall, delicately built, slump-shouldered man in his late forties, hobbled along in the center of a group of monitors, holding a compress against his sandy brown hair. Jerry Wagoner was guiding him.

"Who's Allen, Katy?" Livonas asked.

"Chairman of the Texas delegation—leader of the Sun Belt faction within the Western Coalition." The marshals now spread out in a line below the podium while Wagoner and several others helped Allen up the steps. "Do you think they're going to call for secession now?" She sounded apprehensive.

Livonas considered it a moment. De Young must realize that once they pushed through a resolution to secede, the leadership of the Western Coalition faced certain arrest. Then it occurred to him what Wagoner was up to.

"My guess is they're going to try and move the convention out of D.C.," he said slowly. "Can you stop them?"

"We haven't won a vote all week."

She sounded irritated and Livonas squeezed her forearm. "We're on the same side, remember?"

"Sorry." She smiled faintly and turned to Lambert. "Ask Jonathan to take his group around to the floor microphone in the right-hand aisle."

Livonas looked surprised. "Goodwell?"

Katy nodded."What we need is a loud-mouthed lawyer and that's what we're going to get."

The Chair gaveled again for order. "The Chair recognizes Thomas Allen, chairman of the Texas delegation, who rises on a point of personal privilege."

On the podium, Allen limped slowly over to the microphone. There was an ugly welt high on his forehead.

"Coming back from dinner I was accosted by two federal marshals." He spoke in a trembling Texas drawl. "They showed me a paper they said was a bench warrant for my arrest, issued by the United States Supreme Court. I told them the Court had no authority over my actions as a delegate and then I said good night." Allen paused to rally his strength.

Lambert now brushed past Livonas followed by four other men and two tall, solemn-faced young women. They arranged a barrier of empty folding chairs around where Livonas and Katy and other Federal Coalition delegates were sitting.

On the podium, Allen sucked in a breath. ". . . then they grabbed me and told me to shut my 'fucking cracker mouth.' They said by tonight every member of the convention's leadership would be in jail for contempt of court."

His voice turned shrill. "When they tried to handcuff me, I broke away. They chased me right to the doors." He pulled his left hand from his pocket and raised it above his head. The theatrical spots above the stage glinted off the chrome handcuffs that dangled from his wrist. A roar of outrage filled the hall.

"Liberty or death!" Allen shouted. The convention started to take up the chant, then was gaveled into silence by the grim-faced chairman.

"The Chair recognizes Jerry Wagoner, chairman of the California delegation."

"If he calls for secession now," Katy said, "it'll pass."

"He won't," Livonas said with a confidence he didn't quite feel. He turned to watch the woman in the bulky Pennsylvania state sweater take a small transistor amplifier from beneath it and pass it over to Lambert, making sure to keep it below chair level and out of sight.

"Fellow delegates." Wagoner looked sternly out over the floor. "The Second Constitutional Convention is under siege. We have to decide whether to fight or surrender."

Shouts of "Fight! Fight!" filled the hall. Before it could settle into a chant, Wagoner silenced it with a raised hand.

"The federal government, the Congress, the Supreme Court and the Executive—and it doesn't matter if it's President Massey, who is an easterner, or Acting President Whitman who acts like one—have opposed this convention from the very beginning. First, they ignored it. Then they belittled it. Now they're suppressing it."

Wagoner paused to let the tension mount. "Thomas Allen is not the only victim. Let's not forget the mysterious murder of the young California intern, Steven Hart, nor the harassment that delegates experience daily, and finally, this threat of arrest for any of us who stand by our duties at this Second Constitutional Convention—the only governmental body that is truly responsive to the interests of the people of this country."

He waited until the applause had peaked, then waved for silence. In addition to his other talents, Livonas thought, Jerry Wagoner was an accomplished demagogue.

"There is a solution, a solution our Founding Fathers used over two hundred years ago."

Livonas felt Katy's fingers dig into his arm, her face white. "He's going to call for secession."

"In 1776 when the British threatened to arrest the members of the Continental Congress for treason if they convened their convention in Boston, the first American patriots moved to the safer territory of Philadelphia where they drafted the Declaration of Independence."

He was right after all, Livonas thought, relieved.

"Washington, D.C., is hostile territory. Delegates have been threatened with arrest, beaten, even murdered. The city of Denver, whose deputy mayor, Ted Brown, is a delegate from Colorado, has opened its arms to us as a refuge. I therefore submit as a motion that the Second Constitutional Convention, unable to discharge its duties in the District of Columbia, adjourn immediately to Denver, Colorado, where we will reconvene at the Convention Arena at nine in the morning, December twenty-sixth."

Wagoner, with a slight bob of his head, stepped back from the podium. Shouts of "So moved" and "Second" rose above the applause. Lambert leaned in front of Livonas and handed Katy a microphone. He knelt down to plug the other end into the amplifier hidden under Katy's chair and covered by a paper bag. Two sets of leads ran beneath Livonas's feet, one to a woman's oversized carpetbag and the other to a blue coat that had been dropped on the floor between two Vermont delegates.

Lambert scrambled to his feet. "I learned my lesson when they pushed the Supreme Court resolution through. This baby delivers two hundred watts a channel."

After a hurried consultation, the chairman reclaimed the microphone. "The question before the body is resolved: The Second Constitutional Convention will adjourn immediately and reconvene December twenty-sixth at nine A.M. at the Convention Arena in Denver, Colorado.

"Because the well-being of the members of this body is in jeopardy, the Chair rules that the previous question is a resolution to adjourn and hence cannot be debated or amended or have subsidiary motions attached."

Katy gaped. "That sleazy son-of-a-bitch!"

"Point of order, Mr. Chairman!" Livonas could hear Goodwell's voice from across the hall even though his microphone was dead. "I call for a division of the question! Two motions have been made, one to adjourn, which requires no debate, and the other to relocate the convention more than fifteen hundred miles away. I submit that a debate is in order."

The chairman turned to look in Goodwell's direction. "The Chair has ruled that the motion is indivisible, Mr. Goodwell. The physical safety of our membership is in jeopardy. Your point of order is overruled."

"I challenge the ruling," Goodwell shot back.

Livonas watched as the monitors began working their way over to the other side of the hall where Goodwell was standing.

"Will the delegate from New York please be seated? You are disrupting the convention. I have already ruled on your point of order."

Goodwell stepped into the aisle. "You have ruled incorrectly!" he shouted.

"Go get 'em, Jonathan," Lambert muttered.

"You're out of order. Will the sergeant-at-arms please remove the New York delegate from the floor so that we may proceed."

"Point of order! The challenge must be put to the body for a vote!" A tide of red blazers were closing in on Goodwell.

Katy stepped up on a folding chair, using Livonas's shoulder for balance. In front of them, delegates took the speakers out of the carpetbag and from beneath the blue coat. The other delegates around them stood up, forming a human barricade.

"Mr. Chairman, I rise to a point of personal privilege affecting this assembly." Katy's voice boomed throughout the hall. Lambert was right, Livonas thought, delighted. The rig was almost as powerful as the central PA system.

The chairman sounded exasperated. "Madame Delegate, state your question."

"We have listened to Jerry Wagoner slander, vilify, and degrade the Supreme Court of our country—"

"Madame, you are out of order. State your question." The chairman's voice had developed an angry edge. Livonas tensed. Monitors were streaming toward them.

"Mr. Allen's story is as phony as those handcuffs that could have been purchased in any pawn shop in the city or borrowed from a member of the sergeant-at-arms's goon squad. If Mr. Wagoner had spoken with the clerk of the Supreme Court at any time throughout the day, he would have known that contempt warrants were never issued."

She had succeeded in getting the delegates' attention, Livonas thought. Even some of the members of the Western Coalition were listening.

"Or if Mr. Wagoner had taken the time to read the interview with Justice Burger in the *Washington Post* this morning, he would've known that these so-called warrants don't exist, that the Chief Justice stated he has no plans to issue any."

Strobes were now flashing at Katy from every direction. The chant of "Bullshit!" began to spread through the Western Coalition as the first monitors waded into the wall of delegates surrounding them.

Livonas rushed forward to where the fighting had begun but the barricade of delegates held. Above him, on the chair, Katy was cutting her speech short. The sergeant-at-arms now angrily pulled his men back. It had been a mistake to initiate a physical confrontation on the floor. All you had to do was look at the sympathetic faces of the uncommitted delegates as they strained to hear Katy's words above the chant of "Bullshit!"

Katy finished in a hurry. "Therefore, Mr. Chairman, I strongly urge that the convention vote 'no' on the previous question."

The chanting competed with the chairman's gavel as he fought to regain control of the floor. Stu and Livonas helped Katy down from her perch, then Lambert took her place to survey the hall.

"The question is," the chairman bellowed, " 'Resolved, the Constitutional Convention is hereby adjourned to be reconvened at nine A.M. Mountain Time, December twenty-sixth, at the Denver, Colorado, Convention Arena.' All those in favor, stand."

Livonas looked around the hall. The right side of the auditorium, where the Western Coalition sat, was a forest of standing bodies. Toward the center, the standees thinned out dramatically. He glanced at Lambert, who was smiling broadly. Not only did it look like they had carried most of the uncommitted delegates, but they had made slight inroads among the Western Coalition.

"All those opposed?"

Lambert stared out over the center section, his smile turning into a pinched frown. He hopped down off his chair. "They're not voting with us, either."

Livonas guessed that the uncommitted delegates, unsure who to believe, were abstaining. Lambert looked totally disgusted, his disappointment spreading to the other delegates around him.

"The convention is adjourned."

Katy poked him in the ribs. "Don't be such a hard-ass, Lambert. If the center abstains, the West doesn't get their three-quarters majority. With a little more work, they won't even have a two-thirds."

"Yeah, you're right," Lambert admitted.

The delegates filed out of the hall while the convention secretary droned out the charter flights for Denver that night and the following morning. De Young wasn't wasting any time, Livonas thought.

The core of the Federal Coalition was filling up the chairs around them now and Lambert announced that a caucus was scheduled in the main meeting room of the Mayflower Hotel in an hour. Joanie Spero, the girl who had hidden the amplifier under her sweater, eased in beside Lambert, who put his arm around her. Livonas wasn't sure who moved close to whom but found himself slipping his arm loosely around Katy.

"New York wants to walk out." A disheveled Jonathan Goodwell edged through a cluster of folding chairs and joined them.

Tom Evarts, still looking outraged, nodded in agreement. "I'm for it, tying a move to Denver together with a motion to adjourn was totally out of order."

"We could call a press conference for tomorrow and announce the walkout," Goodwell said.

"How many delegates would actually leave?" Livonas asked.

Everybody looked at Lambert, who pulled out a note pad. "I'd say two hundred would walk and six hundred would go to Denver—the other hundred and fifty could go either way."

Livonas shook his head. "Most of the one-fifty will go to Denver. Parliamentary niceties aside, the fact remains that's where the convention is going."

Katy nodded. "Livonas is right. If the uncommitted delegates had voted with us, it'd be different. If we call a walkout, it'll look like we're giving up."

Just behind Livonas, Debbie Spindler said, "A lot of the Western Coalition didn't vote, either. I was counting in the center section."

Katy sounded more positive. "A boycott would formalize the East-West split."

She'd convince the rest of them, Livonas thought. It would be better if he stayed out of it. The delegates would resent any federal interference.

The group started to break up. "Anybody for a bite before the meeting?" Lambert asked. A half dozen peeled off with him and headed for the doors.

Livonas pulled Katy away from the group. "Is everything going to be all right?" He couldn't keep the worry out of his voice. A boycott now would be absolute disaster.

A tired smile brushed across her face. "It'll be all right, just a long meeting is all." She shook her head. "What a way to spend Christmas week—I don't think I've even seen a tree."

"If necessary, make some broad hints about the secession." Livonas's mind was still on the caucus.

She slipped into her coat. "Don't worry—I've got it covered, all right?"

"You know, we're in a lot of trouble," he said. "Once the convention's in Denver, de Young will have an even tighter hold on it."

"We did the best we could," she said, half-angry.

He changed the subject. "There's an eight o'clock meeting at the White House tomorrow morning. Bob would appreciate it if you could make it."

She nodded. "Of course."

They were alone in the deserted hall and the lights started to wink out around the sides. Katy was beautiful even when she was tired, he thought.

"What are you doing after the caucus?"

"Nothing, absolutely nothing." She looked up at him. "I'd invite you to my house but it's a total mess—I was half packed before I decided I wasn't going back to Seattle."

"How about my place?"

"Why not?" she kissed him lightly on the lips, then turned to catch up with the others.

He stood in the middle of the ocean of empty chairs and watched her until she had vanished through the doors.

Livonas sat at his kitchen table reviewing the latest intelligence briefings on Vincent de Young: a speech in Los Angeles; a trip to Portland and Las Vegas; a list of foreign dignitaries reported to have visited him in Sacramento during the last week; and a pointed memo from the NSC reporting that the governor now flew with a fighter escort from the California Air National Guard.

Then the doorbell rang. Katy brought in the crisp smell of the night air mixed with the faint scent of her perfume. They smiled at one another and embraced, a mixture of awkwardness and desire that made him tentative and unsure.

Katy tilted her head back. "God, it's cold out there tonight." She pressed against him. "You're so warm," she said, and sought his lips.

Livonas slipped his hands beneath her clothing and Katy did the same to him. Her fingertips danced down the length of his spine, massaging the muscles of his shoulders, pulling him against her.

Livonas's hands kept returning to her breasts, delighting in their shape, their tautness, and the pleasure his touch gave her. He pressed against her, forward, back, to either side, their legs between each other's. His hand slid over the soft contours of her stomach and through the silky forest of her sex. Then her hands slid around the front of him, running up and down his length.

"Let's go to bed," he finally said.

They stumbled through the bedroom door, collapsing together on the quilt. Livonas undressed her, touching her and kissing her, and while he did so, marveling in the lean softness of her body.

Katy, naked, sat up, turning to push him flat on the mattress. "Your turn," she said. Livonas let himself be undressed, taking pleasure in her delight in touching him. Then, naked, they lay slightly apart, exploring each other's bodies with their hands until

Livonas could no longer stand the waiting and pulled her to him. Katy reached out and guided him inside her.

Livonas lost himself in the sound, the smell, and the movement of their lovemaking, putting off his orgasm, feeling hers until he lost control and thrust deep as the spasms shot up through his groin and spread throughout his body. He clung to her until the sensations started to slow.

Then they lay against each other, still joined, his hand resting on her cheek. And finally, they slept.

Sometime in the early morning, they made a dinner of ale and smoked oysters that Katy had found behind a can of tomato soup. She set the table—a napkin spread out between them on the bed— and they sat with their backs against the wall, not saying much of anything as they speared the oysters from the tin with toothpicks and passed a single bottle of ale back and forth between them. "Glasses are a pain in the ass in bed," Katy had said.

Livonas watched her as she glanced around the bedroom. His apartment was the top floor of a two-story nineteenth-century townhouse with the bedroom in back, overlooking a vine-covered garden. Katy's eyes kept coming back to the silver-framed photograph of Wendy that he kept on the dresser opposite the bed. It was a small color shot that Gus Frankel had taken of Wendy standing in front of a beach ball, laughing.

"That's my daughter, Wendy," he said quietly. "She died when she was three."

Katy looked at him, her eyes brooding. "It must still hurt."

He speared another oyster. "Not so much now. Sometimes I dream that she's still alive, grown up." He looked away.

Katy leaned over and traced the vein in the side of his neck with her finger. "You're a very private man, Andrew Livonas," she said in a husky voice.

He reached up and took her hand and pulled her to him. Then they made love until the clock radio reminded them of the morning meeting at the White House.

December 22

8:00 A.M., *Tuesday*

"We have five days until Governor de Young calls for the secession of the West from the United States. Five days," Whitman repeated, looking around the Cabinet Room.

The room was stuffy from too many bodies and Livonas could feel the start of a headache. He sat between Katy Houseman and Hugh Ramsay, now de facto energy chief. Whitman was at the head of the oval table with the military delegation to his right and the congressional delegation to his left.

Katy nudged him in the ribs. "I don't see Roger Anderson," she whispered.

"Resigned," Livonas said.

"Tibbetts isn't here either," she added.

Livonas looked sour. The FBI director had left for the coast with four deputy directors in a Lear jet full of files, one jump ahead of a contingent of Rudd's Black Berets. Jeff Saunders was now acting director. Tibbetts's defection explained why the Massey Administration had been kept in the dark about de Young's plans. It also shed some light on the murder of Steven Hart. Saunders had found an entry in one of the night-duty logs with notes from a call Hart had made to the FBI an hour before his death.

"Mr. Reynolds?" Whitman looked over the top of his glasses at the Secretary of State.

Al Reynolds started to speak, then broke into a fit of coughing. There was a nervous stir in the room as they waited for the frail Secretary of State to recover.

"I don't think there's any doubt that the moment de Young announces the formation of the Western States of America, a number of countries will grant diplomatic recognition. Not only the Pacific Rim bloc, as Mr. Livonas calls them, but certainly the Soviets will, as well as a whole host of other countries that perceive a weakened United States as being in their best interests."

Whitman turned to Rudd. "General?"

"The military situation isn't quite as bleak as Mr. Livonas

painted in his report earlier, Mr. President." Rudd smiled slightly as he said the title. "There are strong federal bases in the West."

Rudd was dealing too much in supposition, Livonas thought. "Loyal troops?" he interrupted. For a moment, he was afraid Whitman was going to tell him to keep quiet. Instead, Whitman settled back in his chair, obviously wanting to hear some debate.

"What makes you think they're not?" Rudd countered. "Aside from the defection of an occasional commander."

"I'm sure pockets of troops would be loyal," Livonas said. "But General Bolles isn't the only commander who's defected. And in Bolles's case, he's not just a supporter of de Young but, from all we can tell, a co-conspirator. I think we can assume that over the past few years Bolles has used his position and his contacts to winnow western bases of most eastern troops. The bottom line is that de Young can depend on the loyalty of western bases more than we can on the loyalty of eastern."

Rudd's face grew hard but Whitman cut in before he could object. "General, see if we can get some sort of loyalty check on the top commanders. Have the computers do a breakdown by state of residence of both enlisted men and officers. After that, we can draw up plans for transferring various units and try to make a realistic assessment of our military strength."

He turned to Ramsay. "Hugh, how badly can de Young hurt us?"

Ramsay looked unhappy. He pulled a few sheets from his briefcase.

"Five days from now, they'll have us by the short hairs. If those states west of the hundredth meridian, along with Texas and Alaska, secede and cut off the oil flow, we'll lose seventy percent of the crude oil production in this country plus all the output of the synfuel plants in Utah, Wyoming, and Colorado.

"If we lose Louisiana too, we lose more than eighty-two percent of our crude oil production as well as the natural gas reserves of the Tuscaloosa Trend—the largest in the country. I would assume the westerners would cut the East-West oil pipeline and the natural gas pipelines feeding north from the Trend. Plus we have to consider the hydroelectric power the West feeds into the national power grid. If that were cut off without warning, it could black out the eastern half of the country."

A small red light blinked on and Whitman picked up the phone, listened for a moment, and murmured, "Bring it in."

The young army lieutenant looked pale as he handed Whitman a sealed envelope. He saluted and left. Whitman broke the seal and read the message through twice. The others in the Cabinet Room stared at him, curious.

He cleared his throat, then read in a steady voice: "Regret to inform you that President Thomas Massey committed suicide by hanging himself from the lighting fixture in his room at Walter Reed. Estimated time of death 0730. Signed, Captain Frank Edmonds, Walter Reed Army Medical Center."

General Rudd stood up. "I'm sure all of us share with you a sense of grief at this tragedy, Mr. President. But President Massey's suicide will result in a serious questioning of the method and manner in which he was relieved of office. The press will speculate—it's only a matter of days, probably hours, before the extent of the current crisis becomes public knowledge. We should put whatever leeway we have to good use."

The shocked silence was broken next by Manny Cudahy. "Mr. President, General Rudd is right. Once this gets out, there'll be trouble."

Rudd urged, "I can have a battalion of Black Berets in Sacramento in three hours; we can arrest de Young for treason."

Whitman stared at Rudd, his face betraying nothing. Livonas felt his stomach knot. Rudd was pressing. He had argued the same course of action yesterday and Whitman had vetoed it. Using Massey's death for leverage, Rudd was trying to go over Whitman's head. He hoped to drum up support for the plan in the meeting and use collective pressure to force Whitman to okay it.

Whitman's face still showed no reaction.

Rudd hardly glanced at Whitman. He was playing to the room. "In my opinion, decisive action is necessary if the Chief Executive is not to lose credibility, especially among the military." The generals who flanked Rudd nodded.

Whitman smiled. Livonas guessed he was the only one present who knew Whitman's smile was anything but friendly.

"General Rudd, by the Chief Executive, I presume you're referring to me?"

Rudd relaxed visibly, assuming he had forced Whitman to agree. "You are the Chief Executive, sir."

Whitman caught Livonas's eye; the glance clearly meant stay-out-of-this-Andy. He wanted to see how the people in the room would choose up sides.

"I think General Rudd has a point, Bob." James Hartwell, Livonas noted, surprised. He had pegged the Massachusetts senator as an appeaser. "If we don't think it's politically advisable to use the military, we could send in a group of U.S. marshals to arrest de Young."

"What about declaring a national emergency and federalizing the national guards of all the states, including those west of the hundredth meridian?" Attorney General Knox was hastening to back what he perceived to be a trend.

Livonas stirred uneasily in his chair. He had thought Knox was more clear-headed than to make such a harebrained suggestion. The national guards of the western states would refuse to be federalized and they would be faced with an open rebellion right then.

It was Katy Houseman who spoke up next. "It's not yet a hundred percent certain that de Young will win in the convention."

Rudd glanced at her, dismissing the statement. "I think we're giving the Constitutional Convention too much weight. The Supreme Court has enjoined it; let's close the damn thing down and call de Young's bluff."

Livonas glanced around the room. Rudd was taking over the meeting, coming off as a leader, a man of action. And he was swaying others.

"If there's going to be a civil war," Rudd continued, "what difference does it make if it starts now or five days from now when de Young announces his plans to secede. Either way, we've got a fight on our hands." He turned to Whitman. "The key thing is to reestablish the credibility and authority of the federal government."

Whitman slowly got to his feet, pointedly ignoring Rudd. "Andy, see that a statement is released to the press that President Massey died suddenly at Walter Reed Medical Center this morning."

Rudd started to object. "It won't wash—"

Whitman turned angrily to Rudd, cutting him off.

"General, we could give the press the thread count of the sheet with which Tom Massey hanged himself and the press would speculate that he actually jumped out the window instead. I don't give a damn what the press says—it can't help speculating about such matters any more than a dog can help pissing on fire hydrants. Tom Massey *was* a desperately sick man and he certainly died suddenly. Out of deference to his widow, if for no other reason, this office is not going to comment on the morbid details."

Rudd remained standing, trying to face Whitman down. Livonas smiled. The general was six inches too short for that.

Whitman's voice was ice. "I'm really surprised that you seem so concerned about the credibility of this office, General. I've spent the last three years watching you push and bully President Massey. When he needed his confidence bolstered, you undercut it. When he needed advice, you withheld it. When he needed support, you belittled him."

"I don't—"

"I'm not through yet, General. I've sat here in this very meeting and listened to you propose an obviously dangerous course of action and then imply a possible military insurrection if I didn't go along."

Rudd paled. "Mr. President, I didn't mean to—"

"Crap, General, of course you meant to." Whitman let his voice soften. "But you were just bluffing, or should I say bullying."

Whitman paused, letting Rudd's embarrassment fill the silent room. "General, I'm not going to ask for your resignation. What I am going to do is ask for your loyalty." He stood over Rudd, staring down at him. "Now, do I have it or not, General?"

Rudd looked up, his face white. "Yes, Mr. President," he said in a low voice. "I know I can speak for the Joint Chiefs as well." The general seemed oddly relieved.

Whitman returned to his seat. "Seeking a political solution to the present crisis will remain the strategy of this Administration. The following steps will be taken immediately.

"One—I will declare a state of national emergency. This will give the executive the necessary powers to deal with the contingencies of the next few days. At my request, Attorney General Knox has already drawn up the orders.

"Two—Senator Kennedy and Congressman Gorman will call both Houses of Congress back into emergency session for the duration of the crisis.

"Three—we will federalize the national guards of the various states and put them on active duty under the command of General Rudd." He looked directly at the general. "However, there will be no attempt to enforce the federalization in states west of the hundredth meridian.

"Four—we will form a smaller standing task force to deal with the current situation. It will consist of Andy Livonas, General Rudd, Mr. Ramsay, Attorney General Knox, Al Reynolds, FBI Director Saunders, Mr. White of the Central Intelligence Agency, and Kathleen Houseman, leader of the Federal Coalition at the Constitutional Convention. Until further notice, we'll convene in the Cabinet Room at seven thirty each morning to review the situation and make whatever adjustments are necessary to deal with it."

He glanced again at Rudd. "Finally, General Rudd will draw up a military contingency plan to be considered in the event our attempts to solve the crisis by political means fail." He stood up. "I guess that pretty much covers everything."

Not quite, Livonas thought. "Mr. President"—the title still sounded strange to him when he was talking to Whitman—"you should be sworn in as soon as possible. Perhaps everyone could wait here until the Chief Justice is located? And we should invite in the press."

Whitman nodded. "Let's give ourselves an hour and then we'll reconvene in the Lincoln Room for the ceremony." Livonas thought he looked profoundly sad. "It seems like the appropriate setting, doesn't it?"

December 22

11:00 A.M., *Tuesday*

Whitman leaned back in the green leather swivel chair and watched the snowflakes swirling among the trees that bordered the Ellipse. He thought he could still smell the faint odor from the Scotch that Massey had spilled. The image of Massey that popped into his mind right then wasn't of the drunk they had relieved yesterday morning but of the Massey who had been their host when he and Viv had joined him in the presidential box at the Washington Senators opening game. For a brief few hours, Tom had relaxed and regaled them with anecdotes about Philadelphia. He had been very funny and very human . . .

"You're not listening," Livonas said.

Whitman sighed and turned in his swivel chair to face Livonas, pacing in front of the desk. He didn't want to discuss Rudd.

"Andy, this afternoon I'm going to have to browbeat a dozen different ambassadors. I'm going to have to say a little but imply a lot, and, above all, not show weakness of any kind." He drummed his fingers on the desk top. "Funny. In a lot of respects, the job *does* require a Thomas Massey, somebody familiar with makeup and lighting, as you once put it."

"What happens if, in Rudd's opinion, things don't work out?" Livonas asked bluntly.

Whitman was annoyed. "Rudd's our link to the military establishment. He's a son-of-a-bitch but he's our son-of-a-bitch and he commands the military's respect. He also has the respect of the international military community, which means the Russians. So get along with him."

"Sorry, Mr. President," Livonas said stiffly.

"Come off it, Andy. 'Bob' to you." He yawned, his flush of anger fading. "You know, you and Rudd are a lot alike."

"You mean we're both arrogant pricks?"

Whitman laughed. That was the key difference between the two men. Andy could laugh at himself. He doubted that Rudd ever had.

"Not arrogant, particularly—forceful would be more like it. What I meant was that, like you, Rudd saw catastrophe coming and tried to do something about it."

Livonas considered it for a moment. "There's one thing you can put Rudd to work on right away."

Whitman blinked. "What'd you have in mind?"

"Louisiana," Livonas said slowly. "The offshore oil rigs. From Ramsay's report, I think it would be important to secure them."

Whitman frowned. "There's a certain contradiction there, Andy."

"I know," Livonas said. "But we can't let ourselves get boxed into a position where we avoid confrontation at all costs."

"When you say costs, what are you thinking of?"

Livonas flushed. "I think we should get Rudd's opinion on that."

Whitman nodded. "I want to meet with the crisis task force right after the ceremony. I'll bring it up then."

Livonas sat down, teetering back in his chair and lacing his fingers behind his head. "Have you thought of a candidate for Vice-President?"

"I've decided on Hartwell. He has national stature and, most important, I think he could heal the wounds between the two regions. He's got strong ties in the West but he's certainly loyal to the federal government."

Livonas let his chair down so all legs were on the floor. "Last time de Young was in Washington, he and Hartwell were pretty chummy."

Whitman wasn't in the mood for another argument with Livonas and was about to say so when the intercom buzzed. "The Chief Justice is here, sir," a faintly metallic voice said.

Whitman thumbed the talk switch. "We'll be right there." He turned back to Livonas. "For Christ's sake, Andy, a lot of people were chummy with de Young. The man's a national figure. In any case, Hartwell seems to have a pretty hard position on de Young now. And incidentally, we should include him on the crisis management team. Ask him to join us at this afternoon's meeting."

Livonas started to protest but Whitman held up his hand. "Check him out, but I'm going to announce his name later today and I want a joint hearing of the judiciary committees of the House and Senate as soon as there's a quorum back in town."

He stood up, cutting off any further discussion. "Let's not keep the Chief Justice waiting."

December 23
9:00 A.M., *Wednesday*

Hartwell was right on time, Livonas thought, but then he'd hardly expected him to be late. The senator entered the hearing room flanked by Secret Service agents and accompanied by a stolid-faced, heavyset man carrying a thick black-leather attaché case. Livonas stood up to shake the senator's hand, hoping for a quick glimpse of the personality behind the bluff exterior.

"Good morning, Andrew, hope I'm not late." He turned to the man beside him. "I'd like you to meet my attorney, Mr. Salter— Mr. Livonas."

Livonas nodded, then they took their places at the witness table, Salter and he on either side of Hartwell. It was only a few minutes past nine but the main hearing room of the Rayburn Building was jammed with spectators, half of them reporters. Fran Murphy, Cudahy's aide, had spent the previous afternoon and evening simultaneously hunting up a quorum and lobbying for a speedy hearing. He had hoped to have Hartwell's nomination on the floor of the House and Senate by the morning of the twenty-fourth, when the emergency session of Congress was scheduled to convene.

Livonas exchanged glances with Murphy, who sat on the dais between Senator Tucker, chairman of the Senate Judiciary Committee, and Manny Cudahy. They had two more members than necessary for a quorum and Murphy had reported that his informal poll showed everyone was willing to go along with Hartwell's nomination. The day would be strictly pro forma. With a two-hour break for lunch, Hartwell's nomination should be out of committee by four o'clock that afternoon.

Livonas stirred uneasily in his chair. The smoothness of the hearings so far should have been a source of satisfaction but he couldn't overcome his own doubts about Hartwell. It wasn't just the friendly meeting between Hartwell and de Young at Elizabeth Packard's party, it was a feeling that Hartwell was somehow managing to be all things to all people. Who was it who said never trust a man who has no enemies?

"Sir." The sergeant-at-arms, a deferential white-haired man in his early sixties, had leaned over to talk to Hartwell in a stage whisper. "We've been holding four seats for you"—he nodded at the empty chairs behind the senator—"but if you won't be needing them, perhaps I should release them to the press."

Hartwell flashed a smile, nodded. "Go right ahead; my son's laid up with the flu and it was too short notice for the rest of my family to get here from Boston."

He had included Livonas in his smile and Livonas said diplomatically, "Things are happening pretty fast for all of us, Senator."

Hartwell turned back to study the crowd, and Livonas took a legal note pad and Hartwell's file from his suitcase. He flipped quickly through the file. Fifty-six years old, a widower of ten years, a teenage son—James, Jr., a self-described moderate Democrat. He owned an eight-room house in Milton, Massachusetts, and a modest cattle ranch plus minor business investments in New Mexico.

There was nothing there. He wished he knew more about the substance of the man. If the image of Hartwell and Vincent de Young and their overly friendly handshake would only go away . . .

Senator Helms and Congressman Macher took their seats and Chairman Tucker cleared his throat and rapped politely with his gavel. "The joint hearings of the House and Senate Judiciary Committee are now in session."

Livonas settled back in his chair, faintly bored. His presence was a matter of protocol. Hartwell's lawyer would handle the financial disclosure and then Hartwell and the members of the committee would go back and forth attesting to their mutual admiration for each other, God, country, and President Robert Whitman.

The four reporters started to file in for the vacant seats behind them and Livonas pulled his chair closer to the table, glancing back to see if he recognized any of them—he didn't. They eased down into the chairs originally intended for Hartwell's guests.

Strange, the man is nominated for Vice-President of the United States and doesn't bring one friend or relative to the confirmation hearings. But then his explanation had been plausible enough—just twenty-four hours' notice, his son in bed with the flu and his relatives in Boston. And since he was a widower, there was no proud wife to sit at his side, beaming as the network cameras focused in on them.

Then something occurred to Livonas and he half rose from his chair, searching the crowded hearing room to see if she was seated somewhere else.

Why wasn't Elizabeth Packard at the hearing? For the last year, Hartwell had been her escort on the Washington social circuit; there had even been rumors of an engagement.

She wasn't in the hearing room. Livonas frowned and turned slightly to study Hartwell's profile. The senator was listening attentively to Chairman Tucker as he delivered a compliment-studded history of Hartwell's senatorial career. He looked good, Livonas thought: intelligent, forceful, stern. He'd look a lot better on TV than Massey had.

Maybe Elizabeth Packard had the flu, too. Maybe.

Then he made his mind. He'd call Packard from the telephone in the lobby. If she was home, he'd drive out to Chevy Chase during the luncheon recess and talk to her.

He very much needed to know Elizabeth Packard's opinion of James Hartwell.

"Chilly day, isn't it, Mr. Livonas?" Jamie, Elizabeth Packard's social secretary was, as usual, all smiles. "Let me take your coat." The young, slightly built man helped Livonas off with his overcoat and handed it to the black-uniformed maid at his side. "Mrs. Packard's in the study."

Livonas followed him through the walnut-paneled living room and down a back hallway into the study. Elizabeth Packard was sitting at a small eighteenth-century desk, staring out at the snowflakes dancing around the barren cherry trees in her garden. She stood up as they came in, smiling and walking over to take Livonas's hand in hers. She was in her early fifties but only a light network of wrinkles around her eyes gave away her age.

"Merry Christmas, Andrew, even though the season could be happier. Sit over here by the fire with me."

She sat down in an antique rocker by the hearth and cocked her head, her brown eyes curious. "Now what's this all about? You sounded so mysterious over the phone."

Livonas glanced at Jamie, standing discreetly by the study door. "I realized this is an inconvenience, Elizabeth."

She followed his glance. "That will be all for the moment, Jamie, thank you." Jamie disappeared and she turned back to Livonas. "Christmas is such a busy season. One of these years I think I'm just going to forget about it all together." Her smile faded into one of sympathy. "I imagine you find yourself on a busy schedule these days, too. When things let up a little, maybe you could stop by some evening for drinks. I could have Kathleen Houseman over—a lovely girl."

Livonas smiled in spite of himself. He leaned back in the white-damask upholstered chair. "Elizabeth, as you know, we're conducting confirmation hearings on James Hartwell."

A shadow crossed her face and her voice became more formal. Her eyes turned cautious. "I was aware of them, of course."

Livonas wondered how to go about it. He couldn't just ask her what she thought of the whole deal. Or could he?

"I don't follow the gossip columns, Elizabeth, but my impression is that you and the Senator are quite close." Her eyes became even more remote. "I was somewhat surprised that you weren't one of the Senator's guests at the hearing this morning."

She looked at him with a smile that had a trace of pain in it. "I was invited as a guest. I chose not to go."

He looked at her, alert. She offered no explanation and he said, "He had no guests there at all. His son is down with the flu."

It was her turn to look surprised. "I thought Jimbo had left for their ranch in New Mexico for the holidays."

It was making even less sense than it had before. He sure as hell wouldn't have sent his son to spend the holidays in the West. Not this year.

"You positive, Elizabeth?"

She nodded. "We had lunch last weekend—the senator, Jimbo, and I. Perhaps he got sick afterward."

Livonas hunched forward in his chair. "I'm not sure you realize just how serious the confirmation of James Hartwell is, Elizabeth. You've heard the rumors around Washington, the possibility of secession by the western states." He paused. "We face a civil war."

She turned to touch the leather-framed photograph of her late husband on the nearby mantel. When she looked back at Livonas, her face was ashen. "I'm confident that our Republic will survive despite its enemies, Andrew. With God's help and under Bob Whitman's leadership, I'm sure we will endure."

She stood up and walked over to her desk. She was about to flick the intercom and ask Jamie to show Livonas out when he said, "The Vice-President is next in line for the Presidency, Elizabeth. In Bob Whitman's case, that's more than a technicality. There's a good chance that Jim Hartwell will be our next President—and sooner than we think. I would like to know if you'd have the same faith in James Hartwell's leadership as you have in Bob Whitman's."

She stared at him, shocked, then slowly sat down.

Livonas said, "At your party, I was outside when the Senator was escorting Vincent de Young to his car. They seemed overly friendly." He realized how flimsy it sounded. Maybe he was chasing shadows.

"He was, after all, the unofficial host."

"I understand that," Livonas said. "I guess when it comes right down to it, I want to know what you think of James Hartwell."

She looked again at the photograh of her husband on the mantel. "I wish I could clear up your doubts about James but I'm afraid I can't. My impression is that James admires the Governor, although he has never said so directly. The reason I decided to end our relationship—I'm sure you guessed that—is because I discovered that I really didn't know the Senator very well and didn't think I ever would."

She squared the corner of the desk blotter against the side of the desk, then looked up. "I'm afraid that's not much help, is it? The vague complaints of a woman who's not getting any younger."

"Nothing more than that?"

"I don't deal in gossip, Andrew. You've known me long enough to know that."

"I know, Elizabeth, but this is important. What gossip?"

She sighed. "Jamie reported that the Senator and Governor de Young had a private discussion in one of the upstairs sitting rooms. He didn't hear much of what was said but it struck him, as it did you, that they were overly friendly."

"Exactly what did he hear?"

She shook her head. "It was nothing of substance, Andrew."

Livonas could feel himself start to sweat. "I have to know what they said, Elizabeth, no matter how unimportant it may sound."

She looked at him with faint disapproval. "Jamie only heard the end of their conversation. The thing that stuck in his mind was the Senator saying, 'You know where I stand, Vince. In the next few days, if there's anything I can do, you can count on me.' Jamie remembered only because he hadn't thought the Governor and Senator Hartwell were allies. Like almost everybody else in town, he follows the political gossip."

"How do you feel about James Hartwell being next in line for the Presidency, Elizabeth?"

She took a breath, measuring her words. "I would have to say that I'm deeply troubled by it. Deeply troubled." She hesitated. "To be blunt, Andrew, I don't admire the people around him. And James, I'm afraid, is a bad judge of character."

Livonas glanced at his watch. The afternoon session was due to begin in forty-five minutes. His suspicions still lacked any foundation in fact and whatever he did would be strictly on his own. Bob Whitman would feel that he had undercut him—and he'd be right.

Elizabeth Packard read his face. "I'm sure you must be in a hurry; let me show you out." She paused at the door. "Despite everything I've said, I'd be a liar if I implied that all my feelings about the Senator are negative. In some very personal respects, I'll always be very fond of him."

Livonas fell in step beside her as they walked down the hallway, her arm in his. First, he'd have to pressure Murphy to postpone the hearings. Then he'd have to get Saunders to launch an even more intensive investigation of Hartwell in the hope that something might break loose.

He had to trust his instincts, he thought, despite his lack of facts and despite Whitman's opposition—if he found out.

James Hartwell must not be allowed to become the Vice-President of the United States.

December 24
6:30 A.M., *Central Time, Thursday*

Captain Lou Downes hunched forward next to Scully, the 'copter pilot, and watched the quiet waters of the Gulf slip beneath them. It was just before dawn and the faint glow of the sun on the horizon had gilded the water with a trace of gold. The morning was quiet and windless; there were no whitecaps and large patches of the Gulf were bluish glass.

They were close enough to the water so that the drilling platform hadn't yet appeared on the horizon, though it wasn't more than ten miles away. Downes glanced at the six men behind him. Robinson and Gomez had dozed off, McCarthy, Topping, and Hanson were dull-eyed and yawning. Sergeant Asher, a thermos top of coffee in his hand, was staring glumly out the side window at the ocean speeding by below.

It had been a bitch getting the assault launched. Colonel Worden had asked for volunteers for an important but unspecified assignment, then Worden had arbitrarily eliminated almost half of them. Once the colonel had told them what it was all about, it was easy to figure out why there wasn't one marine from west of the Mississippi in the entire two hundred-man assault team.

Asher stretched and yawned, rubbing a calloused hand over his unshaven jaw. He shifted in his seat, moving his M16 carbine to a more comfortable position. "This is a dumb operation, Captain—we're going off half-cocked."

Downes turned back to face the front. "You're just upset because you missed your breakfast, Asher."

He could hear another prodigious yawn from Asher. "I should've packed one."

"You can get breakfast on the drilling barge—I hear the food on them is great." He squinted through the window. "Wake 'em up, Asher, we're getting close."

The crew on the barge shouldn't be any trouble. They'd shake the men down for weapons, then put them under guard until they were airlifted off . . .

"What's happening?" Robinson was awake now and fingering his M16. A small, nervous black kid from Boston, this was his first mission. He'd been looking forward to it despite Colonel Worden's prediction that there wouldn't be any action. Kids like Robinson always worried Downes; they were too anxious to start a fight and too slow to stop it. Street-wise punks, you couldn't tell them anything, they'd seen it all.

Scully turned his head slightly. "The rig's coming up."

Downes nodded. "Keep it low going in."

Behind him, Topping grumbled, "Let's get it over with." Then everybody fell silent as the drilling platform was highlighted on the horizon by the rising sun, its three massive legs poking two hundred feet above the water. Two minutes later, they were circling the barge. The water was so clear that Downes could see the foundation "mat," the anchoring platform for the huge legs, sitting on the sandy bottom.

Hanson's flat Indiana twang was loud in his ear. "Doesn't look like anybody's home." Then a crewman ran out on the helipad to wave them in. The Sea King settled slowly toward the pad. There was a clatter of metal as the men behind Downes adjusted their packs and picked up their M16s.

The 'copter touched down. "Stay with it, Scully." Downes hopped out the door, his carbine at the ready. The man who had waved them in stared uncertainly at them, wide-eyed. He wore faded jeans and rubber nonskid boots; his belly bulged out from beneath an oil-stained T-shirt.

Downes waved his carbine at the crewman. "Watch him, Topping. Hanson, round up everybody on the production deck. Robinson, Gomez, crew's quarters are one deck below. Shake 'em out of the sack and get 'em up here—Asher and I will take the control room. Move it!"

The crewman stuttered, "What the hell you guys think you're doing?" He looked more startled than frightened.

"This barge is now under federal control," Downes grunted.

The crewman pointed at Topping. "Then tell this bastard to be careful with his goddamned gun."

Downes ignored him and jogged over to the ladder that led to the production deck and the hundred-and-fifty-foot high derrick. The platform had looked small from the air, but seen from the helipad on the stern, it was enormous. The production deck itself was probably an acre in size, a snarl of pipes and machinery and oil drums. The only spot of color in the landscape of gray and crude-oil black were three bright-orange escape capsules, each of them capable of holding twenty men, hanging off the starboard side of the platform.

Robinson and Gomez had disappeared below and Downes sprinted for the stairs. "Let's go!" he yelled at Asher over his shoulder. Behind him, Hanson was prowling through the stacks of equipment on the production deck and Topping was squatting on his heels, holding his carbine loosely in his hands, staring slit-eyed at the frightened crewman.

Downes took the steps two at a time, trying to remember the diagram of the drilling barge from Colonel Worden's briefing. At the bottom of the steps, he took a sharp left and burst into the control room. He leveled his rifle at the radioman hunched over the transmitter in the corner.

"Turn it off!" The radioman's hands shot up in the air. "You got a name?"

"Pollard—Mike Pollard."

Another guy who talked like he had a mouthful of grits. Downes gestured with his carbine toward the doorway. "Okay, Pollard, up on deck. Asher, take him up."

The next room was the galley. It was empty, though apparently a dozen men had been eating, their half-filled plates still on the table. He took it all in, from the huge stoves to the long table and the half-filled garbage can and rack for trays at the door. He plucked a link sausage off a plate and pushed open the door to the next compartment, a machinery room where two mechanics were stripping down an engine. He prodded them up on deck where Robinson and Gomez were already lining up the men from below. Like the radio operator, most of them seemed more frightened than sleepy.

Asher had disappeared again, then showed up escorting a fat, middle-aged man in whites. The sergeant was smiling and Downes knew without being told that he had located the cook.

Then it struck Downes as all wrong and he didn't know why. Something he'd seen had been the clue but he couldn't put his finger on it.

He glanced at his watch. Ten minutes since they'd landed on the helipad, a half hour until the Hueys arrived to lift off the drilling crew and the support team. Time enough for breakfast before they lost the cook.

Breakfast. Something about breakfast.

The platform crew were staring at him and he said, "This drilling platform has been commandeered by the federal government of the United States pursuant to Executive Order Number 178. You'll be lifted off and put down near Grand Isle. After the present emergency, an attempt will be made to return your personal effects, but no man will be allowed below decks from now until the choppers arrive. That clear?"

Nobody said anything and once again he felt a crawling in his gut. A slight breeze had sprung up, but the Gulf was still covered with gold leaf. The men lined up in front of him looked apprehensive and he wondered why. Nobody was going to hurt them.

And then he had it.

"Robinson, where'd you find the men?"

Robinson looked surprised. "Sacked out, there was nobody else—"

Then who the hell had been eating in the galley? And at least two shifts had been served, judging from the garbage can at the door. And while everybody had seemed scared and keyed up, nobody had looked sleepy.

They had walked into a setup.

Time shifted into slow motion. He turned toward the far end of the platform, knowing instinctively where to look. Shadowy figures were climbing out of the escape capsules and disappearing into the jungle of coiled cable and mounds of drill pipe at the base of the derrick.

"Everybody to the chopper! Move it!"

Even as he shouted, there was a sparkling from around the derrick area and the sound of bullets ricocheting off the helipad behind him. Asher sat down on the deck, a look of surprise on his face.

"Come on, Asher! Move it!"

Bullets started to chew up the wooden decking around him. Robinson and Topping had thrown themselves flat, leaning on their elbows so they could fire their carbines. Robinson, cursing, aimed at the top of the derrick. Downes could hear the scream even above the shooting and a figure fell from near the top of the derrick to bounce once on the planking below.

The platform crew had hit the deck, too, one of them face up, staring blank-eyed at the sky. On Downes's right, McCarthy scrambled behind a steel barrel for cover.

Downes screamed, "McCarthy, get away from there!" and then the barrel exploded in a fireball. For a moment he could see McCarthy outlined in the flames, jerking like a marionette. Then the heat hit him. He got off another round at the derrick and lunged for the ladder leading up to the helipad.

How many men had been hiding in the capsules? Twenty? Thirty?

Flaming oil was running across the deck and he screamed again at Asher, who didn't move. He hesitated, then turned away from the ladder, crouched low, and ran across the slippery deck toward the sergeant, racing a stream of burning oil.

Asher was sitting on the deck, the faint surprised look still engraved on his face. The bullet hole was almost invisible, hidden just below his shirt pocket. The deck behind him was drenched with blood.

Downes wanted to vomit. Robinson tugged at him. "Let's get the fuck outta here, Captain!"

"Where're the others?"

"Topping and Hanson are dead, I don't know where McCarthy is. I saw Gomez get in the chopper. Let's go!"

The flames were more intense now and members of the platform crew were crawling off the deck and dropping into the water.

He ran for the ladder and scrambled up it, feeling bullets plucking at the air around him. Then the bullets stopped. Scully was standing in the door of the chopper spraying the far end of the barge with automatic weapons fire. Downes climbed on board, turning to haul up Robinson. Scully threw him the machine gun and leaped for the pilot's seat.

They lifted a few inches off the deck, swayed for a moment in the wind, then slowly turned. Scully dropped the Sea King close to the water, using the stern of the barge for cover as they sped away, skimming the surface of the Gulf. A few hundred yards away, they climbed up into the bright blue sky. One of the windows shattered and then the sound of gunfire dwindled and died.

"You all right, Captain?" Robinson was staring at him.

"Yeah, I'm okay." He was still thinking of Asher—they had been part of the first team into El Salvador. He shivered. The hole where the bullet had gone in was so small you could hardly see it.

They'd lost Asher, McCarthy, Topping, and Hanson. He didn't know how many of the westerners they'd gotten.

Robinson lit a cigarette. He looked like a different Robinson, Downes thought. You could see it around the eyes.

"I thought you said it was going to be a piece of cake, Captain."

"It should have been." Downes relaxed his grip on his carbine and climbed back in front with Scully. Worden had given them several alternate frequencies to use in case things went wrong.

They'd gone wrong, all right. Terribly wrong.

There was a sound in his headset and he cleared his throat, then spoke into the microphone. "Patch me in to Code Charlie Roger, Washington, D.C. Priority One."

He'd lost four good men in what should have been a cakewalk. Somebody had tipped off the western forces. Which meant that things had probably turned out just as bad for the twenty-five other assault teams that had taken off early that morning for the oil rigs in the Gulf.

December 24
11:30 A.M., *Pacific Time, Thursday*

De Young was staring out the windows at the crowds below and didn't hear his secretary when she let in the next appointment. People had been gathering in the streets around the statehouse since early morning, hoping for a glimpse of him. Shepherd had reported earlier that the California National Guard was swamped with young men wanting to enlist.

"That's quite a crowd out there."

De Young turned, an easy smile lighting his face. Luis Rivera, the director of Petrolema, S.A. "It's great to see you, Luis, glad you could take the time."

Rivera grinned. "You're the one whose time is valuable, Mr. President."

De Young waved the comment aside. "It's still 'Governor,' Luis. And for old friends"—he reached out and took Rivera's right hand in both of his—"it'll always be Vince."

He motioned to the chair nearest the desk and offered Rivera the box of cigars that Shepherd had provided. Rivera wasn't much past forty and looked like he had spent most of his life outdoors. He dressed like his Texas counterparts, with subtly stitched leather boots, a custom-tailored suit, and a conservative narrow-brimmed Stetson to complete the uniform. The slight bronzing of his skin could have come from the sun as easily as from his ancestry. Even his accent was strictly Texan—refined, no doubt, while getting his MBA at Texas A&M where he had been a classmate of Ed Teillberg's.

Rivera took a cigar and lit it, savoring the first puff. Then he put the cigar carefully down in the ashtray, his face solemn. "I wanted to talk about three million barrels of oil," he said blandly. "As I understand it, forms still have to be filled out for your federal government."

He wasn't going to renege this late in the game, de Young thought. Or was he? He desperately needed Rivera's cooperation and Rivera knew it.

"I thought we had already gone over that. Gulf Coast Oil will be the importer of record, Petrolema S.A. the supplier. The IRS and customs forms will be taken care of by Gulf Coast."

Rivera concentrated on the cigar. "I was wondering if a slight delay would really matter that much. We're anxious, of course, for the best relations with the Western States of America." He hesitated, then continued smoothly: "At the same time, we see no reason to needlessly antagonize the United States."

Rivera wanted it both ways. So had the Japanese trade minister, Fukuda, who had shown up earlier that morning. He had hung tough with the Jap, but Janice McCall wouldn't play ball on promises alone; the oil would have to be in the pipelines. The greaser had him by the balls and both of them knew it.

"You know Mexico would have favored status, Luis."

Rivera looked up. "Which Mexico, Vince?" He let it hang there.

Of course, de Young thought. He recalled Ed Teillberg's thumb-nail profile of Rivera. "Don't make the mistake of thinking of Luis Rivera as a Mexican, think of him as a Conquistador," Ed had said.

De Young leaned back and laced his fingers behind his head. "That's entirely up to you, Luis. But let me assure you: The re-sources of the Western States of America will be at your *personal* disposal. Economic, political, and military. We have no particular fondness for the current government of Mexico. But as you men-tioned earlier regarding your relations with the United States, nei-ther do we want to foolishly antagonize them."

Rivera smiled and stood up. *"Feliz Navidad,* Vince," he said softly.

After Rivera had left, de Young walked back to the window and stared out at the crowds in the street. He'd be walking a tightrope through next Sunday. But then, he'd been on one for the past year and hadn't fallen off yet.

Shepherd and Bolles arrived at one thirty sharp, along with a tray of sandwiches and a pot of coffee that his secretary wheeled in on a tea cart. Shepherd was whistling off-key.

"Good news, Herb?"

Shepherd grinned and reached for one of the sandwiches. "I wouldn't say it was bad."

He trusted Shepherd much more when he was being pessimistic. Shepherd glanced over at General Bolles, who was also smiling. "It's Herman's story, let him tell it."

De Young poured himself a cup of coffee and leaned back in his chair. "What's up, General?"

Bolles cleared his throat. "At dawn this morning, federal forces launched an assault on the oil rigs off the Louisiana coast."

De Young tensed. They had been warned that such an assault was being planned but Whitman had acted quicker than he thought he would, quicker than he thought he *could.*

"What happened?"

Bolles was searching through the sandwiches for a ham-and-cheese. "We didn't lose a single rig."

Better than he had figured on, de Young thought. "What about casualties?"

Bolles shrugged. "Maybe thirty federal troops and a dozen of ours."

"Congratulations, General," he murmured. His first feeling was one of elation, his second one of caution. The federal forces had suffered a defeat—and one with Whitman at the helm. And the West had retained the rigs, an objective which would have been a tremendous shot in the arm for the federals.

But they were drifting out of the political arena into the military one, toward a full-fledged civil war. It was a risk he didn't want to take, didn't *have* to take.

"I've got a news conference ready to go in New Orleans with Governor Charlie Long," Shepherd said.

"Make sure he calls it an act of eastern terrorists," de Young warned. "Don't let him imply there was anything official about it." They weren't at war with the United States, not yet. They certainly didn't want to make a case over the rigs. The opening gun of secession was three days away at the convention, they didn't want to blow it before then.

The federal government would play it down, too. They had thought they could take the rigs without firing a shot. It hadn't worked out that way, but they weren't about to go to war over a blunder of their own making. Nevertheless, there'd be rumors and the rumors would grow. By Sunday, the East would have suffered a crushing defeat and the West would look a sure winner.

"I think we overestimated Whitman," Shepherd said, smug.

De Young felt a flash of irritation. If it wasn't Wagoner going overboard, it was Shepherd.

"Don't count him out, Herb; he's got some smart people around him, not assholes like Massey had." He thought again of Livonas; some day he'd catch up with that bastard. "And don't forget, unlike Massey, Whitman's popular in parts of the West."

Shepherd's enthusiasm wasn't dampened at all. "Whitman won't have much influence at the convention. Besides, we got a message from Hartwell an hour ago. There's been another slight delay, but he's expecting to be confirmed no later than tomorrow."

"Anything more on Whitman's health?"

Shepherd shook his head and reached for another sandwich. "Just what Hartwell told us the other day. Whitman has a bad heart problem and could go at any time."

De Young stood up and walked back to the window to look out, as much to walk off his euphoria as anything else. The crowds were still there, the young kids hanging on the wrought-iron fence. Somebody spotted him and he could hear the faint cheering through the glass. He waved and the cheering grew louder.

He turned back to the room. "Any word on why Hartwell's confirmation was delayed?"

"From what we can gather, it's just a procedural matter." Shepherd reached into his briefcase and pulled out a list and held it out to de Young. "More defections. It doesn't matter whether Whitman's President or not, people still know when they're on a sinking ship."

De Young glanced at the list. A half dozen ambassadors, most of them in sympathetic countries around the Pacific Rim. A few key officials in the State Department—Al Reynolds couldn't hold the line there, either. Events were moving too fast for Whitman.

"What do you think Whitman will do?" he mused aloud. "Declare martial law? Suspend the Constitution? We can't depend on him just sitting there."

Shepherd laughed. "I hope he does try something like that, he'll lose whatever popular support he has."

De Young turned to Bolles. "What about the military situation?"

Bolles lit his pipe and leaned back in his chair. "Most of the military bases in the East are in a state of confusion. I suspect that will continue for another week or two at least."

Long enough, de Young thought.

Somebody was leading a chant outside the window and he smiled slightly and went to the small kitchen off the office. He came back with a bottle of California champagne and three glasses. He stripped off the foil and untwisted the wire, then pushed out the cork with a satisfying pop and filled the glasses.

"Here's to us, gentlemen." He took a sip, then added: "And here's to Freedom Day."

Bolles looked puzzled. "Freedom Day?"

"Sunday, December twenty-seventh," Shepherd said. "The first holiday of the new Republic of the Western States of America. We're organizing massive demonstrations around federal land and office complexes in the West."

De Young took another sip of the champagne. There'd be a live

broadcast of his speech from the Denver Arena announcing secession once the convention passed the amendment. The celebrations
would begin then; Shepherd had already drawn up the plans.

He grinned and raised his glass again. "Here's to us, gentlemen,"
he repeated. "And to the West."

Then he wondered if Herb had any inkling of the potential of
Freedom Day if they got into trouble between now and Sunday.

He had always made it a rule to have a contingency plan ready—
just in case.

December 24
2:00 P.M., *Thursday*

The helicopter was flying over Manhattan's West Side now and
Whitman glanced at the city below with interest. They were close
enough that he could see the people on the sidewalks. As they approached midtown, he could even make out the trampled paths in
the snow in Central Park.

There was only an occasional wisp of smoke from a chimney and
damn few rooftops where the heat in a building had melted the
snow. The city was freezing.

Next to him, Livonas leaned over for a glimpse of the United Nations Building, a dazzling glare in the winter sun, then settled back
in his seat. It was a beautiful day, Whitman thought, then clenched
his fists, remembering the failure of the oil rig assault earlier that
morning. Somebody had tipped off the westerners . . . But there was
nothing to be done about it now.

"I did what I thought was right," Livonas repeated, still talking
about Hartwell. He sounded like he couldn't make up his mind
whether to be apologetic or defiant.

"I asked you to speed up the hearings, Andy, not delay them."
But Livonas's suspicions had made him uneasy. "Saunders find out
anything?"

"Not so far." Livonas sounded embarrassed.

Whitman sighed. "I want to see Hartwell's nomination out of
committee and confirmed by Congress tomorrow. Is that clear?"

"Yes, Mr. President."

Whitman didn't tell Livonas that between them it was still "Bob." There were times when he had to remind himself that he was the President; Livonas might as well be reminded, too.

The Pan Am Building was a huge monolith on their left now. The 'copter gained altitude and headed for the helipad on its roof. Livonas said, "It's two thirty; we're late."

"I don't think they're going to go anyplace."

"You still seeing Michael Bernstein first?"

Whitman nodded. "His offices are right there—and he might give me some hints on what I'll run into." He'd first met Bernstein when the then president of Offshore Minerals had been a witness before the Senate Banking Committee five years before. Bernstein had been argumentative but forthright and his committee appearance had developed into a personal friendship.

Whitman glanced down. The 'copter was hovering over the helipad. The snow had been cleared away from the pad and a building guard was waving them in. A dozen other men were standing close by the doors to the stairwell. The down-draft from the chopper's blades whipped open the coat of one of the men and Whitman could see the submachine gun slung over his shoulder.

"Those the FBI agents?"

"Saunders said he'd assign a dozen of them."

Whitman wondered whether he'd actually have to use them.

"Care for a drink, Mr. President?"

Whitman leaned back in the huge leather sofa and laced his fingers behind his head. "Coffee's fine for me, Michael—but you go ahead."

Bernstein glanced at the young male secretary waiting in the door of the study. "Coffee for the President, Joseph. Bourbon straight up for me."

The room's decor reflected Bernstein's personality, Whitman thought—dark-hued and polished. The floors were an oak parquet, the furniture was richly upholstered in leather, bookcases and hunting prints lined the walls, and a two-foot antique globe in an ornate walnut cradle stood in front of the large picture window overlooking upper Manhattan.

Bernstein hadn't changed much in semiretirement—too heavy

for his own good, thinning brown hair plastered to an almost perfectly round head, and sharp, black eyes set in a rosy, cherubic face that could turn to gray cement when he was crossed.

Then his attention was caught by a large glass-fronted cabinet in the corner. Bernstein noticed his glance and motioned him over to the case. "Have a look—I think you might be interested."

Whitman walked over to the cabinet and peered through the glass at the armies of tiny soldiers spread out on the shelves before him, frozen in serried ranks.

"I know," Bernstein said, grinning. "I'm too old to be playing with toy soldiers." He opened the case and took one out, handing it gently to Whitman. " 'Miniatures' is a more accurate expression. Some years ago I ran across a shop in the French Quarter of New Orleans that specializes in them. Exquisite workmanship, the best of its kind."

The tiny French fusilier was about two-and-a-half inches tall. He stood at parade rest, his left hand on his hip, the other holding his musket against his side. He was complete with black stockings and blue army coat with bobbed tails, a brown backpack and bedroll, and a black shako with red braid and golden eagle on the front and a red-tipped plume on top. The artist had added a minuscule moustache and a fierce expression to the Lilliputian face.

"They represent armies from all over the world," Bernstein said, walking back to his chair. Joseph had silently set the coffee and the bourbon on the coffee table and just as silently vanished. "These are from the Napoleonic era, when uniforms tended to the colorful and exotic. Damned little from this century, there's not much a miniature painter can do with khaki."

He settled back in his chair and took a sip of the bourbon, letting it linger on his tongue before swallowing it. Whitman thought of a bear relaxing in its den.

"You honor me, Mr. President, though I must confess I'm a little curious why you've come. You're a busy man these days."

"You've heard about the meeting downstairs?"

Bernstein grinned. "Of course."

Whitman cleared his throat. "You know most of the leaders in the petroleum industry not only here but overseas. When you were president of Offshore Minerals you used to wield a great deal of power in the international business community—I think perhaps you still do."

Bernstein nodded, his face sympathetic. "Yes and no. But go ahead."

"The country desperately needs oil," Whitman continued slowly. "Could Offshore Minerals get it—if you really wanted to?"

Bernstein studied him. "You using me for a dry run?"

Whitman smiled. "To a degree."

"All right, I'll play devil's advocate. Let's assume I'm still president of Offshore Minerals. What makes you think I could get them to shill for oil for the United States?"

"Offshore Minerals has had drilling contracts with both the Saudis and the United Arab Emirates for years. You must have some influence over them."

Bernstein shook his head. "When it comes to oil, I have some influence. When it comes to Arab nationalism, I'm regarded as an American, and a Jewish one at that. Among other things, the embargo is inspired by Arab nationalism."

"Offshore Minerals could increase its oil allotments to other western countries."

Bernstein looked sour. "So they could reship to the United States? You've already tried that ploy. The Arabs invented math when the Gauls were still counting on their fingers. Worldwide, they know oil demands and usage as well as we do—frankly, they know them better."

"Not every country you deal with is Moslem. Couldn't you shift allotments yourself?"

Bernstein got to his feet and walked back to the cabinet containing the miniature soldiers. "This is my private army, Mr. President. French fusiliers, British dragoons, soldiers from Russia, from Germany, from Spain." He paused. "Offshore Minerals isn't a U.S. company—like my collection, it owes its existence to many nations. If its stateside business should vanish tomorrow, sixty percent of Offshore Minerals would still be intact."

He returned to his chair, sank into it, and picked up his glass of bourbon. "At one time," he mused, "the government looked upon multinationals as an asset. It saw them as promoting the American way of life, exporting our marketing and banking techniques, our legal system, our political philosophy—right up there along with Coca Cola. It didn't see the other side of that coin."

He eased forward in his chair.

"Take Offshore Minerals. Its major source of supply is in the

Emirates, its corporate headquarters are in Brussels, its drilling gear comes from Germany as well as the United States, and its oil experts come from all over Europe. It has chemical plants in Sweden, a board of directors that meets regularly in London, and stockholders spread around the world. When I was chief executive officer, Offshore Minerals didn't do what *I* wanted it to do, I did what *it* wanted me to do."

The secretary came in with more coffee and bourbon, and Bernstein drained his glass and picked up a fresh one.

"It shouldn't surprise you that Offshore Minerals might consider the farmer in Bangladesh who depends on oil-based fertilizer as valuable a customer as the studio executive who lives in Beverly Hills and needs gasoline so he can drive to work in Culver City. In short, they're not going to let one starve so that the other can ride. Offshore Minerals considers itself a global corporation with global responsibilities and global obligations."

Whitman stared at Bernstein. "You believe all that, Michael?"

Bernstein shrugged. "Some of it. Remember, they may not be as rich but there are a lot more farmers in Bangladesh than studio executives in L.A." He took another sip of his bourbon. "But you asked me to play devil's advocate and that's the argument they're going to give you downstairs."

Whitman said softly, "Then I'll have to use a different approach."

The boardroom was immense—probably the largest in the Pan Am Building, Whitman thought. It had an acoustic-tiled ceiling, recessed lighting, and thick beige carpeting. In the center of the room was a huge oval conference table of rosewood surrounded by high-backed leather chairs with a water decanter and glass in front of each. Tiny bits of grillwork built into the table's surface hid high-fidelity microphones to subtly boost your voice.

There were no windows and despite the room's size, Whitman felt claustrophobic.

He stood in the doorway a moment and studied the fifty men gathered around the table, almost all of them hostile. There were a number of others he would like to have seen there but those present were a healthy cross-section of the men who ran America's business—bankers, corporate directors, presidents of multinationals, American executives of foreign-owned companies ... Men of wealth, position, and power.

He had met most of them in Washington over the years, either at committee hearings or various parties. A brief handshake, a broad smile, some casual conversation, but seldom any insight into the real personality.

He walked into the room, nodding to those he recognized. Livonas and the FBI agents filed in behind him, the agents taking up positions along the wall. Two more agents flanked the closed doors, grease guns hanging from their shoulders. The men at the table stared silently at the agents, their faces curious. A few were pale.

Whitman walked to the far end of the table. "Good afternoon, gentlemen." He sat down and Livonas eased into the chair on his right.

There was no answering chorus of "Good afternoon, Mr. President." Midway down, a man stood up. Clay Ferguson, Whitman recalled, president of the New York Banking Corporation. Late fifties, thin face, a solarium tan.

Ferguson nodded at those around the table and said, "The others here have chosen me as their spokesman." He talked with a clipped New England accent.

Whitman fished for his pipe. "Then you must have a lot to say, Mr. Ferguson."

"I do," Ferguson said. The respect in his voice was tissue-thin. "As representatives of the corporate sector, we find the events of the past two days highly damaging to the business community and corrosive to our prestige internationally. What's perhaps most disturbing is there have been no indications from the White House as to your attitude toward the commercial sector. So far there have been nothing but rumors and 'no comment.' "

Ferguson was hewing to the theory that the best defense was a good offense, Whitman thought. A third of them had probably spent most of the morning trying to cut deals with de Young, convinced that Washington had become a paper tiger. He took his time filling his pipe, careful to keep his voice calm and even-tempered.

"The condition of the country requires immediate action, Mr. Ferguson, you're quite right. In all candor, I must say that some of the steps planned by the Administration will be difficult for you."

The expressions of casual contempt around the table subtly altered. He could sense the rising anger and apprehension. He hardened his voice.

"None of the actions I'm about to take will be rescinded. In fact, they're just the beginning." He took a breath. "Gentlemen, I need your cooperation—and I mean to have it."

Ferguson's face reflected shocked surprise. They'd been expecting an olive branch. Whitman nodded in his direction. "I'll be brief, Mr. Ferguson"—he smiled—"I know you want to get back to your office."

Another pause while he tamped tobacco in his pipe. "First of all, at noon today I declared the country to be in a state of national emergency. Under the powers available to me I've closed the Federal Reserve Bank of New York and established protective custody over all stocks of gold therein, both foreign and U.S. owned. Those vaults will remain sealed until further notice. In the meantime, all trading in gold has been suspended."

He glanced at his watch. "Fifteen minutes ago, all other banks in the United States were closed pending reopening Monday morning. In the meantime, gentlemen, there is a complete freeze on both cash and credit transactions of any kind through the national banking system."

The faces around the table were stunned, then the roar of protests began. Whitman gave them a minute, then pounded on the table with a paperweight in front of him.

"You said you were spokesman, Mr. Ferguson?"

Ferguson's face was a dull red beneath his tan. "You don't have the authority . . . Congress hasn't granted . . . the courts will overturn . . ."

Whitman stared at Ferguson, curious what de Young might have promised him. "With the absence of a large number of senators and congressmen from the western states, Congress has problems of its own, Mr. Ferguson—the emergency couldn't wait. And precedents indicate the courts will back me." His voice became sardonic. "But I didn't come here to be told what I can or cannot do."

Their apprehension returned. "When the banks reopen Monday, I want all the credits you've extended to Governor de Young suspended. I wouldn't suggest any of you try to ignore that. In the opinion of the Attorney General, those credits may prove an indictable offense—treason, to be precise."

Closing the banks and impounding the gold had cut de Young off at the pockets. The men in the room would have the weekend to reconsider any further cooperation with him.

Ferguson raised his voice. "That's an in—"

"I haven't finished, Mr. Ferguson," Whitman interrupted. "For those of you in positions of authority with the various petrochemical conglomerates, I want all tankers chartered or owned by your companies and carrying crude from Mexico, Canada, Venezuela, and other countries in the Americas to be diverted to East Coast ports. Our military satellites know the location of each of your tankers. If you don't comply, those tankers will be seized and their cargoes confiscated"—he smiled slightly—"with reimbursement to their owners, of course."

Clifford Marantz of United Fuels had difficulty choking back his anger. "What about those countries due to receive such shipments?"

Whitman shrugged. "They'll have to make other arrangements. The United States is suffering from an oil embargo, the others aren't. They have room in which to maneuver. We don't."

At the far end of the table, George Burton slowly got to his feet. Whitman could feel Livonas, sitting next to him, stiffen. Burton was the head of the California National Bank. They had both spotted him as soon as they walked into the room and knew that he, not Ferguson, would be de Young's spokesman in the group.

"Mr. President, gentlemen." A slight nod to the others at the table. "With all due respect, Mr. President, a number of us here, particularly those in oil and international banking, represent multinational companies. They haven't been American companies for quite a while now. They're organizations with a world outlook."

Burton's voice was easy, though a little patronizing and overbearing. "In most cases, Americans are a minority of our stockholders, of our managers, of our customers. You can hardly expect us to be"— he paused as if searching for the right word—"nationalistic. Our organizations have other interests, other loyalties—"

Whitman blew up then, uncoiling from his chair, his face red with anger, his voice exploding with a bellow.

"Listen, you son-of-a-bitch, you're a United States citizen and these are United States FBI agents and you either cooperate or you're going to a United States jail!"

The shock was palpable. Those nearest him went white. Burton stopped in midsentence, floundering, not certain just what approach to use. Whitman didn't give him time to choose one.

"I've had this split-loyalties crap up to here. Your country—and I do mean *your* country—can't afford split loyalties, so forget the bullshit, Burton. We've heard it all before and I won't insult the intelligence of anybody here by forcing them to listen to it all over again."

He took a moment to control his anger, then turned to the others at the conference table.

"The United States has also sealed the headquarters of all foreign-owned American corporations pending congressional action on the nationalization of their U.S. plants and properties. Similar action will also be taken, on a selective basis, concerning foreign investments in this country."

How many billions of foreign petrochemical dollars had been invested in the United States? Whitman wondered. Enough to bankrupt several dozen sheikdoms?

He looked at Burton and added blandly, "I'm referring specifically to those corporations in which Americans are a minority of the stockholders, managers, and customers."

He sat down, watching Burton sink back into his own chair. Most of the faces around him looked gray. Once again, everybody seemed painfully aware of the agents standing against the walls.

"We were talking about financial support, either overt or covert, for Governor Vincent de Young." He glanced at Livonas next to him, smiling slightly. It had gone better than he had hoped.

"I'm assuming that all of you gentlemen are loyal, patriotic citizens of the United States and will wish to cooperate. I suggest we adjourn for an hour and then we'll reconvene and work out the particulars with representatives from the Departments of Energy, Commerce, and the Treasury."

He added almost as an afterthought: "I sincerely hope I'm not mistaken about your cooperation."

He didn't try to conceal the threat in his voice.

Chistmas Day

8:00 A.M., *Friday*

Livonas studied Hartwell as the senator adjusted his tie and smoothed back his hair, then relaxed in the chair behind Manny Cudahy's desk. He had nothing on Hartwell, Livonas reminded himself. As of last night, Saunders hadn't been able to find a thing. And Whitman had already given him his marching orders; the President wanted Hartwell confirmed as soon as possible.

"Well, Andrew, it shouldn't take long to wrap this up." Hartwell checked his wristwatch. "Incidentally, Bob briefed me on his health the other day." He shook his head and murmured, "Tough, damned tough. I had no idea."

The hell you didn't, Livonas thought, then said aloud: "I think the doctors exaggerate—personally, I haven't seen him look better in months." Which wasn't true, the afternoon naps were getting longer and yesterday, before leaving for New York, Whitman had complained of poor circulation in his legs.

They were due in the committee room any minute. He had time for one last attempt, Livonas thought. "Excuse me a moment, Senator, I've got to make a call and then we'll go downstairs."

Hartwell reached for his briefcase and pulled a pair of reading glasses from his pocket. "Fine, Andrew, I'll just go over the statement I've prepared for the committee."

Livonas walked through the reception area of Cudahy's suite of offices into Fran Murphy's cubicle and picked up the phone. After what seemed an interminable delay, he was told by Saunders's secretary that the director was out and unable to be reached on his car phone.

That was it, Livonas thought. There was nothing more he could do about Hartwell's nomination. All he'd ever had to go on was a gut feeling, a farewell handshake, and secondhand gossip from Elizabeth Packard's social secretary.

He reluctantly returned to Cudahy's office. Hartwell was leaning back in Manny's swivel chair, staring out at the snow that swirled past the window.

"All set, Senator?"

"Yes, of course." Hartwell shoved his papers back into his briefcase and stood up. "I should have said this before, Andrew, but I'm looking forward to working with you. In the unfortunate event that the worst should happen, I'll be counting on you to stay on the team. I know how much Bob has relied on you; I know that I could do the same."

Livonas stared. The bastard was good, *really* good. He said it like he meant it. For a moment, he felt himself waver, then stiffened. As Whitman had once said of a fellow senator who turned out to be a crook, there was nothing definite—just that Hartwell didn't smell right to him.

One thing for sure, if anything happened to Bob, he'd never work for Hartwell.

"I don't think we have to worry about that in the immediate future, Senator." He held the door open for Hartwell. "I understand you and Vince de Young were once good friends."

Hartwell didn't miss a beat. "I don't know whether 'friends' is quite the right term. I knew him politically—we served on two presidential commissions together. I believe we even collaborated on drafting a report on National Water Use, or rather our aides did."

Livonas couldn't help himself. "It must have been a pleasure to renew your acquaintance at Elizabeth Packard's party." The moment he said it, he regretted it.

Hartwell looked at him sharply and stopped in the middle of the corridor. "If anything's bothering you, Andrew, I think we should thrash it out now."

He ought to smile and apologize, Livonas thought, but he wasn't going to.

"I don't know where you really stand, Senator," he said coldly.

Hartwell read the expression on his face and colored. He lowered his voice, his face hard.

"Don't take me for a fool, Livonas. I know what's been going on for the past twenty-four hours. I know damned well you worked to get the hearings delayed and I know you're responsible for the FBI agents going up one side of my block and down the other, talking to my neighbors. You've exceeded your authority and I intend to apprise the President of it. If it's a struggle for power, Livonas, you won't win it."

Livonas turned away, contemptuous. "We shouldn't keep the

committee waiting, Senator." They walked to the elevator and rode down in silence.

As the elevator doors opened, Livonas was almost blinded by the kleig lights. The reporters closed in around them and they moved at a snail's pace toward the hearing room doors, flanked by reporters, television technicians, and Capitol Hill police.

Somebody called out "Livonas!" but he ignored it. Right now, he didn't trust himself to talk to the press, especially when he was sure some of them sensed where he stood with Hartwell. There was a tug at his sleeve and he whirled, annoyed. It was the field agent Saunders had put in charge of investigating Hartwell.

"Sorry, Mr. Livonas—Director Saunders wants to see you." He nodded at a nearby cloakroom. Fran Murphy was standing by the door. Livonas ran to catch up with Hartwell.

"I'll be with you in a minute, Senator."

Hartwell looked at him sharply. "Livonas, I—"

Livonas ignored him. He squeezed through the throng of reporters and slipped into the cloakroom, Murphy close behind him.

Saunders was standing in front of an oak conference table, looking grim.

"We've got him."

"Enough to stop the hearings?"

Saunders nodded. "We started working out in constantly widening circles from Hartwell's house. We got lucky at a People's Drugstore four blocks away. One of the checkout clerks said Hartwell always walks his dog down there in the evening and buys the bulldog edition of the *Post*. She remembered that both Tuesday and Wednesday nights, Hartwell asked for change so he could use the phone in the rear of the store—a lot of change, like a couple or three dollars' worth. We checked with the phone company and both nights calls were placed from that phone to a Sacramento number."

Saunders paused. "It's an unlisted number, belongs to Herb Shepherd. In both cases, the times of the calls jibed with the times the clerk said Hartwell was in the store."

Despite his suspicions, the reality of it was still a shock to Livonas. "Tuesday was when we decided to move against the Louisiana oil rigs," he said harshly. "Hartwell attended the meeting. We lost thirty men."

Murphy paled. "Jesus H. Christ, I didn't know Hartwell was at that meeting."

"They vote in a matter of minutes," Livonas added in a tight voice. "You can't let it go through."

"Of course not."

"I don't think we have enough evidence for an indictment but I'd certainly be willing to arrest the son-of-a-bitch." Saunders's voice betrayed his anger.

"Let's not forget the man is President Whitman's choice for Vice-President," Murphy said.

They were interrupted by an authoritative knock on the door, promptly followed by an angry James Hartwell pushing into the room.

"Livonas, this is damned embarrassing—" The words died in his throat. For a moment, they were a tableau frozen in time while Hartwell's expression changed from anger to apprehension.

Saunders said, "Senator Hartwell, on Tuesday and Wednesday nights you used a pay phone to call Herb Shepherd, Governor de Young's aide, in Sacramento."

He let the accusation hang there while the three of them waited for an explanation they knew wouldn't be forthcoming. The silence stretched while Hartwell looked from one to another. His face was waxen.

Livonas said, "Tuesday, you were at the meeting when we first discussed hitting the oil rigs off the Louisiana coast, Senator. Wednesday night, we firmed it up."

There was another long silence. Hartwell finally turned to Livonas, his face strained. "So you even tapped the pay phones around my house." He put his briefcase on the table and fumbled with the catches. "I have a letter I'd like somebody to give to Elizabeth Packard."

He said it with a touch of melodrama and Livonas grimaced.

Then all three of them were looking at a small caliber pistol that Hartwell had taken from his briefcase. His voice was shaky as he tried to strike an heroic pose. "I know very well the position I'm in, gentlemen. I value my life; I assume you do yours."

It was the last thing Livonas had expected, then he caught himself wondering how Hartwell had smuggled the gun past the metal detectors. Saunders, at the far end of the table, directly opposite Hartwell, was open-mouthed. Fran Murphy, just as surprised, was a little to Hartwell's left while he was midway between the two of them to Hartwell's right.

"Somebody's bound to come in any minute," Livonas said casually.

"We won't be here long." Hartwell sounded near hysteria. His hand was trembling and Livonas guessed he really didn't know how to use the gun, which made him doubly dangerous—the man might shoot at anything. "The three of you are going to walk me out of here. You in front, Livonas. If Mr. Murphy or Mr. Saunders forget themselves, you'll be shot first."

Hartwell was playing a role, Livonas thought. The western patriot escaping from the clutches of the federal government.

"You'll never get out of Washington," Murphy said.

Saunders thought of the gambit first, shouted, "Cover him, Joe!" and dove for the floor.

Hartwell swung his gun down to cover Saunders. Livonas tackled him at the same time as Murphy. Hartwell gasped and went over backward. Livonas grappled for the pistol, felt Hartwell's hand and wrenched it backward. Hartwell screamed and dropped the gun. Murphy grabbed for it. Livonas continued to force Hartwell on his side, then on his stomach. He twisted Hartwell's arm up behind his back and planted one knee firmly at the base of his spine.

"You can let him up now, Andy," Saunders said.

Both Saunders and Murphy were on their feet, Saunders covering Hartwell with his own revolver.

Livonas let go of Hartwell and stood up. "That's it, Senator."

Hartwell struggled to his feet, holding his injured wrist. "It wasn't a bad try, was it, Andrew?" He said it in a stiff-upper-lip tone of voice.

Livonas felt a wave of disgust. Thirty dead and the prick wanted a pat on the back for courage. "I thought it was pretty feeble myself, Hartwell." He turned to Saunders. "Let's see if we can get him out of here without the media seeing him."

The faint smile of bravery faded from Hartwell's face. He'd probably spent the past year considering himself the West's Nathan Hale, Livonas thought.

Now the fantasy was over and reality was setting in.

Christmas Day
        11:30 A.M., *Pacific Time, Friday*

The rain drummed against the tinted windows of the private dining room in the Dome Restaurant. De Young stared out at the
rainswept Los Angeles airport. There were bound to be problems,
he reminded himself; the important thing was to keep the proper
perspective. And the proper perspective was that somebody had
fucked up. He shoved aside his small glass of sherbet and stared,
disbelieving, at Shepherd.

"You know how the hell they got him?"

Shepherd said, "Livonas was responsible for the delay in the
hearings to begin with. He must have put a tap on Hartwell's
phones." He hesitated. "Hartwell was hardly a professional spy."

"Hartwell was seen leaving the building with Livonas and that
nigger FBI director and two of his agents," Hewitt added.

Livonas. De Young took a sip of his coffee and stared again at the
sheets of rain sweeping across the tarmac. A 747 was lumbering
down a far runway for its takeoff. They had lost a big advantage, but
then they had never counted on Hartwell being selected for Vice-
President in the first place. Things balance out, he decided. At least
Hartwell had been around long enough to warn them of Louisiana.

He turned to Wagoner, toying with his eggs benedict. "What
about the convention, Jerry?"

"Nothing's really changed," Wagoner said, offhand.

De Young felt a flash of irritation. "Jerry, at two o'clock on Sunday I address the convention. How big a margin will we have?"

Wagoner met his eyes. "Big."

De Young slammed down his fork. "Don't bullshit me, Jerry.
How big?"

Wagoner looked apologetic. "You have to understand, Vince, the
convention has a life of its own—I can't give you a nose count. But
we've still got it locked up. New England and the Atlantic Seaboard
are firmly with the East. Some of the southern states—Louisiana,
Mississippi, Georgia—will vote with the West. And then there are
the border states and midwestern states like Illinois where we're
solid."

"The margin, Jerry."

"Enough." Wagoner hesitated. "Though we don't have quite the edge we once had."

That was what he wanted to hear, de Young thought, while there was still time to do something about it.

"Why not?"

Wagoner fiddled with a breadstick. "Two reasons. Houseman is proving to be an excellent leader for the federal forces. She understands parliamentary maneuvering, she's convincing, and the delegates admire her guts."

De Young reached for a cube of sugar, stripped off the paper, and dropped it in his coffee. He turned to Hewitt sitting quietly at his right, half in the shadows, listening impassively to the conversation.

"Do something about her, Craig." He turned back to Wagoner, who looked relieved. "What's the other reason?"

"Whitman himself. Since he became President, some of the doubtful delegates are back in the eastern column and some of those we were counting on are starting to waver."

Whitman was a sick old man but he was still powerful. De Young swore to himself. "A close vote is no damned good, Jerry. When I call for secession, I want the convention to be howling its head off." Then another thought occurred to him. "Any chance Whitman might address the convention?"

"I've heard rumors but I don't know how true they are. I doubt that his doctors would let him attend."

"I don't want Whitman addressing that convention," de Young said slowly. "He could make a big difference." He glanced at Hewitt again. "I don't want Whitman to even touch the microphone."

His eyes wandered back to the tinted window. Five years ago the airport was packed, with planes landing almost every minute during a busy stretch. Today was Christmas and it was almost deserted; they were lucky if a flight took off or landed every fifteen minutes. Within a year, all that could change—only the flights would be coming in and going out over the Pacific, to Japan, Taiwan, China. In people's minds, New York would be as far away as London.

He finished his coffee and pushed away from the table. "We haven't talked about the possibilities of Freedom Day."

Wagoner cocked his head, puzzled. Shepherd stared at him, trying, as usual, to figure out what was on his mind. Bolles was thinking of something else, he was only half listening.

"The mass demonstration in Colorado will be at the new experimental federal synfuels complex that's being built in Colorado Springs. As I understand it, the complex will be guarded by federal troops." He looked at Bolles. "What do you think the federal government will do about the demonstration, General?"

Bolles glanced up from filling his pipe, surprised at being asked a question. "Probably order troops to keep demonstrators out of the complex. Standard riot duty."

The general had always dealt with the overall military strategy. He had never been included when they had discussed some of the grimmer aspects. Now there was no longer a choice.

"The governor of Colorado expects there'll be half a million demonstrators there, General—they'll come from all over the state."

Shepherd and Wagoner exchanged glances. They were way ahead of Bolles. Hewitt, of course, was already involved in the planning.

Bolles frowned. "There's a considerable risk of a confrontation at all the Freedom Day demonstrations."

De Young nodded sardonically. "That's right, General." He turned to Wagoner. "Jerry, I want you to make the arrangements for a direct audiovisual hookup between the convention and the synfuels center." He leaned closer to Bolles, his eyes fixed on the general's. "The synfuels center will be guarded by a contingent of federal troops. Somebody in the crowd is bound to take a shot at them."

Bolles paused with a match halfway to his pipe. "Those troops will fire back into the crowd if they're fired on," he said curtly.

De Young was ironic. "I wanted a military man's opinion on that." He turned to Hewitt. "You've made arrangements to guarantee the situation, Craig?"

Hewitt nodded. Shepherd had obviously guessed what he had planned and was staring out at the rainy airport, expressionless. Wagoner looked nervous.

Bolles put his pipe down on the table, appalled. "You're planning to provoke a confrontation. Our own supporters will be killed!"

De Young stood up abruptly, almost knocking over the chair he was sitting on. He leaned over so his face was a foot away from Bolles's.

"That's exactly right, Herman. Innocent people will be killed, slaughtered by federal troops. It will ruin Whitman. It will outrage the convention and guarantee the passage of the secession amendment. It will so blacken the reputation of the federal government that there will be no popular support for any efforts to make war on the West."

Bolles leaned forward, desperately trying to face de Young down. "We have to maintain our sense of honor," he said stiffly. "Otherwise, we're no better than—"

"What's your alternative, General?" De Young cut Bolles off, not bothering to hide his contempt. "I'll tell you what it is—a civil war that grinds along for years, that bleeds both sides white, that turns the world over to the Soviets. You're absolutely right, innocent people will be killed. Go head, General, make the moral choice: a few hundred on Sunday or a million in a civil war. You pick it."

Bolles sagged back in his chair. "It's a question of morality . . ." His voice drained away.

De Young ignored him. "I'll be on the podium at two o'clock. General, you and Hewitt work out the logistics and coordinate them with Jerry."

"Hewitt can handle everything," Bolles said, trembling. "I don't want anything to do with it."

"You don't?" de Young said politely. His voice became gentle. "You didn't get to where you are without having to do some dirty work, general. Didn't you ever have to clean out a latrine?"

He reached over and plucked a piece of lint from Bolles's lapel. "Just imagine you're in basic training."

Christmas Day

4:00 P.M., Friday

Livonas stood behind his cluttered desk and watched the presidential limousine come to a stop at the West Wing entrance. Whitman, coming back from Christmas services at the National Cathedral. It must have been relaxing to sit and listen to Christmas carols, he thought with a twinge of jealousy. But if anybody needed a break, it was Whitman.

He flipped through the stacks of papers on his desk, searching for his notes for the four-fifteen meeting. He found them just as Hugh Ramsay rapped on his office door and walked in.

"Time to go, Andy." He grabbed Livonas's sport jacket off the coat rack by the door and threw it to him. Livonas slipped it on and hit the light switch as they left.

"How's it look?"

Ramsay shook his head. "It couldn't get much worse unless an Ice Age hit." He took a report from his briefcase and handed it to Livonas. "Read the first page, that gives you the picture."

Livonas scanned it. In ten Frost Belt cities, vital services had been cut off and entire neighborhoods were without heat. The morning *Post* had reported riots in six of them.

The timing was perfect, Livonas thought—for Vincent de Young. He folded the report and stuffed it in his pocket.

"So what are you going to do, Hugh?"

Ramsay lowered his voice as General Rudd stepped out of his office up the hall. "Just support me at the meeting."

Rudd nodded and joined them. "Merry Christmas, gentlemen."

"Such as it is," Livonas murmured. The Louisiana debacle had chastened Rudd, but with the arrest of Hartwell, the general seemed his old self again—the failure of the oil rig assault could be blamed on a civilian. But he was being unfair to Rudd; he had suggested the assault to begin with, not the general.

Whitman was already in the Oval Office, stripped to the waist, with Dr. Mills, stethoscope at the ready, listening to his heart. He impatiently pushed the doctor away when they came in and grabbed for his shirt. "Greetings, gentlemen." He stuffed his shirttails inside his pants, pointedly ignoring Dr. Mills, who glanced at Livonas, shrugged, and stalked out.

A minute later Jeff Saunders, Attorney General Bob Knox, CIA Director Ed White, and Al Reynolds had joined them. Ramsay handed out copies of his report as everyone pulled their chairs around the President's desk.

Livonas reached into his folder and took out the notes he had made during his conversation with Katy earlier that afternoon. He gave the others a few minutes to finish the summary.

"I'd like to bring everyone up to date on the situation in Denver so we can discuss Hugh's report in that context." He glanced at Whitman, who nodded and pushed his reading glasses down on his nose so he had a clear view of everyone in the room.

"To make it brief, Katy Houseman reports the Western Coalition is arguing that the oil-starved states—roughly the same ones mentioned in Hugh's report—would be better off supporting the right of the western states to secede. As an inducement, they're offering oil credits if they support secession."

"Bribes, you mean," Rudd interrupted.

Livonas shrugged. "Whatever. The fact is, de Young can deliver oil and we can't. If we could, we'd have a bargaining chip at the convention. As it is, de Young's going to have enough votes to pass the secession amendment."

Al Reynolds looked confused. "What about the diversion of tankers to eastern ports?"

Ramsay shook his head. "They won't arrive in any number for three days. Then figure in time for off-loading plus through time at the refinery and you're talking about a minimum of two to three weeks. The Amerada-Hess complex in the Virgin Islands can refine crude to residual fuel oil for industrial use and ship that direct—that may save us something."

Whitman glanced at Livonas. "De Young hasn't that much of a lead."

"They believe de Young, they don't believe us," Livonas said.

Saunders hunched forward in his chair, frustrated. "We can set up a distribution system for when the tankers get here, advertise allocations, announce the steps the new Administration has taken to meet the problem——"

Rudd interrupted again, bitter. "Letting the convention leave Washington was a mistake. Here, at least, we could have exercised some ultimate control."

"We've been over that, General." Whitman turned to Livonas. "Andy, who's leading the Frost Belt forces and what's their strength?"

Livonas glanced at his notes. "Janice McCall and the Chicago delegation are acting as brokers—they're enough to make a difference. Their actual delegation strength is small but according to Katy, it's enough to give de Young a victory. Katy says McCall is planning to come to Denver."

"What about Jeff's suggestion that we launch a press campaign?" Whitman reached for his pipe. "We've made some progress. Within three weeks, we'll be able to supply emergency relief."

Livonas shook his head. "We don't have three weeks, we've got two days. Under normal circumstances, it might work. But the atti-

tude of convention delegates toward the federal government is negative; we can't deal in futures."

Ramsay stirred in his chair and Whitman said, "You've got an
idea, Hugh?"

"There's a solution that might work on a short-term basis, Mr.
President, though I'll admit it creates other problems." He shot a
sidelong glance at Rudd.

Everybody was staring at Ramsay now.

"We haven't considered military reserves," he said slowly. "If we
rationed them over the next ten days or so, we might be able to get
through until the first of the tankers arrives and the refineries can
increase their output."

Rudd leaped to his feet. "Mr. Ramsay, we're faced with fighting a
civil war in two days. And you want to deprive us of the ability to
fight it?" He looked at Whitman. "What should be done is to have
Attorney General Knox order the convention shut down. If necessary, I'll move in army troops and do it."

Ramsay couldn't slug it out with Rudd, Livonas thought. He
caught Rudd's eye. "General, could I ask some questions?"

"Certainly, just don't ask me to sanction military suicide." Rudd
was cold, formal.

He'd have to be tactful, Livonas thought, and that had never
been easy with Rudd. "Would our European forces be affected by
the release of domestic military oil reserves?"

Rudd shook his head. "No, of course not. In Europe, our NATO
allies are responsible for fuel supplies. The same holds true for other
parts of the globe. But we're faced with a war right here in the
United States."

Livonas turned back to Ramsay. "What we're talking about is a
two- to three-week delay before we could affect civilian deliveries,
right?"

Ramsey nodded. "That's right."

"And we should be able to replenish military reserves then,
right?"

"In my opinion, yes."

"I'm not debating our position overseas," Rudd said slowly.
"What you'd be taking away is our ability to launch a quick-strike
military move to put down secession. If we're faced with a three
weeks to a month hiatus, everything will harden and the result will
be a drawn-out civil war."

Rudd was persuasive. Livonas glanced around the room. It was obvious the others thought so, too.

Rudd was looking at him now. "Let's say you win—that you've got the oil to buy the votes so de Young loses in the convention. What's to prevent him from saying, 'Fuck the convention, we're seceding anyway, and if you don't like it, come and get us'? Only, of course, we couldn't—not for at least three weeks or more, which gives him plenty of time to consolidate his position, both politically and militarily."

"Without the sanction of the convention, he'd lack popular support," Livonas objected.

"Would he?" Rudd asked. "In the East, yes, maybe in the border states. But passions are certainly running high in most of the West."

There was a short silence when he finished. Whitman finally said, "The choice is whether we put our chips on a military or a political solution. It's a gamble either way." He looked around the room. "This is a decision on which we should all comment. You first, Al."

Reynolds looked uncertain and uncomfortable. "I think we should release the oil reserves. I can't even begin to calculate the consequences a civil war would have for us internationally." He looked at Rudd. "I'm afraid your strategy would guarantee civil war, Charles."

Whitman glanced at the Attorney General. "Bob."

"I'm afraid I have to agree with General Rudd, though not without reservations," Knox said slowly. "My own feeling is that the secession movement would collapse if we show some strength."

"Jeff?"

Saunders looked at Livonas and shrugged apologetically. "We have to call de Young's bluff. The Attorney General should enforce the Supreme Court injunction against the Constitutional Convention and if necessary, we should move enough troops to Denver to suppress it."

"Mr. White?"

"I have to go with the General."

Livonas slowly exhaled, aware for the first time that he had been holding his breath. He'd picked both Saunders and White as being in favor of a political solution.

Whitman walked over to the window and stood with his back to the room, looking out at the mist-enshrouded Washington Monument. After a moment, he turned around.

"Gentlemen, I'm afraid this is a decision only I can make." He looked at Rudd. "As I recall, Carl Sandburg wrote that Lincoln was advised by his generals that the war with the South would be over in a matter of weeks. I honestly don't know whether you're as wrong as they were, General. But I do know that we should exercise every option that's left to us before we decide that the next civil war is inevitable."

He walked back to his desk. "General, I want a full-scale mobilization of our military forces so that, God forbid, if we're called upon to fight, we'll be in a position to do so. Hugh, you arrange for the immediate distribution of the military reserves to critical areas."

He looked at Livonas, his face drawn. "Andy, my feeling is that if Janice McCall can be persuaded to come back to our side, then we've got a fighting chance at the convention. I think it's worth another trip to Chicago."

He had what he wanted, Livonas thought. But there was no guarantee at all how things would turn out, anything could happen. Then he thought that de Young must realize that they wouldn't be standing still. In fact, he would be prepared for moves by them, had probably been prepared for them all along.

Livonas stood up, thinking the meeting was over. Whitman waved him down.

"I'm not through yet, Andy." He glanced at Saunders and Knox. "I want you to arrange security for me at the convention."

It took them all a moment before they understood what he was planning. Livonas started to lead the chorus of protests and Whitman held up a hand. He smiled grimly.

"Governor de Young's going to address the convention, gentlemen. If the President of the United States doesn't have the courage to stand up to Vincent de Young, why should anybody else?"

"It's walking into the lion's den," Rudd objected.

Whitman smiled sardonically and shook his head. "I don't think so, General. De Young's plan hinges on the legality of the convention; he's not about to endanger that."

December 26
7:00 P.M., Mountain Time, Saturday

Kathleen hung up the phone. Livonas had already left for Chicago; his office had said he'd be in Denver tomorrow morning.

Stu set up the long, folding work table in the living room of their Hyatt House hotel suite and they started going over the tally sheets of the day's voting. All the news wasn't bad, Kathleen reflected, just most of it. Despite some movement in their direction, the West was holding on to its sizable majority.

They worked steadily, picking out the convention delegates who had switched back and forth between the West and the Federal Coalition on the different votes, making cards on them and then assigning members of the coalition to lobby them for their vote. It was a tiring process, the saving grace being that it produced results.

She leaned back and stretched, glancing over at Lester Hamilton, who sat in an easy chair on the other side of the room filling out one of his reports. He'd been so quiet, she'd forgotten he was there. Fiftyish, thick-set, with a few strands of graying red hair in the center of his balding head, Hamilton had been the night duty officer for the U.S. marshals ever since she and Stu had arrived in Denver.

At first, she had resented him. Then, after a few days, she had grown used to him and now admitted that she liked the sense of security he and the other marshals provided.

Stu slammed his pencil down and stood up. "Cocktail time." He jingled the quarters in his hand for the ice machine.

Kathleen hit his hand from beneath and grabbed the quarters when they bounced out. "You get the Scotch." She had introduced Stu to the pleasures of unblended Scotch since their arrival and was wickedly proud of it. He had been strictly a rum-and-Coke drinker before, the thought of which made her gag. It had become their evening ritual. They worked until they couldn't see straight, then she got the ice and Stu got the booze.

She grabbed Stu's down vest off the back of his chair and slipped it on. In the daytime, the sun heated the atrium of the hotel but at night it was freezing cold.

"Les, can I get you something?" She hesitated with one hand on the door knob.

Lester glanced up from his clipboard. "No thanks, Katy, I've got a pot of coffee going." He motioned in the direction of the coffee machine which was busily dripping away.

"Yeah, you can get me a Coke," Stu said. He had come out of the bedroom with a bottle of rum in one hand and Scotch in the other, grinning.

Kathleen made a face to indicate her disgust and slipped out into the corridor. The hotel was built around a huge indoor, glass-roofed atrium extending up six floors and ringed with balconies around the sides that fanned out from it like the spokes of a wheel. In warmer weather, the ground floor served as the lobby. But in winter, the atrium was too expensive to heat and the lobby facilities were moved inside the building, giving the atrium a deserted feeling.

Kathleen pulled Stu's vest around her and walked to the fourth-floor balcony, then followed a corridor at right angles to it. The ice machine was at the end of it, next to a housekeeping and linen-storage area.

She bent over the machine to put in a quarter, then swore to herself. Somebody had jammed the coin slot with a slug. She retraced her steps and took the staircase to the fifth floor, hoping the machine up there was working.

The fifth floor was in semi-gloom. Only the fire exit lights were on and she wondered if the hotel had closed the floor down. Then she heard a snatch of an early seventies pop tune from a room along the corridor ahead. She turned left off the balcony and was halfway down the corridor when a room door opened and a man in a green jacket backed out, fumbling with his key.

The floor wasn't closed after all. She walked around the man and, when he turned, noticed that his mutton chop whiskers joined a dirty blond moustache. Appropriately western, she thought.

Then another door opened ahead of her and a man in a blue watch cap and maroon scarf stepped out, staring at her. On instinct, she whirled. The man with the green jacket was walking toward her, grim-faced. From the room farthest down the hall, somebody turned the radio up louder.

The slug in the ice machine had been a setup and she had walked right into it. They had been watching her, knew her schedule.

At the far end of the hall, another room door opened and a

slightly built young man edged into the corridor. She was trapped now, with two men ahead of her and one behind.

She turned to see Green Jacket running toward her. She spun around. The man with the maroon scarf was almost up to her and the young man at the far end of the hall had drawn a pistol.

The man with the gun was trying to aim it at her but couldn't get a clear shot. Then Green Jacket lunged for her. She ducked, twisted her ankle, and dropped to one knee. The man in the green jacket rammed into her shoulder. The shock almost threw her flat but it also knocked the wind out of her attacker. She scrambled to her feet and ran for the long corridor that led back to the atrium-lobby, screaming to attract attention. A shot ricocheted off one of the metal room doors and then she was around the corner, running for the stairs. Lester was racing up the stairwell toward her, his service revolver in his right hand.

There were more shots and Lester flattened himself into one of the doors at the same time that the man in the maroon scarf tackled her. She brought up her knees and tried to jerk away, then felt his arm tighten around her throat.

Somebody else was shouting now. A busboy was standing at the end of the hall next to the atrium railing with his hot cart, staring wide-eyed at the fight.

Then the man with the green jacket rounded the corner and stumbled over the two of them. Kathleen kicked out and struggled to her feet again. "Run!" Lester yelled. She dashed for the end of the corridor.

It was nothing more than a stinging sensation, as if somebody had lightly scraped her right thigh with their fingernails.

She glanced down. The right side of her slacks and the top of her right boot were already turning red. She ducked into a small alcove that held housekeeping supplies. Lester was grappling with two of the men, trying to free his pistol. Then the man in the green jacket ran toward the struggling group, holding something metallic. A second later, Lester went down, his mouth wide in a silent shout of pain. His blue wool work shirt was damp with blood.

The slightly built killer yanked free of Lester and faced her, his feet wide apart. He brought up the pistol and aimed. There was a shot and all expression slid from his face as he collapsed on the dark carpet.

Behind him, Lester was swaying on his knees, gripping his pistol in one hand while he tried to hold the man wearing the maroon scarf with the other. The man broke away and darted for the end of the corridor, toward the busboy, who was screaming for the police. He had just reached him when Lester fired once more, then vomited blood on the corridor rug and slowly folded on his side.

At the end of the hall, the man threw up his arms, did a slow-motion pirouette and collided with the busboy and his cart. They crashed against the thin atrium railing. The railing tore away and the two men and the cart plunged over the edge.

Lester was moaning, his eyes glazed. The young assassin was sprawled on the floor, not moving, so close Kathleen could touch him.

Then Green Jacket crawled out from behind Lester, holding a bloody knife in his hand. He bent over Lester, hesitated, and glanced up at her. He wasn't after Lester, she thought, weak with fear. He was after her.

She squeezed back into a corner of the alcove and felt the edge of a metal dust pan dig into her back. She turned and grabbed it, whirling at the same time Green Jacket dove for her. She caught him in the face with the edge, slicing deep into his cheek.

"Bitch!"

It was the only word that any of the killers had spoken.

He almost fell, then caught her arm just below the elbow and tried to twist it behind her, bringing his knife up against her throat. She braced herself against the wall and jammed her left knee into his groin. He doubled up, still trying to grab for her. She ducked underneath the knife and ran for the end of the corridor.

She tried to scream but was out of breath, her lungs and sides aching. She could hear him padding after her.

Then Stu was somewhere close by, yelling, "Katy! Katy!" There were the sounds of sirens in the distance. Green Jacket pulled his knife back to thrust, hesitating when Stu yelled again from the stairwell off the atrium balcony. He glanced in that direction, then turned back to slash at her. She twisted frantically to one side, lost her footing, and grabbed at the broken railing to keep from falling over the side.

The elevator doors opened and Green Jacket turned and dashed for the stairwell. Two marshals ran out of the elevator, confused for the moment as to what was happening.

Kathleen heard a scream from the stairwell. Then more marshals were pouring out of the other elevator, running toward her. One of them looked down the corridor and said, "Jesus Christ, it's Les! Call an ambulance!"

She felt faint. Her side was burning and her right leg was soaked with blood.

"We better get you to the hospital, Miss Houseman." One of the marshals took her arm to steady her.

She was half-dazed. Where was Stu? She had heard him shouting her name. She shook off the marshal and limped toward the stairwell. Stu had been running up the stairs.

"The ambulance will be here in a minute—"

She ignored him and started down the stairs, almost falling. Stu was sitting on the landing, slumped against the wall. A marshal was bending over him and for a moment all she could see was part of Stu's face. She hadn't seen him look so white since the day he had fainted in Washington. She pushed the marshal aside.

Stu's shirt was drenched red from the neck to his waist. There was no expression at all in his eyes.

Then she saw the gaping wound deep across his throat and screamed again.

December 26
8:00 P.M., Central Time, Saturday

" 'Then Job answered and said, How long will ye vex my soul, and break me in pieces with words?' "

Livonas pulled his overcoat tighter around him. He stood in the shadows in the back of the First Abyssinian Baptist Church on Chicago's South Side. Janice McCall, wearing the black robes of a church deacon, gripped the sides of the lectern with gloved hands as she read from the church's Bible. Between the lectern and the first row of pews were eight caskets, six of them white, on funeral home gurneys.

" '. . . the Lord blessed the latter end of Job more than his beginning . . . He had also seven sons and three daughters . . . And in all the land were no women so fair as the daughters of Job . . . After this lived Job an hundred and forty years, and saw his sons, and his son's sons, *even* four generations . . .' Amen."

The mayor stepped back from the lectern, her place taken by a gaunt, stern-faced minister. "Let us pray. 'The Lord is my shepherd; I shall not want. He maketh me to lie down in green pastures: he leadeth me beside the still waters . . .' "

The congregation joined in so that the whole church rocked with the cadence of the Twenty-Third Psalm. Livonas could hear the sounds of sobbing from a broad-shouldered black man in the first row. He guessed it was Jesse Williams, a twenty-year veteran of the Chicago police force whose family of eight had been wiped out in a fire started by a hand-rigged kerosene heater.

" 'Surely goodness and mercy shall follow me all the days of my life: and I will dwell in the house of the Lord for ever.' " Livonas joined in the final words of the psalm, wishing in his heart that he still believed in them.

From the balcony above him, the choir's voices floated out over the congregation. "Swing low, sweet chariot, comin' for to carry me home." He felt a tap on his shoulder and turned to face a tired Sergeant Chernig. "The Mayor's waiting for you in her car, Mr. Livonas." Livonas eased out into the aisle and quietly followed Chernig outside.

McCall sat in the far corner of the back seat of her limousine, looking small and fragile beneath a heavy blue lap rob. She was repairing the damage to her makeup caused by her tears. Her face tightened as Chernig opened the door for Livonas.

"I don't even know why I'm wasting my time on you." She put away her compact. "Why do you want to see me?"

Livonas got in, sitting on the edge of the seat. "I assume I don't have to tell you what de Young's plans are."

"You do not."

"And you're going to support him?"

McCall leaned forward. "Sergeant, let's drive Mr. Livonas back to the airport." She turned to face Livonas. " 'Contrary to conventional wisdom, cities are not permanent.' Do you remember that little homily? Or perhaps you recall the phrase, 'people-oriented, not place-oriented.' " She was angry now, her face lightly flushed. "Or my favorite: 'Growth and decline are integral parts of urban life.' "

She shook a cigarette from a pack, her voice deceptively calm. "Tell me what the United States government has done for the cities in the past ten years except wish we'd disappear—like the Jesse

Williams family laid out in those coffins." Her hand holding the lighter shook slightly. "You're strangely quiet, Mr. Livonas—I was expecting a patriotic speech. We could drive out to the cemetery, maybe you'd like to deliver it at the burial. I'm sure it would be appreciated."

She leaned back and laughed bitterly. " 'Sorry, Janice, we can't do it.' Remember? I'm quoting Andy Livonas who told me that just ten days ago after seeing me almost order my own citizens shot down in cold blood."

She let her anger build. "You know what patriotism has meant for Chicago and the other northern cities? Suicide." She turned away from him and stared out the side window at the ice-bound street. "God, I wish you hadn't come, you make me sick."

Livonas looked at his watch. "Call the control tower at O'Hare, Janice."

She stared at him. "Why on earth should I do that?"

"Three Boeing stratotankers should have landed in the past hour. They're carrying distillate fuel oil; the city will have to make arrangements to transfer it to tank trucks for distribution."

She stubbed out her cigarette, gave Chernig the orders, then smoked another one down to the filter before the tower confirmed the transports.

"That's an impressive gesture," she said sarcastically. "Perhaps the classic example of much too little far too late."

Livonas could feel his own temper start to rise. "It's more than a gesture. We're stripping the military of its reserves. You're to contact Hugh Ramsay in Washington; he's making arrangements for convoys of tank trucks to supply major cities from the military fuel dumps nearest them. Whatever distillate and residual fuels we have will be distributed on a pro rata basis."

She was silent for a long moment and he added, "I don't think de Young could get you any oil sooner than that."

"It'll be a few weeks' supply at best," she said, staring out the window again. "What happens after that?"

"We're confiscating the cargoes of a number of tankers at sea. With good luck, we'll be able to carry you with stringent rationing through the middle of January and then we'll be able to get crude to the Whiting refineries."

She concentrated on her cigarette and he finally burst out, "What do you want, Janice, an act of God? Bob Whitman's doing more than any three people could do. You know the gossip. It's true—he's risking his life to do it."

"He's risking the country, too." Some of the anger had leaked out of her voice. She was already figuring the city's priorities.

"We're gambling. For three weeks, most of the Navy will be landlocked, the Army will be immobilized, part of the Air Force will be grounded."

"What do you want in return?" she asked in a low voice.

"You're flying to Denver tomorrow. If de Young wins, there won't be much left of the country after that. Just separate states and communities that will drift even farther apart. It's your decision even more than it's ours."

He couldn't tell what she was thinking, what decision she was making. "I won't argue with your grudge against the federal government. But you know me, you know Bob Whitman. We can pull things together, we can change things. But we'll need your help."

"And if I don't go along, I'll be a traitor to my country, is that it?" She still sounded hostile.

"That's exactly it," Livonas said harshly. "You'll be a traitor."

They were turning off for O'Hare when there was a crackle from the radio phone up front. Chernig picked up the receiver to answer it, then handed it back to Livonas.

"It's the U.S. marshal's office in Denver, Mr. Livonas. They say it's urgent."

December 27
8:00 A.M., *Mountain Time, Sunday*

Livonas sat at the desk in the corner of the hotel room, going over reports, the lamp turned low so the light wouldn't disturb Katy in the bed a few feet away. The night table was littered with boxes of gauze dressings and bottles of pills—antibiotics, painkillers, tranquilizers. She had woken up twice during the night, once in pain and once screaming for Stu.

He'd gotten there a little after midnight and insisted the doctors transfer her to the Denver Hilton where the presidential party was staying. It was only a flesh wound, even if it was painful, and he felt more confidence in Saunders's security system at the Hilton than in the few guards at the hospital.

He had just forced his attention back to the reports when there was a light knock on the door. He hurried to answer it before Katy woke up. The marshal outside was holding Jonathan Goodwell by the arm and looking apologetic.

Livonas whispered, "He's all right, Graham."

Goodwell came in and stole a quick glance at the bed. "How is she?"

"She's doing fine."

Goodwell nodded. "All the delegates are talking about it. Jerry Wagoner has already expressed his sympathy. He's also issued a statement calling all the rumors of the Western Coalition's involvement in the attack slanderous."

Katy mumbled something from the bed and Goodwell backed hastily toward the door. He handed Livonas several leaflets. "They're distributing these at all the delegates' hotels."

Behind them, Katy said sleepily, "Don't go, let me see one." Livonas handed her one and she snapped on the bed-table lamp. He took his own over to the desk.

He had seen the first leaflet at Stapleton airport. It was headlined "Remember Freedom Day!" and announced demonstrations in front of federally owned land and buildings at fifteen different cities throughout the West. Facilities would be set up so Governor de Young's speech at the convention would be broadcast to each of them.

The Colorado demonstration would be at the Federal Synfuels Development Center in Colorado Springs. Livonas had heard estimates of demonstrators ranging from three to five million throughout the West and up to a quarter of a million at the Springs.

The new flier was titled simply: "Attention Delegates!" He scanned it, then read it more carefully. He looked over at Katy. "They're up to something."

She was fully awake now. "What do you think?"

"They've got spots on all the local radio stations," Goodwell said. " 'Chase the federal government back across the great divide where it belongs!' " he quoted.

It was good propaganda, Livonas thought. De Young's speech at the convention would steam up the demonstrators, most of whom would probably be in an angry mood anyway.

He hit the flier with his open hand. "I think we ought to get together with the others on this."

He couldn't shake the thought that Vincent de Young specialized in overkill.

"I can't help it," Saunders said. "I still think it's insanity for the President to appear on the podium. There's no way we can maintain tight security in the arena, not with that crowd."

Livonas helped himself to a cinnamon roll and coffee from the cart in the middle of the suite. Katy, her cane hooked over the back of her chair, sat next to him. Whitman, collar open and shirt only partially buttoned, was stretched out on the lounger. Saunders was sitting on the edge of the desk, balancing a cup of coffee on his knee, while the others sat on the tan Naugahyde couch.

Rudd, dressed in combat fatigues, pushed forward on the couch, perching on the edge. "If the President is shot, then everything collapses." He looked at Whitman. "Let's face it, if that happens, then any political solution automatically goes up the flue."

Whitman took a bite of his sweet roll, washing it down with a gulp of coffee.

"We went over all this before we left Washington. The fact is, I don't have any choice. De Young is coming to the convention to call for the end of the United States. If the President doesn't have the balls to confront him, who will?" He turned to Saunders. "Get me one of those bulletproof vests or something." He finished off the roll and added, "And somebody better get in touch with the Speaker of the House—he'll be next in the barrel."

Livonas held up the demonstration leaflet. "Everyone read this?"

"Pretty inflammatory," Reynolds said. He stood up to leave.

"Don't go yet, Al," Livonas said, "we've got to discuss this. It's more than it seems. The Western Coalition has been hoping for a three-quarters majority on the vote. From what I understand right now, they might not even get two-thirds."

Whitman frowned. "What's your estimate, Katy?"

Katy turned slightly in her chair, searching for a more comfortable position. "A lot depends on which way Janice McCall goes, your speech, of course, and de Young's. In the last few days, there's been some movement toward us and away from them."

Saunders looked blank. "I don't get it. What's that got to do with the leaflet and the demonstrations?"

"The situation's too democratic for de Young," Livonas said. "There's an outside chance he could lose. It's damned outside but he's not the type to walk up to that podium without some last-minute insurance."

They were all looking at him now. Finally Ed White said, "What sort of insurance you thinking of, Andy?"

Livonas waved the leaflet again. "This. Katy, tell them about the communications setup."

Katy straightened out her leg, wincing. "They've installed a television linkup between the synfuels complex in Colorado Springs and the convention. This morning they hung a twenty-by-forty video projection screen behind the dais."

"Let's imagine the crowd is stirred up by de Young's rhetoric and decides to sack the complex," Livonas said. "What happens then?"

"It wouldn't happen in the first place," Rudd interrupted. "Those leaflets have been circulating for three days now; at most sites a battalion of military police have been assigned to guard duty, backed up by regular army units. They're equipped with tear gas and if that doesn't stop any demonstrators, they've been issued rubber bullets."

The situation was suddenly clear in Livonas's mind. "And if there are provocateurs in the crowd who fire on them?"

Rudd started to answer, then settled back on the couch, thoughtful. "They'd defend the sites and themselves," he said slowly.

All of them had the picture now. "We're gambling a minor show of force against a slaughter that we'd never survive politically," Whitman said, grim. "General, get on the horn and order the Army to withdraw from those sites."

Rudd immediately reached for the phone and Livonas realized he had underestimated the general. Half an hour later, Rudd put it down, worried. "The commanders at every site acknowledge except Colorado Springs. The phone service seems to be disrupted. They're going to try to get hold of the commander by radio."

Tension started to build in the room. Everybody was silent, waiting for confirmation to come back. Five minutes turned to ten. Then the phone rang and Livonas could sense the feeling of relief in the room.

Rudd answered, listened for a moment, then said quietly, "Keep trying." He looked at the others in the room. "Either there's an equipment malfunction or they're not answering."

There was nothing wrong with the equipment, Livonas thought. De Young had probably been planning his Reichstag Fire for months. "How far away is the Springs?"

Katy said, "Sixty miles maybe, by car."

He looked at Rudd. "Who's the army man in charge of the unit at the synfuels complex?"

Rudd looked uneasy. "I'm told a Major Thompson. I don't know him personally but he wouldn't be there if he hadn't been cleared."

"Can you guarantee him?"

"We cleared more than five thousand officers in less than a week," Rudd said, defensive. "No, I can't guarantee him. But that doesn't mean he's pro-western."

"How did Major Thompson end up in command there?" Livonas asked, boring in. This *had* to be it.

Rudd lifted the phone again. When he put it down, his face was hard. "He volunteered," he said dryly.

"I think," Livonas said, "we've got a problem."

Little beads of sweat had gathered on Saunders's forehead. "It's only three hours before de Young's scheduled to address the convention."

Rudd stood up. "I'll go there personally, it's my responsibility."

Whitman shook his head. "Sorry, General, if things fall apart at the convention, I can't have my military commander fifty miles inside enemy territory. I want you at the airport headquarters."

Livonas said, "What about your aide, Colonel Carlson? He's here in the hotel, isn't he?"

"He's got rank on Thompson," Rudd said. "I'll have papers drawn up relieving Thompson and turning the complex over to Carlson. He'll have the troops withdrawn."

It wasn't going to be that easy, Livonas thought. "I'd like to go there with him."

Whitman looked upset. "You can't go, Andy—you're needed here."

Livonas shook his head. "I'm the only one here who isn't needed. Jeff and Ed are running security, we can hardly send Katy, I don't think you want to send your Secretary of State. General Rudd is out, so that leaves me."

Whitman didn't look completely convinced. "Why do you think we should send somebody in addition to Carlson?"

"There are two places where we can lose—either at the convention or at the Springs. There are too many political variables to just send Carlson."

Whitman looked at Livonas, then turned to Rudd. "Send a detachment of men with Andy. Your best."

Livonas said, "See you later," kissed Katy, and headed for the door with Rudd.

This was as close as he was ever going to get to confronting Vincent de Young personally.

December 27
11:00 A.M., *Mountain Time, Sunday*

At ten in the morning, General Charles Rudd closed Denver's Stapleton International Airport to all civilian traffic. By eleven, the airport was "secure." He had deployed one battalion of Black Berets around the perimeter of the field and finished setting up his communications headquarters in a Continental Airlines hangar near the main runways. They could hold the airport against all but a major assault—at least long enough for the arrival of the 101st Airborne from Fort Campbell, Kentucky.

He was standing just inside the hangar doors, drinking coffee and warming himself in the winter sunshine filtering through the dirty windows when Colonel Marks walked over and helped himself to a cup of coffee from the large thermos next to him.

"Intelligence reports that Colorado national guardsmen and regular western army units have set up positions in the Arapahoe National Forest due west of here, Roosevelt National Forest to the north and Pike to the south. And it looks like the Fourth Infantry Divison is moving up from Camp Carson."

Marks added precise amounts of sugar and powdered cream to his cup. "We lost a spotter plane over the Arapahoe," he continued. "Captain Romero radioed in just before he went down." He sipped at his coffee. "He took a SAM in his fusilage."

Rudd knew he'd met Romero once but couldn't conjure up a face to go with the name. He squinted against the sun and studied Air Force One on the tarmac a hundred yards away. President Whitman had guts, he'd give him that. But if anything went wrong, it would be damned difficult to get the President out of the Denver Arena and back to the airport.

Marks was studying him over his cup. "What happens now?"

Rudd shrugged. "For another few hours, nothing. It all depends on what happens at the convention, what the President can do."

Marks turned away to stare at the distant mountains. "The convention is stacked in favor of Governor de Young, that's pretty obvious." He looked back at Rudd, his eyes lidded. "If anything happens, you'll be running the show, General." He said it with a certain sense of satisfaction.

That was something Rudd didn't want to think about. Not yet, at any rate. Not until later on that afternoon.

"I'm hardly in the line of presidential succession, Colonel." He stood up and stalked back to where the technicians were manning the radio gear. He knew what Marks meant. If a civil war started, it would be up to him to win it or lose it. There had been enough of a buildup over the past few days that the West might risk confrontation. The war could start right here.

And for the first time in more than a hundred years, they'd be fighting people like themselves—people who spoke the same language, wore the same clothes, watched the same television shows, read the same books . . .

What had it been like when the North had fought the South? he wondered. When you understood every word that a wounded enemy was screaming?

He stepped through the side door onto the powdery snow that had begun to blow across the runways. He stared out toward the foothills, almost hidden by the smog and low-lying clouds. A war could start so easily, he thought. The westerners were out there in force. It wouldn't take much to start a firefight in the night, to stage an ambush along one of the mountain roads. An attempt to take the Rocky Mountain arsenal and its supplies of nerve gas a mile or two to the north would have to be repelled no matter what the cost—he'd deployed the other battalion of Berets around the arsenal immediately.

But then again, it might even be easier than that. Some western commandos might try to infiltrate the area around the Denver

Arena and secure it, along with the President. They'd have to watch that ... So far, Whitman had been right—the West had made no effort to block their arrival at the airport. They had even let in several battalions of Black Berets and the detachment of federal marshals that had gone with the President to the convention complex. They were treating Denver as an open city and as long as the major units of Berets remained at the airport, it would probably stay that way.

He was starting to feel the cold and swung his arms across his chest. But it wouldn't take much, he thought again, still staring toward the west.

By dusk, the country could be in a civil war.

December 27
1:55 P.M., *Mountain Time, Sunday*

De Young stood at the observation window in the Western Coalition headquarters watching Carl Baxter, white hair flying, arms outstretched, deliver the preliminary address to the convention.

He couldn't hear Baxter through the thick glass but there was no mistaking the chant that kept interrupting his speech: "Time for the West! Time for the West!"

Shepherd nudged him. "We better get back inside."

"Any word yet?"

Shepherd shook his head. "Bolles is still trying to patch into Hewitt at the synfuels complex."

Just the sound of Hewitt's name was reassuring to de Young. With Hewitt in charge, there simply wasn't any chance of something going wrong. He raised his voice to include the rest of his entourage and the bodyguards that lingered a few feet away. "That Baxter's a helluva speaker, isn't he?" He threw his arm around Shepherd and they walked back into the caucus room, trailed by the others.

The room was jammed with staff and reporters. Bolles was in the far corner sitting next to the radio man working the communications equipment. Over the heads of the crowd, de Young caught a glimpse of the television monitor showing the half-built synfuels complex. It looked almost deserted except for the army personnel carriers parked in front of the administration building, forming a barricade. As in the Indian wars, the Feds were pulling their wagons into a circle.

"You really going to call for secession?"

"How's it looking, Governor?"

The reporters crowded around him, shoving microphones in his face.

"What kind of margin do you expect?"

De Young smiled broadly for the cameras, said, "No comment, gentlemen," and ignored the barrage of questions. He brushed past them and buttonholed Wagoner in a corner of the room.

"Try and get those guys out of here, Jerry, they're a pain in the ass."

"No problem." Wagoner signaled a young aide, then turned to walk over to Shepherd. De Young grabbed his arm.

"How's it look?"

Wagoner grinned. "It's a goddamned shoo-in, Vince. Right now we've got a two-thirds margin." He nodded at the TV monitors that showed the convention floor. "If everything goes all right out there, we'll have three-quarters."

For once, de Young didn't question Wagoner's optimism. The time for doubting was past.

He checked his watch and frowned. They should have heard from Hewitt by now, what the hell was the delay? He pushed though the crowd to Bolles and pulled up a folding chair. "How come we haven't heard from Hewitt, General?"

Bolles's face was starchy white, his forehead shiny with sweat. "I just did." He smiled. The effect was like watching somebody crumple a sheet of paper. "The demonstrators in the Springs have left for the synfuels complex. They should be arriving at the main building in ten minutes or so."

De Young coughed to cover an involuntary sigh of relief. He stood up, almost bumping into Sally Craft, sitting quietly on a stool nearby, her back against the wall. Her shoes were off, her stocking feet tucked behind the bottom rungs.

De Young smiled and patted her on the arm. "You'll be out there soon, Sally." He remembered when he'd first met her. She looked a lot older to him now.

"I can hardly wait." De Young's smile vanished and he turned away. "I'm leaving after this is over," she said to his back.

It would be like getting rid of an old car, he thought. "I'm sure you'll be very happy," he said curtly.

Wagoner pushed his way over. "Baxter's winding up, Vince."

De Young could sense the tension rise in the room. Everybody could hear the delegates chanting his name in the auditorium. Baxter had created the momentum, he had to go out there now. He couldn't wait for the first shots to be fired at the synfuels center.

He took a deep breath and walked toward the door, flashing a smile and clasping his hands above his head. Even the reporters began cheering and applauding. He grinned again for the cameras, stopping by Sally Craft to kiss her on the cheek. "Wish me luck, Sally."

She smiled sweetly. "Fuck you, Vince."

He strode past the barrage of strobes into the concrete corridor leading to the convention hall, surrounded by his bodyguards. He motioned Shepherd closer to him, lowering his voice. "As soon as it starts at the Springs, send somebody up with the message. I'll announce it and we'll put it on the screen."

Then the guards pushed open the doors of the auditorium and the cheering exploded out at him. He walked down the aisle, almost deafened by the applause and the shouting. There were streaks of silence running through the mass of delegates but not many, and by the time he reached the stage, euphoria was washing over him.

"De Young! De Young! De Young!"

He climbed the steps and stood behind the microphone with his hands above his head, listening to the roar of the crowd.

Then he brought his arms down and gripped the lectern. A hush swept across the hall.

"Fellow delegates, today history begins anew . . ."

December 27
    2:12 P.M., Mountain Time, Sunday

She'd better check with Stu—Kathleen caught herself. There wasn't anything she could check with Stu, not any more. She turned away from the TV monitors showing the convention floor and walked over to the technician working on the radio gear. She tried to use her cane no more than she had to.

"Have you contacted Livonas yet?"

The technician shook his head without glancing up. "Not yet, Miss Houseman." He was probably getting tired of her asking, she thought. She turned away and limped toward the observation cubicle overlooking the convention hall, brushing past FBI agents carrying machine guns as casually as other men did briefcases. Strange how easily you accepted violence, she thought. Or maybe it just hadn't sunk in yet. Her mind danced from Stu to Lester Hamilton to Livonas, probably somewhere in the synfuels complex by now.

She couldn't let herself think of Livonas any more than she could think of Stu and Lester, she realized. She clung to the railing as she walked down the few steps into the observation nook. Whitman glanced around and gave her a hand and she stood next to him while they watched de Young harangue the convention.

De Young came across as lean and powerful, jabbing at the air with his hands, strutting back and forth behind the podium as he chronicled the crimes of the federal government, sticking out his chest and chin as he challenged the audience to deny the truth of his accusations.

Then she glanced away from de Young to study the delegates in the hall. Most of them were convention veterans with rumpled clothes and short tempers, sitting in grim-faced anticipation of the final act. There was very little whispering among themselves that she could see, or strolling around in the back of the hall. The delegates from the western states applauded de Young's speech at all the right places while the Federal Coalition waited for its chance when Whitman took the microphone.

On the dais below, de Young hunched closer to the microphone as he detailed yet another horror story about the federal government. Kathleen frowned and checked her watch. His audience must have heard it all before, he should have wrapped it up before this.

Then she realized with a start that de Young was stalling—stalling to bring the Colorado Springs atrocity story, live, to the gigantic video screen swaying slightly on its guy wires above the podium.

"We've got it!"

She turned around. In the other room, the video technician was looking up at a monitor, triumphant. She climbed back up the steps and watched as the synfuels complex came into focus on the monitor screen. They had finally managed to patch into the convention hall's televison relay system. They were now looking at the same image Vincent de Young saw on the small screen monitor next to the dais.

"They're closing in," Whitman said beside her. He pointed at the demonstrators, a seemingly endless stream of bodies that snaked down a wide access road toward the barbed-wire topped cyclone fence surrounding the complex.

"How about some sound?" Saunders grumbled.

The technician spun around, irritated. "What the hell do you think I'm trying to get?"

Whitman patted the young technician on the shoulder. "You're doing just fine, Charlie."

Everybody's temper was fraying. There was nothing any of them could do about what was happening up on the monitor. The mob now began to spread out into fields on either side of the road as they drew closer to the fence. One group was carrying a long banner that read: FEDS OUT OF THE WEST! The video image twitched, shuddered, then sharpened again, becoming so clear Kathleen could make out the angry faces of the leaders who were running beside the marchers, urging them on with bullhorns.

Farther back in the line of march were half a dozen trucks and now the demonstrators split to let the trucks through. They roared toward the fence, gaining speed, and crashed into the wire. The supports bent and the fencing slammed to the ground. The mob surged in behind the trucks.

A moment later she could see the faint, smoky trails of the first tear gas cannisters as they hit the ground just ahead of the front ranks. The scene on the monitor almost disappeared in great white puffy balloons of chemical smoke.

"You got Livonas on the radio yet?" There was an edge to Whitman's voice.

The radio man shook his head. "No, sir, nobody's acknowledging the transmission."

"Keep trying," Whitman muttered.

"Look—they've got gas masks." Reynolds sounded indignant, as if some unspoken rule of etiquette had been broken. Kathleen turned back to the monitor. Some of the demonstrators had put on masks, others were wrapping handkerchiefs around their faces while still others were simply splashing their faces with water. Any minute

now they'd go charging through the acrid smoke, de Young's provocateurs would fire on the troops, and then the huge screen in the
convention hall below would spring to life to show the startled delegates the brutality of the federal government.

Unless Livonas succeeded.

She turned to Whitman and touched him on the shoulder. "I
better get down to the floor, all hell's about to break loose."

Whitman said, "Good luck," then added gently: "Don't worry,
Andy will be all right."

She hoped so, Kathleen thought, forcing a smile. She desperately
hoped so.

December 27
2:20 P.M., *Mountain Time, Sunday*

The jeep driver took a dirt cut-off from the Garden of the Gods
boulevard, stopping a few miles later so Livonas and Colonel Carlson could climb out to inspect the synfuels complex below. It was a
sunny day but cold and the wind coming off the mountain sliced
through Livonas's thick coat like it was a cotton T-shirt. Livonas
shivered, shifted the position of his shoulder holster with its
chopped .45, and walked to the shoulder of the road for a better
look.

The complex was larger than he'd expected, covering a good hundred acres or more. The red-brick administration building in front
was backed by low-lying laboratory buildings and a cracking tower
on the right. For a moment he thought he could see figures on the
tower but couldn't be sure. The rest of the area was cluttered with
more towers and lab buildings still under construction with miles of
above-ground piping connecting them.

Cyclone fencing topped with barbed wire surrounded the entire
complex. An access road led up to the small guard shack and the
gates at the front. The road and the area in front of the fencing were
jammed with people carrying signs and banners that blew in the
wind above them. It looked like there were a lot more than a quarter
of a million down there.

A light haze drifted toward them from the complex. Carlson
sniffed. "Tear gas."

Livonas squinted at the movement in front of the red-brick build-
ng. Then his eyes wandered to a grassy knoll a few hundred yards
away. Nearby was a television truck with a small dish antenna on
top. Waiting to relay the action to the convention hall, he thought.

"Let's get down there, Colonel."

Carlson signaled Sergeant MacAteer and the four Black Berets in
the jeep behind them and a moment later they were roaring down
the road to the back of the complex. The nervous guards at the rear
gate checked their credentials twice, then radioed ahead and finally
waved them in. Livonas cursed under his breath. They were dealing
in minutes now.

Major Thompson and a nervous Lieutenant Nash met them in
Thompson's makeshift headquarters in the project manager's office
overlooking the main gate. Thompson was poised, confident, with a
weatherbeaten face, probing eyes, wiry build. He wore his bone-
handle pistol strapped against his side with a certain flair. He looked
like he could have modeled for a recruiting poster and probably had,
Livonas thought.

Nash was rail-thin, late twenties, with a bad complexion and
jumpy eyes and a Boston accent.

The major saluted Carlson and nodded to Livonas. He watched
with mild interest as the Berets filed into the room, then waved to a
large card table set up in the corner and its nest of folding chairs
nearby.

"Have a seat, gentlemen—afraid this is the best I can do for hos-
pitality." He relaxed in one of the chairs, smiling slightly as Carlson
hesitated, then sat down. He jerked a thumb toward the window. "I
take it your visit has something to do with what's happening out
there?"

Carlson nodded. "That's right, Major."

Thompson glanced at Nash. "How about a pot of coffee, Lieutenant? I think we could all use it."

Livonas walked to the window and looked out. Maybe two hundred troops formed a rough skirmish line in front of the building.
Part of the fencing had been torn down but the mob had been
driven back by tear gas. The demonstrators were milling around behind the billowing clouds of gas, but in minutes they'd try again.
Then de Young's men in the crowd would fire on the troops and
the troops would fire back. He checked his watch. De Young was

probably behind the podium right now, steaming up the delegates while he waited for word.

At the table, Carlson was studying Thompson through lidded eyes. "I have orders relieving you of command, Major."

Thompson tried to look shocked. He held out his hand. "May I?"

Carlson handed over the letter of authorization and Thompson read through it slowly, then handed it to Nash. The lieutenant scanned it and glanced respectfully at Carlson. There'd be no trouble with Nash, Livonas thought.

Thompson drummed his fingers on the table. "This is highly irregular, Colonel. You don't mind if I double-check this?"

Carlson's eyes narrowed even more. "I don't care if you double-check it with God, Major. But first I want you to order your troops back into the building. Under no circumstances are they to fire on the crowd."

Thompson looked aggrieved. "No offense, Colonel, but I've never seen you before. What would you do in my shoes?"

Thompson was stalling, Livonas thought, frantic. Within minutes, the mob would be pouring through the shattered cyclone fencing, marching on the building. Why didn't Carlson simply arrest the son-of-a-bitch? But Carlson had settled back in his chair; the colonel was going to play it by the book.

Then Livonas realized that a half-dozen soldiers with M16's had drifted into the room as backup for Thompson against Carlson and the Berets. Carlson didn't have much choice, he decided.

"Then I guess you'll have to check them," Carlson said. He leaned forward and sipped at his cup of coffee. "Great coffee, Major."

The next thing Livonas knew, Carlson had thrown the coffee in Thompson's face and upended the card table. Thompson went sprawling and the four Berets brought up their Ingrams to cover Thompson's regulars. At the far end of the room, an army corporal fumbled with his M16 and Sergeant MacAteer cut him down with a quick burst of fire that flung the soldier back against the wall, his camouflage jacket a bloody rag.

Carlson, pistol out, covered Thompson on the floor. He glanced over at the regulars. "Everybody drop your weapons. MacAteer, collect them." He waved his .45 at Thompson. "On your feet, Major. We're going to go downstairs and you're going to pull your troops back into the building or I'm going to blow your head off." Thompson nodded, his face pale. Carlson glanced at Nash."You, too, Lieutenant."

Livonas said, "Where the hell's the communications room? I've got to get a message to Denver."

The colonel looked at Nash. "Answer the man, Lieutenant."

Nash snapped to. "At the end of the corridor on the front side of the building—it's marked."

Carlson added, "Tell them it's buttoned up here, Livonas. You want one of my men to go with you?"

"I can handle it." Livonas cocked his head. "You better get downstairs, Colonel, it sounds like they're getting ready to march on the building."

The room was where Nash had said it was, with a hand-lettered sign on the door that read COM OFFICE. Livonas didn't even think about drawing his gun but pushed open the door, anxious to get in touch with Denver.

A man in civilian clothes was sitting at a radio transmitter looking out the window, smoking a cigarette. He glanced up, his shaved head glinting in the sunlight through the glass.

"I heard they had sent you along, Livonas." His voice was colorless, flat.

Livonas struggled to remember where he had seen him before and then he had it. De Young's press conference in San Francisco. Craig Hewitt, waiting to personally relay the details of the slaughter to de Young. Hewitt was roughly his own height and weight but gave the impression of a man made of steel rods and coiled springs.

Hewitt scrubbed out his cigarette. "You've been a lot of trouble to Vince." He laced his fingers behind his head and teetered back in his chair. "You don't look the type."

Hewitt was stalling like Thompson had. But he must know that they'd relieved the major, that the troops were being recalled. Only Hewitt wasn't relying on Thompson's men to fire on the crowd. De Young hadn't left it up to chance, Livonas thought, growing cold. He'd sent Hewitt with a squad of G-Troop as backup.

Hewitt had been staring at the cracking tower just outside the window when he'd walked into the room. The same tower that he thought he'd seen people on when they'd stopped on the road to inspect the complex.

Livonas acted on instinct then, grabbing for the .45 in his shoulder holster. At the same time, Hewitt's chair crashed to the floor as he rolled out of it, automatically going into a crouch. Livonas never saw Hewitt grab the heavy ashtray, only felt it when Hewitt threw it underhand with such force it knocked his gun up so the slug he'd fired tore into the ceiling. Then Hewitt had catapulted into him and the gun went skittering across the floor.

Livonas brought up the heel of his palm and caught Hewitt under the nose, then scrambled away. Hewitt got to his knees, bleeding from the nose and mouth. Now Hewitt made a feint toward Livonas, who dodged behind a desk. Hewitt leaped for the door and shot the bolt, locking them in. He immediately whirled and sprang for Livonas. Desperate, Livonas picked up a wooden office chair to fend off Hewitt like an animal trainer would a lion.

Hewitt turned sideways, a knife in his hand. He held it easily, feinting with it, checking out Livonas's reactions and weighing them. Suddenly he picked up a portable typewriter with his free hand and threw it at Livonas. Livonas knocked it to one side with the chair, then felt something cut into his side and clatter to the floor behind him. Livonas fought to control his panic. Hewitt had decoyed him out of position and caught him in the open with the knife.

Hewitt's face registered mild disappointment. He continued to circle Livonas, waiting for his chance to close. Livonas backed away, staring at him. This was the man who had masterminded Steven Hart's murder, who had ordered Gus Frankel shoved out of a window, who had slit Stu Lambert's throat, and almost murdered Katy. A little theatrical makeup and he'd fit her description of the man in the green jacket.

Livonas kept his eyes glued to Hewitt and worked his way back toward the far wall where the gun had slid to a stop. Then Hewitt leaped on a desk top and ran straight for him, hopping from one desk to another. Livonas retreated, backing into a bank of filing cabinets.

Hewitt had trapped him where he couldn't maneuver. Livonas waited until Hewitt was on the desk directly in front of him, then lunged with the chair at the same time Hewitt leaped. The legs of the chair caught Hewitt in mid-air.

Two of the legs broke off at the seat and Livonas swung what was left of the chair to catch Hewitt on the shoulder. Hewitt slid across the desk top, arms outstretched, and Livonas leaped for him. A moment later, they were rolling on the floor and Hewitt pinned Livonas's arms to his sides.

Livonas kicked free and scrambled toward the other side of the room. He went down with Hewitt hanging on his ankles, climbing up his body like he was climbing up a rope.

Livonas flailed to get away. He was winded and could feel his strength ebbing. Hewitt grabbed his right arm and forced it up behind his back, flipping him on his stomach. Then Hewitt straddled him, clamping Livonas's arms against his sides with his legs. He grabbed Livonas by the hair and lifted slightly and Livonas felt a cord of thin leather slip over his face and tighten around his throat.

Livonas bucked with all his strength, frantic. He freed both hands but he was already strangling, his vision blurry. He collapsed on the floor with his arms stretched in front of him, felt something with his right hand and grabbed it. He had been working around the room to where he had dropped the gun and now he had it. He twisted weakly, pushing it between himself and Hewitt.

The muffled sound of the explosion filled the room. The cord around his neck loosened and Livonas fought for breath. It was a moment before he realized Hewitt had gone limp.

He rolled to one side and Hewitt slid off onto the floor. Livonas staggered to his feet, his shirt soaked with Hewitt's blood. He glanced at Hewitt lying face down on the floor, then looked toward the window. There was shouting outside. The mob was on its way back to storm the complex.

Livonas ran down the hall, ignoring the pain of the knife wound in his side. Ahead of him, troops were pouring back through the main entrance of the building. He spotted Colonel Carlson, surrounded by the Black Berets, waving them in.

"The cracking tower," Livonas gasped. "De Young has a squad of G-Troop on top that's going to fire on the crowd!"

Carlson stared at Livonas's bloody shirt. "Who the hell told you that?"

"De Young's man was in the radio room, he was the one really in charge."

Carlson nodded to the Berets and they rushed out of the building. A single shot echoed from the tower and chipped a nearby wall.

Sergeant MacAteer fitted a grenade onto his rifle barrel and fired. The other Berets opened up with their Ingrams. Flame burst from the top of the tower and several figures somersaulted through the air to hit the ground. Then the top exploded and pieces of debris rained around them.

A hundred yards away the crowd stopped, confused and silent. It must be occurring to some of them that they had been bait for a trap, Livonas thought.

He ran toward a frightened young man in a white parka, clutching a bullhorn. He grabbed it from him, then faced the crowd.

"You want the complex?" he roared. "Then take it! It's all yours! The soldiers have been called back, the government's turned it over to you!"

The front ranks surged forward again and started to run through the grounds, shouting. Livonas didn't know whether they'd torch the complex or not. He didn't give a damn. His side felt sticky and hurt like hell.

Carlson was standing off to one side along with the Berets and a few of the soldiers, watching the crowd as it streamed past. Thompson was squatting on his heels, chain-smoking cigarettes under the watchful eyes of one of the Berets.

Livonas walked over, grimacing at the pain that movement now caused him. They'd take over the television truck on the grassy knoll and the Convention would get its television show all right. Only he would be playing talk show host and Thompson and Nash would do the talking.

"Ever been on television, Major?"

Thompson looked stubborn. "I'll be goddamned if—"

"If you'll talk?" Livonas interrupted in a voice he didn't recognize. "Don't kid yourself, Major, you'll talk. Believe me, you'll talk."

But first he had to go back to the radio room and put through a call to Bob Whitman. He had to tell him that the governor's plot had failed, that de Young had finally paid for Stu Lambert and Gus Frankel and Harry Palmer and Steven Hart—a kid whom Livonas had never even met.

December 27
        2:50 P.M., Mountain Time, Sunday

"Time for the West! Time for the West!"

De Young waited for the chanting to die. He'd been on the stage
for more than half an hour and the sweat was running down his face
and his fingers ached from gripping the sides of the podium. Delegates were cheering and hitting the seats of their metal folding
chairs while half a dozen rows back, he could see Governor Barron
with the Arizona delegation forming a megaphone with his hands
and starting a new chant. A moment later, the auditorium was rocking with it.

"Secession! Secession! Secession!"

Now was the time, the delegates were ripe . . . He felt a tug on his
sleeve and glanced down. Griffin, who had been acting as Shepherd's go-for, handed up a note. There was no indication on Griffin's face what it said, which was bad news all by itself.

He unfolded it. *Have turned off Colorado Springs monitors. No
word yet, Hewitt must be in action. Expect to hear any minute.
Stall. Herb.*

He couldn't stall any longer, the moment was already slipping
away. Even the act of receiving the note was something of a capper
for the audience, which was aware that something had happened
and had abruptly quieted down, expectant. This had to be the pay-
off. Now.

Then he knew what he had to do and the moment of panic
passed. Hewitt was in action, directing his squad. Hewitt would take
care of things, like Hewitt always took care of things. He looked out,
his eyes sliding across the blank monitor screen set beside the dais.
They'd turn it back on when Hewitt called in.

"Fellow citizens." His voice was filled with exactly the right combination of indignation and rage.

"We have just received word from Colorado Springs. Federal
troops guarding the experimental synfuels complex there have fired
on the Freedom Day demonstrators. More than three hundred
peacefully demonstrating citizens have been shot down in cold
blood. Hundreds more are reported wounded."

A horrified sigh swept the auditorium. Then the shouting began, with red-faced delegates on their feet waving their fists while others sobbed with anger. The eastern delegates were frightened, apprehensive.

Now, he thought.

He raised a hand and the convention hall immediately stilled. He spoke slowly, his voice resonant.

"When in the course of human events, it becomes necessary for one people to dissolve the political bands which have connected them with another . . . whenever any form of government becomes destructive, it is the right of the people to alter and abolish it. . . . Two hundred and a score more years ago was such a time."

He bowed his head, then looked up to see his own tenseness and determination reflected in the faces of the delegates.

"The time has come again . . . I ask the delegates to the Constitutional Convention assembled here to grant its citizens and the several states that right through constitutional amendment . . ."

The hall erupted then. Cheers, rebel yells, chants clashed like cymbals throughout the auditorium. Delegates stood on chairs throwing hats, placards, sheets of paper—anything they could find—into the air.

De Young remained motionless at the podium, feeling himself a lightning rod for their collective power. The demonstration would go on for half an hour before the Chair could establish order. Then Janice McCall would put a formal motion on the floor, it would be seconded, and they'd call for the vote.

He looked down for just a moment at the blank monitor, then up at the empty expanse of projection screen overhead. Then even that tiny reminder of uncertainty was swept away by the anger and the enthusiasm in the hall.

"Secession! Secession! Secession!"

December 27
    3:37 P.M., Mountain Time, Sunday

"Listen to them." Saunders turned away, disgusted.

Whitman stared through the observation window at the delegates below; the roar of their cheering pulsed through the glass. For a while, he'd had some hope. Halfway into de Young's speech, he'd realized the governor was stalling, that he'd run out of steam. Then de Young had made the announcement.

Whitman heard footsteps and turned. Katy Houseman hobbled in, the news written all over her face. She squeezed his hand.

"We'll have a quarter, maybe less."

Whitman turned back to the window. They were doing everything but carry de Young around on their shoulders. The United States was about to break apart like a piece of rotten wood.

"It's going to be a tough act to follow," he murmured.

"Don't be a fool, Bob," Reynolds said curtly. Saunders shook his head. "I'm sorry, Mr. President, it would be just too damned dangerous. We ought to be thinking of getting you out of here."

Katy pressed his hand again. "There wouldn't be any point to it. I don't think you could get the podium."

"Then I guess I'll just have to march up and take it."

Katy seemed hesitant and he knew she wanted to say that they'd never give him a chance to open his mouth, that they'd hoot him off the platform. The past week had been harder on her than anybody, he thought. Livonas said Stu Lambert had been like a kid brother to her and she was obviously worried sick about Andy.

Andy.

He walked slowly back to the window, looking down at the floor again. He had been so intent on what de Young had been saying that he'd missed the obvious. The huge projection screen over the dais. Why the hell hadn't de Young shown the slaughter? Why didn't he have it turned on now?

"Jeff, is the Colorado Springs monitor back on yet?"

Saunders was back a moment later. "It's still dead."

"I think it's been cut off here in the building." They stared at him and he said, "Maybe de Young was lying and it hasn't happened yet but he took the gamble anyway."

He looked at Katy. "Let's not give up on Andy yet, Katy—right?"

He stayed at the window watching the demonstration on the convention floor. There was no way of knowing if Andy and Carlson had gotten through, but if he could judge from the blank monitor and projection screen, there'd been no slaughter. At least, not yet.

The minutes wore on and his depression began to creep back. He was so intent on the floor that he didn't hear Saunders at first when he said, "It's for you, Mr. President."

Saunders was holding out the radio phone to him, smiling.

He took it, his heart skipping beats. Then he smiled into the receiver, winking at Katy, who looked faint.

"What the hell took you so long, Andy?"

Two minutes later, he gave the phone to Katy and went back to the observation window, grinning as de Young waved to the crowd with clasped hands.

Enjoy yourself, Governor. For just a little longer.

He turned to Saunders. "Jeff, take a squad of marshals and do whatever you have to do to take control of the communications center. I don't want to be cut off at the microphone or have the lights go off. And I want that big screen to flash on when I wave at it." He looked at Katy. "Get hold of Janice McCall. Tell her de Young lied, there was no bloodshed. Ask her to get the floor and yield it to me so I can prove it."

Minutes later, he watched Janice McCall walk to the dais, her face strained. But she didn't hesitate in yielding the floor to President Robert Whitman.

The booing began then. Whitman stayed in the observation room only long enough to check the startled look on de Young's face at McCall's defection and his involuntary grasping of the arms of his chair.

The first of a lot of unpleasant surprises for the governor, Whitman thought.

He pocketed some notes and took his position in the corridor at the center of a wedge of FBI agents and federal marshals. They picked up speed as they marched toward the auditorium.

Just before the doors, there was a sudden shout behind Whitman and sounds of a scuffle. The marshals on either side of him pushed him roughly to the floor, covering him with their bodies. A fusillade of shots echoed along the corridor, then silence. The marshals got slowly to their feet, then helped him up.

"Sorry, sir."

"Don't apologize," Whitman said, shaken. He glanced back to see a marshal lying in a pool of blood a dozen feet behind him, a pistol in his hand.

Al Reynolds came running up, his face pale. "For God's sake, that marshal was aiming at you!"

Saunders appeared a moment later and took one quick look at the marshal on the floor. "We've got a car at the side entrance—there could be others."

Whitman shook him off. "We're going in, Jeff." Catcalls and cries of outrage were still coming from the auditorium.

"You'll be killed!" Saunders said, desperate.

Whitman shook his head. "Don't argue with me, Jeff, you know there's no choice." Saunders still stood there, uncertain, and Whitman clapped him on the back. "The delegates are waiting."

Saunders gave the signal and two of the marshals pushed open the auditorium doors and Whitman strode in. The hissing was so heavy he could almost feel the spit. Over the heads of his guards, Whitman could see the demonstrators, young and mostly male and all of them big, gather in the aisle in front of him. They were chanting, "Feds out!" They stood arms linked, blocking his path to the podium.

The marshals were professional, you almost didn't notice the body blocks and the blackjacks. It was like clearing a path through a patch of manzanita with a chain saw: a little slow and sticky at times but progress was inevitable. Some of the young demonstrators were doubled up along the sides of the aisle, moaning. There was little blood, the marshals had been too expert for that, but cries of "Shame!" were starting to echo from the western delegates.

It wasn't picked up by the convention as a whole, Whitman noted with satisfaction; they'd already seen too much of it from de Young's goons.

He walked down the aisle, ignoring the faces contorted by hatred on either side. Janice McCall was still at the microphone on the podium, studying him as he walked. De Young sat behind the podium with the chairman and the two other convention officials. Their eyes met briefly, then de Young looked away with apparent unconcern.

Janice McCall stepped aside and Whitman took her place, staring grimly out at the audience. There was a roar of boos and a rising chant from the California delegation: "Go back to Washington! Go back to Washington!"

Then Whitman spotted Katy on the floor and soon the federal delegates were shouting, "Let him talk!" The hooting finally died away and the auditorium quieted.

"Delegates of the Second Constitutional Convention. A few minutes ago, we were told that the federal government had committed a terrible crime." There was another round of boos. "Your anger would have been justified and I would have had to accept full responsibility"—he leaned forward, his voice harsh—"if it had actually happened."

He could sense the shock as his words sank in. Then the red light on the monitor started blinking, indicating he could turn on the overhead projection screen.

"The fact is that federal troops did not fire on the demonstrators at the Colorado Springs synfuels complex. No demonstrators were shot, no demonstrators were wounded. On my personal orders, the troops were recalled in order to avoid bloodshed and the complex turned over to the people who came to protest."

The shocked silence lengthened. He could hear a strangled sound behind him and guessed it was de Young. In the California delegation, Wagoner was staring at him, consternation written huge on his face. The matron sitting next to him had put her hands to her mouth as if she were going to be sick. Then somebody in the Arizona delegation obligingly shouted, "Prove it!"

Whitman waved at the screen and it sprang into life, showing the red-brick adminstration building with demonstrators wandering in and out and gathered in little knots on the lawn in front. There were no soldiers in sight.

Now all he had to do was pin down the responsibility, Whitman thought.

"A slaughter was planned, however—had been planned for months. I regret to say that many of the delegates to this convention were taken in by parts of that plan. I regret even more that good people, including members of this convention, were murdered during the course of that plan. And that our country—beset with problems but still *our* country—faced almost certain dissolution because of one man's arrogance and ambition."

There was a commotion in the Arizona delegation as Governor Barron heaved to his feet and started to struggle toward the aisle. He sat down again when he noticed the U.S. marshal waiting for him.

On the monitor, the television camera zoomed in on a group that included Livonas, Colonel Carlson, several Black Berets, and two men in regular army uniform whom Whitman didn't know.

Whitman turned to face de Young behind him, leaning closer to the microphone so his words wouldn't be lost.

"Governor de Young!" His voice boomed out over the audience

and he guessed that somebody had turned up the volume in the communications center. "I accuse you of treason against the United States! Of murder, of plotting a conspiracy against the people of our country." He lowered his voice slightly, letting the words fill with emotion. "And that includes people like myself, Governor, who claim the West as their home and whose delegates are gathered here today!"

De Young leaped to his feet, his face twisted with hatred and desperation.

"You're a liar, Whitman! You're—"

Whitman watched dispassionately as the two convention officials restrained de Young, then glanced up at the huge screen overhead.

"Let's hear what really happened at the synfuels complex, Governor—from the people who were there!"

On the screen, Livonas introduced Thompson and then the major's husky drawl filled the auditorium. Whitman listened to the details again. They weren't all there but there was enough to damn de Young.

". . . what was planned at the synfuels complex, Major?"

The sharp anger in Livonas's voice echoed through the auditorium. The Major's voice was shaky.

". . . then I volunteered to command the federal troops at the complex . . . we'd placed provocateurs in the crowd to fire on the troops and I was to order my troops to return their fire . . . that's right, sir, into the crowd . . ."

There was a murmur of anger in the hall now—as much from western delegates as from those of the East, Whitman noted with satisfaction.

". . . right, sir, Colonel Hewitt had placed sharpshooters up on the cracking tower to return the provocateur fire in case the soldiers under my command balked at orders to shoot into the crowd . . . yes, sir, Colonel Hewitt told me that Governor de Young had requested the unit of California state police . . . that's what I assumed, sir, that the Governor wanted some of the demonstrators killed . . ."

The shouts of outrage began then. Whitman stepped to one side so the delegates had a better view of de Young standing in front of his chair, his face pale and his eyes jumping nervously around the auditorium searching frantically for former supporters.

"Treason! Treason! Arrest the traitor!"

Whitman waited until the shouting died and the governor had

sunk back into his chair, then returned to the podium for his speech of reconciliation.

It was no Gettysburg Address, but it was short and to the point and he liked the ending.

One nation, indivisible . . .

December 27
4:50 P.M., *Mountain Time, Sunday*

Herb Shepherd couldn't believe it. He clutched the back of the chair in the observation cubicle as the chairman adjourned the convention and the marshals leaped on stage to arrest Vince. Other marshals and FBI agents were weaving through the audience, picking out one delegate and then another. Governor Barron, Jerry Wagoner, Mabel Sweet . . . Occasionally there were little knots where a few members of G-Troop would take on the marshals, but there was no organization and most of them had faded from the hall anyway.

It was all over, he thought. Years of plan—

Not quite, it wasn't over.

"Griffin!"

Nobody answered. He turned around. There was nobody else in the observation booth. He walked back into the caucus room. It was empty, except for General Bolles at the radio console in the corner. Papers were scattered around, an unopened bottle of champagne sat in a bucket of melting ice, ashtrays were filled to overflowing.

He hurried over to Bolles. "The troops. What about the Fourth Infantry from Camp Carson? We've got the National Guard and the commandos in the hills, we can take the city, force them to release Vince . . ."

Bolles turned to stare at him, for the first time making no effort to hide his distaste. "Everything that's happened here has been broadcast to the troops. Remember? We planned it that way. It was supposed to be good for morale." He waved at the console, his voice distant. "Nobody wants to be a traitor. They're disbanding. Nobody's answering."

A voice at the door said quietly, "Mr. Shepherd? General Bolles?"

Shepherd turned. Three marshals were standing in the doorway, one of them with a sub-machine gun slung over his shoulder.

"You're under arrest."

Shepherd started to deny it, to deny everything, when there was an explosion immediately behind him that almost deafened him. He turned, his eyes widening in horror. General Bolles had blown his brains out, and bone and blood had spattered all over the back of Shepherd's silk suit and onto his Bally shoes.

Shepherd was still vomiting when the marshals led him away.

January 3
7:30 A.M., *Sunday*

"I don't know," Livonas said. "Between preparing for the vice-presidential confirmation hearings of Congressman Gorman and everything else, I really hadn't thought about it." He ladled more sugar into his coffee and studied Whitman out of the corner of his eye. "I guess I figured I'd leave Washington when you do."

Whitman laughed. "You do that, you might be looking at early retirement." Then he noticed the expression on Livonas's face and sobered. "I'm sorry, I shouldn't joke about it. But we're talking about you, Andy. I was getting the impression you had it up to here with Washington."

It was early—not yet eight o'clock—and Whitman was still in his favorite bathrobe. Livonas wondered how many discussions like this they'd had over a cup of coffee in various kitchens and pantries during the past ten years. They were both early risers and seven-in-the-morning meetings had become almost a tradition.

"I'll stick around as long as necessary."

Whitman was right. Somewhere after the fight at the synfuels complex and before Air Force One had touched down at Andrews Air Force Base, he'd promised himself a year. He still had the cabin he and Gus had bought. And at one time they had tossed around the idea of buying a small weekly in the Russian River country and trying to do something with it. It wouldn't be as much fun without Gus but it was still something he wanted to do.

"That's not what I asked," Whitman said. He put on his Lyndon

Johnson drawl. "Come on Andy, out with it. This is your President speaking."

"I'd like to take a year or so and do some thinking," Livonas mumbled, not looking directly at him.

Whitman tore a small piece off his cinnamon roll and nibbled at it. "On the plane, you and Katy Houseman looked like you were at a drive-in movie."

Livonas laughed. "I didn't think anybody noticed."

"Politicians and newsmen," Whitman chuckled. "They're the nosiest people in town." He walked over to the kitchen window and looked out at the gray morning sky. "I think you ought to take your year, Andy. I planned to do the same thing myself a number of times." He turned around, shoving his hands deep into his bathrobe pockets. "Came pretty close this last time."

Livonas stood up, he was already late at the Executive Office Building. "That's the price of greatness, Bob—you don't get to take vacations."

Whitman clapped him on the shoulder and they walked through the hall to the door that separated the private quarters from the more public part of the White House.

"You know, Andy, I don't regret anything I've done—the good has always outweighed the bad." He said it with a fierceness that surprised Livonas. He stopped at the door, his hand on the knob. "The next decade will be so damned important for our country." Whitman's eyes filled with a sadness that disconcerted Livonas. "De Young exploited the grievances of the western states for his own ends. But they were legitimate grievances, Andy—grievances that we've got to deal with if we want to prevent another demagogue from taking advantage of them. They're like wounds; we can't let them fester."

He put his hand on Livonas's arm. "I couldn't have gotten through the last two weeks without you, Andy. The country owes you a debt and so do I—a very personal one."

Livonas felt his face grow warm. "I'll see you at two—we have to go over the statement on de Young's indictment."

Whitman smiled, understanding his embarrassment. "Neither one of us does very well with sentiment, do we, Andy? But I'm not worried about the indictment, Knox will take care of de Young." He looked mock serious. "Katy Houseman is another matter. I'm responsible for that girl coming to Washington and I expect you to take care of her. People still get married, don't they?"

Livonas started to reply but Whitman shoved him out the door. "Aren't you late for work?"

By mid-afternoon, Livonas realized he couldn't concentrate on work, that he kept thinking about Whitman's last comments about Katy. By evening, he'd given up on all the reasons why marriage was impossible and found himself walking up the icy path to Katy's small cottage.

He hadn't been able to think of anything else all day.

They sat on a rug, their backs against the couch, in front of a crackling fire. Katy's living room was still filled with half-packed boxes and framed photographs piled in stacks in the corners.

Livonas fumbled with his wineglass, silent and awkward, realizing that he had never really proposed before. He and Ellen had just sort of come to an understanding.

He felt Katy's fingers drift across his shoulder and tug at his shirt collar. "Why so solemn, Livonas?"

He turned. Their faces were so close that through her smile he could see her as she was now, as she had been as a young girl, and as she would be as an old woman.

"I was just wondering if you'd like to . . . get married." He said it offhand.

Katy continued to play with his collar. "I'd like to get married to you. I don't know about anybody else."

"I meant me."

She grinned, tracing the line of his upper lip with her forefinger. "I thought you were a confirmed bachelor."

"I was," he said, "but things have changed." He bit her finger. "I'm thinking of leaving Washington."

She looked around the room. "I'm packed already."

Livonas turned to her and they wrapped themselves around each other.

"It's warmer here than in the bedroom," Katy said.